The
GREAT WAVE
of TAMARIND

The
GREAT WAVE
of TAMARIND

Nadia Aguiar

FEIWEL AND FRIENDS
NEW YORK

A FEIWEL AND FRIENDS BOOK
An imprint of Macmillan Publishing Group, LLC

Our books may be purchased in bulk for promotional, educational, or business
use. Please contact your local bookseller or the Macmillan Corporate and
Premium Sales Department at (800) 221-7945 ext. 5442 or by e-mail at
MacmillanSpecialMarkets@macmillan.com.

Library of Congress Cataloging-in-Publication Data

Names: Aguiar, Nadia, author.
Title: The great wave of Tamarind / Nadia Aguiar.
Description: First edition. | New York : Feiwel & Friends, 2017. | Series:
    The book of Tamarind ; 3 | Summary: Penny Nelson must face three
    dangerous tasks in order to stabilize the magical island of Tamarind
    and keep some of the magic for her own use.
Identifiers: LCCN 2016024482 (print) | LCCN 2016052961 (ebook) |
    ISBN 9780312380311 (hardcover) | ISBN 9781250116635 (Ebook)
Subjects: | CYAC: Adventure and adventurers—Fiction. | Islands—Fiction. |
    Magic—Fiction. | BISAC: JUVENILE FICTION / Fantasy & Magic. |
    JUVENILE FICTION / Action & Adventure / Survival Stories.
Classification: LCC PZ7.A26876 Gr 2017 (print) | LCC PZ7.A26876 (ebook)
    | DDC [Fic]—dc23
LC record available at https://lccn.loc.gov/2016024482

Book design by Eileen Savage

Feiwel and Friends logo designed by Filomena Tuosto

First Edition—2017

1 3 5 7 9 10 8 6 4 2

mackids.com

To Havilland
And in memory of Tim

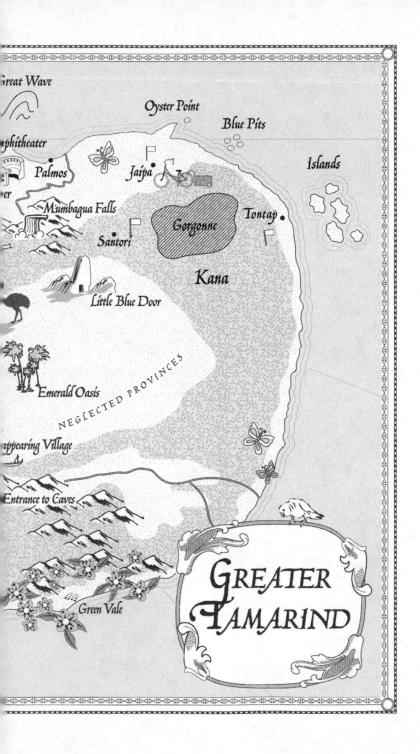

Great Wave

Oyster Point

Blue Pits

...phitheater

Islands

Palmos

Jaipa

Mumbagua Falls

Gorgonne

Tontap

Santori

Kana

Little Blue Door

Emerald Oasis

NEGLECTED PROVINCES

...appearing Village

Entrance to Caves

Green Vale

GREATER TAMARIND

PART ONE

☙ Chapter One ❧

Shark • Penny's Goggles • The Signs • Granny Pearl
• "When the time is right" • Urgent Message

Penny peered through her goggles into the turquoise world below. The water was clear as crystal and there was movement everywhere—swaying, darting, nibbling, tugging. Even the light pulsed in veins across the sandy floor. A school of yellowtail jacks circled restlessly and a spiny lobster crossed an open patch between reefs. With its jointed legs and long, wavering antennae, it looked like a big orange insect. It disturbed a snoozing flounder, which lifted its pancake body briefly and, with a puff of sand, wriggled down deeper.

In the distance, she saw a shark cruise out from behind the rocks. Its belly was white as fresh snow; the rest of it gleamed like sunlit steel. Two unblinking eyes sat on either side of the crude spade of its head. It glided effortlessly, as if unbound by gravity. With only the barest flick of its tail, its rubbery body bent and the creature switched direction, swimming a wide, purposeful circle before disappearing around the other side of the rocks.

As Penny floated there, the sun went behind a cloud, and the water grew suddenly murky. Tiny neon fish that had been zipping around the waving sea rods vanished into a hole, and the school of yellowtail jacks swerved away, re-forming as a spinning, glittering ball in the distance. Penny's lungs began to burn. She'd need to take a breath soon. The shark emerged again from behind the rocks. Its shadow passed over the lobster, which froze for a moment, detecting the disturbance with its sensitive antennae. As the shark came closer, Penny concentrated on keeping her heart rate slow, just as Simon had taught her.

The animal began to rise and bring its circle deliberately in. Its eye was trained on Penny. With each pass, it closed the distance between them. Its skin, somewhere between metal and velvet, shimmered in the dim light.

Penny!

Her name was being called at the surface. Underwater, the sound was muffled.

Penelope Nelson!

The shark passed her, just feet away this time. Then, as if sensing the intent in the voice above, it abandoned its slowly narrowing circles and, with a barely perceptible shift of its sinewy tail, turned and picked up speed and headed straight for Penny. At the last instant, it veered off, a flick of its tail at the surface releasing a curtain of quivering, pearly bubbles, and Penny felt herself being hauled up by the back of her shirt. She was deposited on the ground outside the tank, just as the shark disappeared into the shadows.

"What were you thinking!" shouted Cab, the aquarist. "Do you know how foolish that is—what could happen? I felt sick when I saw you there! For the last time—stay OUT of the tank!"

"But I wasn't *swimming* this time," said Penny, pushing her faded black goggles up over her head, water streaming down from her wet hair and shirt. "I was just leaning in. And," she said confidently, "you know people think sharks are way more dangerous than they really are. You're more likely to die in the bathtub than you are in a shark attack."

"You're not supposed to be in the staff area," said Cab, exasperated. "No one else would come up here, let alone put their head in a tank with a six-foot shark!"

"But," said Penny, "I just . . ." She trailed off. She looked for the shark, as if the sight of it would prove to Cab how she just hadn't been able to help herself, but the big fish was hidden behind the reef.

"Penny, are you up there?" A moment later her mother appeared on the platform.

"I found her in the tank," said Cab.

"Not *all* the way in," said Penny quickly. "Just *leaning* in a little."

"Again, Penny?" cried her mother. "I'm so sorry, Cab," she said. "That's the last time."

"It had better be," said Cab self-righteously as he shuffled off.

The open-air platform above the tanks at the Bermuda Aquarium, where Penny's parents were marine biologists, had been declared strictly off-limits to Penny ever since she had been caught swimming in the tank last month. But today, after walking to the aquarium after school, Penny had grown restless as she'd waited for her mother in the main hall, watching Oscar the shark circle. In the end she couldn't resist sneaking up to the platform above the tank.

"Why do you have to be so reckless?" said her mother after Cab had left. "There are rules for a reason—why don't you think you have to follow them just like anyone else?"

"I follow rules that make sense," said Penny, water dripping on the concrete as she wrung out her wet hair. "But come on, Mami, Oscar won't hurt me. You know he's hand-fed—he's not like a wild shark." She looked longingly down at the beautiful dusky shark swimming peacefully. She had come so close to reaching out and brushing his dorsal fin with her fingertips.

In the tank, the lobster had safely ended his stiff-legged venture. A pair of parrotfish scraped algae from the reef, their fused beaks leaving tiny white crosses on the rock. Purple sea fans bowed in the current and fluted sponges reached up toward the fading light. As Penny watched, a lettuce-green eel emerged from its cave and—like a long scarf set loose by the wind—stretched to its full length and billowed across the water.

She couldn't explain to people like Cab, or even her mother, the powerful pull she felt to be in that other world, close to such a magnificent creature that moved so flawlessly through its element. She couldn't describe how, when she was near the shark, she felt not fear but a deep, potent sense of being alive, a feeling more vivid and real than anything else in her day, in her whole *life*, even. But already the sensation was fading. The clouds thickened, transforming the reef and its creatures into shadows.

Her mother sighed. "I'm going to talk to your father about this," she said. "But right now let's go. I want to get home to Granny Pearl."

Hearing the urgency in her mother's voice, Penny grabbed her school backpack. She felt suddenly chilly in her damp shirt, and a familiar nervous feeling quickened her step. Leaving the darkened tank behind, she hurried after her mother down the staff stairs.

In the car, Penny wound down her window and let the wind dry her hair. She used to take the bus home. Her mother driving her was a new thing; ever since Granny Pearl had been having what Penny's parents called "the episodes," at least one of them tried to come home early. After so long without them being there, Penny found it strange to have them around all the time. She was still thinking about floating in the cool blue world of the tank, remembering how close she had been to the shark, when Mami nodded at the road up ahead.

"Looks like girls from your school," she said.

Penny looked up to see a group of girls walking along the shady verge under the oleander. She shrugged and hunched down in her seat.

"Isn't that Angela with them?" asked Mami, squinting. "It is. Should I offer them a lift?"

"No," said Penny quickly. "They're going the other way!"

"I haven't seen Angela in ages," said Mami. "Are you two still arguing?"

"We're not arguing," muttered Penny. "We're just not friends anymore."

"That's a shame," said her mother. "You've been friends since you were little kids. Don't you think you can try getting along again? Angela probably misses you, too, you know."

Penny didn't answer. It was typical that her mother had no idea what was going on in her life. As if Angela missed her! She had a whole other group of friends now. It wasn't as if *Penny* had wanted things to change—Angela was the one who had turned into a different person overnight. Penny looked the other way as they drove past the girls.

She told herself she didn't care, anyway. She didn't have time to worry about problems at school now, not when things at home—important things—needed her attention.

For weeks now, strange signs had been appearing around Granny Pearl's house.

First, a dozen harbor conches had appeared overnight in a perfect circle on the shore of the cove.

They were followed, days later, by the leaves of the orange tree turning silver.

Then, deep within her plumage, the parrot Seagrape's quills had begun to glimmer.

There were other things, too: little things in the garden and the cove, just out of the ordinary enough to be notable. Granny Pearl said they were like warnings that appeared in the days before a big storm—in the same way that silk spiders moved their thick yellow webs from high in the tree-tops to low in the trunks of the spice trees to escape the rain, or the way your ears popped from subtle pressure changes in the atmosphere.

"On their own they don't mean much," said Granny Pearl. "But all together like this . . . It's been seven years since I've seen anything like it. Something is on its way, Penny; some big change is about to happen. I can feel it."

"Should we tell Mami and Papi?" Penny had whispered as she looked wonderingly at the pewter luster of a leaf cradled in Granny Pearl's palm.

"Better not," said Granny Pearl. "I don't think they'd understand."

"No, probably not," Penny had agreed.

To be honest, Penny wouldn't have paid much attention to any of the signs if her grandmother hadn't seen them and been so sure. But Granny Pearl had always been attuned to things in the natural world that no one else noticed. She knew what the shapes and tints of the evening clouds predicted for the next day's weather. She knew that monarchs spun their cocoons in milkweed and that cloudless sulfurs flocked to cassia trees. On summer evenings, after a full moon, she would take Penny down to the shore, where she could time to the minute when the glowworms would shimmy up to the surface—first one, then two, then dozens of little whirring, bioluminescent spirits, before one by one they'd ebb and sink back down into the silt. Darkness would have seeped in unnoticed in their wake and the last of the sunset drained away, so that when the spectacle was over, the world would have transformed, leaving the cove a glossy black disc beneath the moonlight.

So, when she told Penny that the signs meant that something important was on its way, Penny believed her.

What that something might be, Granny Pearl refused to say.

"When the time is right," she'd tell Penny. "When I'm sure."

It seemed to Penny that since the signs had begun appearing, Granny Pearl had been growing weaker. It was as though the mysterious thing approaching was sapping her strength, making her forgetful and confused, inclined to leave faucets running, or to wander and forget where she was. At the rate things were going, Penny thought that whatever was happening had to happen soon. *Maybe*, she thought, looking out of the car window at the eerie, sallow sky, *maybe even today.*

She and her mother had reached the pampas grass, which meant they were almost home. A breeze rustled restlessly through the razor-sharp blades. Dingy plumes shook on long stalks above the grass, like surf kicked up by a roiling sea, and released fluffy, dirty-white seedpods that whirled thickly in the air. Penny had never seen so many. She twisted around in her seat to see out of the window behind them as her mother turned the car down the bumpy dirt road through the trees to Granny Pearl's house. The gray afternoon dimmed further as the trees met in a roof over the road, forging a gloomy green tunnel. Seedpods from the pampas blew in and were held aloft like tiny parachutes on currents of breeze, eventually coming to lie in yellowed drifts in the hollows of the earth.

"Do you see them all?" asked Penny. "They're never out like this until late summer! And I've never seen so many before!"

"You mean the pampas seeds?" Mami asked. She glanced out the window. "They're the same as always, aren't they? They always make a huge mess."

One blew in the window and landed on Penny's knee. Her heart quickened. She picked it up and examined it. It looked perfectly ordinary—a tiny, soft hook with a shock of blond fluff at the end—but she knew it wasn't. She looked back outside. Her mother was wrong. They were every-where, more numerous than she had ever known, falling like dirty snow, obscuring the day.

She would have to tell Granny Pearl right away.

The green parrot was waiting.

The old yellow-hulled sailboat, the *Pamela Jane*, lay on her mooring in the sea at the foot of the garden. Perched atop the mast as it knocked gently back and forth in the salty breeze was Seagrape the parrot, in the post she kept every day from three o'clock until Penny got home. Far below, tangled in the mooring chain, burned-looking clumps of sargassum drifted dreamily in the tide. The school of snappers that lived below the hull was off at the other end of the cove. A sign hung from the stern, squeaking in the breeze: CLUBHOUSE—KEEP OUT!

At the rumble of wheels, Seagrape cocked her head, then dropped down from the mast and flew, faster than usual, to meet Penny. Penny jumped out before the car had fully stopped, ignoring her mother's irritated shout. She stretched out her arm, and Seagrape landed heavily. Agitated, the bird shuffled from talon to talon, muttering and ruffling her feathers.

"What are you so excited about?" Penny asked. She stroked the parrot's silky wings, looking for the glimmer that Granny Pearl had seen in her quills, deep within the glossy green plumage. But in the sallow light of the overcast afternoon it was hard to discern.

With a squawk Seagrape flew ahead to the porch. Penny kicked off her shoes and peeled off her socks, muddy from the field at school, and ran barefoot the rest of the way to the house.

"Granny Pearl!" she called, dashing up the porch steps, past the row of conch shells.

"I'm home!" she shouted, barging through the screen door into the kitchen.

No one answered.

"Granny Pearl!" Penny sang as the screen door banged shut. But the kitchen was empty. Her parents' lab coats from earlier in the week lay rumpled and soiled in a heap on the floor by the laundry, waiting to be washed. Penny dropped her shoes inside the door.

"Hello!" she shouted again. "I'm home!"

Seagrape flew in through the open kitchen window. The house was dim. The living room, with its faded old furniture and stacks of marine biology journals, was empty, too. The creaky ceiling fan was off, but the faint breeze coming from outside turned it, so slowly it barely moved at all. Penny ran down the hallway, tossing her backpack in her room as she went, but no one was in the bathroom or in her grandmother's small and tidy bedroom. The violet, its leaves fuzzy as bumblebees, sat silent on the windowsill. Across the hall, Simon and Helix's old room, nearly bare now, was quiet.

All of a sudden the house felt hollow, but the musty, undisturbed air closed in claustrophobically. Penny hurried back through the living room, past her parents' bedroom to her father's study. The eyes of sea creatures preserved in jars of alcohol—unblinking year in and year out throughout Penny's childhood—stared down at her from the shelves, and a few ophalla stones from Tamarind glowed stubbornly on the desk, but they were the only things there. Granny Pearl wasn't in the house. The uneasiness building these past weeks rushed to the surface. Seagrape landed with a thump in the doorway.

Penny ran back to the kitchen when she heard her mother come in.

"She's probably just down in the garden," said Mami, but beneath her mother's calm Penny could detect the same sharp fear they all felt these days.

She bolted out the screen door, took the porch steps in a single leap, and raced down the hill. Seagrape ducked out the open kitchen window and flew after her.

When Penny reached the vegetable garden, she saw her grandmother's basket, half full and abandoned in between the rows, but no Granny Pearl. She kept running down the hill to the cove at the end of the garden, where the *Pamela Jane* was moored. It wasn't until she saw her grandmother standing on the rocks near the cove's entrance, looking out to sea through a pair of binoculars, that Penny slowed down. Granny Pearl had shrunk in the past months and her cotton housedress billowed like a mainsail in the breeze, its pattern faded from hundreds of sunny afternoons spent drying on the line. Penny looked back to see her mother standing at the top of the hill and waved to indicate that everything was okay. Her mother returned to the house and Penny ran the rest of the way down the hill.

"There you are!" said Penny, drawing up breathlessly alongside her grandmother.

"Oh good, you're home," said Granny Pearl, not lifting her gaze from the binoculars.

"I didn't know where you were," said Penny.

"It's not like you had many places to look," said Granny Pearl after a moment. "I don't go very far these days, do I?" She lowered the binoculars and sighed impatiently. "Have you been listening to your parents again? They worry too much! Don't do this, don't do that! I'm eighty-six years old and I can tell you—they don't know everything!"

Penny was in hearty agreement that her parents didn't know everything. She felt foolish and somehow guilty for having been frightened. Solidarity with her grandmother reaffirmed, she took the binoculars that Granny Pearl handed to her.

"Here, you look," said Granny Pearl. "My eyes aren't good enough anymore. Tell me what you see."

"Where am I supposed to look?"

"I don't know exactly; I'd try near the far reefs."

Penny squinted at the ragged cuffs of surf along the

breakers half a mile out. A few seagulls wheeled in the sky and the horizon was stacked with dirty-looking clouds.

"Well?"

"Some gulls," said Penny. "A rain cloud on the horizon. Doesn't look like it's coming in. It might just pass us."

"What else?"

"I don't see anything else."

"You're sure?"

Penny looked out to sea again. "Nothing," she said.

"Hmm," said Granny Pearl. "It's still too bright. We'll have to wait until it's dark."

"How are we going to see anything in the dark?" Penny asked. "And what am I even looking for, anyway?"

Her grandmother didn't answer. Penny scanned the water once more, slowly. There was nothing there. The rain cloud was tracking along the horizon, not coming to shore. She followed the waves all the way in to the cove, where the *Pamela Jane* lay lonely on her mooring, and lowered the binoculars.

Penny had been just a year old when her family had left life on the sea, living aboard the *Pamela Jane*, sailing from port to port, and had moved in with Granny Pearl. Her grandmother had already been an old lady then, but now she was magnificently old, her hair white as cotton and her face a mass of soft, deep wrinkles. Penny was twelve now. She had a sister, Maya, and a brother, Simon, who were much older than she was.

When Penny was young, her parents had been so deeply immersed in their work, noses in their microscopes, skin pale from so many hours logged in their lab, that Penny had been left in Granny Pearl's care. Her siblings—and Helix, too, when he had lived with them—had always been off doing their own thing, so most afternoons it was just Penny, Granny Pearl, and Seagrape in the little house by the sea. That was fine with Penny. She loved her grandmother more than anyone. Unlike the others, she always had time for Penny. Granny Pearl never got irritated with her or scolded her or treated her like a pesky little kid to be shaken off. She enjoyed Penny's company, always.

When Penny was old enough, she joined Granny Pearl on her early-morning swim out to the big anvil rock and back. They'd garden together and feed fish in the cove, watching out for the one big greedy snapper who always stole from the chubs. It hadn't been that many years ago that Granny Pearl had built the tree house for Penny in the great, broad-armed old poinciana tree. She'd climbed a ladder with planks of wood on her shoulder, hammering them into the branches herself. Penny's parents had tried to stop her, but she had done it anyway. It wasn't like either of *them* had time to build Penny a tree house. They didn't even have time to cook dinner. Until recently Granny Pearl had done that, too, with potatoes and carrots and onions fresh from the garden, the kitchen windows fogging with steam from the pots, the house smelling like the handfuls

17

of oregano and chives and mint, warm from the sun, that she rinsed in the cool tap and lay, beaded and dazzling, on the countertop.

In those days, come dinnertime the kitchen would be crowded, full of noise and life. Penny's parents' lab coats would have been washed and crisply ironed and left on the backs of their chairs for the next day. But eventually Maya had left for college and then to work in a city in America, and Simon was right behind her. Now they only came home for brief visits once or twice a year.

A swell came through the mouth of the cove, and the *Pamela Jane* strained on her mooring, as if she would have gladly broken free if she could. Penny's gaze roved over the seashore and up the garden. On such a gloomy day, certain things seemed to cast their own light, a soft burnished glow, as though illuminated from within—a bright-leafed bush, fruit glowing on the end of a branch, the hard curve of Seagrape's beak. Granny Pearl's hairpins, the ones she washed in vinegar, gleamed softly in the bleached-out light.

Seagrape was a few feet away, perched on a rock. A gravelly, discontented rumble stirred deep in her throat, like thunder in the distance.

"You feel it in your quills, don't you, old lady?" murmured Granny Pearl. "It's on its way, isn't it?"

Penny's shoulders stiffened. "What is it, Granny Pearl?" she asked. "What's on its way?"

But her grandmother seemed to have forgotten she was there. Penny was reminded of how you're never supposed to wake a sleepwalker. Out on the water, the *Pamela Jane* creaked uneasily, bow into the wind. Her brass portholes caught the low light, making perfect golden circles. Inside the boat it was dark. The day felt like it was pressing in around Penny, suffocating her.

"Granny Pearl," she repeated softly. "What is it? What's on its way?"

Suddenly the garden looked wild, its shadows damp and unpleasant, and the sea cold, creased by mean currents. A strange menace had entered the afternoon, but it wasn't from the light or the sea. It was something inside Granny Pearl herself, as if she were being erased from within.

There was little that frightened Penny. Not sharks, not teachers, not cranky old Cab at the aquarium, not diving off cliffs, or swimming into the shallow cave at the far end of the cove. But there in the familiar garden of her home, with her grandmother beside her and her mother just up the hill in the house, Penny suddenly felt deeply afraid.

Another swell surged into the inlet, rocking the *Pamela Jane*, and for several seconds Penny thought she saw something reflected in the portholes, not the clouds, not the garden, but some strange scene: tangled vines in a great canopy of trees, creatures crossing on branches high above the earth, bell-shaped flowers trembling beneath their paws, turtles lumbering on a hot shore below. The boat swung to face the breeze, and the brass portholes once again became opaque. Granny Pearl snapped back, brisk and ordinary once more, and turned abruptly from the sea.

"Come up to the garden with me," she said. "We need to get a few more things for dinner. I want you to have a good meal tonight. You're going to need your strength."

"Strength for what?" asked Penny.

"You'll find out soon enough," said Granny Pearl. "Now," she said, firmly changing the subject, "tell me about your day."

Whatever had happened was over. If anything had even happened. Penny wanted to believe that she had just imagined it. They walked slowly up the hill.

"I scored two goals at lunch," said Penny. She was eager to put the strange feeling in the garden out of her mind and happily summoned the satisfying sensation of running with the soccer ball down the field, the wind on her face, the ground blurring beneath her feet. "That was great. After that . . ." After that it had been as awful as every other day that year, full of tiny humiliations and spells of profound boredom. "It's another girl's birthday and they're all going to her house. Angela, too, of course. Since she's one of *them* now. Mami wanted to know why I wasn't invited."

Penny knew that Angela was right—they *were* too old for the things they used to do. Even Penny couldn't muster the enthusiasm for the games that once came so naturally. But she was certain there was more to life than sitting around giggling about boys and combing her hair. She was sure there was something else, something *bigger*. Something that felt truly important. Still, she couldn't escape the feeling that something bigger was happening for everyone else, and she was the one being left behind.

It had been a shock when Angela stopped being friends with Penny, but when Penny looked back, she could see it had been happening slowly for a while. They seemed to have lost the ability to play, but nothing else had come along to fill the space. Angela wasn't interested in dares, like seeing how far down the coast they could swim, or in just riding around on their bikes. She had started making excuses not to come over. She no longer cared about how much fun they'd had playing pirates with the yellow flags that Granny Pearl had sewn for them, or camping out on the *Pamela Jane* on summer evenings, when Granny Pearl would wave a white dish towel on the shore before she rowed a picnic basket of dinner out to the boat. It was as if those times had never even happened.

Penny saw Angela with her new friends each day, sitting under the shade tree at lunch, giggling and whispering about boys. Stupid boys, too—show-offs who did everything for attention. Penny couldn't believe that Angela might really like any of them. Or like any of the boring girls she hung out with now. It made no sense how everything had changed so much from just last year. Then, all the girls still played ball at lunch. Now they spent the whole time combing their hair and secretly putting on makeup, and when they got in trouble, they smirked and only pretended to wipe off their lipstick.

Granny Pearl was the only one Penny confided in about their final argument, tearfully on the porch one afternoon before her parents came home.

"She said, 'Don't you see, I don't want to play stupid games—we're not little kids anymore, Penny. You're embarrassing me!' She told me I was *embarrassing* her."

Granny Pearl had hugged Penny and kissed the top of her head. She always comforted Penny, less by what she said, which was usually something mild like, *It won't always be this way,* or *No one ever looks back and wishes they grew up any faster,* and more because she was the one person who seemed to really know what was going on in Penny's life and to understand how she felt. She was the only one who knew how hurt and bewildered Penny felt this year, how much she hated going to school every day.

Penny's feelings were hurt on Granny Pearl's behalf, too. If Angela didn't want to hang out with her anymore, at least once in a while she could have visited Granny Pearl, who had practically been like her own grandmother, after all. Penny consoled herself with the thought that Granny Pearl and Seagrape were all the friends she really needed—even if the latter was inclined to get grumpy and nip.

"It isn't even like I want to go to their dumb party," she said. "All they're going to do is sit around and talk about boys and clothes. It's so boring!"

But today Granny Pearl didn't comfort her.

"You need other people, Penny," she said. She sounded tired. "You need to find a way to get along with people."

"I have you," said Penny. "I'd rather be with you than with anyone else."

But Granny Pearl shook her head. "Not me," she said. "You need people your own age."

Hurt, Penny fell quiet. Was Granny Pearl mad at her? They were halfway up the hill now, almost at the garden. They passed Penny's bike leaning against a tree. It was Simon's old bike, which he had painted and polished for her on a previous visit home. For a moment Penny imagined jumping on it and riding as far away as she could. That reminded her of what she had seen on the drive home earlier.

"I forgot to tell you," she said to her grandmother, eager to bring back the good feeling between them. "I saw thousands of pampas seedpods on the way home today. They aren't usually out for months, and there are so many of them—I'm sure they're another sign."

"Pampas?" asked Granny Pearl. "You mean on the lane? I don't remember that from before . . . but maybe. It's possible." She paused, leaning on her cane as she considered. "And your brother and sister coming home in a couple of days . . . that may be part of it."

"What do they have to do with anything?" asked Penny.

"I don't know for sure yet," said Granny Pearl. "But," she muttered, "it tells me that there isn't much time." She would say nothing further.

It took a long time to make it up the hill. Seagrape flutter-hopped along behind them. They stopped at the garden to pick up the basket.

Penny bent down to pluck a few sage leaves, velvety soft as rabbits' ears. Granny Pearl seldom made it down to the garden anymore, and it wasn't the bountiful, shipshape plot it used to be. It was shrinking, its edges scraggly, caterpillars chomping their way through the tomatoes with new brazenness. A few rows at the end had been lost to the saw grass. Penny picked up the basket to carry to the house, feeling the familiar weight of carrots and muddy potatoes against her hip. Foamy leaves of parsley tickled her leg, and the bristles of the basket pricked her every now and then. She had been carrying the basket up from the garden for as long as she could remember. When Penny was very small, Granny Pearl had just pretended to let her help, then they had taken it together, and now Penny carried it on her own, walking slowly alongside her grandmother, who moved stiffly, pausing to rest a few times as they went up the last bit of the hill.

Across the garden, from the dark mouth of the lane, Penny saw a breeze blowing seedpods out of the trees, buoying them into the sky where they swirled, a mute flock of messengers bearing their urgent, secret message into the dull afternoon.

⊰⧸ Chapter Two ⧸⊱

The Drawer • Maya's Journal • A Frightening Episode
• "All of these things have explanations" • A Mission

Penny left the basket with her mother and grandmother in the kitchen and sneaked down the hallway to her bedroom.

Something that Granny Pearl had said in the garden had stuck in Penny's mind. She said that Seagrape knew something. *You feel it in your quills, don't you?* It was true that Seagrape had been temperamental lately, agitated and restless and more intolerant than usual. Penny's fingers bore the scars of impatient nips. But what the parrot might know Penny had no idea.

Granny Pearl had also said that Maya's and Simon's visit home might have something to do with what was happening.

Simon hadn't been home in close to a year now, but Maya had last been home six months ago. The city had made her sister elegant, and Penny had felt a little shy of her for the first few hours after she was back. She felt newly aware of her own tangled hair, her chin scabbed from a tumble on the soccer field, a fresh bump on her forehead from when she had tried to jump from the railing of the

Pamela Jane through the hatch into the cabin earlier that week. Angela was right—she looked like a little kid.

Penny had helped her sister lug her suitcase down the hallway.

"Everything always looks so small when you come back," Maya said.

"It's the same size it always was," said Penny.

"Well, your perspective changes," said Maya.

Whatever that means, Penny had thought, with a flicker of irritation. She had sat swinging her legs on Simon's old bed while Maya unpacked. Maya had been showing off in her city clothes, but the humidity was already making her dress limp and curling her hair. Soon enough her feet were bare, like they always used to be.

No mention was made of Maya's boyfriend—James or Julian, no one could seem to remember his name—who had been in the wings for the past year. Though he had come to visit the family once—and, as they all said, he was perfectly nice—none of them warmed to him. Even Maya herself didn't seem thrilled about him. Seagrape had brayed rudely at him anytime he came near until eventually Mami made Penny shut the parrot in her room, an act of betrayal that Seagrape rewarded by shredding a blanket with her beak.

"You two are still inseparable," Maya had said, pausing from unpacking to reach out to Seagrape on Penny's shoulder, letting the parrot gnaw her knuckles gently. "Helix knew you'd take good care of her." A soft, wistful glimmer came into her eyes. Through the window the breeze had sighed in the darkening orange grove.

"It seems like forever since we've seen him," said Penny.

"Seven years," said Maya. "It's been seven years."

She had been about to say something else but stopped herself.

In that moment, even with her sister right there, Penny had the sensation of missing her, or as if part of Maya was missing. When Maya was just a girl herself, she had carried Penny through the jungle in a sling and kept her and Simon safe. She had crossed mountains, lived in the treetops, and escaped from pirates—she had been brave and free and done all these amazing things in Tamarind. Now she was restless and preoccupied with a mysterious life far away and thoughts she never shared with Penny.

The old Maya would have wanted to know about the signs. She might have even known about them already. So that was where Penny was going to go: to the old Maya.

Penny went into the room she had once shared with her sister. She waited until Seagrape ducked in, then shut the door behind her. Penny slid a chair against it. She didn't want to get caught.

Furtively, she felt under the dresser's ledge until she found the tiny key, then jiggled it in the lock of the top drawer of Maya's old dresser. When Penny was little, she'd loved snooping through Maya's things. The contents of the locked drawer had been especially irresistible. Sometimes Maya would catch her and then Papi would say that anyone would think a murder was under way, with all the hollering that would break out. Penny liked Simon's things, too—a compass, books about insects, fossils, a math kit in a tin, random scientific gadgetry—but they were never intriguing to her in the way that her sister's treasures were.

It had been a long time since Penny had even thought about the drawer, but now, slowly, she opened it.

She inhaled its musty, botanical smell of old cedar and leaves, a whiff of Tamarind that reminded her of long walks through the jungle. She had been to Tamarind twice before. The first time she had been a baby, and Maya and Simon took turns carrying her in a sling. She didn't remember anything from that time, but she'd heard the others' stories so often that they felt like her own memories. But the second time—*that* she could recall vividly. She had been five years old. She remembered a lake where houseboats had come together like a jigsaw puzzle on different currents into a village that formed every night and disbanded every morning, and she remembered the strange old woman, Milagros, with bird droppings white as ice on her shoes, who had known many of Tamarind's oldest secrets. She could still picture Helix's feuding aunts, the señoras, whose ferocious quarrel they had witnessed, and she remembered how she had kicked the general's trunklike shins when she thought he had been hurting Simon. And she would never forget Helix quietly asking her to take care of Seagrape right before he jumped overboard and swam back to shore as the *Pamela Jane* headed across the Blue

Line toward home. She could almost hear the surprising splash, like the sound of something breaking.

She rummaged gently through objects with secret meanings, castoffs no longer useful but too precious to throw out—old fishing weights, pressed flowers, an ostrillo feather—until her fingers touched something cool. A tooth. It was smooth, its serrated edges blunted by time. It was attached to a worn leather strap. Helix's shark's tooth necklace, the one he had been wearing the first time they had seen him, the day they had landed in Tamarind and gone trekking in circles through the jungle, getting more and more lost until he had dropped down out of a tree—literally— and rescued them. Years later, when he had stayed behind in Tamarind, he had left it in the cabin on the *Pamela Jane* for Maya. For a very long time, Maya had worn it, even when she went to sleep at night, but eventually she had abandoned it in the drawer.

Penny heard her mother's voice down the hall and froze, ready to slam the drawer shut, but her mother's voice grew distant again. She was still in the kitchen with Granny Pearl.

Penny took out the necklace and turned it over in her hand. Seagrape came over and nibbled the leather.

"Shall I put it on?" Penny whispered. The parrot didn't answer, just cocked her head and looked at Penny. Maya had given up her claim to the necklace when she left it here— it belonged just as much to Penny by now. Penny slipped it over her head. The tooth was cool against her throat, as

29

though it had been deep underwater all this time. She felt some strange power, as if she were Helix, a hunter in the shadowy light of the jungle, adept and sure.

But what Penny was looking for was still inside.

Carefully, she reached in and withdrew one of Maya's old journals from the back. Penny heard footsteps and paused to listen, but no one came down the hall.

The journal's spine was cracked, its glue melted from the humidity, and it creaked as she opened it. The paper was mustard yellow with age.

I keep expecting him to show up one day, to just walk through the door, barefoot. It just doesn't seem real to me that he's gone and won't be coming back....

Maya was the one who had pined most openly for Helix (though it was obvious she had thought it was secretly). But Penny had missed him, too. She was little enough that the memories she did have got lost in the shuffle, squashed by the others' noisier and more powerful ones. Sometimes her family even corrected her. Since she'd been so young when he had left, no one thought she could miss him as much as they did, which wasn't true. Reading what Maya had written about Helix made him feel close, and had been worth risking her sister's wrath.

There were letters to him, too, written on pages that had never been torn out. Penny knew they weren't the type

of letters that ever got sent, even if there were an address to
send them to.

> *Dear Helix,*
> *I miss you more each day, not less. It's been three years*
> *since I last saw you, and I would think it would be the other*
> *way around, but the more time passes the more I miss you.*

Fearful of being discovered, Penny scanned the pages
quickly. Maya was not a faithful journal keeper. There were
often long lapses between entries. Once, a whole year was
skipped. Penny put the book back, shuffled through the
books until she found the one she wanted, written seven
years ago, when Granny Pearl had last seen the signs. Penny
skimmed the pages, waiting for some detail to jog her
memory, for something her sister had written to shed light.
But if there had been signs then, too, Maya had been oblivious to them. There was nothing here to help Penny.

Seagrape began to grouse under her breath.

"She left it here, didn't she?" said Penny. "That means
it doesn't really even belong to her anymore. If it was that
important, she would have taken it with her. Anyway," she
said, "I thought there might be something in here about
the signs, but there isn't, so I'm putting it back now."

Seagrape did that thing where she gazed at Penny without blinking. When Penny was younger, she had been convinced that Seagrape could talk but simply refused to.

Penny heard the murmur of voices in the kitchen. Her father was home. She sighed, knowing she was about to get in trouble about the tank. Reluctantly she closed the journal and returned it to the drawer.

When Penny reached the kitchen, she realized that there would be no lecture about the tank this night. Granny Pearl was in the middle of one of her episodes. She was sitting at the kitchen table, muttering under her breath, kneading her knuckles. Penny couldn't make out what she was saying, but there was an undercurrent of urgency in her tone. Penny's parents sat across from her, looking distressed. Evening had fallen and it had begun raining. The wind was blowing the rain around, and everything solid in the garden had merged into a single silhouette. The smell of wet earth crept in under the door. Penny stood in the doorway for a second, then tiptoed in and joined them.

Seagrape flew in behind Penny and landed on the back of a chair. Granny Pearl's gaze drifted to the bird.

"There you are," she said. "Is Helix here? Is he with you?"

"Helix?" said Mami calmly. "Pearl, Helix isn't here. He hasn't been in a long time."

Penny was frightened. Helix was in Tamarind. The Blue Line had sealed behind them years ago—surely Granny Pearl remembered that. She looked down at her grandmother's hands. They worked restlessly. Her knuckles were like burls, her skin thin and papery, a faint bluish cast in the hollows between bones. These strange spells had happened several times now. Scared, Penny had let her parents do the talking, but this time she felt desperate to do something to make her grandmother return to normal right away.

"Granny Pearl," she said cautiously.

"Maya?" asked Granny Pearl, looking right at Penny with a glazed, faraway look. "I thought that perhaps you'd be there, too, but Penny has to do this on her own."

Penny felt like the wind had been knocked out of her. It took a few seconds before she could get her breath back.

"It's me, Granny Pearl," she said in a small voice.

But Granny Pearl had slipped into the past, where Maya and Helix still were, and the world she was seeing was invisible to other people.

A sudden wind funneled up from the sea, through the garden, and howled through the few inches of open window over the kitchen sink, spraying droplets of rain across the counter and floor. Seagrape squawked and flapped her wings.

Mami got up and closed the window, shutting out the menace in the evening and closing the family in together.

The sound of the window broke the spell. Granny Pearl was fully with them again. She blinked a few times and looked around, as if she had just realized where she was. "I'm going to bed," she said abruptly, and stood up from the table. "No, stop fussing, I don't need help."

But Penny's mother went with her. Penny stood up to

go, too, but her father told her to sit down. They waited in unhappy silence.

"Take your goggles off at the table," he said at last.

Penny had forgotten that they were still on her forehead. She didn't take them off, but pushed them up higher. Her hair still had a whiff of the aquarium water. She picked up her fork, but the sight of the food on her plate turned her stomach. Granny Pearl had looked straight at her and not known who she was. Nothing like that had ever happened before, and the awful moment replayed over and over in Penny's mind.

Mami came back into the room. "She's in bed," she said, joining them at the table. "She'll be better after some sleep."

Her parents began to eat, but Penny had lost her appetite. She sneaked a glance at them. Recently Papi had shaved the snowy-white beard he'd had most of Penny's life, revealing a face that was gaunt and surprisingly foreign to her. Her mother's nails were short, her hair briskly brushed. She always looked like she got ready in a hurry, which she did. Their faces were lined from years of living on the boat, but tonight they looked older and wearier than usual. Suddenly Penny had an overwhelming urge to talk to them, to confide Granny Pearl's secret, even though she knew what they would say.

"It's because of the signs," she said at last, taking a bite at the same time so her voice was deliberately muffled. She took a deep breath. "I think they make her really tired. She'll be herself again once they're over."

"What signs?" asked Mami, only half listening.

"Things have been happening," said Penny. "In the garden, in the water. Granny Pearl says it's like signs that happen before a storm—you know, like spiders building their webs lower, that kind of thing. She says they mean that something big is about to happen."

Mami stopped eating and listened.

"What's about to happen?" asked Papi.

"I don't know," said Penny truthfully. "Granny Pearl won't tell me yet. But even Seagrape's quills are changing color."

"Seagrape's quills?" asked her mother, frowning and looking over at Seagrape, perched on the top rung of Granny Pearl's empty chair.

"They've started to shimmer," said Penny. "See?"

"Not really," said her mother.

"You need to be in the right light," said Penny. "But it's true."

Penny's mother looked at her father. "What else?"

Penny knew they didn't believe her—she had known that they wouldn't. But now she was determined to convince them.

"Lots of things," she said. "We found a bunch of harbor conchs lined up in a circle on the sand at the cove. That was the first thing. A wild cockatoo was sitting on the roof one day—he stayed there for an hour before he flew off. The leaves on the orange trees are turning silver—"

"I don't see that the orange trees are a different color," said Mami, looking out the window.

"It's raining," said Penny. "You can't see properly. I saw them, though—Granny Pearl showed me. And she says there's a cloud that forms right over the mouth of the cove every day at lunchtime. And today there were more pampas seedpods than ever before—"

"Penny, stop," said her father, interrupting her. "Any clouds out there are just clouds. The seedpods are no different than any other year. And it's probably a fungus that citrus trees get. I'll take a look at them tomorrow."

"There are other things," said Penny desperately. "Seagrape, show them your quills." But Seagrape wouldn't let Penny lift her wing.

"Sweetheart, all of these things have explanations," said Mami.

"Are you saying that Granny Pearl is making all this up?" said Penny indignantly. "If she says it's real, it's real!"

"Lower your voice," said her father sharply.

Penny stared miserably down at the food that had grown cold. Why wouldn't they listen?

Her mother put her hand on her father's and spoke calmly to Penny.

"Everyone's upset," she said. "Penny, Granny Pearl is very old now. Her mind is wandering. She's mixing things up—things from the past, imaginary things. Sometimes she believes things that aren't real."

Penny shook her head. "Maybe that happens to some people when they get old, but not Granny Pearl," she said. "I spend more time with her than anyone. If something were wrong, I'd know. She made it all the way down to the cove today. She hasn't done that in ages. It means that she's getting stronger again. She'll be like her old self as soon as the signs stop and whatever is going to happen happens."

"Penny, nothing's about to happen," said Papi. Suddenly he no longer looked angry; he was just sad.

"You don't *know* that," said Penny. "I'm surprised you haven't noticed any of the signs yourself. I thought scientists were supposed to be observant."

"We all love Granny Pearl," said Mami gently, moving to touch Penny's shoulder, but Penny shrugged her off.

"Then believe her!" said Penny, glaring at her mother.

"Penny," said her mother. "We think that what's going on with Granny Pearl is serious enough that we asked Maya and Simon to come home to see her. We didn't want to leave it any longer. Do you understand?"

It felt like a lump of food had stuck in Penny's throat, except that she had barely touched anything on her plate.

"Nobody told me that's why they're coming," she mumbled.

"I didn't think we had to," said her mother. "You already know that Granny Pearl hasn't been herself lately . . . that she's been spending more time in her own world."

"What's happening—what's really happening here— is something we can't stop," said her father.

None of them had ever talked about what was happening with Granny Pearl so openly before, and doing so was making it all horribly real.

"But," said Penny. "But she's still okay. She's still Granny Pearl."

She looked at her parents. They looked sadly back at her.

"Of course she's still Granny Pearl," said her mother softly. "But . . ." She trailed off.

Penny couldn't sit there any longer. She needed air. She stood up from the table quickly, the legs of her chair scraping noisily across the floor.

"You'll see," she said. "Granny Pearl is fine—she's FINE. The signs mean something is going to happen— when it does, you'll wish you had believed her!"

She stumbled down the dark hallway. She stopped outside Granny Pearl's room and pressed her forehead to the wall. She felt sick and dizzy. This wasn't how it was supposed to be. The silver orange trees. Seagrape's quills. The conch shells and the cloud and everything else. It was all real. She had seen all these things with her own eyes.

The only person who could reassure Penny now was her grandmother. Penny badly needed to hear her voice, to have her say something that would erase everything her parents had just said. Penny listened, but it was quiet behind Granny Pearl's closed door. She must already be asleep. Penny waited there another moment, then continued unhappily down the hall.

In her room, the shutters were still open and pale moonlight spilled in through the window, lighting the windward side of the furniture and casting outsized shadows from the lees. Penny was about to step through the doorway when a shadow moved and a figure stood up in the moonlight.

~~~

"Granny Pearl," said Penny when she had gotten over her fright. "What are you doing?"

"It's time," said Granny Pearl, getting creakily to her feet from the chair by the window. In the moonlight her hair was lit as white as surf. "I told you I'd let you know when I was sure. Come on, Penny, hurry—you have to catch the tide."

"The tide?" said Penny. "What do you mean?"

Penny noticed her backpack on the ground beneath the window, a life jacket sitting on top of it. Seagrape perched on the open sill.

"The signs," said Granny Pearl. "I saw them seven years ago, too, right before the four of you left for Tamarind. I thought that maybe the others would be with you, but now I can see you have to do this on your own."

For the first time, Penny felt angry at her grandmother.

"I don't know what you're talking about," she said.

Granny Pearl leaned closer, and Penny could see her eyes behind the moonlit lenses of her glasses.

"You have to go to Tamarind," Granny Pearl whispered. "There's something there you need to find, that only you can do."

Penny's heart began to pound. There was a low buzzing sound in her ears. She looked at her grandmother in disbelief.

"To Tamarind?" she asked.

"Shhh, whisper," said Granny Pearl. She had been holding Penny's raincoat, which now she pushed into Penny's hands. "Yes, Tamarind."

"B-but . . ." stuttered Penny. "It's impossible—the Blue Line is sealed, we closed it when we left the last time. It goes all the way around the island. There's no way back. . . ."

"There's a way," said Granny Pearl. "Take the rowboat. Row out of the cove, out past the anvil rock, out to the far boilers. Find the big brain coral, you know where it is, the biggest one, that leads to the crooked cut between the reefs. Wait there. I've packed everything you'll need in your backpack."

"You want me to leave *now*?" asked Penny. "But—I'm not allowed out in the rowboat at night." She looked out at the darkness. "Can't I go tomorrow instead?"

"No," said Granny Pearl. "It has to be now or you'll miss it."

The darkness felt palpable, pushing like velvet through the salty white screen. A breeze carried in the troubled rumble of the surf out by the far breakers. Penny looked helplessly at her grandmother.

"Shouldn't we tell Mami and Papi?" she asked.

Granny Pearl shook her head.

Penny put on her raincoat in a daze. She had grown up around the water. She knew how reckless it would be to take a small rowboat out alone half a mile offshore on a dark, rainy night. And in the past it had taken days of sailing to reach Tamarind—how was she going to get there in a rowboat? It couldn't be done.

"What am I supposed to do in Tamarind?" she asked weakly.

"You'll know when you get there," said Granny Pearl.

The moonlight lit the frames of her glasses like two silver pools. She reached out and touched Penny's cheek. "Everything will become clear," she said. "Don't be afraid, Penny."

But it wasn't the thought of being alone in the wobbly little rowboat in the dark night that frightened Penny. It was . . . what if *nothing* was out there? If she went out and found nothing, it would mean . . . what it would mean was unbearable. Her grandmother's hand on Penny's face had been dry and soft. Penny closed her eyes. She knew the faded print on Granny Pearl's housedress so well that she could still see its pattern, could smell the comforting scent of laundry soap and mint leaves mingled in the fabric.

"Granny Pearl," she said softly, afraid she might cry.

But she steadied herself. To refuse to go would be to admit that her parents were right. This was her chance to prove that the signs were real, that nothing had changed and that Granny Pearl was still herself. Penny took a deep breath.

"Okay," she said. "I'll do it."

She grabbed her life jacket and backpack and opened the window. Seagrape squawked quietly once and flew into the darkness. Before she could change her mind, Penny swung her leg over the ledge and dropped down into the garden.

Helix

He was headed to see the Great Wave, somewhere on the far northeast coast of Tamarind, in Kana, a place he had never been before. For the past seven years, he had been living in a small, sleepy town with his father, a retired general who kept groves of fruit trees—row upon orderly row of citrus that supplied all the nearby towns with polemos, tanguis, and tart suisallies. Helix had gotten to know his father for the first time in his life and had helped him with the citrus, expanding their reach to more far-flung areas. Then a year ago his father had died unexpectedly. He'd been an old man, asleep in bed in the middle of the night— a surprisingly peaceful death for a man who had spent half his life fighting. Without a clear sense of what to do next, Helix had stayed on, tending the groves, selling the crops, but becoming increasingly lonely, dissatisfied, restless.

A few weeks ago, during an early-morning inspection

of the groves, he had found a trespasser sleeping under a polemo tree, clothes damp with dew, empty peels on the ground beside him. Secretly grateful to meet someone living free, off the land like he used to do, Helix shared breakfast with the man, who he learned was from the east and was on his way back there to see the Great Wave and the Bloom. As Helix listened to the roaring—and no doubt exaggerated—stories about this amazing spectacle, this wonder of the world, he began to feel as if some color that he had forgotten was missing had suddenly been restored to the spectrum. The world suddenly seemed brighter and clearer, the things within it more sharply delineated, pulsing with life that gathered strength and seemed to propel him forward.

By the time he had returned to the house, the traveler had departed, the sun had burned off the dew, and Helix knew that he would be going east. It wasn't just curiosity. Even when his father was alive, the town had never fully felt like home. The sense that something was missing— something critical—had only grown stronger as time passed.

Helix needed a change.

So he had begun the long journey across Tamarind, through humid jungles, across mountains where the air was thin and cool, over barren deserts where any breeze that came released animal bones from shifting yellow dunes, rattling them across the scorching sand. The journey boiled life down to its simplest terms. He had only to find food and dry ground to sleep on each night. Usually he slept in the open air; on rainy nights he pitched a small tent.

He had grown up during the war in Western Tamarind, and he was happy to feel the atmosphere change as he entered the region known as Kana. It was a relief to leave behind the old scars in the landscape—the guns rusting in the grip of feverish vines, the ruins sinking into the mud— and be in a place that had not endured years of fear, a landscape not burdened by his own memories. Even on its outskirts, Kana was lush and bright. Food was plentiful. Everywhere was drooping, swishing, kinetic greenery, singing with all the life in it.

After weeks of walking, he was now only a day or two from Tontap, where he had been told the festival would begin. He was walking through an open, empty field when he saw the green smudge of a parrot in the clear blue sky. He stopped and shaded his eyes. He felt a surge of hopefulness, as he always did.

When he was a child, she used to perch beside his shoulder while he slept each night, after his mother had died. She had watched over him for years, until he'd sent her to be with the family. He still missed her company, but it comforted him to know that some part of him was still with them.

He squinted up through the glare. But as the bird neared, he saw it was too small, its feathers striped with crimson. It wasn't her.

And never will be, he told himself.

He wiped the sweat off his face with his arm and kept walking.

He had ample time to daydream as he walked, time for the silent, ephemeral churn of memory to overtake him. He recalled the little house on the cove—the sweet scent of the allamanda flowers blooming on the trellis, the green cloud of the vegetable garden, and the tiny butterfly cocoons shivering in the light breeze through the milkweed patch. Another world, another life. He would have thought that the memories might have faded. Detail blurred, it was true, but only as if to clear away clutter, allowing him to feel the essence of those he missed in pure, potent form. Maya, Simon, Penny, their parents, Granny Pearl—sometimes they seemed more real to him, more present, and certainly more beloved, than most of the people in his daily life.

He remembered the last time he had seen Maya and Simon and Penny. He had dived off the port side of the *Pamela Jane*—he could still feel the cold shock of the water on his skin. On land he had climbed a tree and sat, hidden in the swaying foliage, his hair still wet as he watched the yellow-hulled sailboat vanish into the mists of the Blue Line. He had stayed in the tree long after the boat was gone and the salt had dried white on his skin. Then, without even the parrot to keep him company, he had climbed down and begun the journey to find his father. That had been seven years ago.

Feelings drifted aimlessly, changed shape, dissolved, gave way to new ones, like the cottony white clouds in the sky above him as he drew slowly closer to Tontap. He heard something and stopped to listen, ear to the air. There was a faint tremor in the earth beneath his feet, a minor perturbation in the atmosphere, registered only by him and a sloth, who paused a moment from his lugubrious chewing to glance curiously up at the bright blue sky. A breeze rose, cooling his face, stirring and silvering the leaves. For the first time, after many days deep in the interior of the island, he smelled salt on the air. He wasn't far from the coast now. The breeze faded. Deciding that the disturbance he had sensed must have been nothing, he resumed walking.

❧ Chapter Three ❧

Flags • Following the Lights • A Wish • A Door Opens

Seagrape mumbled excitedly and flew after Penny down the hill. The rain had tapered off; only a light patter still dripped under the trees. Pampas seedpods were strewn across the grass. Penny reached the foot of the garden, where the tiny crescent beach shone stark white in the moonlight, its crust of sand dimpled. Bobbing on the swells, the *Pamela Jane*'s yellow hull emitted a dull glow. The sign on her stern squeaked back and forth in the wind: CLUBHOUSE—KEEP OUT! Her portholes reflected the moonlight, perfect, deep wells into an even greater darkness. Outside the shelter of the cove, the growl of the open sea roared in Penny's head.

She flipped over the rowboat and dragged it down to the shore. Moonlit foam laced the surface of the water surging toward her. Beyond, the ocean was black. The rowboat seemed smaller and flimsier than usual as she stepped in. Seagrape murmured nervously on her shoulder. Penny dug in with the oars and rowed hard toward the mouth of the cove. She gazed back at the house, standing there as it always had—safe, solid, lit, warm—as she headed away from it into the darkness.

Then the outgoing tide caught the rowboat, and for the next stretch it took her full concentration to navigate through high reefs and craggy rocks rustling with crabs. The oars clicked rhythmically in the oarlocks, and after a few minutes she passed the black anvil rock that she and Granny Pearl used to swim to each morning. As she rowed, the peculiar joy of being alone in a small boat on the ocean at night— the thrill of slightly perilous freedom—overtook her.

When she reached the outer boiler reefs, she stopped and let the rowboat drift. A flashlight had been tucked in the outside pocket of her backpack. She clicked it on and searched the water with it until she found the crooked cut, like a crease in plush black velvet, leading out to deeper water. A violent snow of fry massed in the turquoise beam. And then there it was—the great mustard-yellow globe of brain coral, a bright yellow orb, like the cold ghost of a sun sunk long ago.

"That's it," she whispered to Seagrape. "Now we just have to wait. Something will happen." The parrot grumbled and ruffled her feathers, staring hard into the darkness.

There was a light but messy chop in the water, and the boat rocked gently from side to side. The scent of chimney smoke and spice trees hung on the land breeze, but from the low vantage of the boat the island kept dropping from sight behind the black swells. In the other direction, toward open water, only the barest distinction existed between the dark sea and dark sky. Now that she had stopped rowing, Penny felt the chilly night air creeping through her clothes.

She shivered. Waves sloshed against the hull and the minutes ticked past. How waiting there, so close to shore, was supposed to get her to Tamarind, she had no idea. Seagrape sat stoically on the bow.

When the boat wandered on the current, Penny rowed just enough to stay near the coral. The rest of the time, she drew her legs to her chest and sat as close to the center of the boat as she could, trying not to think about bold, blunt-nosed sharks knocking into the hull, or a tentacle rearing up, meaty and cold, snatching her out of the boat, dragging her and the boat under with a woody crunch, a noisy slurp, before she even had time to make a peep.

She remembered the backpack, and to distract herself she opened it. Granny Pearl must have prepared everything earlier that day.

A canteen of water. A sandwich. An apple. Penny's heart sank a bit when she realized that her grandmother thought she might have to wait out there long enough that she would get hungry. But she hadn't had dinner, so she began to eat the sandwich. She rummaged deeper. Her bathing suit, Simon's old penknife and compass. The final thing in the bag made Penny stop. A slow prickle of dread crept through her.

She took out a small yellow flag and held it up in the moonlight. A sunny yellow rectangle with a green parrot stitched into the middle of it, wings spread in flight. Two others, almost identical, were crushed in the bottom of the bag. Granny Pearl had sewn them for Penny long ago. Helix had helped her create a secret code with them—a flag upside down on an allspice tree meant that Simon was home, two flags midway up the old cedar meant that Penny and Maya were out on the boat, and so on. Later Penny and Angela had used them when they had played pirates, hoisting them up the mast of the *Pamela Jane*, letting them flutter from the branches of the conquered orange grove.

The flags belonged in games, in make-believe.

What sort of mission would require something used in a game?

No mission would.

No real one, anyway.

Only one invented by an old woman whose mind was wandering.

Penny sat there numbly. The parrots on the flags were faded and frayed, their threads loose, as if the birds were losing feathers. A school of tiny fish jumped nearby, startling her. Penny could almost feel the shock of the cool night air on their scales during their brief, breathless flight. They chattered down and there was only the chilly silence again.

The flashlight beam had been growing gradually weaker. Now it died altogether. Instantly the moon reflected off the surface of the water, black and bright as oil, sealing away what lay beneath. As if cast loose when the flashlight died, the boat was being swiftly ferried along by the current. When Penny looked back toward land, she was alarmed by how far she was from where she had started. The lights of land had shrunk to intermittent twinkles.

New, clear-eyed dread spread through her. It had been foolish to come out here like this. The current was against her, and getting back to shore was going to be a long, hard haul. Hands shaking, she had just slipped the oars back in the oarlocks when Seagrape squawked loudly, a warning.

Penny noticed a light farther out to sea. It was riding low, like the remnant of a shooting star that had landed in the water.

It was too far away to tell what it was, but her heart quickened. Was this what Granny Pearl had sent her out there for?

To reach it, Penny would have to leave the last of the reefs and venture a short distance into the open ocean. She hesitated, glancing back toward land, then began to row toward the glow. She rowed cautiously at first, and then harder, but each time she saw the light it was a little farther away, bobbing on the swells like a floating lantern. Finally it dropped behind a swell and didn't appear again.

Penny looked around and saw another glimmer, this one off starboard. She turned and rowed as powerfully as she could, and this time she kept the light in her sights and drew alongside it.

She looked down upon a large jellyfish grazing the surface, the moonlight reflecting off its pale, diaphanous bubble. Bioluminescent tentacles drifted dreamily down into the deep. A few small fish, stung to death, hung suspended stiffly in the tangle.

Several other jellyfish glided up ahead, a small fleet of

ghostly night travelers, passing silently by. What looked like fine electrical filaments emitted a buzz of pinkish light within their bubbles. Penny had never seen anything like them before and rowed slowly to keep pace. Had Granny Pearl meant for her to find them? What was she supposed to do now?

Absorbed by the strange creatures, Penny was oblivious to the thickening clouds moving in, snuffing out the stars one by one. The jellyfish floated on ahead and began to spread out, scattering faster than Penny could keep up with.

When the last of them drifted from sight, Penny found herself in pitch blackness. She looked all around frantically, but the lights of land were gone. It was as if a low, opaque roof had closed over the sea and the rowboat was drifting inside a closed vault, into which a great, rushing, jetting darkness spilled. She couldn't even see her own hands in front of her. All that was left was the sound of her ragged breathing, whistling a little in fear. In the panic of sudden blindness, she reached for Seagrape, relieved to feel the parrot's silky feathers and warm, small body.

With every fiber of her being, she wished that she had never left home, that she was still in her cozy room getting ready for bed, her parents and grandmother just down the hall. Fear shocked her into clarity, and she reasoned that, without any other markers to orient her, her best chance of returning to land was to row against the current that had brought her here. She turned the boat around and began to row. Her back and arms soon ached, but she was too afraid to stop. If she rested for just a moment, the boat drifted rapidly back, losing sea it had cost her so much effort to gain. She forced herself not to cry and settled into a numbing, thoughtless, interminable rhythm.

Sometime later, she jerked awake.

She must have fallen asleep for only an instant or two, so exhausted that her chin had nodded forward onto her chest, but an oar had slipped from her hand. She searched the surrounding water, but it was gone. It took all her strength to pull the remaining one into the hull, as though it were made of iron and not wood. She lashed it to the gunwales so it wouldn't get lost if a wave tipped the boat in the night. Exhausted and cold, she lay down in the hull, pulling her knees up to her chest, resting her cheek on her backpack. She drew Seagrape close.

"They'll find us in the morning," she said.

Penny had no idea how much time had passed, but when she woke she instantly had the feeling that she was somewhere very different from where she had begun. There was no sign of Seagrape. She was alone in the boat. The night was over, but the daylight was muffled by fog that hung thick as cotton in the air. She yawned and it filled her mouth. It was like being in an airplane up in the clouds, except that she could still hear the gurgle of water against the row-boat's hull. She was stiff from sleeping on hard planks and her stomach growled.

"Seagrape!" she called. Her voice echoed back to her, as if it had bounced off a mountainside.

Something was pinching her. She reached up to find that her goggles were still on her forehead. She felt unduly comforted by the discovery of this small, precious thing from home. She shifted them a bit and rubbed the indentation they had left in her skin. Helix's shark's tooth necklace was still around her neck, too.

She wished the fog wasn't so heavy so she could see where she was.

Suddenly, up ahead, she saw a giant strobe blink on and off. Moments later came another flash, closer to her, as if someone had flicked on a spotlight and just as quickly turned it off again. Was there a boat up ahead?

"Hello!" Penny shouted. "Is anyone out there?"

Through the mist she heard the sound of beating wings.

Seagrape, feathers brilliant green and lustrous with fog, landed heavily on the bow, the boat rocking gently beneath her weight.

"Seagrape!" Penny cried, overjoyed to see her.

The parrot had something in her beak. She squawked and it fell out, landing with a ping and rolling across the hull. Penny picked it up. A berry stone, copper-colored, the size of a marble. She clutched it and looked all around, but the fog obliterated everything beyond the rowboat itself.

"Where did you come from?" she asked Seagrape urgently. "Which way is land?"

Seagrape balanced on the bow as the boat settled, but gave no indication where she had come from.

Penny opened her palm and looked at the stone. A few fibers of wine-red fruit still clung to it. It was unlike anything she knew from home. Could it . . . was it possible? She peered into the fog.

Suddenly and deeply, Penny wanted to see Tamarind, wanted a glimpse of its emerald slopes, its brilliant blue water feathered in the breeze, small waves breaking whitely on its shores, to see the glossy sheen of the jungle's canopy, hiding the dark, damp richness that lay within. She wanted to be where she had been before, with her brother and sister, where they had met Helix. She wanted with all her heart to be where Granny Pearl had sent her.

A sideways pillar of light shot across the water nearby. It no longer looked like it could be from a ship. It was as though a door had opened in an invisible wall and light was spilling through from the other side. For an instant, Penny thought she heard another bird, but none appeared. She had only one oar left, but she picked it up and began to paddle toward the light. Just before it went out, she glimpsed a dark blue seam in the water, running into the fog in either direction.

She knew at once what it was.

Her heart began to pound.

The Blue Line.

She was at the border of Tamarind.

A new gap appeared in the line and again light blazed through. The gap was open for just a few seconds before sealing abruptly, creating a swell that surged toward the rowboat, rocking it violently, slopping water over the gunwales. Seagrape squawked and flew off the bow. Again Penny heard a strange birdcall, and for a brief second she was sure she had heard voices, too. She put on her backpack and seized the oar, then knelt at the bow and began to paddle with all her might, but the gap closed again before she could get there.

"Hello!" she shouted.

She was feeling panicky that she might be stopped here, on the edge, when she saw a flash off the rowboat's starboard. She turned in time to see light pouring through another breach in the dark blue seam.

The blaze of heat and light burned away the fog and lit the water electric blue. Instead of being pushed away, this time the line pulled her toward it. Water poured through the gap like the tide rushing in under a bridge, lifting the rowboat with it. Penny saw schools of neon fish speeding around her. White birds tumbled like wheels spinning through the air. In a great gush, the rowboat was drawn through. Seagrape flew through a split second before the invisible door slammed shut behind them.

The rowboat teetered on the crest of a swell. Penny had lost the oar and gripped the gunwales. She was looking out over a bright vista of somewhere else entirely. The sky was hot and clear. A peacock-blue lagoon stretched before her and, in the distance beyond it, a smattering of green atolls were lit as bright and vivid as a grasshopper's wings in the sun. Penny hung on for dear life as the boat plunged down the swell into the new world.

She felt warm water engulfing her legs and looked down to see that the rowboat had taken on water and was foundering. Before she could even begin bailing, the water was up to her waist. She heard voices and looked up to see a small, swift wooden boat under a bright crimson silk sail drawing alongside her. As the rowboat sank beneath her, Penny reached up to the hands stretching down for her and was hauled out of the slop and churn of the sea and onto the deck of the new boat.

❧ Chapter Four ❧

New Children • *The Bloom* • *The Competition*
• *No Ordinary Monkey* • *The Whorl in the Trees*

The boat rocked on the settling sea, a fizz of bubbles popping around her hull. The rowboat had vanished. Penny crouched in a pool of water from her soaking-wet clothes near a net full of silvery fish while two boys and a girl, all about her age, stared down at her in amazement.

"I *told* you I heard someone out there," said the girl, then she whispered, "Kal, did you really open a whorl?"

One of the boys looked nervously back at the Blue Line, once again solid as a fortress, then turned back to Penny.

"I . . ." he said. "I mean . . . yes, I must have—" He gazed, dumbfounded, at Penny.

"It was a coincidence," said the other boy. "You were just messing around. No one can *open* the Blue Line."

"But a whorl opened and she came through," said the girl. "We saw her with our own eyes. You did, too, Jebby."

"I'm not saying I didn't," said the boy. "I'm saying that *Kal* didn't do it. He couldn't have. Whorls open all the time before the Bloom; it doesn't mean Kal had anything to do with this one."

The girl turned to Penny and shook her head. "An Outsider. And *we* found her."

Penny, no stranger to feeling like an outsider these days, had never felt as much like one as she did then.

"Are you all right?" asked the girl.

Penny got to her feet, looking down at her arms and legs, which no longer felt like they quite belonged to her.

"I think so," she said.

She was confused and afraid, but she still had her goggles and her backpack, and was reassured by the sight of Seagrape, who was ticking serenely back and forth on the starboard gunwale. Surely Seagrape wouldn't be so calm if Penny were in danger.

She looked past the children at the distant patch of brilliant green islands that she had first glimpsed from the other side of the Blue Line.

"Am I in . . . Is this Tamarind?" she asked.

"That's Tamarind up ahead," said the girl. "The northeast coast, to be exact—Kana."

Kana. The name jogged no memory, and the islands were still too far away for Penny to make out clearly.

"How do you know where you are?" asked the girl.

"I've been here before," whispered Penny. She felt a surge of emotion as she looked toward Tamarind. She wanted to tell Granny Pearl she had been right, that the signs had been real. That she was sorry for having doubted her. Then her heart lifted: Helix was there—somewhere in Tamarind.

She turned back to the children. "I'm Penny," she said. "This is Seagrape."

"I'm Tabba Silverling," said the girl. "This is my brother, Jebby. And this is Kal."

Tabba and Jebby were small and wiry and looked like twins. They had bright, dark eyes and hair so black it shone blue in the sunlight. Tabba's hair was cropped at her chin and a few fish scales glimmered on her faded tunic. The boys were bare-chested and wore loose-fitting fishermen's trousers. A carved wooden whistle hung from a string around Jebby's neck. Kal looked a little older than the others, perhaps a year or two, and while they were lean he was heavyset, with strength born more of size than of health. He had a yellowed bruise on his forehead, beneath a scrape that had almost healed. Tabba and Jebby seemed friendly, but Kal stood half in the shadow of the gently luffing sail, staring at Penny suspiciously, as if now that his shock had passed, he was beginning to question the wisdom of what he had called forth.

"Let's take her back near the line," he said to the others.

Penny felt a moment of horror—they weren't just going to abandon her there, were they?

"It's too late," Jebby said to Kal. "However that whorl opened, it's shut now."

They had been sailing along slowly, parallel to the Blue Line. Penny looked back to see it, a sealed band of darker blue that was already fading back into the sea. The gap she had come through—the whorl, if that's what it was called—was no longer there. There was no sign of exactly where it had even been. There was no way back across. Home—where Penny's parents and Granny Pearl were, where her brother and sister would be in a few days, where the *Pamela Jane* still lay at anchor in the peaceful cove—seemed impossibly far away. The rowboat was gone, and the islands in the distance were too far to swim to. Penny's knees suddenly felt weak, and she held on to the gunwale to steady herself.

"I'll open another one—watch," said Kal.

He put his hands on his temples and closed his eyes tightly, concentrating. But, when he opened his eyes a moment later and looked at the Blue Line, nothing had happened.

"We need to be closer," he said.

"You'd better be careful," said Tabba darkly. "Or the mandrill will show up right on the deck of this boat."

"Forget it, Kal," said Jebby. "She'll have to come home with us."

"Two against one," Tabba said firmly when Kal protested. "We're taking her to shore."

There was no doubt in Penny's mind that if Kal had been on his own, he would have left her here. But Jebby turned the tiller to starboard and the boat tacked. The boom swung neatly across and the crosswind caught the sail, then the boat settled into an easy, steady run toward the islands.

"After we get to shore, you're on your own," Kal told Penny.

He took the tiller from Jebby, who let him, and settled in the cockpit. Seagrape flew ahead, and Tabba and Jebby joined Penny on the port rail.

"Don't worry about him," Tabba whispered. She smiled at Penny. "You're lucky," she said cheerfully. "You're here just in time for the Bloom, and you came through the line in the right place! Our town, Tontap, is just behind those hills. Everything starts there tonight. People come from all over Kana—from all over Tamarind!—to see the Bloom, but I never heard of anyone coming from the Outside before!"

"What's the Bloom?" asked Penny cautiously. Her hair had begun to dry stiffly in the wind, and she pushed a stray strand behind her ear.

Kal snorted. Tabba and Jebby ignored him.

"It will be in the Great Wave, four days from now," said Jebby. "It only happens once a generation. There's a competition to be the Bloom Catcher—the one who will go out to the Wave to get the Bloom."

"The kids in the competition are called Bloom Players," said Tabba. "They're mostly thirteen or fourteen—no one can be older than that or they'll be too big for the Wave. There are three trials, and the player who passes them all becomes the Bloom Catcher. No one knows what the first trial is yet. It won't be announced until tonight, and the players don't leave until tomorrow morning. Jebby and I are going to Palmos to see the Bloom at the end. There's a

62

big stone amphitheater in the valley and everyone watches from there. We're just going to watch, of course—Kal's actually a Bloom Player."

"Wave," muttered Kal from the stern. "Like it's some ordinary wave. It's a *wall* of water."

Tabba and Jebby seemed eager to talk, and Penny had been about to ask another question, but Kal wielded peculiar authority in the group and made her feel nervous. The Bloom—whatever it was—was clearly very important, and it seemed wise to keep the extent of her ignorance a secret. In the hull, the fish were still, their molten scales like empty armor.

"The Bloom only happens in one place, Palmos," said Kal, looking coldly at Penny. "There's an ancient stone dial in the valley there. That's how everyone knows when the Bloom is going to happen. Before the Bloom starts, the tide goes out, out, out—way farther than it ever does, ever—and all the water gets sucked up into this enormous wave. A towering wall of water. You can see straight into it; it's like glass. That's where the Bloom happens."

Kal fell into sullen silence. The wind hummed in the sails and made Penny feel cold in her damp clothes. The children waited.

"Well," said Jebby grudgingly. "You've started, so you may as well tell the whole thing."

Kal sighed. After a moment he continued, as if he was doing them a favor.

"On the morning of the Wave, thousands of people

wait in the hills all around Palmos," he said. "At exactly the right moment, the Bloom Catcher starts to walk out to the Wave. He walks, every step sure and steady, even though he's looking up at this wave so huge that he's the only one in all of Kana brave enough to just walk up to it like that."

The wind whistled softly over the sea, breaking its surface into a confusion of dazzling panes. No one interrupted Kal, and he dropped his voice, making the children lean in toward him.

"Everything is silent," he said. "No one rustles. No birds chirp. The only thing that moves is the Bloom Catcher. He walks all the way out to the bottom of the Wave . . . and then . . . he dives in!"

Kal lunged forward a few inches and Penny recoiled, nearly slipping off the gunwale. She winced as she felt a splinter slide into her palm, but she kept her gaze steadily on Kal's.

"Suddenly the Bloom starts bursting out everywhere in the water," said Kal, raising his voice, sweeping his arm through the air to mirror the grand scale of the Bloom. "Like dozens of fires underwater, lighting everything up. Every creature from miles around shows up. The water is crammed with shoals of fish, flocks of birds diving in, sharks appearing out of nowhere, turtles, octopus—everything—all there to feed on the Bloom. It's total chaos."

Kal had begun by trying to frighten her, Penny knew, but his vision of the Bloom was more powerful than his desire to impress her, and he seemed to have forgotten that anyone was even there.

"But the Bloom Catcher isn't scared," he continued in a low voice. "He's strong. He can hold his breath underwater for longer than anyone else. He swims and gathers some of the Bloom. When he has everything he needs, he steps out of the Wave and walks—he *walks*, he never runs or looks behind him—and gets back to shore just before the water comes tumbling down. But by then he has the Bloom. He's the only one in all of Kana—in all of Tamarind—who has it. He pours it in the Coral Basin to save Kana, and everyone knows who he is. Even people outside Kana hear about him. He's the most powerful person anywhere."

Kal's story had woven a spell over them and it took a moment for anyone to speak. Penny realized she had been holding her breath. They had strayed slightly and now Kal corrected their course so they were once again heading toward land. The islands were closer now and appeared larger. A steady sea breeze rippled the foliage, making the hills shimmer like a mirage rising up from the sea. Clouds soaked the peaks, shadows darkened the dreamy slopes, and the whole place faded in and out behind a thick salt haze.

"Well," said Tabba at last. "At least we *think* that's what happens. We've never seen it. A Bloom only comes once a generation. We weren't even alive the last time there was one."

"It's what happens," said Kal. "Believe me."

"Stop pretending you know so much," cried Jebby in exasperation. "I don't care what else you've done, Kal. When it comes to the Bloom, you're just like us—you've never seen it either. And you don't know that you'll even make it past the first trial, let alone the second two! The Bloom Catcher could be anyone."

"It can't be anyone," said Kal quietly. He kept his gaze on the land now, hand firmly on the tiller.

Penny's curiosity was swiftly growing greater than her fear of Kal.

"What *is* the Bloom?" she asked. "It happens in the Wave, but what is it?"

The children paused.

"I know that each bit is very, very tiny," said Jebby. "It looks like glowing sand stirred up in the current. So bright it hurts your eyes."

"No," said Kal. "It looks more like blue-green fires. But underwater."

"Most people say it looks like turquoise clouds of pollen that burst open," said Tabba.

"But what does it do?" asked Penny, eager to find out before the children began arguing among themselves. "Why does everyone want it?"

"The Bloom is the biggest, most powerful thing ever that one person can have," said Kal. "There's nothing else like it."

"It keeps Kana safe," said Tabba. "From the whorls

and the mandrill. When it's poured into the Coral Basin, all the whorls that opened before the Bloom close, and the mandrill is forced to go back to the Gorgonne."

"But the Bloom Catcher is allowed to keep a tiny bit for himself," said Jebby. "They say it makes him strong and wise and helps him live a long time."

"The Bloom is just . . ." said Tabba, struggling to explain. "Ma and Da say it's . . . life."

Penny's heart began to race. She tried to sound calm.

"Could the Bloom Catcher give the Bloom to someone else?" she asked. "You said it makes the Bloom Catcher strong and helps him live a long time. . . . If someone were sick or old and they were given the Bloom, would it help them?"

"Probably," said Tabba. "I mean, if it works for the Bloom Catcher, I don't see why it wouldn't work for someone else, too, right?"

The children kept talking, but Penny was no longer paying attention.

Warmth spread throughout her whole body. She didn't know how she would do what she had to do, or how she could return home again after, but she knew one thing: Granny Pearl wasn't crazy. What she had been talking about was real. She must have known about the Bloom and had sent Penny to Tamarind to get it—the thing that would make her well again and restore everything at home to the way it used to be.

Wild, giddy joy seized Penny. She felt fresh and alive.

The gloomy past months of worry and the sharp terror of the night in the rowboat had been rinsed clean, and in an instant life had opened up and anything and everything had become possible again. She looked ahead eagerly to Kana. The clouds had moved off the peaks, the haze had dispelled, and Tamarind appeared larger and brighter and more solid than it had been before. The sun streamed down and the shadow of the ruby-red sail raced alongside them on the water. Seagrape was far ahead now, a bright green star in the blue sky, leading them in. Kal let out the sails and they rushed toward Kana.

The sea was shallow in some places, deep in others, and Penny looked down into water that was by turns azure and indigo and emerald, animated by flashing schools of bronze fish and sea bats that fluttered by on their darkly ruffled capes. Several times she saw silent fleets of the same jelly-fish that had drawn her to Kana, their glow dulled by the daylight, their tentacles gently trawling the current. The wind coming off the land swelled the red silk mainsail, which Kal adjusted, turning the boat toward a passage through the islands.

Where once there had been just a cloak of green, now individual trees came into view as the boat approached land. What had looked like boulders on the beaches revealed themselves to be snoozing tortoises who roused and shuffled off, their heavy, lumbering bodies leaving surprisingly fine, feathery traces in the sand. Jebby blew the whistle around his neck, and a flock of gangly yellow birds wading in the shallows raised their heads and trilled back.

"That's what I heard on the other side of the line—your whistle!" said Penny, recognizing the sound she'd heard through the fog. The whistle was carved neatly out of pale wood, and Jebby held it sideways, like a flute, his fingers jumping nimbly in sequence to imitate the cries of the yellow flock.

"I made it myself," he said proudly. "I can do fifty different calls with it."

He began demonstrating various calls, and the lemony flock turned, alarmed, and retreated on long stilts of legs into the mangroves.

The boat rounded a head, and a town came into view, nestled deep in a green harbor.

"Tontap!" said Tabba proudly. "It was chosen as the place for the competition to start for the Bloom."

It was not the deserted fringe of shore that Penny, Maya, and Simon had first landed on, or the flinty coral fortress town they had approached on their second time to the island. This Tamarind teemed with human life. Palm-thatched huts sprang from the shores all around the harbor. Carts laden with fresh produce rattled over bridges. Boats heeled under bright silk sails. The air seemed clearer, the colors more vivid than Penny remembered. Here, the ghosts of scents that had lingered in the pressed leaves in Maya's drawer at home were rich and alive—smoke from cooking fires, herbs drying on sun-baked stones, the sour sap of trees, and the waft of damp earth. Sounds of squealing and growling and honking and chirping burbled inside the hot shadows of the jungle and traveled effortlessly across the water.

"Look at all the people," said Jebby. "Way more than when we headed out this morning!"

The coastal road into the town was jammed with travelers, walking in noisy groups or riding in carts pulled by bristle-maned gray mules that swayed beneath the weight of their passengers.

"See over there," said Tabba, pointing to a group of young men with thick yellow ribbons knotted above their elbows. "Those are Bloom Players—they all wear yellow arm sashes."

"They're just showing off," said Kal, frowning at the group. "You're not supposed to wear your sash until tonight."

"Why can only one person be the Bloom Catcher?" Penny asked as casually as she could. "Wouldn't there be better chances of getting it if a whole bunch of people went out to the Wave?"

"The Wave is big, but it's very fragile," said Tabba. "If more than one person dives through it, it will collapse. That's why a kid has to do it—only a kid is small enough."

"Who gets to be a Bloom Player?" asked Penny.

"You have to do something that no one else has done," said Jebby. "Then Elder—or whoever your town elder is—decides if you qualify."

"It has to be something really hard or scary," added Tabba.

"Like what?" asked Penny.

"One guy walked across a rope over the Naino Gorge," said Jebby.

"Another caught twelve Tagor eels with his bare hands," said Tabba. "That kind of thing."

"What did you do, Kal?" Penny asked.

No one answered for a moment.

"We're not supposed to talk about it," said Tabba.

"Drop me off first," Kal interrupted.

They were nearing a wooden dock on one of the tiny islands dotting the small green harbor they had just entered. When they drew close to the dock, Kal hopped lightly onto it.

"But what do we do now?" Tabba whispered to him.

"You're the ones who wanted to pick her up; you figure it out," Penny heard him say as he reached down for the small net of fish from Jebby.

They watched him hoist the catch onto his back and disappear into the trees. Though Penny was relieved to see him go, she knew that Tabba and Jebby would soon leave her, too. She wasn't looking forward to being on her own.

Without Kal there, Tabba and Jebby relaxed. Jebby took the tiller, and Tabba stretched out her legs as they sailed across the harbor. Seagrape, who had been cutting emerald swaths in front of them, returned, coasting in and landing on the bow where she perched, feathers folded crisply, curved beak pointing into the wind.

"How do you know Kal, anyway?" Penny asked.

"We've known him ever since he came to Kana," said Tabba. "He was seven or eight then."

"He's just a year older than us," said Jebby.

"Oh," said Penny, surprised by how disappointed she felt. "So you really are friends."

"I wouldn't go that far," said Jebby. "Kal's just . . . Kal."

"He doesn't really *have* friends," said Tabba. She reached out and stroked Seagrape's head with a knuckle. "But Tontap's so small. Everyone knows everyone else. He wanted to go fishing for this kind of fish that school out by the Blue Line that are supposed to be lucky. We like going out near the line, so we said we'd help him. After all, he *is* a Bloom Player."

"We're supposed to stay away from the line," said Jebby. "But everyone's so busy getting ready for the festival we figured no one would notice."

"Kal's wanted to be the Bloom Catcher forever," explained Tabba. "Ever since he got to Kana. His mother sent him to live with his aunt and uncle in Tontap, but he hates it here. He used to tell everyone how great it was at home and how he was going to go back there, but no one ever came to get him."

"It's his own fault he's never fit in," said Jebby. "He

thinks he's better than everyone else. For ages now he's been acting like he's already the Bloom Catcher!"

"Ma says he'll get himself in trouble, messing around with all the things he messes around with," said Tabba. "That's how he got the mandrill to appear in the first place."

"Tabba!" snapped Jebby.

"Sorry," she said.

The children had mentioned the mandrill a few times now.

"Is it a real mandrill?" asked Penny. "A monkey? Have you seen him?" She remembered seeing a color photograph of a large, burly monkey with a brightly colored face in a book her parents had at home. It was the creature's skin that was brilliantly pigmented, as though he had walked through a rainbow and it had soaked into his body.

"He's no ordinary monkey," said Jebby.

"He opens whorls," said Tabba. "Before the Bloom, he can be anywhere he wants in Kana. He opens whorls all over the place. Look—see that there? In the trees?"

Penny looked where Tabba was pointing and saw something peculiar in the jungle along the shore: a blurred, swirly, oval patch, as if a giant's thumbprint had smudged the surface of the canopy. She'd never seen anything like it.

"It's the whorl the mandrill left through, the day he came to Kana," said Tabba.

Before Penny could ask any questions, Jebby tacked sharply to avoid another boat, and she had to move to the starboard rail. When she looked up again, the funny patch had slipped from sight and they were approaching the edge of town. Seagrape flew off the bow toward the trees along the shore.

"We'd better take you to Elder," said Jebby.

That was fine with Penny.

Elder was exactly who she wanted to see.

❧ Chapter Five ❧

The children secured the boat on a shallow mooring and waded to shore just outside the town. Penny called to Seagrape, who was devouring small mulberry-colored fruit from the spiky branches of a tree Penny had never seen before. She noticed the same coppery, marble-sized seeds as the one the parrot had dropped in the rowboat scattered below the tree.

Penny trotted after Tabba and Jebby toward a street paved with flat, sea-smoothed stones. The air was hot and smelled of woodsmoke and the spicy cassava pies cooling on the ledges of windows that opened onto the streets. The town was a huddle of small wooden homes built along the shore and up into the hills. The roofs were thatched with tightly woven palm fronds that formed a rustling patchwork of sloped rectangles. Most were burned to dull pewter tones by the sun, but every now and then amid them a newly pitched roof shone green and glossy.

"The town square is that way," said Tabba, nodding to where the sounds of hammers on boards rang out from deeper inside the town. "They're finishing the last bits and pieces before tonight. We live way over there, on the other side. And Elder's house is just up ahead."

People walked briskly past the children, carrying baskets of shining fish or vegetables still damp from the fields. Others stood on ladders stringing dully glowing white bulbs between rooftops. Freshly picked flowers decked the corners of the eaves. Kitchen gardens burst over the tops of rickety fences and rainwater drums stood outside each door. In the tiny gardens, bright multicolored domes of tents being set up for visiting families were popping up like mushrooms after a rain.

"How come you guys aren't in the competition, like Kal?" asked Penny, hurrying to keep up with the others.

"Us?" laughed Tabba. "We tried! But no luck! Our feat wasn't good enough. We climbed the cliff at Malmo, but so did a lot of other people. I told Jebby we should do something harder, but he wanted to be safe."

"Most players are a couple of years older than us," said Jebby defensively. "Kal's probably the youngest one in the whole competition."

"How many players *are* there?" Penny asked.

"Around fifty, I think," said Jebby. "But hundreds tried."

"What are the trials going to be?" Penny asked.

"They could be anything," Jebby told her. "Every Bloom they're different. One time players had to climb down these sheer cliffs before the tide rushed in, to get a type of barnacle that only lives at the bottom. Another time they had to build boats to sail down a very rough river in the north. The only thing anyone knows for sure is that the first trial is always underwater—what it is exactly no one has any idea."

"Why are there trials and a festival at all?" Penny asked. "Why not just let one person go out to the Wave?"

"The trials determine who the strongest, best person is to go out to the Wave, the one who is most likely to get the Bloom," said Jebby.

"And the festival—it's a chance for families who live far apart to see each other," explained Tabba. "It keeps people's spirits up while the mandrill is on the loose."

Penny savored Tabba and Jebby's company; she knew that after they got to Elder's she'd be on her own. The farther they went, the more nervous she grew. They left a warren of streets and headed down a broader thoroughfare in a quiet part of town, where the gardens were bigger and trees drizzled green light over the road. Seagrape caught up with them and landed on Penny's shoulder.

"Is Elder nice?" Penny asked.

"As long as he gets his nap," said Tabba. "If you wake him when he's napping, he gets grouchy."

"He won't be napping," said Jebby. "The elders from other towns are starting to arrive. They'll probably be having lunch in the garden right now. Here we are, anyway."

The town elder's house was set back from the road. It was built on short wooden stilts, its woven-grass shutters closed against the noon heat. A chicken and her chicks were pecking around in the dirt yard in front of the porch. Elastic towers of cane grass swayed nearby in the hot breeze. A bright snaggle of bougainvillea sprang over the garden wall. Penny tiptoed to peer over it and saw a group of people eating lunch together in the jewel-colored light beneath a canopy of thin sails strung to provide shade. Seagrape flew to the porch railing, and Penny followed the others up the steps. Butterflies churned in her stomach as Jebby knocked on the door.

A woman in an apron answered and went to fetch Elder.

Moments later, from inside the hut Penny heard a voice say irritably, "What am I being interrupted for?" followed by the sounds of sharp footsteps approaching. She glanced at Seagrape to shore up her courage.

A wiry old man emerged, blinking in the bright afternoon sun. Over time his title had become his name, and the people of the town referred to him only as Elder. A few white hairs sprang from his bare chest, his fingers were stained deep orange, and he wore a bright saffron cloth wrapped around his waist. His bald head shone with coconut oil, and he had an expression—part aggrieved, part distracted—that was familiar to Penny from the faces of almost all the adults she knew. He listened as Tabba and Jebby introduced Penny.

"A young girl—alone across the line?" he said in astonishment. He peered past Penny, as if he expected others to be there, too.

"We saw her do it ourselves, Elder," said Jebby. "Just a

little while ago. A whorl opened in the line and she came through."

"What is a whorl doing out at the line?" muttered Elder. He glanced over the rooftops to where the Blue Line shimmered out at sea. "It's all starting," he murmured. "Things, even people, ending up where they don't belong. . . . The Bloom is almost here." He turned his attention back to Penny. "Don't worry, young lady," he said crisply. "You've stumbled across, but we'll find a way to get you back."

Though relieved by the reassurance that there was a way to return home, Penny had no intention of leaving yet.

"I don't want to go," she said quickly. "Not right away. My grandmother sent me here for a reason."

It was evident that this was not what Elder had expected to hear. He hesitated, though whether in suspicion or just surprise, Penny couldn't tell.

"What reason is that?" he asked.

Penny knew it was important to look strong and capable, so she squared her shoulders and stood as tall as she could. She opened her mouth.

But no sound came out. She couldn't speak.

Nothing like this had ever happened to her before. How could it be happening now of all times, when it really mattered? She felt a bead of sweat trickle down her temple. Penny wasn't afraid of adults. Not her parents, not Cab at the aquarium, certainly not her teachers when they berated her for unfinished homework or rapped their knuckles on her desk to wake her from a daydream. But now she found herself standing there, mouth dry, palms sweaty, heart banging away inside her chest.

Elder waited.

"Because . . ." she croaked. She tried to swallow, but her throat was too dry. Suffering, she stopped. Sunlight crawled up the steps. Beyond the porch, the hot white light of noon burned patches of glare on everything. Bees swarmed in the bougainvillea, rattling it. Penny couldn't bear it anymore. She took a deep breath.

"I want to be the Bloom Catcher!" she blurted out, more fiercely than she had meant to.

Tabba elbowed Jebby sharply in the ribs. "I *told* you," she whispered.

"I mean, I want to be a Bloom Player," said Penny quickly. "My grandmother needs the Bloom. That's why she sent me."

It took Elder a few moments to get over his surprise at such an abrupt pronouncement.

"I'm afraid you have the wrong idea," he said at last. "The Bloom is for Kana. It must be poured in the Coral Basin to close the whorls and send the mandrill back to the Gorgonne. The Bloom Catcher is only permitted to keep a few drops."

Penny was barely listening to Elder. All she cared about was getting the Bloom for Granny Pearl, and to do that she had to persuade Elder to let her be in the competition. Everything else she could worry about later.

"I've done a feat that qualifies me to be a Bloom Player," she said, and this time she kept her voice strong and steady. "Last night I left home in a small boat, alone, in the dark, and I rowed and I rowed until I got here, and then I crossed the Blue Line. It turns everyone back, but I got through. Because I'm supposed to be a Bloom Player—I know I am!"

"You may have crossed the Blue Line," said Elder. "But you have no idea how challenging the Bloom trials are—"

"I can do them," said Penny vehemently, interrupting him. "I'm strong and I'm fast. Faster than all the boys I know. I can swim underwater for a long time. I'm not afraid of heights—I climb the mast of my boat every day. I'm not afraid of the dark or spiders or anything. I've even swum with a shark. Whatever the trials are, I'll do them!"

She had become louder as she spoke, and now she stood there, trembling but defiant, feeling sick that she had been too brash and gone too far, and Elder might refuse her.

"So you're brave, or possibly just reckless," said Elder. "That's only half of it. You've only just arrived—you're alone in a strange place you know nothing about. How will you know even the first thing about what to do or where to go?"

"I—" said Penny. Elder was right. She knew nothing about Kana. And an hour ago she had never even heard of the Bloom, let alone the competition to get it. All she knew was that she wanted the Bloom—*needed* it—more than she had needed anything in her whole life.

"I have a friend here in Tamarind," she said.

"And this friend, he knows you're here?" asked Elder.

"Well . . . no," said Penny. "Not yet. But . . ."

Elder sighed. "I understand that you came here hoping to help your grandmother," he said, his tone softening. "You must love her a great deal. But you don't realize how serious this competition is for Kana—and how dangerous it can be. Being the Bloom Catcher is the greatest honor in all of Kana. Young people train for it for many years, learning about the island, honing the skills the contest calls upon. Bravery and desire aren't enough. I'm sorry," he said gently. "Coming here was a mistake. Tonight you'll stay here as a guest of Tontap. Once the players depart tomorrow morning we'll figure out how to get you back across the Blue Line and on your way home."

He turned to leave, the matter sorted. Penny felt her chance slipping away. She didn't know what else she could say to convince him. She turned helplessly to Seagrape, but there was nothing the parrot could do either.

Suddenly the yard grew darker, and Penny became aware of a breeze bowing the cane grass by the road. The air grew cold; a chill wind had plunged out of season into the sunny day. The world drew in closer; the borders of objects seemed to blur. Penny thought at first that it was her—she was dizzy from the shock and fatigue of the past night and day, from sheer disappointment. Then she realized that the others had felt the same thing. Tabba and Jebby froze where they were. Elder turned back to the yard and gazed slowly around. Seagrape growled and her feathers puffed up, the way that fur will rise on a startled cat.

It felt like a storm was coming, but when Penny glanced up at the sky it was discordantly bright. Rooftops shone in the distance. The crisp scrawl of palm shadows still marked the sunny road. Only the yard in front of Elder's had been transformed, sinking into a plot of shadow. Penny saw a murky puddle leaking from a rain drum, where she hadn't noticed a puddle before. She caught a whiff of dank, rotting wood, of decaying matter. Mildew crept like evening shadows over the walls of the hut. The world within the yard felt sealed off, as if she were trapped inside one world looking out at another, and she suddenly thought that no one there could have heard her if she had shouted. Goose bumps prickled her arms and legs. The hen pecking for grain in the sand clucked in alarm and herded the tiny yellow puffs of her chicks away.

Elder's grizzled beard lifted in the creeping cold breeze. Penny followed his gaze across the yard, where a strange, hazy cloud hung in midair above the sandy, chicken-scratched earth. It was oval, about three feet at its widest. Like a greasy thumbprint on a pane of glass, it distorted what lay behind it. It was from this that the cold, dark feeling was coming, funneling through on the strange draft. Penny saw a flash of movement, the dull shine on the matted fur of a paw.

Then, abruptly, there was a small, crisp clunk, as though a door had shut. The blurry patch disappeared. The breeze died; Elder's beard fell. The yard was bright again, the air clear. The normal day resumed. Sunlight prickled the leaves, the tiny chicks reappeared chirping across the road, and the silk sails diffused colored light onto the guests in the garden, who seemed oblivious to what had happened. Seagrape's feathers settled. The only scent was of hot grass in the sun and spices from the lunch on the other side of the hedge. The strange malaise had lasted only a moment or two, but had spooked even Elder.

"Elder," whispered Tabba. "Was that . . . ?"

"It was the mandrill," Elder answered finally. "He's gone now." He turned to Penny, studying her as he had not before. "He opened that whorl to see *you*," he said. "He's curious about you. You'll have to be careful."

"The thing that was in the air over there," said Penny. "The blurred patch. That was a whorl?"

"Yes," said Elder. "A whorl, a doorway that the mandrill opens to travel between places. Usually he can't leave his home in the Gorgonne, but before the Bloom, Kana becomes more porous, and the mandrill's free to roam wherever he pleases."

"Where did that whorl lead to?" asked Penny.

"Only the mandrill knows that," replied Elder.

"A whorl opened at the Blue Line today," said Penny. "That's how I got here."

"Kal opened it," said Tabba.

Elder frowned. "He's up to that again?" He looked

angry. "If you see him, send him to speak with me. He has to stop this before he finds himself in trouble he can't get out of," he muttered.

"We're not certain it was him," said Jebby quickly.

"Could it have been?" asked Tabba.

Elder paused. "I'm surprised he could open a whorl powerful enough to let someone cross the Blue Line," he said carefully. "But it's happened before—that people have opened whorls before the Bloom. We believe Kal did it, the day the mandrill came to Tontap. But it's rare— extremely rare. And dangerous."

Elder paused, observing Penny as though some clue about her might explain what her unexpected presence meant for Kana. But after studying her tangled ponytail, bruised shins, and scuffed old backpack, he shook his head.

"I don't know why you're here," he admitted. "But there's nothing I can do to stop you from being a Bloom Player— crossing the Blue Line is an extraordinary feat. It surely qualifies you. It's only for your own sake that I advise you to go home now. You're alone here and you know nothing about Kana. It may be hard for you to imagine today, but the Bloom is an extremely dangerous time.

"Treacherous places lie on the other side of whorls. The change that happened in the yard just now—that was only from a small whorl, opened for a moment and then closed. But the mandrill's power grows before the Bloom. He starts opening more and more whorls. They get bigger and stronger, and things start coming through from the places on the other side of them. Storms, floods, fires, wild animals, darkness . . . all manner of chaos and destruction."

Penny didn't know what to think or say. It was becoming clear to her that the Bloom was no simple elixir, but was part of something much bigger and stranger, something potentially ominous. She couldn't give up, but she had no idea at all what to do next.

Tabba and Jebby had been whispering to each other, and now Jebby cleared his throat.

"Elder," he said.

"What is it?" asked Elder impatiently.

"Lots of Bloom Players go in teams, don't they?" said Jebby. "Even though only the person who did the feat can be the actual Bloom Catcher."

"That's correct," said Elder.

"Well," said Jebby. "Penny did the feat, and Tabba and I know Kana. What if the three of us go together—a team?"

At first Penny didn't understand what was happening. She gazed speechlessly at Tabba and Jebby. No one had been on her side for such a long time now that it hadn't occurred to her she might not be alone.

"And how will you travel?" asked Elder briskly. "Your family has no animals for you to ride. Nor a boat of your own."

"We . . ." said Jebby. "Um . . ."

"Well?" asked Elder.

"We have a way," said Tabba confidently. "It's just that we can't say what it is yet."

Several people had come and were waiting behind the children with questions for Elder. He frowned at the garden, where his lunch was growing cold, then back at the shuffling line awaiting his attention.

He turned to Penny.

"You want to be a Bloom Player, fine," he said briskly. "But it isn't a game. The last bad Bloom nearly destroyed Kana. If the Bloom Catcher fails, there will be suffering—terrible suffering—for a whole generation. *That* is why Kana needs a Bloom Catcher. The Bloom must be poured into the Coral Basin immediately after the Great Wave."

"I understand," said Penny breathlessly. "But, if I were the Bloom Catcher . . . would I be able to keep a few drops of it . . . for my grandmother?"

Elder nodded impatiently. "The Bloom Catcher has always been allowed to keep a very small amount," he said.

He rapped on the door frame and the woman in the apron appeared. "Yellow arm sashes!" he cried. She went inside the hut and scurried back out a moment later to hand the children three folded silk sashes, which they accepted in disbelief.

"Quick," whispered Tabba, steering Penny off the porch.

"Thank you, Elder!" they called over their shoulders as Elder turned to address the waiting people, who were looking curiously at the children as they thundered down the stairs.

"Go," said Jebby. "Before he changes his mind!"

～～～

Penny, Tabba, and Jebby dashed, ducking down sandy side streets until they were a safe distance from Elder's hut. They stopped beneath a stand of palms to catch their breath, Tabba and Jebby beaming. Penny couldn't quite believe what had happened. She was free to try to get the Bloom, and she wouldn't be alone doing it. She, Tabba, and Jebby were a team now. It seemed so long since she'd had friends that she'd forgotten just how much better it was than being alone. She felt lighter than she had in ages. Overwhelmed by such unexpected happiness and relief, she became suddenly shy.

"Thank you," she said.

"Don't thank us," said Jebby. "We would never have been Bloom Players if you hadn't crossed the Blue Line!"

"Bloom Players!" exclaimed Tabba. "*Us*—can you believe it?"

They took out the yellow arm sashes to have a closer look at them. The silk, soft as water, was the same brilliant yellow as the *Pamela Jane*'s hull, which Penny believed must be a good omen. But then Jebby's face darkened.

"Put them away," he whispered, looking around to make sure the yellow cloth hadn't attracted anyone's attention. "We should keep this a secret for as long as possible, until we've got everything we need. Ma and Da are going to kill us, you know," he added.

"So?" said Tabba giddily. "Come on, Jebby—we've never even been that far out of Tontap! And now we're Bloom Players!"

But Jebby's rush of excitement had been tempered by sobering practical matters.

"We're probably the youngest players," he said. "And we aren't prepared at all. The first trial is always underwater and we don't have anything for it, let alone whatever we might need for the other trials."

"So we'll get kelp pods and sea lights now," said Tabba. "There's a kelp bed just past the cliff with the sea lights."

"What are kelp pods?" asked Penny.

"They're round, hollow pods that grow in the kelp," explained Tabba. "They're filled with air. They'll let us breathe underwater if we have to swim very deep. And the sea lights will help us see if we have to go very deep, or into a cave or something."

"More important," said Jebby, "how are we going to get anywhere? Elder's right—we have no animals to ride. And I know you didn't really have a plan when you told Elder we did."

"Well, of course I didn't have a plan," said Tabba. "But I didn't want him to say no."

"How is Kal going to get around?" asked Penny, eager to contribute something.

"He has a lumphur," said Tabba.

"What's a lumphur?" Penny asked.

Jebby raised his eyebrows at his sister, as if to say, *She doesn't even know what a lumphur is!* Tabba paused, chewing her lip as she looked at Penny, as though she, too, were having second thoughts. Penny realized that now the first hurdle had been crossed she was of woefully little help. Kelp pods, sea lights, lumphurs—she had no idea what any of these things were or where to find them.

"Is there anyone we can borrow an animal from?" Penny asked. "Any animal?"

"No one's going to lend us one now," said Jebby. "The festival moves around from town to town after the players—everyone will be using their own animals to travel."

"Well . . ." said Penny. "What about a boat?"

"Wind's dropping out," said Jebby. "And after the first trial, the rest of the competition is always inland. A boat won't help us then. Our family doesn't have one, anyway. That was Kal's we were on earlier."

"Jebby!" said Tabba, exasperated. "Stop just saying no to everything and think of something we *can* do!"

The children were at a loss. Overhead the palms rustled, and the sound of construction echoed in the distance from the town square.

"I have an idea," said Tabba suddenly, jumping to her feet. "Come with me!"

❧ Chapter Six ❧

Penny and Jebby followed Tabba through the town as it climbed the big hill to the edge of the jungle. Near the top, Tabba crossed the road toward a small wooden storefront.

"Bellamy's?" Jebby asked doubtfully. "What are we going to do here?"

Tabba didn't answer. She waited for a customer carrying a parcel wrapped in banana leaves under his arm to exit, then she pushed aside the curtain and the children stepped into a hot, dim room.

Bellamy's was a sort of general store. Crates of potatoes and gingerroot and baskets of crinkly mushrooms were stacked in the middle of the room, and musty barrels of grain and nuts stood along the back wall. Above the barrels were shelves that hosted a ragged miscellany—hand-sewn dolls, turtle-shell bowls, crudely hammered fishhooks, collections of missing parts whose original purposes were mysterious. Coiled in the corner was a large ship's rope, home to a family of darting mice. The only person there was a girl the children's age who was sweeping behind the counter, the bristly broom vigorously scratching the wooden planks.

"Are you here to rub it in?" she grumbled. "I've been stuck here all day—I'm missing everything! He says we won't close while people keep coming in. But every time I think we're done, someone else shows up, needing something that they could have bought just as easily yesterday! Tell me, I'm desperate—what's going on out there?" She vigorously swept the last bit of dust under a basket, then looked up and noticed Penny. "Who's she?"

"This is Penny, from the Outside," said Tabba. "Penny, this is our friend Rai."

"What are you talking about, Penny from the Outside?" asked Rai suspiciously, putting aside the broom. "I saw you just last night; you didn't know anyone from the Outside then—what's going on?"

"Shhh," said Tabba. Then she took out the yellow arm sashes and pushed them across the counter.

"What do you have *those* for?" Rai asked incredulously, picking one up, rubbing the yellow silk between her fingers.

"*Shhhh!*" Tabba leaned over to whisper to Rai. "We don't want Bellamy to hear yet."

"Jeez, Tabba, you could have asked me to go!" said Rai enviously. She looked at Penny, sizing her up. "Oh, Ma never would have let me anyway. I can't believe yours is letting you." She paused. "Wait . . . Are you telling me she doesn't know?" She whistled. "Good luck to you."

"We'll worry about Ma later," said Tabba. "Right now

we need to find a way to get around Kana; that's why we're here."

"What can *I* do?" asked Rai. "You know my family only has the one mule, and my parents are going to be using it to travel around for the festival. And those two Bellamy has in the back are ancient—they wouldn't make it out of the yard." She frowned. "Oh . . ." she said slowly, but suddenly she looked interested.

"What?" asked Jebby warily. "What's going on?"

"But you saw it; it's falling apart," said Rai. "And we never figured it out, anyway."

"But Penny could," said Tabba. "It's from the Outside, isn't it? I bet she'd know. And if it needs a little work to fix it up, we could do that, too."

"What are you talking about?" Jebby demanded. "Tabba, what have you been up to?"

"Bellamy has this thing," said Rai, turning to Jebby. "He got it off an old wreck, a ship from the Outside. It has two wheels and a seat in the middle. I showed it to Tabba before and we tried to ride it."

"You mean a bicycle?" asked Penny.

"Yeah, that's what Bellamy calls it," said Rai. "So you know what it is?"

"Sure," said Penny. "I have one at home."

"See?" said Tabba triumphantly. "I told you she'd know."

"Are there really no bicycles here?" asked Penny.

Rai sniffed. "This is the only one *I've* ever seen."

"But three of us couldn't go on one bike," said Penny.

"There's a cart, too, a little one, that he built to go at the back of it," said Rai. "He used it to carry stuff when he was a trader."

"Will you talk to him for us?" asked Tabba excitedly. "Ask him if we can borrow it?"

"If Bellamy ever said yes to anything, I wouldn't still be here today," said Rai. She sighed. "Come on, Tabba, you know I'd help you if I could." She glanced at the curtained doorway behind the counter. "Look," she said at last. "He's napping right now. Why don't you just come in and take a look at it?" She nodded to Penny. "It's *really* old. She might see it and say it's no good. But if it is, then she should talk to him herself. He loves anything to do with the Outside."

"All right," said Tabba. "Let's see it."

Tiptoeing, the children followed her through a rough curtain into a room at the rear of the store.

It took Penny's eyes a moment to adjust to the dim, mossy light that filtered in from a single window, overgrown with plants, in the opposite corner. It was a storeroom: Bins and barrels and boxes were piled everywhere, a jumble of odds and ends poking out of them. The window looked over a small dirt yard built into the stone hillside. Slouched in a deep chair in the dusty light in the far corner was a white-haired old man, fast asleep. His eyes were shut, his breathing even, the handkerchief that covered his face luffing with each inhalation and exhalation. His legs were very long, so that, even though he was sitting, his knees were a long way from the chair.

The children followed Rai, picking their way between mounds of heavy fishing net and lopsided towers of crates. Tabba stubbed her toe on a wooden pole, which rolled over with a clatter. The children froze, but the old man didn't stir.

Rai stopped in the corner, in front of something lumpy that lay hidden beneath a grimy sheet. Very quietly she began to pull back the edge of the cloth. Just as Penny caught a glimpse of rusty metal, she heard a noise across the room. Something creaked; a shoe scraped the floor. The children turned to see that the old man had woken and was sitting straight up in his chair. His wild white hair was askew and his foggy eyes were wide open, staring at them as if he wasn't sure if he was dreaming. With a deft flick of her wrist, Rai whisked the sheet back over the bike.

"Rai!" the old man bellowed. "What's going on here? Who are these people snooping around my stockroom while I'm sleeping? Are you stealing from me?"

"Of course we aren't *stealing*," said Rai with exaggerated indignation. "They're Bloom Players. They wanted to see your bicycle. I already told them it was no good, but they insisted, and I didn't think it was worth waking you."

Sheepishly the children crossed the room and stood in front of Bellamy.

"I'm Jebby Silverling," said Jebby politely. "This is my sister, Tabba. And this is our friend Penny."

"Silverling? Your father's the carpenter?"

"That's right," said Tabba.

"I know who you are," grunted Bellamy. "And who's she?" he asked, nodding at Penny.

Rai shoved Penny forward. "She's from the *Outside*."

This information had an immediate effect on Bellamy. Abruptly he abandoned the tirade he had been about to launch into. He studied Penny carefully, his eyebrows working like two great caterpillars that had been disturbed.

"The Outside?" he asked at last. "Is that true?"

Penny nodded.

"Come closer," he barked. "I can barely see you from here."

Penny took a few steps forward, into a slow carousel of dust motes turning in the weak light. "My name is Penny Nelson," she said. She spoke loudly, since she figured the old man was likely to be partly deaf, too. "I've come to ask about your bicycle!"

"What do you want with it?" Bellamy asked cautiously. "I salvaged it myself off a wreck. That ship ran aground years before I rowed out to it, and no one had ever bothered with it. The bicycle had been underwater so long I had to hammer barnacles off it when I got it to shore." He leaned forward and shook a long, pale finger at her. "So don't think you've come to lay claim to it now, after all this time!" He settled back in the chair, like a buoy easing into stillness after a wake had passed.

"Not claim—borrow," said Penny calmly, taking another small step closer. "We want to ask if we can borrow it for the Bloom competition."

"You mean—you want to take it away, out of my shop?" Bellamy said. His impressive brows massed like cumulus clouds, seeming to expand as Penny explained how she had returned to Tamarind and what she was there to do.

"We just need it for a few days," said Jebby. "The competition will be over then. We'd have it back to you safe and sound right after that."

"We would be extremely careful with it," added Penny.

"*Extremely* careful," said Tabba, nodding vigorously.

"They're my friends," said Rai. "I can give you my word that they'd take care of it. And, if you ask me, Bellamy, the bike would be a lot better doing a few laps of Kana than rotting away in here."

"Well, I didn't ask you, did I?" muttered Bellamy.

The children were expecting a battle, but to their surprise, after a moment of hesitation, he relented.

"Go and get the bicycle, Rai," he said. "Let our visitor take a look at it."

Before he could change his mind, Rai quickly returned to the corner. With a flourish, she yanked the sheet clear and tossed it to the side. She smacked away some spiders, kicked aside a rope, and wheeled a dusty, squeaking contraption out to the middle of the room, stopping in front of Bellamy and the children.

Penny could feel Tabba's and Jebby's awe as they gazed at it.

"There she is," said Bellamy, reaching out to pat the handlebars lovingly.

"Wow," breathed Jebby. "I've never seen anything like it."

"I'm curious, young lady—is it a very good one?" Bellamy asked Penny.

Penny paused. It was as if the bicycle had wheeled out of the past, from a time Penny knew only from books. It was ancient, probably eighty years old at least. She had only ever seen such an old model in fuzzy black-and-white photographs. Her heart had sunk when Rai had unveiled it. Spots of rust grew like ruddy lichen on its frame. The worst were the tires, though. Age and humidity had rotted them to a few shreds of what looked like bark clinging to the banged-up metal rims, from which rose a whiff of decayed vegetation that permeated the stale air in the room. Both axles had squawked and squealed the whole time that Rai had wheeled it over to them. A small cart was attached to the rear axle by two shafts. It was lopsided, scratched, its interior netted with cobwebs. A brown spider cowered in a corner of it. It looked as though the weight of a sunbeam might cause it to crumble to dust.

But it was all they had. She swallowed.

"Yes," she said decisively. "It's an excellent bicycle. Maybe the best of this model that I've ever seen."

"I knew it was a good one," said Bellamy, satisfied. "I suppose there are a lot of them on the Outside?" he asked eagerly. "That's something I'd like to see. I used to love the feel of the wind in my face, the burn in my legs. Weather never bothered me. The bicycle never needed to stop or drink water or rest for the night. I went all over Kana on her, as far as Andusay! Well, try it, young lady—see if it still runs."

Penny took it from Rai and rolled it forward and backward. To her surprise, the brakes still worked. The axles screeched, but it was nothing a little grease couldn't fix. She could see the dents where the barnacles had been, but when she dug at a spot of rust with her thumb, she found that it was superficial: The frame was solid. Even the leather seat was still intact. Impressed by her knowledge of the unfamiliar machine, the others watched with almost reverent respect as she examined it.

"The problem is the tires," she said at last. "The rubber's worn away; only the frames are left. And without tires I'd be afraid to even sit on it right now in case the frame bends."

"That's easily fixed," said Bellamy. His defensiveness upon being startled awake had fully dissolved, and his excitement about having his prized possession called into action for the Bloom was growing. He had anticipated the problem with the tires and was gleefully ready with its solution.

"Sapsoo vines!" he said. "There were only scraps of the original tires left when I got it off the wreck. I tried

99

everything I could think as an alternative. Finally it was sapsoo vines that worked."

He peeled off a piece of a vine from the frame and held it up in the muddy light that filtered in through the dirty window.

"Miraculous things, sapsoos," he said. "Remarkably fast growing—you could cut one from the tree, then plant the cutting days later, and it would grow almost before your eyes. Even this may have some life in it, believe it or not, if it had a little water."

He rubbed the chalky strip between his fingers, and Penny watched it crumble and fall to the floor like ash.

"It doesn't look like there's any life left in it," whispered Rai.

"In any case," said Bellamy. "We need new ones. You can find them in the sapsoo grove over the ridge above Tontap. You'll have to climb a tree for them. Get the young, spongy ones—they give the smoothest ride. It'll be like floating along on a cloud. Bring me some of those and we'll be in business."

"So . . . we can borrow it?" asked Jebby.

"What use is it to me anymore?" said Bellamy. Now that his mind was made up, he was generous and jovial. "It deserves to be used for what it was made for, not moldering away in here. The Bloom has called it into service for Kana! Rai! Reach me that palm oil from off the shelf, then close up the shop!"

The room was suddenly buzzing with high spirits and

goodwill, and the children chattered excitedly, thanking Bellamy. Everyone reached out to pat the cool metal of the bike.

"Why don't I get the sapsoo vines and come back to work on the bicycle with Bellamy?" Jebby asked Penny and Tabba. "And you two go and get the kelp pods and the sea lights? We can meet in the palm grove on the way home when we're done."

The girls agreed, and the children said good-bye to Bellamy, then shuttled back out to the front room of the shop, where Seagrape had been helping herself to seeds from the bins along the back wall.

"Glutton," Penny whispered, picking up the bird and putting her on her shoulder.

"Sorry that you're stuck here," said Tabba as Rai got the key to lock the door behind them.

"He's in a good mood now; he'll let me go soon," said Rai affably. "Anyway, I don't mind helping with this—it's the closest I'll get to really being part of the Bloom!"

She opened the door and the children stepped out onto the bustling street.

"Hey," Rai said suddenly from the doorway. "I just thought—does Kal know you're Bloom Players?"

"No," said Tabba merrily over her shoulder. "But he'll find out soon enough!"

Jebby left to get the sapsoo vines, and Penny and Tabba headed for the far side of Tontap where Tabba said there was a dugout that could take them out to the kelp beds. It seemed wise to keep the fact that they were Bloom Players a secret for as long as possible, so they avoided main streets and ducked through mossy channels of back alleys until they were safely in the jungle just outside the town, where they trotted quickly along a thin hunting trail.

"Not that anything in Tontap is a secret for long," said Tabba.

Muted golden light spilled from the high canopy. Small whiskered monkeys jibbered as they groomed themselves, and the ceaseless murmur of birds underpinned the hot, humid air. Shimmering processions of leaf-cutter ants marched up and down the trunks, waving their tiny flags. Penny saw sloths hanging upside down, napping their lives away. They were the only creatures in Tontap that didn't seem caught up in the excitement of the festival. Seagrape flew in front of them, the light dappling her wings.

"You told Elder you had a friend here," said Tabba. "How do you know someone from Tamarind?"

"I've been here before," explained Penny. "Not Kana, another part of Tamarind." She found herself describing how her family had been to Tamarind, and how Helix had come into their lives. She hadn't talked to anyone so freely in a long time, but it didn't feel strange. Tabba was easy company.

"Helix is great," Penny said. "I bet you'd like him. He used to be a hunter. He can climb to the top of a tree in, like, ten seconds flat. His hair is really messy. And he hates wearing shoes—I remember that. The only time he would ever wear them when he lived with us was when he went to school."

"Where is he now?" asked Tabba.

"Somewhere in Western Tamarind, I guess," said Penny. "That's where he lived."

Penny's memory of Tamarind was not dim; on the contrary, it was the most vivid memory she had, but the things she remembered were not the most useful things when it came to questions of basic geography. She could conjure in a heartbeat an afternoon that she had leaned against Maya as they traveled down a river, the comfort of her cheek resting on her sister's shoulder, hear as clear as day her brother's voice as he pointed out the funny blue birds that had filled the bushes all along the shores, but her sense of geography was slippery, and any attempt to pinpoint where that river was on a map ended in fog.

"Western Tamarind is ages away," said Tabba. "But people come from all over for the Bloom Festival. Even from Western Tamarind. Maybe he'll be here. Though if he's coming, maybe it won't be until later in the competition, right before the Wave. That's what a lot of people do."

Something occurred to Penny. It was obvious, but somehow she'd never really thought about it before. She had been five years old the last time she'd seen Helix—he might not recognize her now. And maybe she wouldn't even recognize *him* anymore. Who knew how he had changed in the past seven years?

Seagrape had flown on and was waiting for them on a branch up ahead. When the girls reached her, they paused to catch their breath.

"I wonder . . ." mused Tabba. "You said Seagrape used to belong to Helix. Do you think that she could find him?"

"I don't know," said Penny. Seagrape was not a pet, like a dutiful dog, anxious to please its master. She was not a pet at all, in fact. She had been given a task years ago—to watch over Penny—and she had done that faithfully. She had stoically borne indignities—being dressed in doll's clothes or enlisted in boisterous games of pirates—out of secret fondness for Penny, or duty to Helix, but she remained deliberately private, as observant and inscrutable as a servant. She had moments of genuine affection, of course: When Penny was very young and frightened of thunderstorms at night, Seagrape would come and perch beside her on the edge of her bed, and Penny knew that Seagrape loved Granny Pearl as much as she herself did. Penny had long believed that the parrot could talk but chose not to, either out of pure stubbornness or—Penny imagined—in fidelity to some secret vow. In her old age she was increasingly stubborn and cantankerous. Who knew what she really thought about anything? Now that she was back in her home after many years away, Penny wasn't sure what to expect.

"Seagrape," said Penny. "Do you know how to find Helix? Can you find him?"

The light caught the oily sheen in the bird's feathers. She cocked her head, her sage, crafty eye unblinking. Penny sighed.

"She only ever does things when she feels like it," she said.

"I have a better idea," said Tabba. "There's a message pole in every town in Kana where people leave notes for other people. Why don't we stop at the pole in the square and leave something for your friend? He won't be expecting anything, so he won't check it, but if you can think of something he'll recognize, something obvious near the top, maybe he'll see it."

Penny was about to say that she didn't know what she could leave, when it struck her.

"The yellow flags," she murmured. "How on earth did Granny Pearl know I would need them?" She stopped in the middle of the path. "I have these flags that my grandmother made," she said excitedly. "We used to play this game with them when I was little. If Helix saw them, he'd know right away that I was here. It's a great idea, Tabba! Thank you."

Pleased, Tabba led her on a quick detour back into the town to the square, where in a corner was a tall, skinny wooden pole, a repurposed ship's mast, which stood twenty feet high. Pinned to it were hundreds of notes on leaves and scraps of fabric, fluttering and rustling in the breeze. From a distance it looked like a great raggedy flock of butterflies had settled on it.

When they reached it, Penny saw there were evenly spaced pegs on the sides so people could climb to the top. Holding a flag in her teeth, she ascended quickly, as if scaling the mast of the *Pamela Jane*. She shook out the flag and secured it firmly to the top of the pole, where a high breeze lifted it and held it gently aloft so that the stitched green parrot appeared to be in flight. The sun shone through the thin fabric. If Helix were here, he wouldn't be able to miss it. Penny looked over the town. More and more people were arriving in Tontap each hour, and the streets around the square were clogged with the newcomers. She climbed back down, and she and Tabba escaped the crowd as quickly as they could.

Tabba recovered the dugout from its hiding place beneath a stack of fallen palm fronds on a desolate patch of the coast facing the sea, far from the town and harbor. Soon she and Penny were heading out toward the kelp forest.

The sky was hot, the water deep blue. Seagrape flew ahead of them. Tabba took the first turn paddling. Penny looked back at the green silhouette of the island. Every now and then she had the feeling that her senses were failing her. There was a chameleon quality to the landscape, something amorphous and protean. She saw the same shimmery smudge that she had seen when she had first sailed into Kana. It had not moved.

"It's started to fade; it was much brighter at first," said Tabba, who saw what Penny was gazing at.

"Why is it still there?" Penny asked. "The ones at Elder's and at the Blue Line were only open for a few seconds."

"Some close right away; some stay open and fade gradually," said Tabba. "They say that if it's a bad Bloom, the whorls *never* close. More and more just keep opening, and everything keeps getting worse and worse. But no one alive really remembers the last bad Bloom. Even the very oldest people alive now would have only been small children."

Penny remembered the menacing feeling that had infiltrated Elder's yard, how the world had warped, a dark wash come over it. She squinted at the shore. This whorl didn't seem dangerous at all. It appeared blameless and dreamy, like the shimmer of heat in the distance on a drowsy summer day.

"It looks harmless," she said.

"I agree," said Tabba. "It *looks* harmless. And maybe some of them are. But that's the one the mandrill left through, the day that he came to Tontap."

"Were you there?" asked Penny. "Did you see him?"

"Jebby and I were there," said Tabba, drawing hard on the paddle. "But we didn't really see much. Kal had gathered some people in the town square to see his feat. Elder was there. Me and Jebby. A few other kids. Most people hadn't listened to him, though, so there weren't that many. None of us had any idea what he was going to do. We were all standing around Kal, and suddenly a whorl appeared, right beside him. Jebby and I didn't know what it was at first—we'd never seen one before. It was very faint, not like the one in the trees there but like a tiny cloud hovering in midair."

"What did Elder do?" asked Penny.

"I don't think he could believe it at first either," said Tabba. "Kal asked Elder if it meant he would be a Bloom Player. Elder said yes, but that whorls were dangerous and he had to close it right away. Kal was so excited. He tried to close the whorl—you could tell he really was trying—but, instead of closing, the whorl started getting bigger and darker. Before it had looked like a little bright cloud on a sunny day, just sitting there, no breeze. By then it was as black as a storm cloud. The air smelled like something under a rock—mud, earthworms. Jebby started pulling me away from it."

She paused, letting the dugout coast for a few moments. "That's when the mandrill came out of the whorl. Jebby and I were already at the edge of the square by then, but we turned back long enough to see him jump out of it. He looks like a very big monkey with dark, shiny fur. He was moving so fast his face was a blur, but we saw it was brightly colored, like a mask. Kal had been standing right next to the whorl and was knocked over when the mandrill jumped out—that's how Kal got that bruise over his eye. Everyone started screaming and running inside to get away from the mandrill. Jebby and I ran and ran and didn't stop until we got home. Later we found out that he wandered around the town for a little while—people hiding in their houses could hear him outside their windows. Then he went into the jungle just outside the town, climbed a tree, and opened the whorl that you saw back there. He disappeared into it and didn't come back.

"Kal got into trouble," Tabba went on. "But Elder knew he'd only meant to open a whorl, not make the mandrill show up—Kal had been more surprised than anyone when the mandrill jumped out. And you couldn't deny that he'd done an amazing feat—something no one else had done or could do. So he was still allowed to be a Bloom Player, but Elder made him promise not to open another whorl. I think he decided that Kal had learned his lesson—the mandrill had given him a bad scare, and had hurt him, too. As far as I know, until today he hadn't opened another one, but who knows? Maybe he was practicing secretly. A few days after the mandrill appeared, people started saying that maybe Kal *had* made him appear on purpose. You know how people talk and stories get started."

"Where did the mandrill go when he left?"

"Back to the Gorgonne, I guess," said Tabba. "That's the place in the middle of Kana where he lives. They say you can't even see inside it; its edges are all blurred. No one knows what's inside because no one can get in. There's a force that pushes you back if you try to get close."

"It pushes you back," said Penny. "Kind of like the Blue Line does."

"I guess," said Tabba. "Anyway, all the mandrills used to live there. All the others are gone—he's the last one left. He's been around forever. He's only able to come out right before the Bloom."

Penny thought about the strange creature living by himself in a place he couldn't leave, a place where no one ever went.

"Sounds lonely," she said. "No wonder he shows up all over the place while he has the chance."

Penny and Tabba switched places and Penny took over paddling.

"How close did you get to it?" asked Penny. "To the whorl in the tree?"

"The next day we went to see it," said Tabba. "On the way we found the mandrill's footprints in the mud. Five toes, deep gouges from his claws, heavy heel. We got close enough to the whorl to look right up at it from under the tree. It was brighter then; it's faded a bit now."

"What would happen if you tried going through it?" asked Penny.

"Are you crazy?" said Tabba, laughing. "No one would ever do that! Do you know what could happen to you?"

"No," said Penny curiously. "What?"

"You'd get sucked in and you'd disappear forever," said Tabba. "You might even explode."

Penny frowned. "How do you know that if no one's ever tried to go through one?"

"I don't know," said Tabba. "But my mother says that in the last bad Bloom, people used to disappear into them all the time."

"But I came through one," said Penny. "That's how I crossed the Blue Line, right?"

"True . . ." said Tabba. "But the mandrill didn't open that whorl; Kal did. It's different. You know, Jebby doesn't believe that Kal is really doing any of these things. He thinks it's got to be some kind of trick, or luck, or something. He thinks that whatever Kal was doing just irritated the mandrill somehow and that's why he showed up."

"What do you think?" asked Penny.

"I think Kal *is* doing something," said Tabba. "I just don't know how."

"What I don't understand," said Penny, "is, if the mandrill's so dangerous to Kana, why doesn't someone just catch him? Lock him away or something."

Tabba laughed. "Impossible," she said. "No one's ever caught him, and no one ever will. He's too smart and too fast. All he has to do is open a whorl and disappear into it. By the time an arrow's left a bow, he's vanished into a whorl. He senses a net falling—zip, he's gone. Anyway—if you tried to hurt him, he'd hurt *you*. If you ever do see him anywhere, you're supposed to run for your life."

To run for your life. Penny scanned the jungle in the distance, half expecting to see the strange creature leaning

111

out from a high branch, peering at them out there in the tiny dugout, but they were too far from land now to have made him out clearly even if he were there.

"Now," Tabba said briskly. She stood up so she could see farther, and the boat rocked precariously. "We must be getting close. I know it's out here somewhere. . . ." She shaded her eyes with her hand. "There!" she cried at last, pointing. She took over from Penny and began paddling swiftly.

Penny smelled the kelp before she saw it—a briny, vegetable odor mingled in with the salt air. The Kelp Forest—or the very top of it, anyway—was a vast fleece of rumpled, shining leaves swaying like a mirage on the surface of the water. Blue-footed seabirds paddled around its edges, taking flight every now and then to cruise over it on tilted wings. As they drew closer, Penny could see that what had looked like flakes of snow being buffeted about were actually small white sea butterflies, pollinating the kelp. One alighted on her shoulder for a moment, tiny feet cold, as if a snowflake had fallen on her.

Seagrape landed on the kelp and squawked in annoyance as she began to slide through the waxy leaves. She flew to perch on the gunwale of the rowboat, where she picked out a glossy wet rag from her talon: a long, draping leaf, dark green as spinach. Tabba guided the boat through the stalks and then stopped paddling.

The kelp pods were near the surface. Golden bubbles—tough and leathery, about the size of birthday balloons—they were attached near the tops of the kelp stalks, buoying the stalks up toward the nourishing sunlight. They could be gathered from the boat. Penny joined Tabba in cutting them free and tossing them into the hull. They were light, almost weightless, but strong and nearly impossible to pop, and they gathered in a big amber froth at the girls' feet. Tabba broke off a few tips of kelp stalks, which poked up here and there like stiff reeds. She sharpened them with her knife. They were empty inside, like straws. Exhaling noisily, she punctured a pod with a straw, then put the straw to her lips and breathed in the oxygen from the pod.

"You try it," she told Penny.

Penny took a straw and after a few attempts punctured a rubbery pod, then drew a deep breath. The air from the pod tasted like salty, overcooked vegetables, but it was air. Each pod held several breaths' worth.

When they had all the pods and straws they needed, they stuffed them into a fishing net and rowed toward a shoreline cliff, where tiny, lustrous orbs of sea lights were nestled in tide pools in the tiers of the cliff. The girls tied up the boat and hopped onto the rocks. They climbed nimbly and gathered the sea lights, which were as lightweight as pumice and small enough to fit in their palms. The lights glowed only dimly now, but Tabba assured Penny that come nightfall they would burn brightly. When the girls had what they needed, they returned to the boat and headed to shore with their haul.

By the time they stowed the boat and hurried back to meet Jebby, the afternoon was waning and the light beneath the palms was mellow. It was hard to see Seagrape, her wings dappled with light and shadow as she coasted from branch to branch ahead of them. It was a lazy hour when no creature had to try very hard to blend in with its surroundings. Jebby was already waiting at the appointed spot in the palm grove.

"The new tires are on," he said. "I think it's going to work! Bellamy said to come and pick it up tonight, after Elder announces the first trial. It will be safe there until then. And Rai's gone to find us a map. How'd you do?" He peeked into the bags with the kelp pods and sea lights. "Wow—this is great!"

"So it looks like we're almost ready," said Penny happily.

"I think so," said Jebby. "I came back through the town. There are Bloom Players everywhere. They're all walking around in their yellow sashes already. Some of them are huge—they look really strong. Also, I ran into Sol and his sister. Someone saw us getting the sashes from Elder. People already know; that means Ma will, too. She hears everything!"

"Great," groaned Tabba.

"Come on, let's get it over with," said Jebby. "Just don't argue with her. Da will help smooth things over."

"We hope," muttered Tabba.

They walked through the palms and emerged in a clearing with a tidy, palm-thatched hut. A woman was raking the sand outside the door. Colorful hammocks were strung between the palms. Several small children were swinging in one of them, trying to tip out the littlest among them. When they saw Tabba, Jebby, and Penny, they tumbled out and came running over. The woman dropped the rake.

"Da—they're here!" she shouted.

As Tabba, Jebby, and Penny approached sheepishly, Ma Silverling assumed a posture common to mothers on both sides of the Blue Line: hands on hips, glaring down at them.

"Did you think I wouldn't find out?" she cried. "Do you have any idea what you've gotten yourselves into? How many times have we told you to stay away from the line? Who are you?" she asked, turning to Penny. "Does your mother know where you are? How have you put this crazy idea into my children's heads?"

Penny shifted her backpack with the yellow sashes in it behind her protectively. Experienced at weathering their mother's rages, Tabba and Jebby were compliant and apologetic.

"Don't blame Penny," said Jebby soothingly. "It was our idea to go, Ma."

"You don't have to worry," said Tabba. "We've spent the whole afternoon getting ready—we have everything we could possibly need for the first trial. We have a bicycle and we have kelp pods and sea lights—"

"Kelp pods!" Ma Silverling snorted. "Kelp pods! Da, I

guess we don't need to worry anymore—they have kelp pods!" she said to the man appearing now from behind the hut.

Da Silverling was a calm, affable-looking man, unperturbed by his wife's fury. He had been working and his skin was covered in sawdust.

"Hi, Da," said Jebby.

"Da," said Tabba, her eyes shining. "We're going to be Bloom Players."

"Bloom Players!" moaned Ma. "You've never even been out of Tontap on your own before! Da—tell them."

"Elder said—" began Tabba.

"Elder said!" interrupted Ma, swatting away the littlest Silverling child, who was trying to climb her skirt. The other children stood around silently, staring curiously at Penny. "Does Elder feed you and clothe you? Who is *Elder* to say you can go gallivanting across the countryside?"

Da Silverling had been studying the children. Now he put a steadying hand on Ma's shoulder.

"I said it before," he said. "We can't stop the Bloom."

"Of course we can't stop the Bloom," exclaimed Ma. "You know that's ridiculous. But why do they have to be involved? It's gone wrong—it's happened before. The whorls are *dangerous*." She turned to the children. "I've told you my grandmother's stories about the last time there was a bad Bloom—about what happened to Kana, how people vanished into whorls and never came back. Children would be playing in a garden and suddenly a whorl would open and swallow them up. Sometimes men didn't make it home at the end of the day—they wouldn't see a whorl on the road right in front of them in the darkness and they'd disappear into it. And things came *out* of whorls, too—fires, freezes, floods, wild animals. . . . My grandmother knew a woman who watched her child carried off into a whorl by a jaguar, right before her eyes."

Penny glanced at Tabba and Jebby. They hadn't told her about *these* stories before. She wondered if they were true, or if Ma Silverling was exaggerating, the same way her own mother would if she wanted to impress on Penny the danger of something that Penny was bent on doing.

"Come on, Ma, those are just stories," said Tabba. "Who knows if they're even true? No one from then is even alive anymore."

"Things don't usually go wrong," said Jebby. "There've been good Blooms since then. Every single one. Right, Da?"

"The last bad Bloom was a long time ago; it's true," said Da Silverling, who looked cautious but not fearful. He turned to Ma. "This is a new Bloom," he said calmly. "And it's called them."

"Called them?" Ma laughed. "Called them—since breakfast?"

The children stood quietly and pretended not to hear as Ma and Da dropped their voices.

"If the Bloom goes wrong, it won't matter where they

are," said Da soberly. "We know that. They have an amazing opportunity right now, one they won't have again. The next time the Bloom comes around, they'll be grown. So now . . . they'll see a little more of Kana, they'll learn a few things, someone will get the Bloom, and then they'll be home safe and sound."

Ma shook her head miserably. The kelp pods glowed dully; the scent of sea moss rose from the basket and expanded in the pink evening air. Ma looked at Da, Tabba, Jebby, and the little children gathered around her feet. Seagrape perched on Penny's shoulder as the seconds ticked slowly by. One of the little children hugged Tabba's leg and grinned up at her. She wiped his nose and patted his head. Ma reached down and drew her smallest child to her, pressing her cheek against the baby's face. Penny saw that she had given in. The baby wriggled free and began crawling after a beetle trundling across the dirt. Ma tucked Tabba's hair behind her ear, brushed sand off Jebby's shoulder. She shrugged helplessly.

Tabba and Jebby were trying not to smile, which Penny knew from her own mother could provoke an abrupt reversal of ground that had been won.

"We can go?" asked Jebby.

"It's done, isn't it?" Ma asked stiffly. "What does a mother matter when it comes to the Bloom?"

"Ma! Thank you!" cried Tabba, throwing her arms around her. "You'll see—we'll be okay!"

"Enough wasting time!" said Ma. "I still have things to do because certain people disappeared all day and left me high and dry on the busiest day of the year!" Enlivened by anger once more, she turned on her heel and marched back toward the house.

"She'll be all right," Tabba whispered to Penny. "She never stays mad for long. She's too busy. Da, thank you—you'll see; it's going to be great."

However, with Ma gone, Da was newly stern. "It isn't a game," he said gravely. "If the Bloom goes wrong, there's not going to be anything we can do to protect you. Do you understand?"

Penny wondered what he meant exactly. Surely Ma Silverling's stories were just that—stories, weren't they? And Tabba was smiling, and so was Jebby.

"Yes, Da," said Tabba, beaming at him.

"I don't think you *do* understand," said Da, shaking his head. "Now"—he went on in a lighter tone—"I suggest you stay out of your mother's hair until it's time to leave for the square!"

⌇⌇⌇

Penny, Tabba, and Jebby retreated a short distance from the hut. The three littlest Silverling children followed them, staring at Penny.

"Go on!" Tabba said, shooing them away. "She's from the *Outside*—she doesn't need you pestering her!"

The little ones hung back and watched as Tabba and Penny used rough leaves to scour the sea moss off the sea lights so they would burn brightly. They wrapped the burnished globes in wet banana leaves and placed them in a basket, covering the top with a cloth to keep the light hidden when night came. The kelp pods were secured in a fine-mesh fishing net. Penny watched Jebby deftly fashion weight belts out of rope, which they would need if they had to descend to any depth with the buoyant kelp pods. Tabba foraged for berries and bark, which she ground into a paste in case they got blisters, and Jebby returned with three spears he had borrowed from Da Silverling. After watching how Jebby did it, Penny began sharpening one of the blades against a stone. She felt a thrill. Spears. They needed *spears* for what they were going to do. She thought about Helix— this was exactly the kind of stuff he used to do in Tamarind.

When everything was ready, the children laid their precious objects on the sandy ground between them and gazed at the collection. Along with the kelp pods, kelp straws, sea lights, and spears, they had knives, fishing line, mosquito nets, and ointment for blisters. Tabba and Jebby had simple sackcloth packs, and Penny had her backpack. To the offerings on the ground, Penny added the contents of her bag: Simon's compass, her goggles, and the remaining faded yellow flags, the third one of which was already hanging on the pole in the square.

She held the goggles up for a moment. They were very old. The scratched plastic frames had faded from jet-black to seal-gray, and a knot was tied in the rubber strap from where they had broken a long time ago. Penny touched the lenses, then tucked them away carefully in her bag.

Tabba yawned and suddenly they were all yawning, tired from the day's exertion and excitement. Seagrape, who had sagely waited out Ma Silverling's rage at a safe distance, had tucked her head beneath her wing and was napping on an overhead branch. The children walked down to the sea to bathe, then returned to the hut where, her battle lost, Ma had thrown all her energies into preparations for the children. Enough food had been packed to last them a week. She had repurposed one of Tabba's old tunics for Penny to wear. She had sewn shells onto the hem, and in the luminous evening light through the palms they gleamed as if they were still wet from the sea. Tabba wore a similar tunic, and Ma Silverling clipped two pink tellin shells in her hair. Jebby wore a new pair of flowing dark fisherman's trousers and two strings of triangular shells that crossed in an X over his chest. But the best of all were the bright yellow sashes, which they wore on their left arms. The cool silk was as glossy as Seagrape's feathers, the knot soft and square, and the children could barely take their eyes off the lemony yellow glow, like sunshine in the dimming grove. Even Penny, who only cared about getting the Bloom for Granny Pearl, sensed for a moment that she was part of something very old and bigger than herself, a feeling that seeped out of the earth and air of Kana itself.

Ma chased the smallest Silverling children around, scrubbing their faces one last time despite their protests, and then the company set out for the town. Their hair still damp from the sea, Penny, Tabba, and Jebby hurried along the path with a spring in their steps. The sound of firecrackers and music and jangling merriment grew louder as they approached. The dirt path became a stone-paved street, and Seagrape flew down to perch on Penny's shoulder. The children turned a couple of corners and emerged in the middle of everything.

Helix

Following the rain early that morning, the day was clear. He guessed that he could be in Tontap within a few hours.

The solitary part of his travels was ending. After days alone with his own thoughts, there were more and more people around. All of Kana was on the move. The closer he got to Tontap, the first town on the festival route, the more people he saw, droves of them: on foot, in carts, on the backs of bizarre creatures. He was only one among thousands who were heading east, traveling between the towns on the festival route, all eventually destined for the narrow crescent of a bay on the northeast coast where the monstrous wave would rise. The discovery that he was part of a great migration was strangely disorienting. He had come on a whim, in what he had believed to be a wholly independent act, but now it seemed that all along he had been compelled by something beyond himself.

Sometimes he listened to people's chatter, caught their excitement, but as much as he could he avoided main roads and kept to paths through the jungle, preferring his own company. He wanted his thoughts free to roam, unintruded upon by the needs of strangers eager to talk about the Wave, the Bloom. Every step he took made it clearer to him how stuck he had felt for so long, and how much he wanted to keep moving.

Helix ducked off the busy road he had been on and walked along a quiet dirt track that ran alongside a wide stream. When he found a good place to stop for lunch, he dropped his bag and gathered sticks to build a fire. While it crackled to life, he waded into the water. The air in the clearing was shady and green. Silver-barked trees leaned gracefully. The breeze rustled in their tiny round leaves, a sound as fresh and light as spring yet somehow wistful at the same time. The stream gurgled over smooth stones, and he knelt and splashed his face with cold, clear water. Waiting there until his legs turned numb, deftly he snapped his bare hands together and caught a small bronze fish. He quickly clubbed its head on a stone and instantly it was dead. Returning to shore, he speared it on a spit and set it to roast on the fire. He pulled roots from the earth and washed them, watching the mud drift away in the current, then sliced them and added them to the spit where the fish was slowly blackening.

He sat quietly and waited for his meal to cook. Something about the place, the tranquillity and the quality of light, reminded him of the trees behind Granny Pearl's house and brought him back to being there with Penny one afternoon when she must have been about five years old. After much begging on her part, he was teaching her how to track.

You don't look for the whole animal, just part of it, he told her. So, if you're hunting a jaguar, you may just see its tail or a foot hanging down from a tree branch.

Maya and Simon were out with their friends, as they often were, but he was home. He never tried to shrug her off like they did; that's why she liked him so much.

Look for broken branches, torn leaves, any signs that things have been disturbed. You have to make yourself very still. It's about balance. If you're still, something else will eventually move and you'll know where it is. You want to hide in the undergrowth and make yourself secret— very quiet and very still.

That's hard, she whispered.

She was silent for less than a minute.

Helix?

What?

This is getting boring.

Shhh, he said. *You have to be patient. When you've been still for a while, you'll start to see more things.*

I see Seagrape over there on that branch. She's watching us.

That's good, he said. *The other thing you have to learn to do is to breathe slowly and slow your heartbeat.*

She frowned as she concentrated on slowing her heartbeat.

What about painting mud on our faces? You told me in Tamarind you painted mud on your face if you were hunting.

You're right, he said. *I guess we'd better.*

She scooped up a handful of mud. This was her favorite part, he knew, though she didn't understand the purpose.

To camouflage yourself, so you blend in with the background, he explained. *And so that no creatures can catch your scent and find you.*

Oh, said Penny.

He watched her rubbing handfuls of mud on her arms with quiet glee. She would have to go swimming to wash it off before her mother came home.

They lay on their stomachs, listening.

Eventually you become attuned to everything around you—to the vibrations, the sounds, to every chirp and breaking twig and footstep. Understand?

She nodded happily, though he was sure she didn't know what *attuned* meant.

I see a kiskadee over there, she whispered loudly.

Very good, he told her. *Now . . . you have to learn a creature's habits and patterns, where they like to go and when.*

Like Maya will be coming home at four thirty?

I guess—yes, he said.

Granny Pearl appeared, carrying the basket overflowing with freshly picked lettuce.

Granny Pearl, said Penny. *Helix is teaching me how to track*.

A useful skill, said Granny Pearl with a smile.

The fish was ready. Helix took it off the spit and let it cool on a banana leaf.

"Hi—do you know if this is the way to Tontap?"

The man had obviously been trying to get his attention for a few moments. A cart had stopped at the stream and its passengers were arguing about which road to take.

"I think so," Helix said, trying to hide his irritation. "But I'm not from here either."

"Mind if we join you?" the man asked. The passengers of the cart were already disembarking, their noisy chatter lifting to the treetops as if a raucous flock of birds had alighted invisibly, and the thirsty horse was drinking from the edge of the stream, its hooves stirring up the silt on the bottom and clouding the water.

The place was spoiled. Helix finished his lunch quickly and gathered his things to go. The fire was out, but he kicked the charred wood into the stream, where it hissed gently. He waved politely to the people and left. On the road, he picked rough, minty lantana leaves and chewed them to clean his teeth, spitting them onto the side of the path as he went.

He needed new twine to mend the strap of his backpack, which had been broken for a few days and was becoming a nuisance. Though he had little desire to see other people, he was looking forward to getting the twine and a few other things he needed in Tontap.

❧ Chapter Seven ❧

When Penny and the Silverling family walked into Tontap, the evening was still light, the air violet in the fresh streams of sky that ran above the narrow streets. Below, the thoroughfares were close and crowded, the atmosphere thick with a dizzying stew of scents from the wooden stalls that lined them: charred wood chips, flowers picked just hours before, fruit cores squashed underfoot, spicy chowders bubbling in giant cauldrons. The children were instantly absorbed into the throng, shuttled closely together as people pushed past, weaving and wending, the crowd moving jerkily forward in the brief moments when a few paces of clear path opened.

On every corner was a different band blowing shells, shrilling reed pipes, drumming empty turtle shells. Singing choruses of men clustered around, already sweaty and rumpled, swigging from flasks of palm wine. In the stalls, grimy-aproned men turned sizzling meat on giant spits. Flames leaped out, almost singeing the hairs on Penny's arm. Rafts of smoke burned her eyes. Women in hats piled high with fresh flowers sailed past, their clothes still crisp and bright, sleeves dripping with neon feathers, hems singing with tiny shells. Homemade firecrackers exploded in the sky. Small monkeys staged bold forays on the food stalls, then fled through the smoke to the rooftops, their brown tails hanging down, ticktocking down the time between raids.

It was impossible to stick together in such a mass of people, so Tabba, Jebby, and Penny, with Seagrape on her shoulder, soon peeled away from Ma and Da and the youngest Silverlings. In the square, Penny saw that the yellow flag was still there, but she didn't let herself feel too disappointed—she had only put it there a few hours ago, after all. The children bought conch fritters from a man selling them from a tray balanced on his head, and gorged on the oily breaded bits as they walked. Penny's mouth watered as they passed tables heaped with ice-white dragon fruit and sour jungle fruits dipped in shimmering crystals of cane sugar, deepwater fish wrapped in big floppy leaves, giant blue crabs steamed over hot stones.

A smiling man stopped the children, nodding at their yellow sashes, and pressed a small bag into Jebby's hands before walking on.

"What is it?" asked Penny.

"Insects," said Jebby, peeking into the bag. "That guy's a Beetler—they come through the towns selling bugs a few times a year. They're giving them to us because we're Bloom Players. These ones have been fried—they're good."

"They're gross," said Tabba, grimacing. "I hate it when Ma cooks with them."

"Try one," Jebby challenged Penny, a merry gleam in his eye. He held out the bag and gave the insects a shake.

Penny wasn't eager to eat a bug, nor was she willing to show any weakness. She reached in, pinched a tiny hardback between her finger and thumb, allowing herself only a brief glance at it—a small, knobby creature with blunt, antlerlike antennae, crisply fried—before she popped it nonchalantly into her mouth. It was salty and crunchy.

"It's good," she said.

"Liar," said Tabba, but she looked impressed anyway.

Rai appeared, making her way through the crowd toward them. Her hair had been swept up, and she was wearing a tunic like Penny's and Tabba's, woven with shiny round shells.

"There you are!" she cried. "I've been looking all over for you. I've got a map for you from my cousin Pallo."

"Oh, great!" said Tabba eagerly. "Let's see it!"

"There's just one thing," said Rai. "He wants something in exchange. . . ."

"What?" asked Jebby.

"Your whistle," said Rai.

Jebby groaned. "My whistle?" he said. "It took me ages to make this one—I can do forty-eight different calls with it!"

"Does it do a silver kingfisher?" asked Rai. "That's what he wants."

"Of course it does," said Jebby glumly.

"You can make another one," said Tabba.

"Easy for you to say," replied Jebby. "It's the best one I've ever made."

"Sorry," said Rai. "I would have just given it to you. I tried to make him. But you need a map, and Pallo says it's the best he has. I looked at it—it's a good one. Trust me."

"Come on, Jebby, just give it to her," said Tabba.

"He won't even know how to do half the calls it can make," grumbled Jebby, but he took the whistle off his neck, looking at it a last time before grudgingly handing it over.

Rai blew the whistle a few times, testing it. Seagrape cocked her head. Satisfied that her acquisition would pass muster with her cousin, Rai slipped the whistle into her pocket and handed them the map. Jebby opened it long enough for Penny to catch a glimpse of blue inlets and slivers of roads wending through jade-green jungle dotted by towns before he let the roll snap shut.

"All right," he said with a nod. "Looks good." He handed it to Penny to put in her backpack.

The children bought slices of cassava pie from a vendor and kept wandering. The sky had passed from violet into starry darkness. Strings of swaying sea lights zigzagged across the streets.

"So," Penny said matter-of-factly, "of the other Bloom Players, who's our main competition?"

"Um, everyone," answered Rai, giggling.

"But who does everyone say is the best?" Penny asked.

"There are two brothers from Dorado who everyone's talking about," said Rai. "They swam the Zalla Channel in a storm. Then there's a boy from Mamano who's really good, too. He caught an eight-foot-long oarfish with his bare hands and wrestled it to the ground."

"That's probably just a story." Jebby sniffed. "I don't see how anyone could do that."

"Well, he did," said Rai. "Everyone says. And there's a guy from Lamlo who you're going to have to watch. They say he can dive deeper than anyone else in all of Kana—a girl dropped a ring into Dallo Lagoon. It's so deep you can't see the bottom, even on the sunniest day. They said he was underwater for ages and when he came up he wasn't even out of breath. And he had the ring. And look, quick—over there—that boy is from Tuptow." She nodded across the street. The others sneaked a look and saw a beefy guy with bulging arms and a barrel chest, who was leaning on a wall, eating charred meat on a stick.

"That's not fat; it's muscle," Rai went on. "He rolled a giant boulder between two villages. And see that guy over there—yeah, the short one in the red trousers—he swung from vines all the way from Maum to Moloro without touching the ground."

"So, that's the Dorado brothers, Oarfish, the Lamlo Diver, Boulder Guy, and the Vine Swinger," said Penny.

Rai blinked. "Good memory," she said. "But those are just a few. There are plenty I haven't even heard of yet. And some others I have heard of who are really good—like him over there, see?" she whispered, nodding to a tall young man passing on the other side of the street. "People have been calling him Grasshopper Boy. He's from the southern edge of Kana. Apparently he ran for three days and nights without stopping—even to eat or drink. He just grabbed fruit off trees as he went."

Grasshopper Boy's long, lean limbs had earned him his nickname. He had a lanky, aloof sort of grace and seemed strangely untouchable as he glided alone through the crowd, not talking to anyone. He didn't bluster and brag, like so many of the other players they had seen. He was perfectly relaxed, his expression mildly amused. He reached up once to gently tug the tail of a monkey that had just stolen fruit from a stall. Even after he disappeared into the crowd, the impression he had made lingered.

The children kept strolling, searching for other players, whom they recognized by their yellow arm sashes. Penny dismissed some of them immediately, the ones who didn't seem serious enough as they joked around, play-fighting with one another, indulging in too much food. For them it was just a lark, a game. Others looked deadly serious, and the sight of them made her feel nervous and jittery.

"Everything everyone has done . . . they're all just feats of strength or endurance," said Jebby thoughtfully. "Not brains or knowledge about anything in particular. Or any difficult skill at all, really."

"Well, whatever—they're pretty impressive if you ask me," said Rai.

"None of them did anything like Kal did, though," said Jebby.

"Well," said Rai. "If you want to know the truth . . . people *have* been talking about Kal a lot. People from outside Tontap, even. He's getting famous for what he did. But no one really *likes* him. It's not as if anyone *wants* him to win. People like the brothers from Dorado. And the Lamlo Diver. And everyone's really curious about Grasshopper Boy. There are a lot more players you need to worry about than just Kal."

"TABBA! JEBBY!"

Penny looked up to see children running toward them. Moments later she found herself in the middle of a small swarm of kids from Tontap who were all talking at once.

"Tabba, Jebby, are you really going to be Bloom Players?"

"Is that the Outside girl?"

"Did you honestly see her come over the line?"

"Did Kal really open a whorl on the line?"

"How did you get your parents to let you go?"

"How will you get anywhere?"

Tabba and Jebby fielded questions with the self-conscious but self-satisfied generosity that accompanies newfound celebrity. Heads held a little higher, they resumed walking along a wide side street, the other children crowding around them.

"We heard Kal brought her over—he opened a whorl

in the Blue Line and she came through!" said a boy who was about their age.

"That's not what happened," said Jebby irritably.

"But, Tabba," said a tall, lean girl, "all the other Bloom Players are older. And they're boys."

"There have been girls in the competition before," said Tabba.

"Hardly ever," said the tall girl.

"Well," retorted Penny. "There are now."

The other children looked at Penny with a mix of curiosity and respect—after all, she was an Outsider and she had crossed the Blue Line. But they said nothing. Miraculous solo line crossing or not, Penny realized that no one thought she had any hope of becoming the Bloom Catcher.

"Come on," said a boy to Tabba and Jebby. "You don't actually think you're going to get that far, do you? It'll be a miracle if you even make it past the first round."

"People are betting that you'll come in last in the first trial," added another boy.

"Actual bets?" asked Jebby.

The other kids nodded.

This knocked the wind out of Penny, Tabba, and Jebby's sails a bit, but then Tabba said, with false jauntiness, "Well, everyone's in for a surprise, then, aren't they?"

"Hey, Jebby, what about Kal?" asked a boy.

"What about him?" asked Jebby.

"Does he know you're in the competition now, too?"

"I have no idea," answered Jebby.

"Aren't you . . ."

"Aren't we what?"

"Scared of him?" said one of the other children finally.

"No," said Jebby brashly. "Why should we be?"

"Because he can open whorls," said a boy. "No one else can do that. Only the mandrill."

"And because he made the mandrill come to Tontap," said another boy.

"We don't have proof that Kal brought the mandrill here," said Jebby. "It could have been a coincidence. The mandrill appears all over the place before the Bloom, doesn't he? The fact that he showed up here doesn't mean it's because of Kal. Maybe the mandrill knew that another whorl had been opened and he was curious."

The children stopped walking. They had gone a good distance from the square. At the end of the street, the harbor glimmered in the moonlight. Other people had been around a minute ago, but now there was a lull and the children were the only ones left. They turned around to walk back toward the square.

"Look," hissed a kid. "Kal's coming!"

A hush fell over the children as Kal made his way purposefully in their direction. He looked calm but angry. Penny felt her heart begin to beat faster.

Kal stopped abruptly in front of the group. He said nothing, but slowly he moved his arm through the air, like a magician drawing a silk scarf through a ring. Penny had no idea what he was doing. She glanced at Tabba and Jebby, but they shrugged and waited. The children held their breath. The youngest children cowered behind the older ones.

"What's he going to do?" whispered someone.

"Quiet—watch," said other voices.

Across the street from the children stood a scrappy tree, its leaves motionless in the hot night air. Suddenly a sickly, stormy light shone from it. Everyone turned to face the light, even Kal, as if he had not known precisely where it was going to come from.

"It's a whorl," Tabba whispered, squinting through the leaves.

It was a whorl, a small one, smudged and bleary, lodged in a fork in one of the branches. The light that came through it was muddy, as though passing through murky water or a dirty pane of glass. Penny caught the scent of rain on the air and felt a breeze, like the first puffs in advance of a storm. Seagrape bristled on her shoulder.

"Shhh," Penny whispered.

There was a silence, then she heard a very fine patter and saw misty rain blowing in the beam.

She could hardly believe what she was seeing.

The rain was coming only from the whorl, nowhere else. The rest of the street was bone dry, and the surface of the harbor was smooth, undimpled by raindrops.

Seconds later a strong gust shook the whole tree and, with a sound like a belt snapping, a downpour was unleashed. Rain crashed down. The wind snatched leaves from the tree and whipped them through the air. Children squealed and retreated farther down the street, but Penny, Tabba, and Jebby only stepped back a few paces. A puddle was growing beneath the tree, and Penny recoiled when she felt the water touch her toes.

She glanced at Kal and saw him smile a dark, satisfied smile. What he'd done had been effortful and had taken his full concentration, but the hard work was over. He turned to look directly at her, leering, pleased to see he had intimidated her.

Penny knew it was irrational, but suddenly she believed that he had the power to harm them, even with just his gaze.

There was a thud, and the whorl popped shut. The wind dropped out. The rain ceased abruptly. The cloying light disappeared. Penny saw from Kal's face that the whorl had closed without him meaning it to: He hadn't had the strength to keep it open any longer.

The wind had stripped the tree's leaves, blown them around and plastered them on the row of wooden housefronts along one side of the street, so that they looked like a great, scaled creature just waking from slumber. Children huddled, listening to the *drip-drip-drip* of rain under the bare branches. Those who had been closest to the whorl were drenched. They stood there blinking rain out of their eyes.

"Run!" shouted a boy suddenly. "Before he makes the mandrill come back again!"

As the children stampeded away, the triton sounded from the square.

Telling themselves they had to be there to hear the announcement about the first trial, Penny, Tabba, and Jebby turned and fled after them.

The children wove their way through the crowd and climbed a Bobea tree whose boughs overhung the square. The tree was already sagging under the weight of people who had climbed it for a better view, but the children found an empty branch and wriggled out to the end of it. Seagrape disappeared elsewhere in the tree. The shark's tooth necklace swung forward as Penny crawled along the branch. She found a spot and settled in to wait. She tried to forget what she had just seen Kal do, but her clothes were still damp, her blood buzzing through her veins.

The Council of Elders came through the crowd and assembled on the platform in the middle of the square. Elder banged his cane on the stage and, with much shushing and whispering, the clamor of the crowd was reeled in. Here and there came a cough, a sniffle, a shuffle, but the intensity of attention felt palpable, as if the air itself had gone taut.

"Listen," said Elder. "Do you hear the sea?"

Hundreds of ears turned to the ocean. Penny closed her eyes, her legs dangling in the soft night air, and listened until she could hear the swish and churn of the waves.

"In four days, not many miles from here, a Great Wave will rise from that sea and in it will be the Bloom," said Elder. His voice was rich and deep, like an incantation drawing strength from some distant, mysterious source. "Bloom is life for Kana.

"Between now and then, a competition will take place," he went on. "A sometimes gruelling competition of bravery, stamina, and wits. And at the end of it will be left one person, who alone will go forth fearlessly into the Great Wave to gather the Bloom—Kana's next Bloom Catcher!"

As Elder spoke, Penny pictured the Bloom as Kal had described it that morning in the boat—the great, glassy wall of water, soaring upward from the sand, the explosion of creatures within and then the bright flares of the precious Bloom itself, bursting forth like fireworks inside the Wave. For a moment her vision was twinned with Kal's. Goose bumps prickled her arms. She was going to be that person who strode fearlessly into the Wave. She was going to be the Bloom Catcher. A breeze rose and the branch beneath her swayed and she imagined it was the Wave lifting her up.

She realized Elder was still speaking.

"Whorls have already begun to appear," he said. "The mandrill can now be out of the Gorgonne whenever he wishes. I sensed his presence myself earlier today. If the Bloom Catcher succeeds in getting the Bloom and pouring it into the Coral Basin, then the mandrill will be forced to return to the Gorgonne, and Kana will continue in peace and prosperity, as you see it now. But if a Bloom Catcher fails to emerge from the field of players, if the Bloom is not gathered and poured into the Coral Basin in time, the mandrill will be free to wreak his havoc. What is on the other side of the whorls will come through, and all of what you see around you will be altered beyond recognition—or may disappear forever. Kana as we know it will cease to exist."

The crowd was too youthful and their spirits too high to be sobered for long by such a grave warning. Excited whispers rose and people squeezed in close to see as, after a moment, Elder reached into a cloth bag and fished around for something. Penny, Tabba, and Jebby inched farther down the bough and peered through the leaves. Penny held her breath. Elder withdrew his hand and raised it over his head. Slowly he opened his fingers to reveal in his palm a small purple-and-orange sphere speckled with blue flecks, radiant in the torchlight. Guesses about what it was fizzed through the crowd.

"A Molmer egg," he boomed. "Players will depart from this square tomorrow morning, and it will be their task to find a Molmer egg and bring it to the next town, Jaipa, as quickly as they can. Fifty-two teams will leave here, but only the first twenty teams to reach Jaipa with an egg will advance to the next round. I warn players not to think about sneaking off early—all competitors will be logged tomorrow morning here in Tontap, and any player not accounted for will be disqualified.

"Now . . . players, please enjoy the rest of the night's festivities but be ready for an early tomorrow! Good luck and may the spirit of the Bloom Festival be with you!"

A stray firecracker shattered the sky and, its invisible

ties released, the crowd expanded suddenly, diffusing into the streets around the square. The babble of voices resumed, the music struck up again, and meat sizzled back on hot griddles. The branch the children were on began to bob wildly as people streamed out of the tree.

"Do you know where we can find a . . . what is it—a Molmer egg?" asked Penny, shinnying down the trunk after Tabba and Jebby.

"The Blue Pits, I think," said Tabba. "Right, Jebby?"

"Right," said Jebby. "Let's go to Bellamy's—we can look at the map there and pick up the bicycle, too!"

∼∽∼

The crowd thinned as the children climbed the hill toward Bellamy's. By the time they neared the top, the streets were empty. The door to Bellamy's shop was unlocked. The children entered and, calling quietly to him, went into the storeroom. They found him sitting in a wedge of moonlight at a table near the door to the yard.

"Go on out," he said. "She's all ready for you."

The children went out the back door into a little yard cut out of the limestone walls, bathed in moonlight. A pair of ancient mules dozed beneath a scraggly loquat tree. One opened an eye to watch the children. Seagrape had flown over the roof and landed in the tree.

In the middle of the yard, gleaming brighter and newer than Penny would have believed possible, stood the bicycle.

Every last flake of rust had been sanded off, its gears greased with palm oil, its metal frame polished with beeswax. The tires, bound with the newly cut vines, looked springy and strong. Flexible bamboo rods attached the axle of its rear wheel to the handsome wooden cart. The cart had been sanded smooth—no splinters would catch the children's arms leaning on its edges—and painted bright yellow. It would fit two passengers snugly. Grass streamers hung from the ends of the bike's handlebars, and a breeze stirred them, giving the impression of speed even as the bike stood still.

"Wow!" said Penny. "It looks like a whole new bicycle!"

"Give it a spin," said Bellamy proudly.

Penny got on and rode in a circle around the yard, starting slowly then picking up speed so that puffs of white sand spun up from beneath the tires. It was a little big but still a good size for her, which meant that long ago Bellamy must have ridden around on it with his long legs folded up to his ears like a grasshopper. The cart rolled smoothly and willingly along behind. It balanced the bike, almost as if it were a giant tricycle, which would make it easier for Tabba and Jebby to ride, too. The brakes didn't squeak, and the crooked axle on the front wheel had been hammered straight. The rusted bell on the handlebars had been taken apart, its pieces meticulously cleaned, and when Penny pushed it with her thumb, instead of the old hoarse croak it had emitted earlier, it trilled, clear and purposeful as a bird's call.

"It's perfect," said Penny sincerely, stopping back in front of the others. "Thank you, Bellamy."

"Teach us how to ride it, Penny!" said Tabba.

With Penny jogging alongside, Tabba and then Jebby took their first wobbly turns around the yard. Tabba was bolder, going faster immediately, almost crashing into the loquat tree, causing the mules to bray and shuffle a safe distance away. Jebby was more cautious, carving a few slow, precise circles before he was comfortable enough to go faster.

"There!" called Penny. "You've got it!"

Jebby sped up, showing off. The bike fishtailed and almost tipped over. He steadied himself, then got off and left the bike standing securely in the shafts of the cart and joined the others.

The children sat down with Bellamy at the table near the doorway, and Penny retrieved the map from her bag.

"The first trial is to bring back a Molmer egg from the bottom of a Blue Pit," Tabba told Bellamy.

"Not at the bottom," said Bellamy quickly. He looked alarmed. "You'd never make it all the way down to the bottom of a Blue Pit, let alone back up—far too deep." He gave a short, dry laugh. "You'll find that out quickly enough."

"Oh," said Tabba, abashed.

"They'll be in the cave walls, partway down," said Bellamy as Penny fiddled with the string that tied the map together. "Molmers lived in the Blue Pits before the last bad Bloom—they looked like giant lobsters, with huge purple shells and claws that could dig through stone. They carved cubbyholes—small caves, really—in the sheer walls of the pits and laid their eggs there. I remember being a boy and hearing old people telling stories about how the Molmers used to come up and float around on the surface sometimes in the spring—they were as big as rowboats. It was rare to catch one, but when people did, it could feed several families for a week. In those times the pits were teeming with life—they were big fishing grounds. Then the bad Bloom happened and the Molmers went extinct, along with a lot of other creatures. The pits have been barren ever since, and the Molmer eggs that are still down there have turned to stone."

Penny unfurled the map, and Jebby pinned down its corners with stones from the yard. The children leaned in, elbows on the table, and pored over it.

Penny's gaze roved over blue fingers of inlets scattered with jade atolls, luxurious green jungles whose borders were etched with coconut plantations, towns with strange and musical names marked with tiny stars. The whole place was threaded and crosshatched with roads and paths, except for a blank expanse that weighted the middle of the map—the Gorgonne, where Tabba said the mandrill lived. Unlike the rest of the map, which was finely detailed, it was featureless, its depths uncharted.

Penny kept looking and located Tontap on the northeast coast amid a smattering of tiny islands. Then her heart quickened as farther north, in a half-moon cleft on the coast, she found Palmos, where the Great Wave would rise. The waters around it were painted a bright, swimmy, promising blue. That was where the Bloom would happen and where— if they were lucky—they would be a few short days from now. She took a shivery breath.

Then she realized that the others were looking not at Palmos but at several dark splotches shadowing the water farther west.

"There they are," said Tabba, pointing. "The Blue Pits."

The pits were not blue but appeared black, like inkblots— mistakes—and Penny felt a tug of foreboding. Most of them were close together; only one was out on its own.

Jebby chewed his lip. "Everyone is probably going to head to those," he said, indicating the main cluster. "They're closest, and they're all together, so there will be lots to choose from. But it looks like it's dense jungle all along that part of the coast—I don't see any real roads. Players on animals will be fine, but I don't think the bike could do it."

"You're right," said Bellamy. "Past a certain point, there are really only hunting trails out to that part of the coast."

Penny's gaze wandered across the map. "What about this one?" she asked, pointing to the stray blot farther west, at the end of a narrow, broken peninsula. "The one by itself. Off—what's it called?—Oyster Point. It looks like there's a clear road out there at least. It's farther away, but we can cover ground quickly. And from there it's not far to Jaipa."

The children contemplated the solitary Blue Pit.

"It just *looks* lonely," said Tabba. She put her hands in her lap, as though she didn't want to risk touching the pit, even on the map.

"Bellamy, you used to go all over Kana," said Jebby. "What do you think?"

"In terms of getting there, on the bike, yes, the pit off Oyster Point makes the most sense," he said carefully. "But you'll find it . . . desolate. A long time ago it was a bustling fishing town, but it was one of the areas worst hit by the last bad Bloom. Some places never came back, you know— they're just dead zones. The pit there is an empty, dark place."

Jebby frowned as he studied the map. "But what choice do we really have?" he asked.

"I still don't like it," said Tabba.

"You'll like it when no one's there fighting us over the last Molmer egg," said Jebby. "Agreed?"

"Agreed," said Penny. The lonely pit seemed creepy, even on the map, but Jebby was right, it was the best choice.

"All right," sighed Tabba at last. "Me, too."

"We'd better get back home," said Jebby. He rolled up the map and shook Bellamy's hand. "Bellamy, we'll have your bicycle back safe and sound in no time."

"Thank you for letting us borrow it," said Penny.

"Yes, thank you!" echoed Tabba.

"It's an unexpected honor to be part of the Bloom at

my age," said Bellamy graciously. "I'm glad you found your way to my shop."

Penny went to get the bicycle from the yard, but before she could wheel it past Bellamy, he put a large hand firmly on the handlebars and stopped the children.

"The Bloom trials aren't easy," he said. "Fatigue sets in, tempers fray. Make sure you stick together—it's the only chance you'll have."

The children endured this somber caution without really listening. They were on their way: They had supplies for the first trial, a shiny bicycle to convey them swiftly across Kana, and a solid plan. They were on the brink of the greatest freedom any of them had ever known. Nothing could dampen their excitement.

"We will," they sang dutifully.

Bellamy released his hold and the children said good night to him. Penny wheeled the bicycle through the stockroom and shop, past the squeaking mice, into the street.

In the open moonlight on the high, empty street, the bike glittered. The air itself seemed molten, holding everything in silvery suspense. The sounds of the celebrations in the cramped town below hummed like a distant sea, but up here it was still and serene, a final private moment before the great race that so many players would join. Then, with Penny on the bike and Tabba and Jebby in the cart, the children rolled down the sea-stone-paved street.

The bike rode as light as air on the supple sapsoo vine tires, and soon the children were speeding down the hill.

A warm river of night air poured over them, and Penny's hair flew behind her. Seagrape nestled in the cart at Tabba's feet. Through a break in the rooftops, Tabba pointed out the distant cliffs, studded with sea lights, where she and Penny had been that afternoon. Flowers that had been freshly picked a short time ago were crushed now and their fragrance filled the air. The children skirted the town, and soon the bike and cart rolled silently into the clearing outside the Silverlings' hut, where Ma and Da had already taken the littlest children home to sleep. The hut was cozy, lit with an oil lamp. The door was propped open and Ma and Da were inside, Ma wrapping food in banana leaves for the children to take with them the next day. After being admired, the bike was stowed inside, away from prying eyes. The children covered it with a cloth, as lovingly as if they were tucking in a child for the night.

"Have you ever seen a Blue Pit?" Jebby asked his parents.

"No," said Ma. "You children are going to see things we've only heard stories about."

Da came outside with them to set up a hammock for Penny in the clearing between the palms near Tabba's and Jebby's.

"Da—do you really think we have a chance?" Tabba asked him.

He hesitated, then said lightly, "Why not?"

Seeing Ma and Da Silverling made Penny feel a pang about her own parents. She wondered what they were doing right now. She knew they'd be worried about her, even if

Granny Pearl told them she was in Tamarind. She wished she could have talked to them before she left, assured them she would be all right.

Da left, and Penny climbed into her hammock, the gauze of the mosquito net settling mistily around her. It was like being in a big, soft cloud. For a few minutes the children were quiet. Jebby had found a new piece of wood and begun whittling another whistle. Penny could hear the soft scrape of his knife. White flakes sputtered from it like pale sparks in the moonlight.

"That thing Kal did, the storm in the tree," whispered Tabba.

"What about it?" whispered Penny.

"It wasn't a whorl that just, I don't know, just sat there," said Tabba. "It was like Elder said—what was on the other side of it was coming through. That seems pretty scary, that he can do that."

"I wasn't sure before," said Jebby. "But I agree now that Kal's opening whorls." He stopped whittling. "But you know what else I think? That whorl out at the line today—I don't think he opened it. I think *you* did, Penny. And Kal knows it. And he's scared of you. So he's trying to make *you* scared of *him*. That's why he let everyone see him open a whorl tonight—it wasn't to show everyone else, it was to show you."

"I couldn't have done it," said Penny. "How would *I* open a whorl? I have no idea how it happened."

"Well, I'm not so sure Kal does either," said Jebby.

"Or not so much of an idea as he wants us to think. That's all I'm saying. But we should be careful around him, anyway."

"You'd all better get some sleep before tomorrow!" Ma hissed from the doorway to the hut.

"She's right," whispered Jebby.

Penny heard a snap as Jebby folded his knife and put it away. The fall of wood shavings ceased. A few minutes later, Ma stopped bustling around, then the oil lamp was blown out. The palms creaked as Ma and Da got into their hammocks on the other side of the hut. Penny lay there quietly. She told herself that Kal didn't matter. He was no more important in the competition than anyone else, even her. Within minutes, Tabba and Jebby were breathing evenly, already asleep, but Penny lay awake. It seemed hard to believe that at this time just yesterday she hadn't even met Tabba and Jebby. Already she felt as if she had known them forever.

An animal growled from a distant hillside, and Penny stiffened. She lay there listening to the intermittent strange cries of animals, the beasts of burden that the players would ride into the first trial. They had been invisible throughout the evening, tied up in the trees around Tontap. Now the darkness amplified their sounds—grunts, screeches, roars, warning growls, and restless snorts—and mingled them with the crackle of campfires and the odd human voice that traveled across the water. One of the little Silverling children coughed in his sleep.

It was the first time Penny had stopped all day, her thoughts free to wander. Home felt very far away. If she had been there right now, her family would probably have already had dinner and would almost be finished cleaning up the kitchen. She closed her eyes and thought of the scent of oranges in the garden, of the cove dark and luminous and the *Pamela Jane* at rest on her anchor, of the yellow glow of the living room lamp illuminating the tiny print of the marine science journal her father would soon sit down to read, of the pipes wheezing in the walls as her grandmother got ready for bed. Suddenly Penny's chest felt tight and a lump lodged in her throat, and she wished fervently that she could be home, even just for a few minutes. Then she made herself stop that train of thought. She had to concentrate only on getting the Bloom; it was all that mattered. She could go home after it was done. She touched the shark's tooth necklace, cool against her neck.

Penny whistled softly to Seagrape, who flew down from the palms. She lifted the mosquito net so the parrot could slip under it. Seagrape perched on Penny's knee.

"Tomorrow we're leaving to start to get the Bloom for Granny Pearl," Penny murmured. "Then we can go back home and everything can go back to the way it was."

The parrot did not corroborate or comfort but kept silent vigil as Penny finally drifted off to sleep. Some miles down the coast, in the small cleft of a bay, the sea gently milled the shore, waiting in the darkness for the Bloom.

Helix

Halfway down the hill to Tontap, he had stopped.

He wasn't ready to be caught up in the thick of a bois-terous and celebratory crowd, not after being alone for so many days. He needed twine to repair his backpack, but he would wait until late the next morning, after the Bloom Players and the crowds had left.

He turned around and headed back up into the hills. He found somewhere far enough away that it was peaceful and struck camp. He built a fire and warmed the last of the cassava bread from his bag and ate, wriggling his bare toes in the dirt. Soft, dark flutters of moths brushed the air. Lights twinkled in the town far below. On the breeze he heard the murmur of music and voices, indistinct but comforting and pleasantly melancholy to listen to from so far away. He was glad to be on his own. He should bathe before he got too near other humans, anyway.

After he had eaten, he lay on his back, the smoke from his fire keeping the insects at bay as he gazed up at the con-stellations. They had different names on the Outside. The others had taught them to him, lying in the backyard, or on the deck of the *Pamela Jane* at anchor in the cove, bundled up in sweaters on cold, clear winter nights. Orion, Cassio-peia, Ursa Major, Taurus, Perseus, Cepheus, Pisces, and Andromeda, Maya's favorite, though he couldn't remember why. The fire crackled. He dozed, hovering in the intertidal zone between consciousness and sleep.

He was in the kitchen at Granny Pearl's house. Granny Pearl was standing at the sink filling a pot with water. She carried it briskly to the stove and turned on a gas burner. He heard the *click-click-click* and the tiny roar as the orange flame caught. Rain pattered on the window over the sink, and outside he could see the *Pamela Jane* glowing yellow through the rain that blurred the surface of the cove, but inside it was dry and cozy. He could hear everything— the bump of cupboard doors, the whistle of the kettle, the tap of rain on the windowpanes.

Distracted by a cracking sound from the corner, he looked across the room and saw Penny. She was three, maybe four years old, in the corner where she often used to sit, listening to the vague hum of adult conversation but lost in her own world. She was feeding almonds one by one to Seagrape, who was sitting on the floor beside her, tail feathers brushing the cool tiles each time she reached up for a nut.

He looked around the room and then his heart began to beat faster.

There she was.

Maya sat at the kitchen table, leaning in concentration over a book. She was doing homework. The pale winter light glowed on her long hair, and the cuffs of her old sweater hung loosely around her wrists.

She was saying something. Helix could only hear a murmur, a dull buzz. The memory was imprecise, molten at the edges. The actual words, the actual world all this had happened in, were gone. This was just an echo. He watched Maya put her homework aside. She was the brightest thing in the room. Every other part of the room was slightly hazy; only Maya was in focus. She was the source of the radiance. She looked up at him and smiled, and a feeling washed over him powerfully and completely, a feeling of warmth, of peace, of safety. Of love, pure and overwhelming. His heart felt as if it were filling up too fast and would overflow.

Helix rolled over and his foot touched the embers of the campfire. It jolted him awake and he sat up. Instantly the kitchen and the younger versions of Maya, Granny Pearl, Penny, and himself vanished. It took him a moment to remember where he was.

He was alone on the hillside in the soft night air. Tontap glittered far below. He could still hear the sounds of the celebration drifting up over the trees.

He took a deep breath. No dream should feel so real.

Tomorrow he would join the crowds. He'd been on his own too long.

PART TWO

❧ Chapter Eight ❧

The day was still fresh and new when Penny woke. She wrestled her way out from under her mosquito net and swung her legs over the side of the hammock, wriggling her bare toes in the cool sand. There wasn't even a flicker of breeze. Boats sat motionless on their moorings, and the highest palms were so still they looked as if they had been painted on the sky. All that moved was the dazzling creep of the sun across the water, and ivory birds that swooped for fish in the calm shallows, only their wingtips blue, as if they had soaked up the color from the sea. Seagrape had ducked out from under the mosquito net sometime in the night and was now preening herself vigorously on a nearby branch, her dewy feathers spread out to dry. Tabba and

Jebby had woken, too, and were climbing out of their hammocks.

"Good morning!" called Tabba. "It's really happening—I can hardly believe it!"

The children hurried to take down their hammocks and stuff them into their waiting backpacks. Worn-out from their late night at the festival, Tabba and Jebby's little brothers and sisters were still sleeping, but Ma and Da Silverling were awake and the door of the hut was propped open with a coconut.

"Good morning, Bloom Players!" said Da when they went inside.

"You need food in your stomachs," said Ma, pushing warm sweet bread into their hands. "I don't want to hear it," she said when they protested. "You have time—eat! I've packed a few extra things for you. There are dumplings and tapai for your lunch today. Eat that first. Everything else will keep. Get what you can in the towns—Bloom Players will be given food; just show your sashes at the stalls. Keep what I've given you for when you really need it."

She placed a basket of food wrapped in banana leaves into the cart. Everything else was already packed—the sharpened spears, the net of kelp pods, and the basket of sea lights, whose light burned softly through the wet rag that covered them.

The children ate quickly and wheeled the bicycle and cart outside. It was the first time they had taken a good look at the bicycle in daylight. They gazed proudly at it, gleaming splendidly in the sunlight.

"I think it looks pretty great," said Jebby.

The children remembered the yellow sashes and fumbled as they tried to tie them on their arms. The silk was cool against their skin. When Ma helped them, Penny noticed her fingers trembling.

"Now, you listen to me," she said. "The competition is a free-for-all—all sorts of lunatics come in from all over the place. Keep your wits about you and stick together. Steer clear of Kal. I don't trust that boy—I don't care if he is from Tontap. And don't do anything too dangerous!"

"Okay, Ma," said Tabba obediently.

"We won't," said Jebby impatiently, looking past his parents toward the town, where the sounds of animals and people were coming through the trees. "But come on, Ma—we're going to be the last ones there if we don't go now!"

"We'll be in Tontap until Palmos," said Da. "Come back if you need to."

"We won't need to," said Jebby confidently. "We'll see you in Palmos in a few days."

The triton sounded, a low bellow over the water and through the palms.

Penny, Tabba, and Jebby froze and looked at one another—this was it. A deep thrill spread through them. Penny worried the knot with her fingers, making sure the sash was tied securely.

"That's the triton," said Tabba. "We have to get to the square! Good-bye, Ma! Good-bye, Da!"

"Good-bye and good luck!" called Da, putting his arm around Ma and pulling her to him. "We'll come to wave you off!"

The children had agreed that Penny would be the first one to ride the bike. She hopped on, while Tabba and Jebby piled into the cart behind her. The littlest Silverling children struggled out of their hammocks, still bleary with sleep. Dazed, they trotted down the road after the bicycle, then stopped and waved furiously as Penny, Tabba, and Jebby turned the bend through the palms.

The bike glided along effortlessly. The sapsoo-vine tires absorbed the shocks of pebbles and potholes, the brakes were responsive, and the cart cornered easily. The children overtook a team of three Bloom Players astride a serene ivory water-ox, whose long, polished horns gleamed like burnished metal in the sunlight and whose back was as wide as a raft. The young men's legs dangled down, bumping gently against the creature's sides. Penny, Tabba, and Jebby nodded to the other team and slid through the cool blue shadow cast by the animal.

They passed the street where Kal had whipped up the strange storm the night before. The tree stood stark and barren. A few people had gathered to see the shock of its suddenly nude limbs, ornate knots, and burls revealed for the first time, and to remark on the damp jade shadow of the walls, scaly as snakeskin, where its torn leaves had dried overnight. Seagrape flew through two empty branches, into a chunk of raw blue sky, and the children cycled past.

As they drew closer to the square, the crowd thickened, but people saw their yellow sashes and opened a path for them, ogling the strange bicycle as it coasted by. Seagrape perched regally on the handlebars, sleek feathers resplendent in the morning sun, and for a moment the little yellow cart seemed less like a cart and more like a chariot. Penny took a deep, happy breath. It was good to be a Bloom Player, fresh on the first morning of the first trial of the competition! She pedaled with zeal around a corner and into the square.

Only then did she have her first moment of true doubt. She squeezed the brakes too quickly, to avoid barreling into a hippolike creature so solid that the bike's metal would have crumpled upon contact with it, and the bike fishtailed in the sand. When Penny regained her balance, she kept pedaling slowly, gazing around in astonishment.

The square had been transformed into a bizarre, thunderous zoo, a crush of snorting, stomping, braying beasts and their riders. The creatures were fantastical relations of animals Penny knew on the Outside: stout, broad-barreled pigs with barbarously spiked tails; sleek, graceful gazelles with single horns for shearing through the undergrowth; feathered, flightless creatures with four legs and curved canines. The sheer number and variety of creatures struck even Tabba and Jebby speechless. Amid them, too, were ordinary mules, shaggy and docile, furred ears flicked back in dismay at the commotion.

Yellow arm sashes flashed everywhere, like flowers that had bloomed overnight, and were being tugged this way and that on the bright, windy hills and valleys of the swelling crowd. The air was bursting with boasting and bravado, with jokes that Penny couldn't quite catch and laughter that exploded suddenly and startlingly.

It was impossible to stop anywhere—she had to keep steering out of the way of gnashing teeth and tusks and flinty hooves. Within moments, a film of dust coated the bike and cart and made an acrid paste in her mouth. The sun was already baking—it was going to be a steamy day. Uniformed officials moved through the crowd, logging the competitors. Penny recognized a few of the Bloom Players from the day before; others they were seeing for the first time. She caught sight of the Lamlo Diver riding a buffalo-like animal with an ancient face buried deep in its shaggy beard, and the Dorado brothers astride a fidgety pair of striped chestnut horses. From their low vantage, everyone and everything looked bigger, stronger, and more ferocious than the children and their bicycle and cart. As they were pushed through the crowd, Penny saw that the yellow flag was still on top of the message pole, but she had no time to feel disappointed.

"Watch out!" cried Jebby.

Like a flint striking stone, a razor-sharp hoof punched

the earth within inches of the bicycle's front tire. Penny swerved out of the way and the cart tipped to one side before righting. The children turned to see what had almost crushed the tire and found themselves looking up at Kal, high above them astride a nimble-footed, swan-necked creature. More antelope than horse, its legs were long and lean, its striped, brandy-colored coat groomed to a high, electric glow. Muscles rippled like pure coiled energy beneath its hide. Its legs were so long that its neck and haunches were too high to have been touched by the cloud of kicked-up dirt that hugged the ground, and as the children looked up at it through the haze, these high points glinted like mountain peaks on a clear day.

"*That's* a lumphur," whispered Tabba.

Unlike the skittish creatures prancing around, it wasn't frenzied and foaming. It was alert and self-possessed, conserving its energy. It observed them with a cold, sharp eye.

For a moment after he saw the children, Kal's face relaxed and he laughed. It was the first natural, spontaneous response Penny had heard from him: He thought they looked ridiculous.

"It's going to take you a week just to reach Jaipa on that thing!" he called down.

Next to the sleek and mighty lumphur, the bicycle and cart that the children had been so proud of just a short time ago suddenly seemed like an embarrassing miscalculation—a silly, improbable, and unreliable contraption. As the triton sounded again, Kal and the lumphur pushed in front of the children and muscled their way toward the front of the line, the lumphur's tail delivering a stinging swat to Penny's arm as it passed. Penny, Tabba, and Jebby found themselves shoved this way and that until they were at the rear of the crowd of Bloom Players, struggling to see through tossing heads and swishing tails to where the Council of Elders had assembled on the elevated platform in the middle of the square.

The Council wore flowing, jewel-colored robes and carried staffs encrusted with polished seashells whose tips caught the light like broken glass. The Elder of Tontap was among them. He had washed and brushed his beard, which hung straight down in the breezeless air, and his bare head shone with coconut oil. He stepped forward and raised a large and ancient triton shell. There would be no speech or ceremony that morning, no final advice. He lifted the shell to his lips and blew.

A sound emerged, sonorous and otherworldly, as if it came not from the shell but from another atmosphere, out of the past, as it had so many times before to send forth new generations to seek the Bloom. Before its single note began to fade, the horde of competitors lunged onto the road out of the town with a roar.

"Good-bye! Good luck!" called people in the crowd, waving vigorously as they surged after the players. Small children were lifted onto the shoulders of adults so they could see, the elderly given elbows to lead them back to the shade, and soon a growing space had opened between the pack and those who had come to see them off. The children didn't see Ma or Da or the little Silverlings or Rai or Bellamy during the frantic dash. Penny pedaled furiously, the bicycle's tires whirring to keep up with the hooves and paws and talons up ahead.

The competitors began together on the same road out of town but quickly dispersed. Kal's lumphur loped along far ahead of the pack and soon dropped from sight. The team on the hippolike beast charged straight into the jungle. Penny caught sight of Grasshopper Boy ducking onto a shadowy dirt track. A few teams had ventured out in boats, though in the windless day they made little progress, fluttering in circles in the harbor, sails luffing. Penny, Tabba, and Jebby headed north. The dust kicked up by the animals clouded their view. When it cleared, both animals and town were gone. Seagrape flew high above them like a green kite attached by an invisible string. The wheels of both bicycle and cart ran smoothly—no rattling or squeaking—and the grass streamers buzzed in the wind.

As the sun blazed down on Penny's shoulders, it struck her that she had never been so free in all her life. She already had two new friends, a shiny bicycle to take them where they needed to go, and a plan to get a Molmer egg. It was better than the last day of school with summer sprawling out before her, better than one hundred summer holidays back to back!

"We're free!" she cried joyfully. "We don't have to be in Jaipa until tonight!"

"That isn't very much time," warned Jebby from the cart. "You heard Elder—only the first twenty teams back will make it to the next trial. We don't have long!"

Penny braced her arms against the handlebars and pedaled hard. The sun climbed in the sky and beat down on the farm fields and piping-hot road. When her calves began to burn, she stopped to let the others take over. At first she ran alongside them, shouting encouragement and catching the bike if it began to wobble, but soon Tabba and Jebby were as capable and as fast as she was, and she was able to ride in the cart, gazing out at the shining fields and hot blue sky, soaking it all in. Seagrape flew back down to perch on the back of the cart, the breeze glossing her feathers to green lacquer.

The children passed hundreds of people streaming in from all around for the festival. Young and old, everyone in Kana seemed to be on the move. Families rode in mule-drawn carts, piled precariously with everything they had brought with them for their journey. Others traveled light, their few possessions stuffed into the same kind of sackcloth backpacks that Tabba and Jebby carried. People stopping to picnic on the roadsides saw the children's yellow arm sashes and waved and cheered, and the children rang the bicycle bell back. The whole island seemed to be in high spirits. Penny thought that the dark warnings from Elder and Bellamy and Ma and Da Silverling seemed misguided—adults were always exaggerating danger. How could Kana be in trouble? It was too bright and vibrant, ringing with too much life. The whorl she had seen at Elder's was strange and unsettling, sure, but it had lasted so briefly, like a passing mood, easily forgotten.

Jebby pointed out a sapsoo, a tall tree with pale bark and elastic vines waving in the breeze like upside-down garden eels. The vines were the same type that had been used for the bicycle tires. Bellamy had been right—the bike rode so smoothly on the new tires that the children really did feel as if they were floating along on a cloud.

They had just passed the sapsoo tree when a great clattering, scraping sound came from up ahead. When they turned around the next bend, Penny saw a pair of mighty elephantine animals hauling a rattling cargo of empty oyster shells caught in a trawling net. They were compact creatures with round haunches, pale blue hides, and reedy tails that swatted away flies. A couple of men walked beside them.

"They're taking shells to Palmos to build the breakwaters," said Jebby. "So when the Wave crashes, it won't rush up and destroy the town."

"They've been building the breaks for ages now," added Tabba. "Since we were small."

The children moved to the edge of the road to pedal past and caught a whiff of oysters and dung, but soon the clanking shells faded behind them.

Whenever Jebby was in the cart, he worked on the new whistle, stopping to play a few notes on it, then carving the holes to adjust the pitch. The tunes summoned different birds that appeared on the edges of the undergrowth, blinking curiously at the children from beneath fluffy feather caps, or swooping in small neon flocks in front of them, trailing their scraggly shadows across the dusty road. He pointed out different birds to Penny: sagwonds, with frilled purple tail feathers; trilbadors, who made only a single note, a low, mournful G minor; pellucines, who sang only for three minutes at dawn and three at dusk; and a lone bowerbird, a nondescript figure that Jebby claimed built a nest as elaborate as a castle, decorated with tiny treasures he gathered from the jungle. Seagrape sat on the handlebars, nodding to all of them as if she were passing royalty.

"If we get one of the Molmer eggs, we'll be bringing back something that no one's seen since before the last bad Bloom," Tabba mused. "It's pretty amazing."

"It *is* pretty amazing," agreed Penny.

She liked Tabba and Jebby so much. It had been a long time since she had really hung out with anyone her own age, and she had forgotten how much fun it was to be with other people. She remembered Simon's compass and took it out to show them. They marveled at its needle, which pointed faithfully north and could not be fooled, and they used it with the map to guide them ever closer to the Blue Pit.

❧ Chapter Nine ❧

By the time the sun had reached its peak, they had covered a lot of ground, a person in the cart checking off each town on the map as they skirted its edges. The crowds going east to Jaipa thinned, then petered out altogether, until all that was left was the occasional farmer carrying a basket of muddy vegetables or, once, a man driving a mule pulling a cart of clattering mussels. There were no other players, and when the children reached the valley they saw no one at all. Nervously, they pedaled faster. They had taken a chance coming out so far. If they were unlucky, there was no way to make it to the other Blue Pits and still get to Jaipa before the other players did.

They raced across the floor of the valley, but their pace slowed as they began to cycle up its far hill. The sun beat down mercilessly. Rills of sweat coursed down their faces and drenched their clothes. Eventually it grew too steep and they had to get out and push the bike and the cart the rest of the way. At the top, light-headed, they stopped to catch their breath. The other side of the hill dropped abruptly down a series of switchbacks onto a long, narrow peninsula that sat barely above sea level. At the end of it lay the shingly remnants of what must have been, at one time, a town. Beyond it the vast sea undulated in sallow, blue-gold swells for miles before finally ascending into haze on the horizon.

"Oyster Point," said Tabba, gazing down at the stony ruins.

But Penny had lifted her gaze and was staring beyond the town, at the sea half a mile from shore—at a dark hole, an unexplained void in the corrugated surface of the sea.

"The Blue Pit," whispered Jebby as he caught sight of it, too.

Even from so far away, coldness seemed to emanate from it. The children's excitement drained away and a sick feeling lodged in their stomachs. Nobody spoke. Seagrape growled softly. There in the bright sun, Penny's skin prickled with goose bumps and she wanted to pull a blanket over her head and hide. Grimly, Jebby took a reckoning so that they would be able to find the pit from shore, then they began the plunge down the hill toward the empty town.

When the children reached the end of the peninsula and rolled into Oyster Point, tires clattering over shells, it was obvious that they were the only ones there. No other Bloom Players had ventured this far. The town was abandoned, as Bellamy had said it would be. It was becoming hard to see that a town had been there at all, in fact. The homes, once made of shells compressed into bricks, had mostly slumped into piles of rubble, swallowing the streets that had run between them. A breeze whistled forlornly through the cracks. Seabirds sat on the mounds, their beaks tapping on hard, empty volutes and oysters. They observed the children with the watchful, unfriendly stare of those unused to visitors. Mosquitoes not driven off by the stiff sea breeze multiplied in the pools of old rain drums whose tops had rotted away. A frazzled net had washed in and got hooked on the lone, wind-gnarled shrub that still clung stubbornly to the rocks. Sea urchins glistened on the edges of the shore, their menacing points advancing in a slow, pointed creep.

It seemed impossible that in such a short time the children could have gone from the lushness of fields and jungle to a place so devoid of life.

"Hello?" Tabba called as they pedaled through storm-split stones. "Hello!"

It felt like a necessary gesture, to throw something hopeful and human out into the desolation, but all that returned was Tabba's own voice, echoing thinly off the crumbling shell walls. The children put the bicycle inside one of the few intact huts, more to keep it from toppling over in the wind than out of any need to hide it. Something spooked the birds and they took off together, flying seaward, where they disappeared, leaving the town entirely deserted except for the newcomers.

"There aren't any boats left at all," said Jebby, returning from a brief expedition around the shoreline. "I didn't even think of that. . . ."

The children endured a brief moment of silent panic, before Penny said, "The cart—we'll take the cart off and paddle out there in it."

They turned in relief to the little yellow cart.

"I think the three of us can squeeze into it," said Penny.

"I'll detach it from the bike and take the wheels off," said Jebby.

"I'll get the stones for our weight belts," said Tabba.

"And I'll try to find something we can use as a paddle," added Penny.

She stepped quickly and carefully through the ruins. The gurgle of the tide was amplified through the shells. There was hardly anything left—a child's faded toy, a dented, smoke-stained kettle. Finally she saw a paddle—an actual paddle, they were in luck—poking out from between two stones. Bracing a foot against a rock, she yanked it out. It turned out to be only half a paddle—split and splintered, its wood pocked with shipworm holes—but it would do. She returned to the others with it. Tabba had found stones and secured them in the weight belts, and Jebby was just removing the last wheel from the cart.

Together they carried the cart down to the shore. With the cargo of stones, it sat precariously low in the water. It groaned when, one after another, each child eased tentatively into it, but it held steady. Kelp pods and sea lights safely stowed, they set out from shore. As if to lighten the load, Seagrape flew ahead of them, an electric-green volt in the burned-out sky.

When they neared the Blue Pit, the children stopped paddling and let the cart drift toward the edge. The Blue Pit was just that—a pit—a vast underwater hole in the seafloor, as though a place on the earth had ceased to exist and nothing had replaced it. It was impossible to tell its depth. The surrounding seafloor was only ten or fifteen feet deep, but the circumference of the pit dropped abruptly into steep cliff walls. A few shafts of light angled down but were soon swallowed into an unknowable knot of darkness far below. Gloom crept up from the depths like cold, foul vapor, entering Penny's lungs and chilling her. The cart floated over the edge, and a moment later the children found themselves suspended precariously over the abyss.

They realized they had no way to anchor, so someone would have to stay with the cart. They drew straws. Tabba would remain on board, paddling to keep over the middle of the pit. Penny and Jebby divided the kelp pods between them and tied the nubby stalks of each bunch with fishing line. With only two people underwater, the air in the pods would last longer.

"Do you need to practice breathing from them first?" Penny asked Jebby.

"No," he said tensely. "I've done it before."

"Only once," said Tabba quietly.

Tabba had fashioned headbands out of twisted cloth and had secured the sea lights to them, and now Penny and Jebby adjusted the straps until the sea lights rested firmly on their foreheads. They tightened the stone weight-belts around their waists. Penny practiced a quick-release knot until she was satisfied she could drop the weights quickly if she needed to. She tucked the kelp straws into her belt. She and Jebby sat on opposite sides of the cart to balance it. With difficulty due to the weight of the stones, Penny inched around until her legs were dangling over the pit. This was it. She felt excited and afraid, as if she were slightly outside her own body. Carefully she polished her goggles, then put them on, pulling the strap behind her head and lowering the lenses over her eyes. The world blurred slightly. She tied the fishing line with the kelp pods around her wrist. She turned her head to look at Jebby. They nodded to each other and, each taking a last deep breath, slid in.

The stones weighed Penny down, and despite the buoyant kelp pods, she descended briskly. A panicky sensation gripped her and subsided only when she breathed from the pod for the first time and found that it worked. Breathing seemed harder here than it had been at the surface with Tabba yesterday, but she willed herself to stay calm. Every few feet she pinched her nose to equalize the pressure in her ears. The air in the pods tasted like seaweed, and the taste grew stronger as she went deeper. She glanced up to see that Jebby was beside and just above her. They each held a cluster of kelp pods, like people selling balloons in a park.

It felt as though they were dropping down a large, deep well, bounded by sheer walls. They were only able to see the wall they were closest to. Beyond that, the water became too dark and murky, the opposite side too far away. If Bellamy was right, a Molmer egg would be nestled in a nook somewhere in this underwater cliff. If one was here at all, that was. Penny and Jebby stayed as far from the cliff as they could to have the widest perspective possible, but close enough that they wouldn't miss an egg.

The circle of light from the top of the pit shrank to a small disk as they descended. They drifted beneath it as if they were parachuting under a cold sun on a windless day. The water grew swiftly colder and Penny felt very far from yesterday's sunny green kelp forest, dappled and swaying and full of life. Soon she was deeper than she had ever been before. The darkness, thick and heavy, seemed to sink with its own weight. Relics of creatures—gill plates, bones, teeth— rested in the cubbyholes of the cliff. She saw them illuminated briefly by her sea light as she sank past them, like rows of tiny tombs, or a cabinet of curiosities scavenged by some rogue curator. Penny imagined the barren graveyard of creatures that must lie at the very bottom of the pit, sifting down piece by piece over the years. The deeper they went, the brighter the sea lights burned, and she saw that there was life here, brittle and surreptitious. Sea spiders stalked the cold tomb walls, and a pale crab scuttled out of the passing glow of the sea lights.

By the time she and Jebby saw the Molmer egg, they had almost sunk past it: a peep of light from a small, pale oval, not guttering but burning softly and steadily from inside a narrow cave in the cliff wall. They each dropped a weight from their belts to achieve stable buoyancy and hovered parallel to the cave. This was it!

Penny looked at Jebby. He nodded. They couldn't talk, but she could see he was excited, too. Penny smiled as she exhaled a column of bubbles that jittered toward the surface. It had all been quicker and easier than she'd expected. Minutes from now they'd have the egg and be back in the cart with Tabba. They began swimming toward the cave.

Jebby recoiled. Penny didn't know what had happened; she just felt him seize her hand and kick away from the cave, back toward the middle of the pit. When they were a safe distance away, they stopped and waited, still holding hands, kicking gently to stay in place.

What looked like thick black fog was being pumped out of the entrance to the cave. For a second, Penny thought she glimpsed movement inside the inky cloud. She squinted through her goggles, straining to see. Something *was* there and now it was venturing out. The faint outer glow from the sea lights illuminated a cold shine on invertebrate flesh. A shape resolved into limbs as long as Penny's own, and a bulbous, pulsing head, in the middle of which lodged a pinched, stony beak: an octopus, larger than any she had known existed.

The creature had not expected them and was alarmed by the intrusion, its posture defensive. It lingered, alert and suspicious, observing them. Its skin pulsed through a spectrum of patterns—speckled and piebald, striped and mottled. As she watched, Penny's fear receded. The display of patterns was mesmerizing, and she began to swim toward the creature. Jebby tugged her hand and motioned to her to hang back. He advanced cautiously, spear pointed in front of him, attempting to nudge the octopus aside. But the creature refused to budge from the cave entrance. As the children approached, it grew agitated and began changing colors at rapid speed, cycling through a dreary color wheel from ashen to oil-black.

Suddenly the octopus uncoiled an arm and took a wild swipe at Jebby's spear. Jebby stopped where he was but didn't retreat. He waited a moment, then once again began swimming slowly toward it. Another arm shot out like a snapping belt. This time the spear was almost knocked out of his hands.

Penny was confused—why didn't the octopus just swim off? The only thing in the cave was the Molmer egg. But the water enforced silence, and she and Jebby were unable to confer and figure out what to do. Penny looked back at the octopus, hovering outside the cave.

Then she understood: The creature was guarding the egg.

Jebby took a deep breath from a kelp pod and swam, no longer tentatively but purposefully toward the cave. The octopus's head puffed up. Patterns morphed frantically across its skin. Its arms flailed. Then, in a motion almost too fast to see, a single arm lashed out. Anticipating this, Jebby gripped the spear tightly. But this time the octopus didn't reach for the spear. Instead it wrapped its tentacles around the fishing line tied to Jebby's kelp pods and yanked it swiftly out of his grasp.

Without the buoyant kelp pods to counterbalance the heavy stones on his belt, Jebby plummeted. He disappeared almost instantly into the darkness. Penny looked helplessly after him, then back up to see the octopus, arms still curled around the fishing line attached to Jebby's kelp pods, drifting silently toward the lighted surface.

She looked back down and saw her feet, pale in the sea light, dangling flimsy and helpless over the boundless dark. An internal dam broke; panic overwhelmed her. She wanted to help Jebby, but she was terrified to go after him. What could she do, anyway, even if she did let her kelp pods go and follow him down? *Think*, she told herself. *Think. Think. Think.* Air, she needed air. But the straw broke against a pod when she tried to take a breath and, when she fumbled in her belt for a spare, the spare slipped from her fingers. She had only one straw left. Finally she pierced the pod and took a deep, wheezing breath of stale air.

As the air entered her lungs, a calm, lucid thought entered with it: If Jebby dropped his weight belt, he would rise. But would he be able to think clearly enough to do that in time?

She looked back down into the darkness and saw a glow coming back up from the depths, as if a bright bubble were surfacing. Jebby's sea light. He *had* dropped the stones from his weight belt. Penny felt weak with relief. She had never been so happy to see anyone in her life. As he drew alongside her, she gave him one of her kelp pods and he drew a desperate breath.

He motioned to the surface. He was telling her to come with him.

Penny knew there were no more kelp pods in the cart, and they would never be able to make it back down there with the few pods that she had left. Going back up now would mean abandoning the Molmer egg for good—it would mean the Bloom would be over for them.

She shook her head. Jebby gestured again, more urgently. Again Penny refused. Jebby didn't have enough air left to fight with her. He began to swim up out of the pit. As he passed the cave, Penny saw him hurl his spear—a lightless thunderbolt—into the creature's dark lair. He kicked hard for the surface.

Penny was on her own.

She checked her remaining kelp pods. Fear had made her breathe greedily, using up oxygen too fast. Only two remained. She took a breath from one of them, emptying it. The air in the final pod wouldn't last long. She looked for the octopus and was relieved that it was nowhere to be seen. She had open access to the cave now. She could see the Molmer egg still shining there.

She swam to the cliff wall, but the egg was too far back in the cave to reach. She would have to go in. With a single scissors kick, she was inside, the narrow walls and roof closing around her. She swam over a floor littered with cracked shells toward the egg. It was not glowing; the light they had seen was just the reflection of their sea lights on its pale surface. She picked it up. It had calcified and was as heavy and hard as a stone, and would be almost impossible to break. She held it tightly. The cave was just wide enough for her to turn around, which she did, awkwardly, ready to swim out.

She stopped.

The octopus was back, and it was blocking the exit.

She was trapped.

The octopus's shifting, amorphous bulk hovered there for a moment. Then it slid, sneaky, sinewy, shape-shifting, into the cave, where it effaced itself, becoming the color of the rock, lumpy, ridged, pocked as stone. Penny couldn't even see it anymore. As she peered for the creature, she felt her spear wrenched from her hand. In the glow from her sea light, she saw the octopus snap the spear like a twig and toss it out of the cave into the void.

She took a breath from the last kelp pod and to her horror discovered that it was empty. She was out of air. Penny dropped the strings of the deflated pods and they sifted like dead leaves to the cave floor.

She had nothing.

No more air.

No defense.

No way out.

A jet-black cloud of ink began to seep through the cave. It was like being trapped in a room that was filling with smoke—the exit, only feet away, hidden from view.

Suddenly fear made her angry. She was not going to be trapped in here like this! Not when she had the egg, not when she was so close to passing the first trial. She wanted to get out of the cave; she wanted to be out of the Blue Pit, swimming to the surface, popping up into the air and daylight where Tabba and Jebby were waiting for her in the floating cart. She wanted it so much, she began to swim heedlessly toward the exit when she remembered that Jebby had tossed his spear into the cave.

He must have known she might need it.

Keeping low, Penny swam until she saw the spear on the cave floor. She dropped the weights off her belt, seized the spear, and swam for all she was worth.

She almost bumped into the octopus before she saw it, the rubbery curve of an arm with its mat of pale suction cups unreeling before her, but she brandished the spear like a lance and kept kicking. The creature began to swim backward in front of her and Penny drove it out of the cave.

As soon as she was out, Penny kicked with all her might to the surface. Her lungs burned. Darkness dropped away. She held the Molmer egg in her clenched fist, raised toward the blue lens of the surface, which was expanding, becoming sunlit. She had no idea if the octopus was coming after her. She didn't dare look back. She saw the hull of the cart, so tiny drifting there above the darkness, and aimed for it.

Penny exploded out of the water, gasping for air. Treading water, she held the Molmer egg over her head. Tabba and Jebby shouted and paddled the last few feet to her. They helped her into the cart, where she huddled in a heap, shivering, trying to catch her breath.

Jebby sighed in relief, but he knelt, holding Tabba's spear poised over the water in case the octopus surfaced.

"Are you okay?" Tabba asked, sitting down next to Penny.

Finally Penny nodded. Though she knew she was safe now, she was unable to stop shaking. The thrill of being in the shark tank at home was nothing like real-life fear. She realized she hadn't really been angry in the cave: What she had been was frightened. Very, very frightened. Seagrape came and sat beside her, then hopped into her lap. She stroked the parrot's feathers with numb fingers.

"It was a Brazior octopus," said Jebby. "An egg stealer. It must have been waiting for the Molmer to hatch."

Penny opened her hand to look at the egg. It was as hard as marble, and as smooth and cold. A pale, undistinguished oval in the murk below, sunlight revealed shocks of lilac and topaz veins. She wrapped it in a cloth and tucked it safely in her backpack. She looked back down into the pit. Despite the hot sun beating down, her teeth chattered.

"Please," she said. "Let's get away from it."

Jebby began to row and the abyss shrank behind them until they could no longer see it. Without the weight of the stones, they went faster, skimming along the surface, the wind at their backs. They reached the shore and Jebby quickly reassembled the cart's wheels and reattached it to the bicycle. Penny no longer wondered why the town had been left to ruin. No one could live so near such a void. She still felt cold to her core, as if now that she had been inside the pit she carried part of it permanently within herself.

The children set out, rattling past the shell-brick houses and the great lavender heaps of middens beginning to turn golden. The sun was lower in the sky than when they had arrived in Oyster Point, reminding them that only the first twenty teams to make it to Jaipa would advance to the next round. Now that it was so close, they were nervous. The ebullience of that morning was gone. Leaving behind the hollow jingle of the tide through the shells, they raced back along the peninsula toward the valley.

❧ Chapter Ten ❧

*The Twentieth Team • Stories Swirl Round • Jaipa by Night
• A Narrow Escape • A Bad Feeling*

The children barely stopped the whole way to Jaipa, only to change riders, and even then they slowed for only a few seconds. Evening was falling as they coasted downhill into the town, the girls' hair flying back in the wind, the chain whizzing on the bicycle. The roadsides were jammed with people waving and cheering as they sped past. The sights and sounds of so much life seemed almost unreal after the cold vacuum they had so recently escaped.

When they cycled into Jaipa's town square, the Molmer egg was still cold. They rushed to give it to a waiting councilman, who examined it, then nodded—the egg was good. Elder from Tontap was there. He looked surprised to see them at first, then Penny thought she saw a glimmer of pride in his eyes. But he spoke gruffly and she couldn't be sure.

"Have we made it?" she asked breathlessly.

"By the skin of your teeth," said Elder. "You're the twentieth team to arrive."

Just then, two young men on antelopes cantered into the square and pulled up short in front of the councilmen.

One rider swung off his mount and hurried forward with a Molmer egg.

"Too late!" barked one of the councilmen.

The Bloom Player sank to his knees in dismay. The other rider dismounted and stood there, catching his breath, too disappointed to speak. The antelopes were lathered in sweat and their nostrils flared. Penny stared at them, dizzied by a confusing surge of both pity and relief—just a few moments later, and she, Tabba, and Jebby would have been in their place. Nearby, a woman was boiling fruit to make syrup to pour on rice for returning Bloom Players, and the cloying scent wafted over and made Penny feel ill.

Elder took the children's limp yellow sashes, grubby as tarnished brass, and replaced them with the brilliant ruby-red ones that players moving on to the next round would wear.

"You're free," he said. "The next trial won't be announced until morning. I advise you not to linger in town. Find somewhere to camp for the night and stay out of trouble."

He returned to the rest of the Council, and the woman at the syrup pot offered the sweetened rice in banana-leaf cones to the children. Penny had no appetite, but she took it anyway. They thanked the woman and left, wheeling the bike alongside them.

"Well," said Tabba, lifting her elbow to admire the red sash. "We did it."

"But it was close," said Jebby.

"Too close," agreed Penny.

They were quiet for a few moments.

"But . . ." said Tabba finally, "we made it."

Penny took a deep breath. Tabba was right—they *had* made it. They were okay. Suddenly she realized she was famished. The children ate the rice and got more food from a stall. They sat down against a wall to eat and watched the swirl of people around the square. The food revived them. Slowly their fears receded and were replaced by a feeling of giddy triumph. The icy feeling inside Penny's chest that had been there since the Blue Pit finally began to thaw. The octopus, deep in its dark lair, couldn't reach them here.

Since the children had no idea what the second trial would be, there was nothing for them to do or to get. They could enjoy their first victory and recuperate until morning. When they finished eating, they wiped the day's dust and grime off the bicycle and polished the cart. They found Jaipa's message pole, and Penny climbed to the top and raised one of the yellow flags over the town. That done, they decided to wander and take everything in. Warm exhalations from the surrounding jungle wafted through the streets, and the sea lights strung overhead between the eaves bobbed gently. They got food for the next day, and Penny got a packet of seeds and shook them into the cart for Seagrape.

New players were still coming in, collapsing in the square as they learned they were out.

"Do you think Kal made it?" asked Tabba.

"Probably, knowing him," said Jebby. "But I can't wait to see his face when he sees *we've* made it. Remember him laughing at us this morning?"

He hailed a couple of boys who were passing.

"Have you seen a Bloom Player called Kal, from Tontap?" he asked.

"That's the one who made the mandrill appear," one of the boys whispered to the other. "Yeah," he told Jebby. "He was the first one back."

"The first one?" asked Tabba, crestfallen.

"By a long shot," said the first boy. "We saw him—he got here ages before the other teams started coming in."

"How could he have gotten here *so* far ahead of everyone else?" asked Jebby suspiciously after the boys left.

The news of Kal's victory dampened the children's spirits and made Jaipa seem less welcoming. It was bigger than Tontap, and they didn't know their way around. Unlike Tontap, it was not by the sea, and instead was hemmed in by the surrounding jungled hills. It felt as if it had fallen to the bottom of the hills and been caught there, unable to pull itself back out. The streets were crooked and old, the houses that fronted them shabby, their windows dark and secretive. Sometimes the children saw parrots chained to porch railings.

Strangers, seeing their red sashes, stopped to congratulate them, but the children kept mostly to themselves, afraid to attract unwanted attention. They missed Rai, with her ear to the ground and her never-ending patter. To their frustration, over and over again they overheard people talking about how a boy from Tontap had summoned the mandrill. The story was growing—he wasn't just scaring a few kids anymore. He was becoming notorious, described in tones both fearful and reverent.

The only thing that seemed familiar in Jaipa were the other Bloom Players, who were everywhere. Of the fifty-two teams that had started that morning, twenty would go on to the next round. All were a little worse for wear. The sleek creatures that had left that morning had returned muddy-legged, coats stiff with sweat, and the clean, bright clothes the players had donned proudly were darkened with grime.

Teams that had been defeated either melted away to lick their wounds or joined the festivities with gusto, indulging in food and drink in a way that no serious Bloom Player could afford—relieved, in part, to be free of the burden of continuing. Teams bragged about their exploits, their stories growing more epic with each telling: One team was chased by a belligerent reef shark, one player had been ensnared by his own anchor line, another had dived too deep and passed out trying to reach the surface and had to be fished out by his teammates. The players who hadn't made it often seemed to boast more than the ones who had.

Since the children didn't know anyone in Jaipa, the competitors they recognized seemed almost like friendly faces. They were almost happy when they saw teams they knew sporting red sashes. There were some surprises. Oarfish was out—his horse had gone lame, and by the time he reached the Blue Pits all the cubbyholes in the cliffs had been picked over and he hadn't found a Molmer egg. Boulder Guy was out, as well, too heavyset to be able to dive deep enough to reach a Molmer.

The children were bashfully skirting a group of victorious players, too shy to speak to them, when the player named Bagnorio waved them over. They recognized the Lamlo Diver there, too.

"Hey," said Bagnorio. "You're the kids from Tontap and the girl from the Outside, aren't you? We didn't see you at the pits."

"We went to a different one, out on its own, near Oyster Point," explained Jebby.

Penny, Tabba, and Jebby hovered on the outside of the group. The other players were all older, and the children felt intimidated.

"Were there a lot of whorls on the way out there?" asked the Lamlo Diver.

"We didn't see any," said Jebby.

"We saw them the way we went," said Bagnorio. "Three or four of them." He nodded at Grasshopper Boy, who was approaching at a leisurely stroll, a bright red sash tied to his arm. "He got really close to one, you know. He put his hand through it!"

Grasshopper Boy had a pleasant face, but he was always alone and didn't seem to need anything from anyone else.

He barely even carried anything with him—the sackcloth bag slung across his chest was almost empty. He was so tall and long that he looked to Penny like a shadow stretched out on the road at sundown. But he nodded agreeably when he saw the other players and paused on their fringes.

"You went up to one of the whorls," announced Bagnorio.

Again Grasshopper Boy nodded amiably.

"Well?" demanded the Lamlo Diver. "What happened?"

"There was steam coming out of it," said Grasshopper Boy.

"Then what happened?" asked someone.

"Nothing," said Grasshopper Boy. "The whorl disappeared. Everything was normal again."

The fact that it was Grasshopper Boy who had spoken lent authority to his claim. Plus, other than Kal, this was the closest they'd heard of anyone getting to a whorl.

"Did you see inside it?" asked Bagnorio. "Was anything there?"

"It was too dark to see anything," said Grasshopper Boy. "And there was too much steam. Sorry."

Bagnorio suddenly turned to Tabba and Jebby, and said, "If you're from Tontap, do you know that kid who opened a whorl and made the mandrill appear?"

"A little," mumbled Jebby. "Not really."

"How did you get here from the Outside, anyway?" Bagnorio asked Penny.

"I was rowing near the Blue Line and a whorl appeared

and I came through it," she said. "Kal was there on the other side, so I think he must have opened it. It happened so fast, and it closed right away behind me. Tabba and Jebby were there, too—they rescued me." She shrugged. "There was a lot of fog—it was hard to know how it happened. I can't really tell you anything else."

Embarrassed by the older kids' attention, the children slipped away as soon as they could, leaving the others to speculate among themselves about Kal and his mysterious powers.

"I can't believe they knew who we were," whispered Tabba.

"I don't think anybody *did* know yesterday," said Jebby.

The children were walking quickly down the street and almost crashed right into the lumphur. It was tied up to a post. It had been bathed and its coat gleamed in the evening light. Its muzzle was deep in a bucket, and the children could hear the crisp crunch of fruit in its teeth as it ate. Kal came out of a nearby food stall, carrying his dinner wrapped in a banana leaf. He stopped in his tracks when he caught sight of the children and the bright red sashes on their arms. It was hard for the children to hide their glee at his reaction. Kal gathered himself and returned to the lumphur.

"Anyone can get lucky," he said.

"There was a Brazior octopus in the pit we were in," said Penny. "We had to fight with him to get the Molmer egg."

She immediately regretted bragging. Wanting to impress him was a sign of weakness, and he knew it. If he was affected by the mention of the octopus, he didn't let on.

His gaze fell on the bicycle, which the children had been wheeling along next to them. For just a second Penny saw a triumphant expression pass over his face, leaving the hint of a smile at the corners of his mouth when he turned back to them.

"Good luck on the next round," he said casually. He untied the lumphur and headed off down a side street.

"Good luck to YOU the next round," called Tabba. "Did you see his face when he saw us?" she crowed after Kal had gone. "He couldn't believe we made it! Serves him right."

"Don't laugh," said Jebby, but Penny could tell he was pleased, too.

Penny wasn't sure how she felt. The encounter should have been more satisfying than it was. The sight of the strong, steely lumphur had once again reminded her that next to the players' animals, the bicycle and cart were odd and, after the day's hard journey, increasingly worse for wear. And that funny expression that had crossed Kal's face—what was that about?

The children were wandering around Jaipa when night fell. One moment it was still light; the next the final glimmer was lost on the ridges and the hills had darkened around the town. Without their realizing it, the atmosphere had been changing. Other Bloom Players had been everywhere; now suddenly there were none. The Council had retired for the night, and the streets surrounding the square had emptied out as families retreated to gatherings in private gardens or to isolated campsites outside it. The people left in the town square were mostly teenagers and older Bloom Players who had not made it to the next trial, and they were growing increasingly rowdy, a strident edge creeping into their shouts and laughter.

The children began walking out of town to find a quiet spot to strike camp, wishing they had heeded Elder's advice and found somewhere while it was still light. Outside the center, the town was poorly lit. They wheeled the bike and cart, trying to make the tires roll quietly on the bumpy cobblestones. Penny had been in Tontap for only a day, but very quickly it had felt safe and familiar. In the dark, Jaipa did not. Strangers' faces weren't clear until they passed close by. A few times they got lost in the snarl of streets. Silhouettes of the surrounding hills loomed claustrophobically. A mangy stray dog trotted after them, then another joined it, and another, following them but keeping a careful distance. Seagrape rode on the handlebars, not making a sound.

They were on a hill on the outskirts, walking along a deserted street, the strains of music and celebration from the square growing fainter, when they heard loud voices from a street up ahead. A moment later a gang of half a dozen older boys appeared around a corner, heading in the children's direction.

"They're looking at the bicycle," whispered Penny.

"They've never seen one before," said Tabba, trying to sound calm. "Of course they're going to look."

"They're too interested," muttered Penny.

As the boys drew closer, Penny could see that some of the boys were very big. They were stumbling a little, their voices overloud.

"Let's get out of here," said Jebby under his breath.

"Hey," called a large boy, who broke away from the group and came toward them.

It was all the children needed.

Penny spun the bike around, hopped on, and began pedaling. Tabba and Jebby pushed the cart until it built up some speed, then they jumped in. The older boys shouting, the dogs barking and baying behind them, the children fled, bumping wildly down a dark street onto a dirt road that led outside the town. Trees enclosed the road and in stretches it was pitch-black. No one else was there.

"Stop," said Jebby suddenly. "Go back—there's a little path off to the left. Maybe we'll find somewhere to camp."

Penny turned off the main road down a narrow, rutted track and they bounced along until they reached a dead end. She squeezed the brakes and they came to a stop in the little clearing. They had escaped, but she was ashamed of the tremble in her hands. There were no lights anywhere. The ground was boggy and mosquitoes whined in the air.

"Well, we know why no one else is camping here," said

Tabba, smacking a mosquito from her shoulder. "Oh well, it's too late to look for anywhere else."

They set up their hammocks quietly. Seagrape settled on a branch nearby. In their little band of three, away from the crowd, the children felt better, but it was impossible to fully shake the sense of unease. Before he climbed into his hammock, Jebby stopped and turned in a circle.

"What is it?" whispered Tabba.

"I have a bad feeling," he said quietly. Though they were alone, they all spoke in low voices. "Something doesn't feel right."

"You have a bad feeling because those boys just scared us," said Tabba soothingly. "No one will come and bother us—or the bike—in the middle of the night. Not here."

"No," admitted Jebby. "I guess you're right."

Penny looked around. There were no whorls anywhere nearby, and no troubling feeling in the air. It felt like an ordinary place, just dark and humid and humming with mosquitoes.

"Just to be safe, we can sleep in shifts," she said. "And we'll tie the bike and cart to this tree here and we can sleep around it."

The children secured the bike to the tree. Their hammocks surrounded it protectively. They set up their mosquito nets and tucked themselves in. Penny had first watch. She brought the map into her hammock with her and squinted to make out its features in the weak moonlight that filtered through the trees.

"I don't see the Coral Basin anywhere," she whispered.

"It's not on there," said Jebby. "I noticed that earlier."

"What is it, anyway?" asked Penny.

"No idea," said Jebby. "Never heard of it before Elder said it."

"It's such an important thing, you'd think it would be marked," said Tabba. "It seems like it's a pretty thorough map otherwise."

"If I had to trade that whistle, we could at least have gotten a map with everything we need on it," grumbled Jebby.

Penny was straining her eyes, trying to see the map in the dark, so she put it aside and lay back in her hammock. There was a narrow pool of dark sky open in the trees above them, and the stars quivered in it, like reflections trembling on water. She was reminded of the sea lights in the tidal pools in the terrace cliffs she had seen with Tabba. Was that really only yesterday? They had done so much already. The Blue Pit had been just that morning. Penny shivered at the memory. Its coldness had permeated her. Since seeing it, it had become harder to believe in the wholeness of the world. How could such lushness and life suddenly give way to . . . nothing? Everything suddenly seemed more fragile, less solid and permanent.

An animal cry reverberated against the hills. Penny stiffened, remembering stories the others had told her about wild animals that had slunk out of whorls during the bad Bloom. She lay there in her thin hammock and imagined malign presences creeping out from hidden places, prowling through the darkness. She had the sense that the world was not stable, that great shifts were happening invisibly all around her.

At one point, she thought she heard rustling at the end of the track, through the trees. Seagrape squawked sharply. Penny waited alertly, ready to wake the others. But nothing came out of the shadows, so she settled back down uneasily to wait until it was time to wake Tabba for her watch.

Helix

When he had walked into Tontap that morning, the town was empty, clean, orderly. Like a storm that had moved on, even the people who had come for the festival were mostly gone. Palm brooms scraped on stone as a few residents cleaned the streets.

He caught sight of the flag as soon as he had entered the square. It was on top of a tall pole—a message pole, common on this part of the island. A lone breeze funneled through the buildings, opening the yellow rectangle like a sail. When he saw the green-stitched insignia of the parrot, he stopped and stood very still, shading his eyes to look up at it.

It couldn't be.

The breeze died and the cloth fell. He decided to take a closer look. He climbed the pole, retrieved the flag, and slid back down. He held it in his hands, feeling the soft, faded cotton, ran his fingers over the careful stitching of the parrot. There was no mistaking it: It was one of the ones Granny Pearl had sewn for Penny. He did not move for several minutes.

The town was sleepy. Even the scrape of brooms had ceased. It almost looked as if no one had been there at all. Orange light filtered through a flame tree, roving over the packed dirt whenever a breeze stirred the branches.

He knew the flag had been left for him and he knew who had left it.

What was she doing here? Were the others here with her? Was everything all right?

He tucked the flag into the leather satchel slung over his shoulder. Dazed, he forgot the twine to fix his backpack and continued on the road out of town in the direction of Jaipa.

The road was no longer clogged with people and carts, and soon the confused shuffle of footprints and tracks ebbed. He felt as though he were in a dream. The pack on his back was light, an afterthought. He barely noticed the broken strap. As he walked, the edge of the yellow flag, dusty, faded from the sun, stuck out of the top, like a flower that had suddenly blossomed.

❧ Chapter Eleven ❧

A Bad Start • A Strange Scent • New Whorl in the Night •
The Second Trial • A Reluctant Plan

The next morning got off to a bad start. Despite the children's fears, the camp in the little clearing had been undisturbed in the night—dew was the only thing that had touched the bicycle. But the children had slept poorly because of the watches, and they couldn't stop yawning as they untied their hammocks and packed to leave in semidarkness. Penny was stiff from the dampness. An insect had sneaked inside her mosquito net and feasted on her ankles, which she had soon scratched until they bled. All three of them were short-tempered and irritable. Even Seagrape seemed to have absorbed their bad mood. When Penny offered her arm, she refused, grousing softly and shuffling away down the branch she had slept on.

"If that's how you want to be," muttered Penny. She swiped dew off the bike with her shirt and swung her backpack into the cart. She was about to get on the bike when Jebby stepped in front of her and took the handlebars. Annoyed, she joined Tabba in the cart.

Jebby pedaled down the narrow path they had come along in the dark the night before. Seagrape joined them, riding on the back of the cart. Halfway down the path, they wrinkled their noses.

"Ugh," said Tabba. "What's that smell?"

"It's like rotten potatoes," said Penny.

"I think it's coming from the puddle up there," said Jebby.

Up ahead was a small, cloudy puddle that stretched all the way across the path. Jebby slowed down so the girls wouldn't get splashed.

"I think I remember a puddle being there last night," said Tabba, frowning as she looked down at it. "Though that odor definitely wasn't here. But it's familiar. . . . I've smelled it before. Hurry up, Jebby—let's get away from it!"

Jebby pedaled faster. Beyond the puddle the air cleared, and they turned off the path onto the road into town. Gratefully, Penny breathed in the fragrance of damp earth and opening flowers. The first warming rays burned off the mist, and the purple silhouettes of the hills lightened around them.

Before they even reached Jaipa's town square, she saw the message pole, high above the rooftops, and on it the flag she had staked there the night before, its faded rect-angle hanging limply. She felt deeply low for a moment but was distracted when Tabba pointed to the other side of the square.

Perched brazenly on a thatched roof overhanging the square was a whorl. It was round, like a ball that had rolled down the roof and stopped, improbably, on the edge, where it balanced precariously. Nothing came from it, and there was nothing to see inside it, just the sheen on its surface as the sun came up over the town. The fact that it meant the mandrill had prowled the streets while the town slept seemed more a cause for excitement than fear as people clustered around to see it.

The remaining Bloom Players were arriving and the children found themselves shuttled across the square. Spirits were high, but there was a new edge, a nervous energy that circulated through the whittled-down field. Those who remained were the fastest, the strongest, the ones in possession of the finest animals, the ones who most wanted to win. The bicycle threaded squeakily through the crowd, narrowly avoiding getting trampled. Penny knew they were on the fringes of this group of the toughest and the best, but she was undeterred: They'd come this far, and she had every intention of making it past this next trial, too. She was eager for it to start.

She searched for Kal in the crowd. When she finally glimpsed him astride the lumphur, she saw that he had been watching them. He immediately turned and disappeared amid the people and animals. Something about how intently he had been observing them struck her as strange, but she didn't have time to reflect on it for long because once again the children found themselves at the rear of the pack of Bloom Players as the Council of Elders prepared to announce the second trial.

Elder strode to the front of the platform.

"You can all see that the mandrill made an appearance last night," he said, and the crowd whispered and craned necks to look at the whorl perched on the rooftop. "From now on, expect to see more whorls, appearing suddenly, in unexpected places. Beware—not all will be as harmless as this one. The time the Bloom competitors have to prove themselves grows briefer with each passing day, and the consequences of failure grow ever more perilous for Kana.

"Now!" he said. "The first challenge was to determine speed and strategy and, of course, to select capable and fearless swimmers—all necessary skills for the Bloom Catcher. This next challenge, however, allows players the opportunity—if they are clever enough—to use their minds and conserve their energy for the third and unavoidably arduous challenge." He smiled. "This is a problem with a variety of simple and elegant solutions."

He held up a gleaming bullet, pinched between his finger and thumb.

"A Zamzee beetle," he said, projecting his voice over the snorting and braying of animals as their riders jockeyed for a closer view of the insect. "Your next task will be to find one of these and return with it to Santori. These creatures are highly venomous. I urge you to use the utmost caution when attempting to capture one of them. Anyone who gets bitten should return to the next town for the serum at once. Consider yourselves warned."

"Do we have to bring it back alive?" called one of the competitors.

"It would be safer for you to find one that was *not* alive," said Elder. He paused. "This will be the final trial for most of today's players. Only the first five teams to reach Santori with a Zamzee will advance to the next and final round. When I blow the triton, you'll be free to go."

A moment later the deep bellow of the triton once more reverberated through the hot morning air. But, unlike the last time, the competitors did not rush out of the square. Everyone crowded to get a good look at the rare beetle, sitting on top of a box on the platform, guarded by a councilman. Penny, Tabba, and Jebby found themselves shoved to the back, where they waited impatiently.

"Where can we find one?" Penny whispered to Tabba and Jebby.

"I don't know," whispered Tabba. "I've never seen one before. Have you, Jebby?"

He shook his head.

Slowly the other players eddied off to confer in hushed groups around the square, and the children were able to get up close to the beetle.

"Wow," said Penny. "It's beautiful."

The Zamzee was dead. It appeared to be a variety of scarab. It was about the size of a mussel, its body a sleek, hard shell, its turquoise lacquer as sumptuous and opaque as oil. It had two black eyes, two jointed pincers, and rows of powerful legs that had once carried it over rotting logs, up looping vines, and high into jungle canopies. Swirled horns prodded out of its head like miniature antlers. Penny was used to her family taking field notes, so she folded the map into a square and dug around in her backpack to find a pencil.

"I'll sketch it," she said. "So we're sure we get the right kind."

Deftly she drew the creature and scribbled a few details about it:

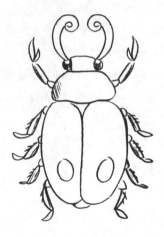

The size of a cowrie shell
Swirled horns
Deep turquoise wings make a hard, polished case
Two fake orange eye spots

When she was done, the councilman placed the beetle in a cloth pouch and took it away.

"Let's look at the map," said Jebby. "Maybe there's something on it that will give us an idea of where to go."

The children wheeled the bike and cart to a quiet lane just off the square, where they stopped in the shade of a bougainvillea vine. They spread out the map on the ground between them and pored over it, but nothing on it sparked any epiphanies about where to find a Zamzee. Minutes passed.

"Bugs are usually under rocks," Tabba offered at last.

"We can't just go around the jungle overturning rocks," said Penny. "That can't be it."

They had been ready to dash off as fast as they could, but now everything had come to a stop. They were stuck. Ideas seemed to be flying out of rather than into Penny's head. This time they had no parents, no friends, no one like Bellamy with expertise or provisions, no one at all to guide them. They had to figure out what to do on their own, and suddenly each of them felt at a loss.

Seagrape flew off Penny's shoulder and settled in the bougainvillea. The light through the brilliant petals glowed pinkly on the map, deepening as the seconds ticked by. The sun was fully up now, the sky blue, and Penny felt like the morning was slipping through their fingers. Fragments of conversation drifted over from the square. Everyone else in Jaipa seemed to be loudly sharing their opinions about where to find a Zamzee beetle: beneath rocks, beside streams, in the crooks of cool, mossy branches, in the sunny heights of the canopy. Some said under the bark of wameda trees.

Some said they were always just outside the Gorgonne; some said, no, they were never that far south. Some were convinced they lived only in deep jungle; others insisted they could be found close to the coast.

Think, Penny willed herself, trying to shut out all the outside noise. *There must be some places that it would be more likely to find a Zamzee beetle than others.* But, if even Tabba and Jebby didn't know, how would she? She picked up a twig and traced anxious lines on the earth with it.

"Everyone's starting to leave," said Tabba, looking toward the square.

One by one, the teams were deciding on a plan and departing. Often they started out in one direction then, once out of sight, veered off in another to throw off anyone who might think of following them. Kal had disappeared without the children noticing. Even the people who had been there for the celebration were packing up and starting to stream out along the main road to Santori, or to the towns of the family they would stop to see along the way. The townspeople were cleaning up the square, dismantling the platform, and clearing leftover food from the stalls. The party was moving on.

How hard could it be to find a Zamzee? Penny thought in frustration. There were bugs everywhere in Kana! Giant ones, minuscule ones, bright ones, dull ones, bugs that clicked and groaned and squeaked like rusty gears, others that whistled and sang from dawn to dusk, still others that only left their damp, mulchy homes under cover of night. She and Tabba and Jebby had to sleep under mosquito nets or be bitten alive. If they stopped to refill their canteens at a slow stream, its surface was rippled from dragonflies taking off and landing. When they ate, industrious little beetles arrived at once to cart away the crumbs. With a slight grimace, Penny remembered crunching on the fried bugs in Tontap on her first night. There were so many bugs that people even *ate* them.

She stopped tracing lines on the ground and dropped the twig. That was it.

"The Beetlers!" she whispered triumphantly, leaning in to Tabba and Jebby. "Those people we saw in Tontap selling bags of insects! I bet they'd know where to find a Zamzee beetle!"

"Of course," cried Jebby. "I can't believe we didn't think of that right away. Tabba—the Beetler who comes at the full moon, the guy Ma always buys from? Where does he come from exactly?"

"From Mud-Dales," said Tabba, suddenly excited. Kneeling, she smoothed out the map, and the children crouched around it. "All the bug sellers do."

"Here," said Jebby, circling a mulchy-looking green-and-brown area far to the west of Jaipa. "This is Mud-Dales."

"Hopper is the main trading town there," said Tabba. "That's right here. And right now we're here. It's far. . . ."

It *was* far. Penny swallowed. Between Jaipa and Hopper spread miles of jungle, interspersed with farms and tiny towns, before the brown humps and valleys of the dales.

The only town in Mud-Dales was Hopper, marked by an unpromising dot, and the only road there, a narrow dirt track for most of the way, wound along a frustratingly arduous route through what appeared to be steep hillocks.

"It would take us until late this afternoon to even get there," said Jebby. "And see these little squiggles? I think that means the terrain is all little hills. Crossing it would hardly be conserving energy."

Penny agreed that it hardly seemed the simple, elegant solution that Elder had described. But she didn't know what else to do, and time was passing. All the other teams were already on their way to get the beetles.

"Maybe we shouldn't rush off," said Jebby. "We might save time in the end if we spend a little longer thinking."

But Penny's impatience won out. She couldn't sit there any longer. Already they were at the rear of the pack. She found Santori on the map.

"We could sit here all day trying to come up with something clever," she said briskly, getting to her feet. "We can think just as well when we're on the road."

Hesitantly, Tabba and Jebby followed her and climbed into the cart and they set out. But, unlike the day before, none of them felt quite right.

❧ Chapter Twelve ❧

Mysterious Presences • Eyes Out for Helix • "Something's not right with the bike" • Mud-Dales • Hopper • "He'll be a man before they come out again" • An Unbelievable Sight

The children were barely any distance from Jaipa when they began to see whorls everywhere, just as Elder had predicted. Every now and then, their conversation would be interrupted by the sight of one: leaning against the trunk of a tree, hanging like a shiny bauble from the end of a branch, even one that wobbled on the shoulder of the road, as if at any moment it might roll across the bicycle's path.

The ordinary world had been breached by these mysterious presences, but, despite their deep strangeness and their growing numbers, the whorls remained benign. Some even sparkled a little if the sunlight hit them the right way. Nothing came out of them, let alone anything nefarious. Rather than being frightening, they seemed to Penny to be a hopeful sign: the life-giving Bloom was almost here, and she was getting closer and closer to being able to bring it to Granny Pearl. As for the mandrill who had left them so carelessly all over the place, he seemed to Penny to embody a creative, haphazard energy, a spirit of joyful freedom—and she felt herself almost liking him when she passed whorls that shone like rainbowed bubbles in the sun.

She wondered if Helix was here somewhere, seeing all the whorls, too. There were ten times as many people out on the roads as there had been the day before. Children sat with their legs dangling over the backs of wooden carts. Other people traveled on foot, singing or keeping time on the road with sticks taken from the jungle near their homes. They cheered as the children sped past on the bicycle. Many people were gathering up relatives and friends on the way to Palmos, and Penny witnessed joyful reunions—people tumbling out of carts into the exuberant embrace of loved ones.

She kept a sharp lookout for Helix whenever there were other people around. She knew that she could be very close and still miss him—he could be hidden behind a cart trundling past, or the bicycle could turn a corner seconds too late. One moment, deep down she felt unaccountably confident that their paths would cross sooner or later; the next it seemed impossible.

"I'm looking, too," said Tabba, who was in the cart with Penny. "If I see anyone by himself who might look like him, I'll tell you."

"Thanks, Tabba," said Penny. It had been a long time since she'd had a friend who understood her so well, who knew what she was thinking without her even having to say. She and Tabba had talked about Helix for a long time the day before. Tabba, ever optimistic and encouraging, always said the same thing: If Helix was there, he *had* to see at least one of the flags and, if he did, it was only a matter of time before he found Penny.

"I don't know, Penny," Tabba said thoughtfully as they sped out of a small town onto a road between farm fields. "Sometimes it sounds like Helix is the one who needs *your* help."

"What would I help *him* with?" asked Penny.

Tabba shrugged. "I have no idea," she said. "It's just the feeling I get. He sounds like he was on his own for a long time before he met you guys."

Penny gazed out over the lush fields. She had never thought about Helix this way. To her, he had always been the strongest and most capable person that she knew. He'd seemed more grown-up than her siblings, despite being only a year older than Maya.

Though Penny and Tabba's capacity to discuss Helix was inexhaustible, Jebby could only sustain interest for so long in something for which there was no new and concrete information, just the same vague, wishful thoughts being constantly remilled. This morning he welcomed taking more than his fair share of time riding the bicycle, when he could tune out the chatter in the cart. He was preoccupied by the bicycle, anyway. Its wheels squeaked and the cart had a new and unexplained wobble that worsened with each new mile they covered. The handlebars were gradually becoming harder to steer. The children stopped repeatedly to check but couldn't find anything wrong. They decided it was their own legs, weary from the previous day's journey, which made each revolution of the tires seem like such an effort.

They were traveling along a wide road through some scrubby jungle when Jebby pulled abruptly over to the shoulder. Penny looked around in irritation. The children knew that they were on the right road, but with no obvious landmarks in sight, they couldn't tell how far they were from Hopper, and Penny was getting frustrated by how long it was taking to get there.

"Hey," she said. "Why are we stopping?"

"Something's not right with the bike," said Jebby. He came to a stop in a dusty tuft of frog grass and hopped off to examine it. The girls climbed out of the cart.

"The vines are twisting a bit; that's all I can see," said Penny. "Bellamy hadn't put new tires on in a long time; maybe he didn't do it quite right. Or maybe they aren't exactly the right-size vines."

"They were fine yesterday," said Jebby.

"Do you want me to ride it?" asked Penny.

"No, it's not me; the bike is different," said Jebby.

Penny didn't say what she actually thought, which was that Jebby just wasn't used to riding a bike.

"Well, it's old," said Tabba reasonably. "We can't expect it to work perfectly. Anyway, take a break for a bit, Jebby. It's time for someone else to have a turn."

Jebby sighed. He looked tired. But before he climbed into the cart, he turned his ear to the jungle, listening.

"Hear that?" he said. "That's a bowerbird." He took out his whistle and made a few short bleats. From deep in the foliage, the bird responded. Jebby smiled. "They're really rare, you know," he said.

"Come on!" said Tabba impatiently. "Like we have time for birds right now!"

～～～

They set out again. After consulting the map, they turned off the main road onto the bumpy dirt track and entered Mud-Dales. The track crossed a grueling series of moguls too steep to pedal up easily and too short to get much of a rest coasting down. The terrain was laborious, but the thought that Kal's lumphur would have loped over the hillocks as if they were nothing spurred Penny on, and whenever it was her turn, she stood up to pedal, her calves burning. The farther they went, the deeper the mud in the troughs grew, and soon they all had to get out and together push the bike up the hills.

At last the lumpy moguls began to ease, and the road shrank to a dirt track that ran over a series of longer hills. Jebby was on the bike, the girls in the cart, and they were coasting downhill when he suddenly started shouting.

"I can't slow down!" he yelled.

"What are you talking about?" said Penny. "Use the brakes!"

"I'm trying! They won't work!" Jebby cried desperately.

He pumped the brakes frantically, but nothing happened.

The grade steepened and soon the bike was going at full tilt, the cart rattling from side to side behind it. The bottom of the hill was coming up fast.

Everyone shouted as the front tire hit the deep mud at the base. The bike stopped abruptly and the cart swung violently around. Penny and Tabba were flung onto the side of the road.

"Are you okay?" Jebby cried, leaving the bike and rushing to help them up.

Penny's left wrist hurt where she had landed on it and a stone had grazed her knee. Blood seeped from a cut on Tabba's forehead. They scrambled to their feet and stood there, getting their balance back. The soft mud had spared them any broken bones, but they were bruised and filthy.

"What did you do?" Penny asked angrily.

"I didn't do anything," said Jebby. "The brakes stopped working!"

The bike was so covered in mud that Penny had to scoop off clumps of it with her hand before she could see the frame clearly.

"The front axle's bent," she said finally. "And the brake wire's twisted; that's why the brakes didn't work. I don't know how that happened. It couldn't be your fault, though," she added. "Sorry."

She untwisted the brake wire and, with a stone from the edge of the road, she hammered the axle back into place. Miraculously, the shafts attaching the cart to the bicycle hadn't snapped.

"That's the best I can do," she said. "But I'm not sure how long it's going to last. Maybe from now on don't slam on the brakes too fast."

"I didn't," muttered Jebby, frowning at the bike.

Tabba had walked ahead, to where the trees broke, and now she called excitedly back to the others.

"Look!" she shouted. "We're here! This has to be Hopper! We almost crashed right into it!"

The children hastily brushed themselves off and hurried the squeaking bicycle and cart around the bend into Hopper. The village was even smaller than they expected and it was all brown—just a few dirt streets and huts thatched with dried and faded palm leaves, built haphazardly around a muddy central market square. There were Beetlers everywhere, buying and selling insects on rough wooden tables, boiling them in vats to makes insect jams and pastes, scooping them into sacks for stubby tan mules to haul to sell in other towns.

But it wasn't just Beetlers who were there.

"It's *crawling* with Bloom Players," said Tabba, aghast.

Penny's spirits plunged. Everyone else seemed to have had the same idea as the children. Teams of Bloom Players were everywhere, running off into the jungle, or returning, empty-handed. Others were scavenging through bugs laid out on the tables or sieving through overturned sacks of beetles, shining like beans in the dirt. Hopper was like an archaeological site that had been raided, a carcass picked over. Demoralized, the children walked the bicycle and cart into the town. They searched among the insects on the tables in the market. There were no Zamzee beetles among them that Penny could see, though it was hard to tell because many were in brittle pieces: a jointed leg, a shell, a wing. If there *had* been any Zamzees, they had been snapped up by faster competitors long ago. There was no sign of Kal anywhere.

A lively trade of "guides" had established itself, youthful middlemen offering to escort Bloom Players to groups of Beetlers collecting insects in the surrounding jungle. Seeing the newcomers, two young boys raced over to them. The boys scuffled and the winner quickly offered to take them to a group of Beetlers working nearby. Disappointed, the loser scowled and wandered off. The children had to trade the last of the food Ma Silverling had packed for them before the boy would agree to take them.

"What choice do we have?" asked Jebby, shrugging.

The boy tucked the food into his bag and headed off quickly. The children followed, falling into single file down a narrow, empty track into the jungle, wheeling the bike alongside them. It was hotter than it had been anywhere else in Kana, and Penny's clothes were soaked with sweat. Each breath felt like steam in her lungs. Barely a breeze stirred, and the air was as thick as soup.

"They're in there," said the boy, stopping abruptly on

the path and pointing into the jungle. He turned around and started back the way they'd come.

"Hey, wait!" called Jebby. "You're supposed to take us right to them!"

But the boy kept going, breaking into a loping jog.

"Where are we supposed to go?" asked Penny. "There's no path anywhere." She squinted into the thick gloom.

"Listen," said Tabba. "I think I can hear people."

"I don't like this," said Jebby. "We can't take the bike with us. It's too overgrown." He scanned the jungle suspiciously. "What if Kal . . ."

"Kal isn't here," said Tabba impatiently. "We didn't see him. He probably had a better idea and didn't even come to Hopper."

The road was empty, the boy already gone. Eerie light drifted hazily through the trees. A cloudy thrum of insects filled the humid air. Seagrape perched on the back of the cart, grumbling softly. A dull thud came from somewhere deep in the trees.

"Stop dawdling," Tabba scolded her brother. "What if the Beetlers move on? We can hide the bicycle in the trees. No one's around."

Jebby relented and the children left the road. They concealed the bike and cart in the dense greenery and set off toward where Tabba thought she had heard voices.

It was a buggy, boggy mess of a jungle. Damp, mulchy earth sucked at the children's feet. The air seethed with ticking and warbling, chirping and slithering. Strange noises came from up ahead: dull thumps followed by frenzied scraping and tapping. The children kept silent.

They arrived in a clearing as a group of people—Beetlers—rolled over a boulder. The men held it while the women, crouching, walked on the balls of their feet to gather blind wriggling worms, hard beetles, and smooth-backed roaches into fine nets, which were then emptied into larger woven sacks. Creatures clinging to the underside of the stone were knocked free with a small mallet and scooped briskly off the ground. The Beetlers spoke among themselves, in whispers no louder than the scratching murmur of tiny wings and legs. A large winged beetle escaped, zigzagging in a final desperate, headlong flight to freedom until a hand, pale as an earthworm, reached out and snared it.

When the Beetlers noticed the children, they let the boulder fall with a soft thump and stood in a blinking huddle to observe the newcomers. They looked as though they seldom saw sunlight: Their skin was wan, and even their irises were pale. Mud streaked their drab clothes and hair. Their fingernails were packed with thick half moons of grime. They had long, tapered fingers, made for plucking unsuspecting grubs out of mushroom stems or needling behind damp bark where stitch-worms burrowed.

Penny was relieved when Jebby was the one who worked up the nerve to speak first.

"Hello," he said. "We're Bloom Players, trying to find a

Zamzee beetle. We were hoping you could tell us where we can find one."

The Beetlers muttered among themselves, never raising their voices above a whisper.

"Zamzee?" asked a man, stepping forward, his voice raspy and low. "They're sleeping. Deep underground. Very deep. You won't find them now." He indicated a young boy standing behind him. "He'll be a man before they come out again."

"What does he mean, before they come out again?" Tabba asked the others under her breath.

"Maybe they're like cicadas on the Outside," Penny whispered. "They live underground for most of their lives and only emerge for a little while to mate." She thought for a moment. "If we know where they like to burrow, we can dig for them."

"Can you tell us where they are underground?" she asked the Beetler. "Where do they like to go?"

"Never together, and never to the same place," said the man. "They could be anywhere when they're underground, then one day you see them at dawn. They crawl and fly around, but by the time the sun is fully up, they've gone again. Even we only see them a few times in our lives."

To demonstrate, he turned to the group to ask how many among them had seen a Zamzee. Only a few people nodded.

"See," said the man. "Very rare."

Penny swatted impatiently at a pair of flies buzzing around her face.

"There must be *some* way to find where they are . . ." she said.

The Head Beetler shook his head. "If there is, *we* don't know it," he said.

The jungle was oppressively hot, and the humid air was making it harder and harder to breathe. Penny's eye fell on one of the Beetler children, who leaned his head back and tossed a wriggling silkworm into the air, then caught it in his mouth. *Crunch*—his teeth came down on the creature, and a little of the juice trickled down his chin. Penny cringed and looked away. An open sack of beetles tipped over and a herd of tiny armored creatures rolled across the jungle floor like beads of water skating across a hot frying pan. Women scrambled to gather them.

The man reached into the sack and withdrew a few mealy albino grubs and handed them to the children.

"For you," he said gravely. "Finer than the finest oysters."

Penny suppressed a shiver of revulsion, but Jebby accepted the creatures without blinking.

There was nothing else the Beetlers could tell the children. Penny, Tabba, and Jebby watched helplessly as the Beetlers hoisted the sacks onto their backs and prepared to move on. They seemed to disappear gradually, the way that light fades. Soon the children heard the crackling of the undergrowth in the distance as another boulder was heaved over.

"Gross—Jebby, let those things go," said Tabba, making a face.

Jebby tipped his hand, and the grubs writhed in the mud, burrowing back down to its cool, dark depths.

"Now what?" asked Penny in frustration. They were back to square one. Finding the Beetlers had been their only plan. "What are we supposed to do now?"

Tabba and Jebby didn't have an answer.

When Penny had heard the Zamzees were underground, she had been prepared to dig to find one—with her bare hands if she had to. She'd been sure the Beetlers could tell them where to start looking, at least. Now she had no idea what to do. She felt claustrophobic. She lifted the hem of her tunic to wipe the sweat off her face, but more just poured after it. She felt like her whole body was turning to steam, as if she was about to drift off in a Penny-shaped vapor.

"Ugh—it's BOILING in here!" she cried, stamping her feet to get the flies off her legs. More buzzed maddeningly around her head. Even Helix's necklace was irritating her, tickling her neck. "Let's get back to the road."

Shoving branches out of her path, she returned the way they had come, recklessly ignoring the thorns nipping her legs. She just wanted to get out of there, to be in the open where there might be even the faintest tickle of a breeze. Maybe then she could think of what to do next.

As she neared the place where they had left the bicycle, Penny sensed that something was wrong seconds before she knew what it was. Tiny branches snapped, dead leaves rustled. Something was moving through the foliage. Seagrape growled. Tabba sucked in her breath. Penny stopped where she was and stared, unable to believe what she was seeing.

The bicycle was upright, gliding slowly across the jungle floor, dragging the cart along after it.

No one was riding it; it was moving of its own volition. Something was oddly stiff about the way it moved, and it took Penny a moment to realize that none of the wheels was turning. They were locked solidly in place, and instead of rolling, they were sliding over the ground. Too stunned to react, the three children froze in their tracks.

"It's the tires," Tabba whispered. "The sapsoo vines—they're growing!"

Tabba was right. All six tires—two on the bike and four on the cart—had taken root in the mud and were growing at a remarkable speed, pushing the bike and cart ahead of them. Without warning, the vines from the cart tires veered off and began to coil around the trunk of a nearby tree. The vines from the bicycle tires kept barreling ahead. Bike and cart were pulled in opposite directions. For a moment they strained against each other before, with a sharp pop, they broke apart. Freed, the cart vines lunged forward, looping around one another in a mad scramble up the trunk, hauling the cart up with them. The cart was crushed almost instantly. Scraps of wood dropped to the ground.

At the same time, the bicycle vines reached another, thicker tree and began to wrap around its trunk. The heavy bicycle was slower to leave the earth than the cart, but, as the children watched, the vines hoisted it up. The sight of it lifting off the ground snapped them out of their shock. They rushed to save it, but by the time they got there the frame had just slipped beyond their grasp.

In horror they watched as the bicycle crashed relentlessly up through the foliage, higher and higher into the branches. A storm of broken twigs and torn leaves floated down in its wake. Then the two vines parted ways, the rear tire vine shooting down a branch, the front tire vine continuing up the trunk. For several agonizing seconds the bike hung suspended in midair. Then, with a dreadful, grinding screech, the frame began to twist like foil, and finally with a groan, it split apart. The handlebars broke free, swinging wildly. A rim spun, whistling against the leaves. The seat vanished into the canopy. The bell croaked desperately before a stray tendril strangled it. Each part was winched higher and higher as the vines charged upward, spurring each other on in a dead heat toward the canopy.

Then, as abruptly and explosively as it had begun, the growth ceased. The vines' mad rush ended as they reached the top of the canopy, where they curled in the sunlight, sated. The fragments of the bicycle came to rest where they were. The trees swallowed, burped, and chips of paint and a stray spoke shook down.

"Bellamy's bike," said Jebby slowly. "I don't believe it."

A lump lodged in Penny's throat as she looked up into the tree. Even if they went after the pieces and chopped them down, each was warped and mangled beyond repair. The bicycle was finished.

"I don't understand how it happened," she said. Her voice sounded small and hollow.

They were silent for a few moments, then Tabba spoke numbly.

"That puddle when we left Jaipa this morning," she said. "That odor—I know what it was."

"What?" asked Jebby.

"Ballawa seeds," said Tabba. "They're a fertilizer. Ma used them in the garden once, a long time ago; that's why I didn't remember it right away. They smelled so bad she never used them again. They were in that puddle, I'm sure of it. That's why we kept having problems with the bike all day—the vines had started growing, getting bigger and messing up the brakes. They couldn't grow too much while we were moving, but as soon as we stopped and left the bike in the mud, there was nothing to stop them. It all makes sense now. I'm sorry," she said miserably. "I should have realized it before; I don't know how I didn't."

Bellamy's words came back to Penny, and she saw him holding the vine between forefinger and thumb. *It would grow almost before your eyes. Even this may have some life in it, believe it or not, if it had a little water. . . .*

"It's not your fault," Penny told her. "None of us knew."

"Would those seeds have just been there?" asked Jebby quietly.

226

Tabba shook her head. "They have to be ground into a powder, and that has to be mixed with water. It had to be deliberate. And we didn't notice it when we got there last night because it wasn't there. Someone put it there in the night."

"Kal," said Jebby. "He knew where we were—maybe he followed us after we saw him in the town."

Penny remembered how a funny expression had come over Kal's face when his gaze had fallen on the sapsoo vine tires, and she remembered Seagrape's warning screech in the early hours of the morning. But Kal hadn't even had to come very near their camp—all he'd had to do was sprinkle the powder in the puddle and slip away unseen. He didn't have to be anywhere near when the tires started to grow. He was probably already in Santori at this very moment, Zamzee beetle given safely to the Council, and was resting with his feet up, the lumphur groomed and fed.

"There's no chance of being the Bloom Catcher now," she said, a choke in her voice. "It's over—we're out."

The bicycle's bell was caught in an offshoot of one of the vines, a curling tendril that bounced gently as it settled. Seagrape flew up and clipped the tendril with her beak, and with an exhausted wheeze, the bell dropped. Jebby caught it before it hit the ground.

"This is all we have left to take back to Bellamy," he said hoarsely.

The children walked back to the road, still hardly able

to believe what had happened. Not knowing what else to do, they consulted the map and decided to begin the slow hike to Santori. For a long time as they walked away they could hear the lonely metallic echo of parts of the bike jangling together in the breeze high in the treetops.

❧ Chapter Thirteen ❧

A Bad Fight • The End of Everything • A Brilliant Idea
• "It's a palace!"

"What are we going to tell Bellamy?" asked Tabba as the children walked along an empty red-dirt track.

"The truth—that Kal destroyed the bike," said Jebby.

"It's my fault," said Tabba morosely. "I should have known what that odor was this morning—I'm the one who helps Ma in the garden. If I'd known, then the vines would never have started growing."

"It's not your fault," said Jebby. "I knew Kal looked like he was up to something when we ran into him in Jaipa last night. I should have been more careful. Anyway, even if we had the bike, we wouldn't have a Zamzee right now. Elder said it should be simple—we messed up, okay? We didn't stop and think about it for long enough; we just ran off to Hopper. We should have known right away that it was too hard."

Penny felt like Jebby was blaming her. "We had to do *something*," she said defensively. No one had a better idea, after all. "We couldn't just sit around waiting. At least, I didn't think we could. Maybe it would have been better if we had."

"It's not anyone's fault," said Tabba.

Jebby nodded.

Penny felt better for a moment, then a surge of anger swept over her.

"But it *is*," she said. "It's *Kal's* fault." As Penny's shock wore off, anger was seeping in and taking over. Very soon the mere thought of Kal made her so searing mad she felt as if she were going to explode.

"When I see him, I'm going to . . ." she said, clenching her fists, but the sudden lump in her throat stopped her from saying more.

It was impossible to believe that it could all be over like this. No Bloom for Granny Pearl—she could hardly bear to think about it.

"He'll get in trouble in the next town," said Tabba. "He won't be able to get away with something like this— he might even be disqualified."

"It's his word against ours," said Jebby bitterly. "He'll deny he had anything to do with it. It was perfect—he was nowhere near when the vines started growing. He never even touched the bike or the cart."

No one said anything. They all knew that Jebby was right.

It didn't take long for everything to fall apart as surely as the bicycle had.

The bike and cart had allowed them to cover ground swiftly. When one of them was pedaling, the other two could rest. Speeding along created a breeze that kept them cool and the insects at bay. Walking was slow and tiring. They were hot and sweaty, their backpacks chafed their shoulders, and they were at the mercy of rafts of greedy insects that drifted out from the nearby Gorgonne. They were on an empty side road that it seemed no one had been on in a long time, and they felt very far away from all the life and busyness of the past days as well as the chance to be part of it in the days ahead.

As Penny racked her mind for some way to miraculously come up with a Zamzee, she lifted Helix's shark's tooth necklace and absently began to tap the tooth with her fingernail, making a soft clicking sound.

"Would you stop that?" Jebby snapped irritably.

"Stop what?" asked Penny.

"You know what," said Jebby.

"I feel like it," said Penny.

"Just because you feel like something doesn't mean *we* do," said Jebby. "Knock it off."

"Don't speak for *me*," said Tabba.

In her exhaustion, Penny's distress and rage spilled over and poured back into the source of all her troubles.

"I *hate* Kal," she fumed.

"We know, we know, you hate Kal," said Jebby. "How many more times are you going to tell us? Anyway, it's Bellamy's bike that's gone."

"It's just a *thing*; it's not the same as the Bloom," said Penny. "You don't care as much as I do because it's not your grandmother who needs the Bloom."

"All of Kana needs it!" cried Jebby. "You know, everything isn't just about you getting the Bloom. Even with me and Tabba, you act like you're the only one in this competition. Without us, you would never have gotten this far! You wouldn't have known what to get for the first trial, or where Molmers were, or anything!"

Jebby's outburst had surprised Penny, but she was feeling too angry and reckless to back down.

"And you wouldn't even be *in* the competition if it weren't for me!" she said.

They stopped in the middle of the road and scowled at each other.

"You know what the funny thing is?" said Jebby. "You're just like Kal! The only thing you care about is the Bloom!"

"Come on, you guys," said Tabba. "Everyone's tired and upset—let it go."

Penny began tapping her fingernail on the tooth again, louder this time.

"If you don't stop, I'm going to take it from you and throw it into the jungle," said Jebby.

"Hah," said Penny.

"I could in about five seconds," said Jebby. "You're not as tough as you want everyone to think you are."

Penny tapped the shark's tooth as hard as she could.

"That's it!" cried Jebby, striding back to Penny to take the necklace. "I've had enough!"

"You wouldn't dare," shouted Penny, stopping and

closing her fist over the shark's tooth. "This is *Helix's* necklace!"

"Helix, Helix, Helix," said Jebby. "I'm sick of hearing about him. If he was so great, maybe he'd be here to help us! He's *not* here. You have no idea if you'll ever see him again." He glared at Penny. "And you don't know if the Bloom even works on the Outside!"

Penny froze. "Of course it works," she said.

"Jebby!" said Tabba sharply. "That's just mean. Penny, calm down and stop provoking him. I don't feel like listening to this the rest of the way to Santori!"

"Whose side are you on, anyway?" Jebby asked.

"The three of us are on the same side!" shouted Tabba.

Jebby glowered at his sister then back at Penny.

Penny felt hot and dizzy. A paste of dust from the road clung to her sweaty skin. The wings of insects shimmered in the bright air and everything began to feel very unreal. What was happening? How had a small disagreement escalated to this?

Tabba sighed and began to walk away up the road. "I've had enough of both of you," she called over her shoulder. "I'll see you in Santori. Or not!"

"Fine!" shouted Penny. "Fine! I don't need you, anyway. Let's just split up now!" She started walking down the road after Tabba.

"That's just great," said Jebby. "Stomp off when you don't get your own way!"

Penny *was* stomping, banging her heels down hard with

each step, her backpack bouncing against her back. Then Jebby overtook her and quickly overtook Tabba, too.

Jebby was in the lead, then Tabba, then Penny, all on the same road because it was the only way to get to Santori, but with distance between each of them.

Penny didn't make it much farther before her shoulders began to shake. She stubbed her toe on a sharp rock and she felt the warm trickle of blood. She trudged along for a few more steps but then walked off to the shoulder of the road and collapsed in the grass. She could see Tabba and Jebby up ahead, but if they had looked back—which they didn't—they couldn't have seen her in the tall grass, so she let herself weep freely, hot, frustrated, regretful tears.

It was all over; she knew it. This was the first time on their trip that they had argued, truly argued. And it wasn't just an argument—it was an argument that meant the end of everything. Just yesterday they had been speeding along in the bicycle and cart, hopeful and happy and full of energy on the way to find a Molmer egg. The Bloom that would save Granny Pearl was out there, awaiting them. Everything had been going so well. Now, in an instant, it was ruined. Penny was alone all over again, just like at home. She had been so lonely before meeting Tabba and Jebby—she'd forgotten how good it was to be with other people, and now she'd messed everything up by being stubborn and selfish and difficult. And Jebby had been so mean to her! She felt miserable. Tears spilled down her cheeks, and sky and earth ran together in a swimmy smudge.

Suddenly, and with her whole heart, all she wanted was to be at home, a breeze wafting through the orange grove, gently swaying the *Pamela Jane* on her mooring, Granny Pearl on the porch in her rocking chair, its runners squeaking softly as she waited for Penny to come home from school. Then the whole horrible reason she was there in the first place rushed back to her. Without the Bloom, there was no home to return to—no home where everything was the way it used to be, where she was safe and happy and loved, where Granny Pearl had always been and always would be. The Bloom was the only thing that had the power to make Granny Pearl better, to restore life to the way Penny needed it to be.

Penny had always been determined. If she wanted to run faster than a boy at school and steal the soccer ball from him, she did. If she wanted to get the highest mark on a math test, she would study furiously for the week before and she would come in first in the class, even if her grades were poor the rest of the time. If she wanted to stick her head in the tank at the aquarium to see Oscar, or root through Maya's old belongings, or take the rowboat out by herself, no matter how many times her mother and father told her not to, she was still going to do it. That's how she was. Stubborn and determined. But now she couldn't make Jebby stop being angry with her, and she couldn't get the Bloom.

And she couldn't erase the terrible thought he had put in her mind: What if the Bloom didn't work on the Outside, if outside Tamarind it lost its power?

Then nothing—truly nothing—could help Granny Pearl.

Seagrape sat on a nearby stump, watching her. Penny thought she looked reproachful and disapproving of this display of self-pity. The sight of her made Penny think of Helix. Jebby was wrong about him. He had to be. Helix was part of her family. Even if they hadn't seen him in a very long time, even if Penny no longer knew where he was, or anything about his life. He was part of them; nothing could change that. She would see him again, she was sure of it. She took a deep, shivery breath and wiped her eyes with the back of her hand. Everything felt hollow and unreal, but she no longer felt despair. She could still find Helix.

She looked up the road, where she could still see Tabba and Jebby walking away without her. Regret filled her. The late-afternoon sun reflected off the suspension of red dirt particles in the air, and orange haze hugged the ground where they had stepped. Jebby had taken out the bird whistle and was running through different calls on it: single notes and nimble arpeggios. A hot breeze stirred from the opposite direction, carrying on it the musical jangle of the bicycle parts swaying into one another in the trees in the distance. Suddenly the birds that had been chirping and twittering in the jungle all along sounded crisper and clearer to Penny. She listened as pitches changed, new melodies began on the heels of old, and calls crossed each other in the air. The sounds fused with the clanging of metal and Jebby's whistle until a motley composition expanded into the air all around her. She closed her eyes and listened.

"PENNY! JEBBY!"

Penny's reverie was pierced. Tabba was shouting, and Penny looked up to see her waving furiously. Jebby stopped and began walking reluctantly back toward his sister.

Curiosity more powerful than pride, Penny took a shuddery breath and wiped the back of her hand, dirty and bug-bitten, over her eyes and got to her feet. On the road she broke into a jog and reached Tabba just as Jebby did.

Tabba was waiting, arm thrust out, palm opened to reveal a shiny shell the size of a button.

"Jebby," she said. "I can't believe we didn't think of it!"

"Think of what?" asked Jebby warily. "What are you talking about?"

Penny came closer to see the shiny object, some type of quartz, that Tabba held in her palm.

"I saw a *bird* drop it from its beak," said Tabba, unable to stop smiling, her eyes shining.

"So?" said Jebby.

"A bird was taking it back for its *nest* . . ." said Tabba.

Jebby looked at his sister as if she might have been out in the sun too long.

"Sometimes birds pick up strange things for their nests," continued Tabba. "And there's *one* bird in particular, who . . . Jebby, haven't you guessed it by now?"

"Tabba!" said Jebby, exasperated. "I have no idea what you're talking about. Just say whatever you're trying to say!"

"A *bowerbird*," she whispered.

For a moment Jebby was silent.

"A bowerbird!" he said slowly. "Tabba—that's brilliant!"

"What about a bowerbird?" asked Penny.

"We heard one earlier today, remember?" said Jebby. "Why didn't I think of it then?" He groaned. "We've wasted all this time and come all this way for nothing. We could have found a bowerbird a mile out of Jaipa and been in Santori hours ago!" He began blowing a series of long and short notes on the whistle, searching for the right sequence.

"Please, someone tell me what's going on!" Penny cried, bouncing on her toes in frustration.

"Male bowerbirds build nests on the ground in the jungle—more like little stick huts," said Tabba, turning excitedly to Penny. "But what makes them so unusual is that they collect objects—usually pretty, shiny things—and they group them together in piles around their huts to attract a mate. The rarer the objects, the better. They'll have a heap of purple flowers here, a pile of red berries there, shells, coins—anything that catches their eye . . . even brightly colored beetles! We've seen a nest once before—Da found one in the hills outside Tontap and took us to see it. There's a really good chance that if we find a bowerbird nest, we can find a Zamzee among the beetles the bird has collected!"

Penny's heart soared. "We're not out of the competition yet!" she cried. "We still have a chance!"

Penny and Jebby forgot why they had been so angry and upset just a short time ago. They looked at each other sheepishly.

"I'm sorry," said Penny. "And I really am sorry about Bellamy's bike. I feel terrible about it."

"*I'm* sorry," said Jebby. "I didn't mean what I said about the Bloom, that it can't help your grandmother. I don't know that. I don't know what the Bloom can do. I've never seen it before either."

"What Jebby meant earlier is that we don't know *for sure* the Bloom will help," said Tabba delicately.

"But why would everyone want it unless it could do amazing things?" said Jebby. "Why would there even be a Bloom competition? We have to try—let's keep going."

Penny thought for a moment she might cry again, this time with relief. All was forgiven, and the Bloom was still within reach.

"Now we just have to find a bowerbird," said Tabba. "Let's go back to where we heard one earlier!"

~~~

The children set off at a fast clip down the road, retracing their steps. Suddenly their muscles were no longer weary, their feet no longer sore. Hope and a new plan of action had revived them. Seagrape flew ahead, soaring and swooping as though she were refreshed, too. Jebby began to blow different notes with his whistle.

"I'm sure you know it," said Tabba confidently. "It's in there somewhere. Maybe just don't think too hard and it will come to you. Maybe it's a bit like this?" she said, beginning to hum a tune.

"Stop," said Jebby. "It's just muddling me."

Obligingly, Penny and Tabba fell quiet as Jebby searched for the notes. Frowning, he ran through a range of calls, a confusing avian babble that drew curious birds to the trees on either side of the road. He tried a cluster of high notes, a lilting alto phrase, a sharp peal. He paused. Then he tried two short bursts followed by a low, warbling hum. He repeated it a few times and smiled. "That's it," he said. "I've got it."

This time they didn't see any Bloom Players as they skirted Hopper. Everyone else must have already figured out what to do and was probably already speeding back to Santori. The awareness of time squandered raised a sour taste in Penny's throat—if they were too late, she didn't know what she'd do.

At last Jebby stopped.

"This was where I heard it earlier," he said. "But the nest won't be near the road, where people could disturb it. We'll have to go into the jungle a bit."

The girls followed Jebby, stepping gingerly over sticks that would snap, mindful not to stir any branches or disturb the creatures that lived there. Jebby repeated the tune on the whistle, stopping every now and then, ear to the jungle. Penny listened, too, but she couldn't distinguish one call from another amid the ebb and flow of chirping that filled the air all around them.

Finally Jebby turned back to the girls, smiling. He blew the whistle again, and this time there was a response, a rich, rococo tune inviting them deeper into the jungle. The children kept going, following the call, which grew louder the closer they got. Two short bursts followed by a low, rumbling warble. Through the undergrowth they could see they were approaching a small clearing. Jebby was in front, and he stopped when he reached the edge. Penny stopped behind him. Peering over his shoulder through the undergrowth, she first thought she was looking over a sort of junkyard piled with strange, half-camouflaged objects. But, when Jebby pulled the last of the foliage away and stepped aside to make room for her, she quickly realized that she wasn't looking upon anything haphazard. Instead she was peering at an elaborate miniature kingdom, surprising and strange and wonderful.

"It's not a nest," she whispered. "It's a palace!"

In the middle of the clearing, a tower of open-windowed rooms constructed from twigs stood eight feet high—the bower. Its roof was steeply pitched, its walls woven with grasses. A small, dark doorway was centered in the front of it. It was not any kind of nest Penny had ever seen.

On the ground all around it, lavish heaps of wampum were artfully arranged. Shiny baubles, grouped by color and texture, overflowed in bright piles: minty-green seeds, silver berries, nuts of different shapes and sizes. Feathers with false eyes were staked like sentries in deep cushions of moss. Shoals of bleached seashells stood on either side of a path leading up to the bower door. Penny noticed that each floor of the bower was devoted to a different collection of treasures: vermillion leaves, electric-blue quills, smooth gray bones, sea-smoothed pebbles, tiny white stars of flowers, colored threads and buttons poached from human clothing, tiny cracked eggshells blue as the sky. Leafy curtains rippled from some of the windows of the tower.

The architect, a young male bowerbird, larger than a seagull, smaller than a peacock, watched the children from the corner of his eye as he kept working. He cracked a violet seed with his beak and painted a smooth white stone with the purple dye, dabbing on spots of color with each tap of his beak.

Seagrape waddled over to steal a juicy red berry that had caught her eye, and the bowerbird dropped his seed and shrilled anxiously.

"Seagrape!" whispered Penny sharply. "It's not yours."

As she was scolding the parrot, Penny's eyes fell on it.

Near the open doorway of the bower was a circle of tiny orange beetles, and in the middle of them reposed the crown jewel. A single Zamzee beetle. In the low light it gleamed like a polished shell in a shallow riverbed. It had been a risk that, even if the children found a bowerbird, there would not be a Zamzee there, and Penny felt flush with gratitude that it had been so simple.

She held Seagrape back while Jebby went to retrieve it. The bowerbird squawked and fluttered its wings and spun in agitated circles.

"We're sorry," Tabba whispered. "We're just going to take this one thing."

Jebby returned, tilting the beetle gently in his palm so Penny and Tabba could see it.

To be sure it was the right one, Penny compared it nervously with the sketch she had made back in the last town. It was the same—the size of a cowrie shell, swirled horns, deep turquoise wing case, the fake orange eye spots.

Tabba gathered sphagnum moss and wrapped the beetle in it gently, and Penny placed it carefully in her backpack.

"Come on," said Tabba. "Let's not disturb him anymore."

Penny took a last look at the bowerbird's palace in the drizzle of diffused light. She plucked one of Seagrape's feathers and laid the offering gently on the outskirts of the bowerbird's garden.

"Shhh," she whispered when Seagrape growled reproachfully. "It's just one feather."

The children tiptoed away, leaving the secret bower once again camouflaged by the thick undergrowth.

❧ Chapter Fourteen ❧

"Like glowing reptilian eyes" • Dust • Santori • Strange Netherworld
• A Single Green Feather

Penny, Tabba, and Jebby hurried as fast as they could the whole way to Santori. They ran for short stretches, fell back to walking, caught their breath, then broke back into a jog. Their legs burned. The closer they got, the more nervous Penny grew. Surely other players had already made it there with beetles. They began to see more whorls, small ones like they had seen earlier, but in the fading light they took on a strange, lurking menace, like glowing reptilian eyes watching the children as they hurried along the darkening road.

The sun was setting when they started to see the dust. It began finely, but within a short distance it coated every-thing in sight. The disparate colors and textures of leaves and bark were reduced to a uniform ashen patina. Trees toiled along the roadside like a phantom procession. Branches slumped under the weight. Flowers had fallen off and been lobbed along the road by breezes, leaving swirling scripts in the thick grit. The children passed carts whose passengers swayed like ghosts, faces and hair eerily pale. All were heading away from Santori.

The children hailed a couple driving one of the departing carts.

"What's going on?" they asked. "What happened?"

Seeing their arm sashes, the couple stopped.

"A massive whorl opened over Santori this morning, and a dust storm poured out of it all day," said the man. "It was so thick it blotted out the sun."

"It looked like the middle of the night by lunchtime," said the woman. "You couldn't even see your hand in front of your face."

"It's stopped falling now, but the town is covered in it," said the man. "We spent the day inside waiting for it to pass. Now we're going where there's clear air."

The children thanked the couple and pressed on. They vibrated with a new, nervous anticipation—this was the kind of thing Elder had warned would happen.

The atmosphere grew thicker as they neared Santori. Seagrape tilted forward on Penny's shoulder and buried her head in the hollow of Penny's neck. Penny brushed dust off the bird's folded wings and bowed her own head to keep the dirt from falling into her eyes. She only looked up when she felt Tabba grasp her elbow.

The trees had ended, exposing sloping fields that encircled a town in the middle distance. Penny and Jebby stopped and followed Tabba's gaze up into the sky.

"Is that a *whorl* . . . ?" whispered Penny when she could finally speak.

The whorl was twenty times the size of any they had

seen before, and it hung high in the sky directly above San-tori. This was no humbly shimmering patch. It was dark and angry, a savage rend in the sky. A light snow of dust sifted from it, blowing this way and that on the muddled breeze. Dust blanketed the town below, filling its streets, mounding on its rooftops. Some roofs had buckled beneath its weight, leaving gaps like missing teeth. The whorl was calm now, but the evidence of its power was all around, and it gave the sense that it might only be resting, that at any time it could once again spring into action.

In an instant, the children knew that everything was different.

The past bad Bloom no longer seemed like a mere story. It was a dormant state that had been in danger of waking to potent and terrible life all along.

They continued on silently. In Santori they found that lamps had been lit early, their palm-oil wicks smoking softly. People were sweeping dust from doorways into drifts. There were fires in the gardens and the scent of food cooking, but there were no festivities on the scale of those in Tontap and Jaipa. There was an unnatural hush—the unsettling absence of a particular element of sound—and it took Penny a while to realize that it was because people's footsteps were muffled by the thick cushion of sediment on the streets. Coughing could be heard everywhere, muted beneath the damp cloths people held over their mouths. Penny felt as if she were in a dream, walking through a blast zone, as they made their way toward the town square.

The children found the Council of Elders on a platform in a corner. One of the councilmen rose and came to meet them. Penny gave him the beetle. Almost at once, the dust in the air settled on it, dulling its lacquer. The councilman rubbed it clear with his thumb, and it shone like a light through fog as he examined it. He nodded.

"Accepted," he said. "It's a Zamzee. Congratulations, you'll be one of five teams advancing to the final trial tomorrow." He took the children's old sashes and tied new ones—these a deep sapphire blue—to their arms. "In a little while, go to the red garden gate on the third street off the square—the teams will be meeting there to discuss the next trial."

The children stumbled across the square in a daze. They were reeling: Just a few hours ago all had seemed lost, and now here they were, hearing that they were still in the competition after all, and yet everything had changed. The lighthearted venture they had been on was over.

Santori had become a strange, dark netherworld. Silhouettes of people bobbed unpredictably here and there, features reduced to forms. The roiling dust made the world feel as if it were spinning. A few fresh gusts through the whorl shook down more powder. Penny put on her goggles and was able to take in the surreal panorama without her eyes watering.

For the first time, it was impossible for her to ignore the grave danger that Kana was in. She had been so focused on getting the Bloom for Granny Pearl that she had spared little thought for Elder's dire warnings or for the frightening stories about the last bad Bloom. But now, as she witnessed the destruction around her, she found herself flooded with emotion about Kana itself. Tamarind had been such a significant part of her and her family's lives, and she felt anew how deeply—how profoundly—she loved the place. Her resolve strengthened—she *must* get the Bloom, not only for Granny Pearl but for Kana, too.

Jebby returned from a stall with food, and the children found a place to sit down to eat. The food was gritty with dust and sand that crunched in Penny's teeth.

Dust lay on everything: windowsills, the backs of stray dogs, children. It dimmed the glowing bulbs strung between the streets. People swept it up, stood on ladders to wipe it from the bulbs and lanterns, sprinkled water on the streets to tamp it down. Sneezes and coughs punctuated the air. Seagrape faded into a pale ghost of herself on Penny's shoulder, every now and then ruffling her feathers to shake loose a dry snow of grains. A pallor settled over the children's new sapphire-blue sashes.

The dust was all anyone could talk about. People stood in clusters in the square, whispering, reddened eyes looking up at the whorl. Though no one had actually seen the mandrill, his presence hung heavy over the night. People glanced over their shoulders, half expecting that at any moment he might materialize behind them.

Still, the natural resurgence that occurs in the aftermath of any disaster was happening, and there were efforts under way to have the festival go on. People who had cowered indoors all day emerged to shovel dust off their rooftops before its weight made them collapse. Tainted barrels of water were dumped into gutters, rinsing small sections of the streets clean. Travelers who had steered clear of the town all day began to trickle in and wander around, though many of them soon left again for the clean air of the surrounding hills. Musicians set up on corners, stopping now and then to wipe instruments clean and spit grit out of their mouths.

The children saw other Bloom Players. Most had failed to even track down a single Zamzee; others had found beetles but not managed to be among the first five teams to reach Santori. No one was bragging this time around. Almost anyone who had come into contact with a live Zamzee had been injured. They limped into Santori, tattered and weary, limbs ballooned from Zamzee stings, and hobbled around on crutches or in slings, arms or legs numb and paralyzed until the toxin wore off in a day or two. Penny could hardly believe it—some tiny beetles had *crushed* these big, strong boys. They heard about one player who had to be rushed, lips foaming, to Santori for the serum. Animals had returned lame, too.

They learned that the other victorious teams were Grasshopper Boy, the Lamlo Diver, the Dorado brothers, and Kal. Kal was nowhere to be found, but among the others, only Grasshopper Boy had emerged unscathed. He was as fresh and springy, lean and rangy and burnished by the sun, as the first morning they set out. Early in the day he had tracked down a retired jeweler and secured a long-dead scarab that had been used in a bracelet, a move considered ingenious.

The Dorado brothers had vigorously dug down thirty feet and, in a stroke of fortune, unearthed a single scarab beetle. Each of them had been stung and the younger brother had one arm in a sling, but they were so happy to still be in the competition that they didn't care.

The Lamlo Diver had heard that scarabs often nested deep in the roots of teuchalia trees, so he had harnessed his buffalo to one, uprooted the tree halfway, and scrabbled around in the dirt on his hands and knees after a beetle, then galloped all the way back to Santori with it.

Word spread about the children's trick with the bowerbird, which was widely admired.

The children discovered that once again Kal was the first player back, arriving in Santori with a Zamzee long before anyone else. The lumphur was not with him; it was rumored to have been lost in a whorl. Kal's fame and the feeling of fear and awe he inspired had been amplified to mythic proportions as stories about how he had summoned the mandrill passed from town to town. Penny was furious that he was so famous, so fearfully admired. He didn't deserve it. What he deserved was to be exposed as the cheater and saboteur that he was—to be kicked out of the competition, even. Fresh anger surged through her. Jaw clenched, she squinted hard, searching through the thick atmosphere until she spied him.

He was standing in a corner of the square, back to a wall, scanning the crowd. Though shrouded in haze, it was unmistakably him. Penny remembered the grinding sound of the bicycle tearing apart. She thought of Granny Pearl coming so close to never getting the Bloom. Rage flooded her. She wanted to know how he was doing everything he was doing. She wanted to punish him for cheating. Without a word to Tabba or Jebby, she sprinted toward him.

She was the fastest-moving thing in the square, and Kal caught sight of her.

He bolted.

Within seconds Penny lost him in the crowd.

She craned her neck to see around the people in front of her and spotted him heading off the square into the tangle of narrow streets. She chased him and this time she kept him in sight. The farther they went from the square, the thinner the crowd, and the easier it was to close the distance between them. The air was heavy with dust and she was coughing when up ahead he pivoted suddenly and disappeared around a corner.

Penny pulled up short in the spot where Kal had turned and found herself at the top of a long, narrow lane. It was empty. Thinking she had stopped at the wrong street, she was about to head to the next one, when she noticed footprints in the thick dust.

The alley was unlit, the windows of the homes that bordered it dark. Dust furred the musty palm-frond eaves. No one had swept the lane since the storm, and a spongy mat of dust lay thickly on the stones, revealing a single trail of footprints that ran down the middle and stopped at a stack of wooden crates.

Penny smiled. Kal was trapped. She began to walk toward the crates. The fact that he was hiding emboldened her, and she clenched and unclenched her fists as she walked.

"I know you're here!" she called. "You destroyed our bike. We know it was you!"

"Stop!" Kal called, but Penny kept going deeper. The alley muffled the sounds of the festival back in the square. It was like listening to the sea in a shell. As her eyes adjusted to the dim light, she could make out more details—an abandoned nest in the eaves, the chipped wooden boards of the crates.

"How did you get a Molmer egg and reach Jaipa so much faster than anyone else?" she demanded. "And how did you get back here so quickly today? What did you do the day I came over the Blue Line? How are you opening whorls? How are you doing all these things?"

Just before she reached the crates, Kal stepped out and faced Penny. He was sweating and he was cradling his right arm, which was bandaged—probably from a Zamzee sting, Penny presumed. He couldn't escape. He'd have to answer her now. There was a squawk in the alley behind her, and then she heard flapping wings. Seagrape had caught up to her.

"Don't come any closer," called Kal, but he edged backward away from Penny. "I'm warning you!"

Penny felt a faint current from Seagrape's wings as the parrot flew past her, heading down the dark tunnel of the alley toward Kal. The breeze stirred the grit on the eaves, knocking loose small silent drifts.

"I'm serious!" Kal shouted desperately. "Stop!"

Just before Seagrape reached him, Kal closed his eyes, as if cringing for a blow, and threw up one arm. A ripple fanned through the air. Instinctively Penny turned away to shield herself. When she opened her eyes again, she saw that a whorl had opened in midair between her and Kal. Seagrape could not veer off in time, and Penny watched her fly into it and vanish.

"Seagrape!" she shouted.

The whorl quivered darkly. Penny became aware of a strange, sulfurous odor, of vegetable decay, the scent of deep, abiding rot. Steam began to fill the alley. Moisture gathered on the walls; dirty rivulets trickled down to the street, tracing snaking lines through the dust.

Without warning, the whorl snapped shut and disappeared.

"Seagrape!" Penny screamed.

There was no response, no raspy squawk, no flap of wings. The steam was gone. The air was a vacuum. Penny felt as if she had been punched in the stomach.

"What have you done to her?" she cried frantically. "Where is she?"

Kal looked all around the alley, his chest rising and falling hard.

"Bring her back!" Penny repeated. "BRING HER BACK!"

"I didn't want to hurt her," Kal said, his voice trembling.

"Then bring her back!" Penny shouted, a choke in her voice.

"I CAN'T!" Then he turned and fled down the alley, leaving Penny alone.

She dashed to the crates and turned them over. They were all empty. She ran up and down the length of the alley, rattling the closed shutters, peering up into the eaves. Seagrape wasn't there. Penny felt powerless, in a nightmare from which she couldn't wake. She had no idea what to do next.

"Seagrape!" she called pathetically.

Beneath where the whorl had been, she saw a single green tail feather on the ground. She crouched and picked it up, cradling it in her hands. The dust had gotten into her lungs and she started coughing and couldn't stop.

She heard running footsteps at the top of the alley.

"What happened?" asked Tabba, stopping, out of breath, beside Penny.

"Seagrape's gone," Penny said hoarsely. "Kal opened a whorl, and now she's gone. He just lifted his arm, like this—"

She raised her arm and the others recoiled, as if perhaps merely witnessing Kal's casual mastery had given Penny powers, too.

Jebby ran down the alley, checking all the same places where Penny had just looked.

"It was my fault," Penny whispered, anguished. "If—"

It didn't matter how righteous Penny's anger had been. Kal's mysterious power was real. She had provoked him, and now her impulsiveness had been punished. She had never felt more awful about anything in her life. She began to cry.

Tabba knelt beside her helplessly. Jebby awkwardly patted her shoulder.

"Stop," said Tabba at last, kindly but firmly. "We know that the mandrill comes in and out of the whorls— that means Seagrape is all right; she's just somewhere else right now."

"Sitting here isn't going to help her," said Jebby. "We have to meet with the Council and the other teams now. You need to put everything out of your mind except the third trial, okay? Whorls are opening up all the time. Think about how many we saw today. Seagrape . . . Maybe she'll find a way back."

Penny let their calm voices draw her back until she felt like she was once again in the world. Clasping the feather tightly in one hand, she let Jebby help her to her feet, and she followed her friends out of the alley.

❧ Chapter Fifteen ❧

Meeting in the Garden • The Mandrill's Maze • A Strange Camaraderie
• Please Find Me • "The farthest we've ever been"

The final trial would not be announced, as the previous two had, to the whole crowd. Instead, the five remaining teams gathered in a private garden behind a cane fence too high to peer over, where the Council of Elders would address them. Dust hung like smoke in the air. The plants and flowers lay stiffly beneath a pale frost of it. The Lamlo Diver, the Dorado brothers, and Grasshopper Boy were already there with the Council when Penny, Tabba, and Jebby arrived. Kal came in right after them. The other players shuffled aside to make room for him, but Penny didn't budge.

She glared at him across the circle. If they had been adversaries before, they were enemies now. The air trembled between them. Jebby nudged Penny and nodded to the Council. Penny took a deep breath and turned her attention to Elder. Everyone drew in close. The night was hot and airless, and sweat trickled down Penny's forehead. The dark canker of the whorl hung overhead. The silt drifting finely down from it caught the moonlight—against the dark night sky it looked like a pale, ghostly curtain adrift on a breeze.

"After tonight, maybe you understand a little better what's at stake for Kana," said Elder. "The whorls will continue to grow more powerful the closer we get to the Bloom. Today it was dust. Tomorrow it could be fire, floods, plagues of insects—any size and manner of chaos you can imagine."

Dust had turned Elder's beard silver. Small ashy heaps gathered on his shoulders and as he spoke slid down in miniature avalanches.

"So what you are doing is terribly important," he continued. "This final trial will be the greatest challenge yet and will determine which one among you will become the Bloom Catcher."

Dust fell, soundless, over the garden. With each breath, Penny felt its grit crunch between her teeth, tasted its sharp metallic flavor on her tongue. Even breathing had become more effortful, more deliberate and dangerous. The Lamlo Diver coughed into a cloth. The younger Dorado brother's eyes were so irritated that they had almost swollen shut.

"Early in the morning, you'll leave here and head to the Gorgonne," said Elder. "Your task is to be the first to find a shell and reach Palmos with it. The winner will be the Bloom Catcher and will use the shell to capture the Bloom in the Great Wave."

The Gorgonne! The players shuffled nervously. Penny remembered the blank patch on the map. The mandrill's lair, the place where no one in Kana could go. She swallowed painfully.

"Usually it's impossible to travel into the Gorgonne, but tomorrow, the day before the Bloom, the border will open and players may enter," said Elder. "The Gorgonne is a strange and disorienting place, a vast maze of the mandrill's own creation. Deep inside are his secret feeding grounds. There you'll find thousands of shells, spread all around the shores of a lake. Each shell is a spiral, clear as glass."

When Elder had mentioned the mandrill, the other players had glanced furtively at Kal. He betrayed nothing, staring steadily at Elder. Whether the news pleased him or frightened him, or if he knew it already, they could only guess.

"Each team will be able to enter the Gorgonne only once," said Elder. "Anyone who leaves will not be able to get back in—the border will seal behind you. You have only a single day to find a shell and get to Palmos. After that it will be too late. The Bloom will happen whether or not a Bloom Catcher is there, but, if the Bloom isn't captured and poured into the Coral Basin, what you've seen here"—he lifted his arm to the gash of the whorl—"will be only the beginning."

Except for Kal, who remained stoic, the players seemed suddenly frailer and less sure. The dust had suddenly aged them, turning their hair gray, snuffing out the color in their cheeks. The garden's hedges morphed into silver walls, like a prison closing in on them.

After arranging to meet before dawn the next morning,

Elder and the rest of the Council bid the players good night and left. Without a word to the rest of the group, Kal quickly slipped out of the garden, too.

The rest of the players stood there, looking at one another. They were different from what they had been two days ago. Something inside each of them had been whittled down. There was no boasting, no bragging. For a brief spell, a strange camaraderie existed between them.

"We have an uncle who lives near the Gorgonne," said the elder Dorado. "He's told stories about people who have gone in and never come out."

"He said there are fires in the water there," offered his brother.

"I've heard it's supposed to be full of whorls," said the Lamlo Diver. "Everywhere you look."

"I met an old couple in Palam who said the whole place is like a giant whorl itself," said Grasshopper Boy.

"I guess we'll find out tomorrow what it's really like," said Tabba.

"What do you think the mandrill will do if he finds us in there?" asked the younger Dorado brother in a small voice.

No one knew.

"You're from Tontap," said the Lamlo Diver suddenly, looking at Tabba and Jebby. "You know that kid, Kal. Were you there the day he made the mandrill appear? Do you really think he did it?"

Penny, Tabba, and Jebby looked at one another.

"We don't know if he did," said Jebby finally.

"Let's hope he didn't," said Grasshopper Boy. "Because if it's true that he has some power with the mandrill, he's going to have a huge advantage in the Gorgonne."

The group contemplated this quietly.

The younger Dorado brother broke the silence. "Hey, where's the parrot?"

Penny looked down at the ground.

"Gone in a whorl," whispered Tabba.

The other players looked sorry for Penny. They stood there, blinking the ceaselessly falling dust off their eyelashes. Nothing left to say, they bade one another good night and went their separate ways into the murky night.

The children found a sheltered place to camp on the outskirts of town.

"We want to find the shell without the mandrill even knowing we're there," said Jebby. "But if we *do* see him, we need a plan. We need something to trap him in. I'm going down to the harbor to see if I can get a fishing net. We have the mosquito nets, but they won't be strong enough. I'll need something to barter, though."

"We don't have anything left," said Penny.

"Our hammocks," said Tabba. "Ma won't be happy with us, but . . ."

"And look," said Penny. "What about this, the buckle on my backpack? No one here has anything like it."

She cut off the metal buckle with a knife, and Jebby left with it and the hammocks. Tabba stayed behind to organize their food for the next day, while Penny went to hang the final flag on the message pole. She was happy to have a task to take her mind off Seagrape.

Her footsteps were silent in the deep dust as she crossed the square. More dust roiled palely in the dark night sky. It tickled her nose as she climbed. It felt so strange not to have Seagrape with her. She hung the flag at the top of the pole and slid back down.

She looked up at it. That was it. There were none left. The insignia of the parrot slowly disappeared beneath the dust. She pictured the others still hanging in the last towns, already fading, the cloth stiffening, seams fraying in the elements. She made a wish.

Seagrape, please be okay.

And then another.

And please, Helix—please see these flags and find me.

Penny returned to find that Tabba had been busy. She had wrapped food for the next day in banana leaves and found herbs to make more ointment for their blistered feet. She had also gathered some hollow wooden sticks to whittle into arrows, in case they were forced to defend themselves.

"And look what I found," she said. She opened a banana leaf to reveal a clutch of red natal plums. "Monkeys love them, and since the mandrill *is* a monkey, we can use them as bait if we need to trap him."

Jebby returned with a net.

"It's made of spiderpod silk," he said, pleased with his acquisition. "It's strong but lightweight and nearly invisible."

Plums and a fishing net helped to restore a degree of cozy cheer among them. Penny even managed to convince herself that Seagrape was all right, just somewhere far away, and that she was already on her way back to them. The children felt satisfied that they were as prepared as they could be. They had only what they could carry on their backs, and each item had been chosen carefully and wisely. The spider-pod silk net was as light as air. Their sharp wooden arrows were strong but hollow. They would carry only a single meal with them, and their canteens were only half full, to be replenished at streams along the way. The only extra thing they were taking was Bellamy's bicycle bell, which they planned to return to him after the competition.

They took out the map to decide on the best route for the morning and found a footpath that would take them to the edge of the Gorgonne in a few hours. On the map, the Gorgonne was a featureless, amorphous mass in the middle of Kana, as if left blank to give their imagination free and fearful rein to fill the space. Penny remembered the octopus in the Blue Pit. Now it seemed like child's play. The mandrill was a much bigger monster. And tomorrow, from barely even wanting to say his name a few days ago, the children would be going in search of his lair.

They decided there was no point in keeping watch that

night. Except for the net, which Jebby folded and used as a pillow to keep safe, they had nothing left to steal. The scent of the tart natal plums that Tabba had found wafted through the campsite. Without the hammocks, they had to lie on the hard ground and, despite their fatigue, none of them fell straight to sleep. They lay still and listened to the howls of wild animals deeper in the jungle.

"Ma and Da and Tontap seem so far away," whispered Tabba. "I know you've come all the way from the Outside, Penny, but I can't help thinking . . . tomorrow will be the longest Jebby and I have ever been away from home, and the farthest we've ever been."

"We can't let ourselves get scared," said Jebby. "We'll be all right." But his voice sounded hollow in the darkness.

"Of course we will," said Penny bravely, wanting to cheer up Tabba. "We've made it this far."

"That's right," said Jebby. "Now, who knows what tomorrow's going to be like? We should get all the rest we can."

"Okay, shhh," said Tabba. "Good night."

"Good night," said Jebby.

"Good night," whispered Penny.

She closed her eyes. Granny Pearl had felt so distant for so long, for longer than just these past few days Penny had been gone, but the Bloom would bring her closer again.

She imagined Seagrape, perhaps somewhere very far away but safe and flying fast, on her way back to Penny. All

Penny could hope was that a new whorl would open and her friend would be released. She pulled her tunic over her mouth so she wouldn't breathe in the dust and waited for sleep.

Over Santori the yellow flag waved, and the threadbare parrot flew without rest, like static in the dark sky.

Helix

He sat in the dark in the hills above Santori. He had not bothered with a fire or a real meal. It was very late when he had approached Santori and seen the giant whorl and the town beneath it blanketed in dust. Until now, the Bloom had been only a thrilling prospect. The fate of Kana had not concerned him. Now he saw that the dangers he had heard about on the road, the whorls and the mysterious creature, the mandrill, were real and imminent.

This was not why he had fled, though.

In the town, he had been close enough to see the third flag hanging from the message pole. He had already found the second in Jaipa earlier that day: proof that Penny was here. And, if Penny was here, it meant Maya and Simon could be, too. He had asked around in Jaipa, but people only talked about one young girl here from the Outside. Still, it didn't mean the others weren't here, too.

He had walked on and found the third flag, as he had expected to.

He had retrieved it, but then before he knew it he was

back up in the hills. He couldn't see them. And he couldn't be seen by them. Not like this, not now.

So much time had gone by—it might be a mistake to see any of them again. It might be best—safest—to leave them as they existed in his mind. To see them now, to hear anything real about them, would be to dispel the people he had carried with him all this time. And . . . Maya could still be angry at his choice, at how he had left without even saying good-bye—he still felt guilty about it.

He'd been having a conversation with Maya in his head for years now; he was always in conversation with her. But who knew what she was like anymore, or if she even thought of him? Seeing the real person again might prove how futile and foolish his thoughts about her were and mean that he would have to put her—and all of them—out of his mind for good. They would evaporate. It was too much to risk.

It was crazy that he was there in Kana at all. He should have been at home in Western Tamarind. If he hadn't happened to stumble upon the man in the citrus grove who'd told him about the Bloom, if he hadn't been so bored and eager for something fresh, if his father had not died, he would not have been here to see the flags. He would have been none the wiser that they had been left for him. Whatever happened to Kana would happen without his knowing. That something so important could have come down to dumb luck, to chance—or, to take an opposing view, that there were forces outside himself of which he was ignorant but which still acted on him—both of these thoughts disturbed him, left him feeling agitated and confused.

He was so lost in his own thoughts that he heard the parrot screech before he saw her, flying low toward him in the moonlight. Before he could even stand, she had landed on his shoulder. She mumbled softly; pushed her head against his cheek.

She had first sat on his shoulder when he was a young boy and his mother had sent her to watch over him before she had died. He knew her better than he knew most people. He closed his eyes, grateful that the darkness hid his tears. The seven years since they had been together felt like nothing, as if he had last seen her just that morning.

"I wondered when you'd find me," he whispered.

He looked, but no one was with her. The hillside was quiet.

"Have you come by yourself?" he asked.

Behind her, dust seeped from the whorl, suspended like the tail of a meteor bearing down on the valley.

With a quiet squawk, Seagrape flew from his shoulder. He knew she wanted him to follow her.

As he watched, a small whorl opened in midair in front of him. It rippled, reflecting the moonlight like a patch of satiny black sea. He hesitated. The parrot circled, waiting for him. There was something she needed him to do.

"Are you taking me to Penny?" he asked.

She didn't answer, but he knew she wouldn't put him in

danger—not anything he couldn't handle, anyway—so he started walking toward the whorl. With one last flap of her wings, the parrot disappeared into it.

Helix followed her into the darkness.

❧ Chapter Sixteen ❧

Seagrape had not returned by morning. The children
whistled for her as they broke camp in the shadows. It
was very early, not yet dawn, and the sky had barely begun
to lighten. The whorl loomed like a strange, unwelcome
planet over the valley. The dust had stopped falling from
it sometime in the night, but a layer coated everything,
absorbing sound. The air was heavy and still.

The Council of Elders had arranged for the Bloom Players to meet on a side road leading out of Santori. The other
players were just arriving when the children got there. Unlike
the mornings of the other trials, there was no fanfare, no one
but the Council to see them off. They would slip away secretly, before the town rose. Few words were exchanged. The
stakes were higher this time around, and everyone had drawn
inward.

Penny sneaked a glance at Kal. For the first time at
the start of a trial, she thought that he looked tired and a
bit scared. He studiously avoided looking at the children.
His soles were painted with a rubbery paste to cushion
them, and he flexed his ankles, bobbing silently on his toes

on the foggy road. The Lamlo Diver's buffalo's chin was wet from drinking at a nearby stream. The Dorado brothers' horses were keen and edgy. Their glossy flanks shone in the milky light, and they pawed the ground, their knees neatly bandaged. The night's dampness had turned the dust from the whorl into a gritty glue that weighed down the leaves of all the trees, shifting everything into a lower register than it had been the previous day.

When the elders gave the signal, the teams disbanded. The horses disappeared in a golden blur and the buffalo thundered behind them. Kal vanished into the trees. Penny, Tabba, and Jebby dodged onto a shortcut through the jungle before joining a path heading north. It would take a couple of hours to reach the Gorgonne, and Jebby kept out the map and compass to refer to every now and then.

They felt strangely free on foot. The bicycle and cart would have been a bumpy, miserable ride on the narrow, rutted track. However, they knew that the other teams were ahead of them, so they walked as fast as they could. To conserve energy, they seldom spoke. The ointment Tabba had made dulled the sting of their blisters, but their legs were still weary.

Dust covered everything for a few miles outside Santori before it finally began to thin. The day was overcast, and even when the sun was fully up, the trees never really shrugged off the shadows. Fields and jungle lay under the pall of a sullen, marbled sky. Penny looked up often, always hoping to see Seagrape. But, even if she had somehow escaped, Penny wasn't sure if the parrot would know how to find her again.

The children passed no one all morning. Most people were already converging on Palmos, miles to the north. Few people had reason—or the desire—to pass this close to the Gorgonne. The path felt ever more desolate, so the children were startled when they heard hoofbeats and saw a man on a shaggy donkey hurrying at a jolting trot toward them. They waited apprehensively as he approached, instantly wary of anyone who would choose to travel so near the most feared place in Kana. When the man saw their arm sashes, he hailed the children as someone alone at sea for days might quicken at the sight of a fellow ship.

"Have you heard?" he shouted.

"Heard what?" Jebby called back.

"The mandrill's kicking everyone out!" said the man as he pulled up beside them. "The Lamlo Diver and Grasshopper Boy were the first to go!"

"What do you mean they're out?" asked Jebby.

"Out of the competition!" exclaimed the man. His beard was filthy, and mud was caked on his broken shoes. "The mandrill chased them right out of the Gorgonne! The Lamlo Diver ended up miles away—he said it was like he had been dropped through a trapdoor. People who saw him said he was scared witless, shaking like a leaf. And Grasshopper Boy was found trussed up on a raft floating out of the Gorgonne near Manalmo. He had to be fished out of the river and cut free. The mandrill caught him and tied him with the same ropes Grasshopper brought to capture *him* with! As if ropes or nets could ever catch that old devil! They tried to go back in, but the Gorgonne rejected them. They'd get close and it would push them back. One chance—one chance only! They're on their way to Palmos now."

"How have you heard all this already?" asked Jebby after the children had gotten over their surprise.

The man blew his nose on a dirty rag he retrieved from his pocket. "I heard it in Nalloma, a few miles back," he said. "It's all true—I spoke to people who had seen Lamlo with their own eyes."

"What about the Dorado brothers?" Penny asked. "Or Kal, from Tontap?"

"No word," replied the man, stuffing the rag back in his pocket. "They may be out already, for all I know. Or the brothers will be. The boy from Tontap has conjured up the mandrill before—he knows a few of his tricks. He'll be all right in there."

He looked at the children, and his eyes glittered like flakes of gold in a dingy stream.

"If I were you, I'd turn right around and run straight to Palmos," he said. "That's the mandrill's country you're heading for right now. He's lived in there for years, making hiding places, laying traps. People who've stumbled in there have never been heard from again. You'll be lucky if he kicks you out!"

"We just need to get a shell and then we'll get out as

fast as we can," said Tabba. "We're hoping we don't find the mandrill at all."

The man laughed, a hoarse, startling whoop, as loud and unexpected as a seagull.

"Never mind about finding him," he said. "He'll find *you*!" He kicked the mule and it lurched forward. As it trotted madly away, the man shouted over his shoulder, "Good luck! Good luck! Good luck! You'll need it!"

～～～

The savage brevity of these ventures into the third trial shocked the children. If the news was true, it meant they were closer to winning the competition than they'd been even a few short hours ago, but instead of feeling excited, doubt settled over them. Penny remembered the other teams in the softly falling dust in the garden in Santori just the evening before. The Lamlo Diver had always seemed so fearless and capable! And Grasshopper Boy—the favorite! They had believed, with all of Kana, that he was the finest competitor, in a class of his own. While all the other players had boasted and bragged, and while Kal had been devious and underhanded—guilty of sabotage, even—Grasshopper Boy had seemed above it all. It was hardest to accept that he was out.

The fact that the man had heard nothing about Kal made Penny deeply suspicious. Kal was the only one who really knew anything about the whorls or the creature who made them. Surely that would give him a big advantage in the Gorgonne, as Grasshopper Boy had suggested. Perhaps—perhaps he was even colluding with the mandrill. Penny had to concede it was possible. All at once the things that she, Tabba, and Jebby had brought with them—a net, plums, arrows—seemed flimsy and feeble, and she felt ill-equipped to face either Kal or the mandrill. As she was thinking this, the dirt track opened onto a scrubby, razed field, and suddenly, across the field, there it was.

The Gorgonne loomed like a swelling green cumulonimbus cloud, stretching from the ground so high into the sky that the children were blinded by the sun if they looked for the top. On either side it bent toward the horizon, as curved and vaporous as a rainbow dissolving from view. It was dense yet insubstantial, masking what lay behind it and revealing only rough outlines. Blurred colors soaked through its filmy layers. As the children watched, it roiled, slowly puffing itself up, as if, Penny thought irrationally, it were turning around to see them better.

"The green—are those trees?" whispered Tabba. "They can't be, though—they'd be so tall. . . ."

Like prisoners being marched to the gallows, the children walked slowly toward it through drifts of insects that hovered in the bleached-out light. The earth around the cloud was barren. As they drew closer, Penny's skin began to tingle.

The Gorgonne's edge was marked by a silver stream that slipped in and out of the mist. Clear, cold water conveyed bits and pieces from inside the Gorgonne: jagged leaves, a drowned dragonfly, delicate-limbed insects pin-wheeling silently on the surface, all of them mute messengers unable to describe what lay within. A draft sucked at the children's heels. A dull, unsettled growl emanated from deep within the mass's murky depths, then came a crackling, as if something were sagging under a great weight. The cloud's ominous bulk swelled, almost seemed to breathe.

"It feels alive," whispered Tabba.

"Don't be silly," said Jebby. But they could all feel it.

A sudden storm of hopping clams made a din on the rocks at the edge of the stream, startling the children, before clapping shut and settling beneath the surface. Penny felt as if she had stepped out of time. The rest of the world seemed very far away—home, family, the pleasant and familiar commotion of other people in the midst of ordinary life in a world both deeply absorbed in and oblivious to its workings.

A path of stones led across the stream into the green cloud. Here and there a stray clam caught in the rocks clapped forlornly.

"Well," said Penny, hoisting her pack higher on her back. She felt an unnatural emptiness on her shoulder where Seagrape should have been. "This is it."

Tabba reached out and squeezed Penny's and Jebby's hands. They squeezed back. Jebby checked the map a final time, then, close on one another's heels, they crossed the stream and went in.

After just a few steps, they had passed through the cloud and found themselves inside a jungle. Inside, it was instantly darker. The leaves grew bigger, the trees taller, the trunks wider, and the children felt that they grew smaller with each step they took.

"The *trees* are getting bigger," said Tabba.

"They can't be," said Jebby.

"But Tabba's right. They are—look," said Penny.

Tabba shivered. "It's giving me the creeps."

"We're barely even in," said Penny, peering up at the bold patterns of spores striping the backs of giant ferns that crossed above their heads.

The trees stretched up endlessly, growing so tall that their tops merged into a dark arboreal sky, and the floor of the jungle abided in a state of permanent twilight. Vines draped from trees like the rigging of a storm-battered fleet. Flowers, fleshy as mollusks, sprang from the crooks of branches. Spiders hung from single threads, revolving slowly, not in the breeze but from the weaving of their softly furred legs. Every now and then there was the sound of something unseen falling in the foliage—ripe fruit, Penny assumed, or else a small creature jumping between branches. A bat as large as a seagull took shuddering flight past them, wings squeaking like an unoiled hinge.

Tabba called out the names of plants as they went along. She ticked off fewer and fewer the farther they ventured.

"There's not a single plant here that I recognize," she said at last, stopping in her tracks to gaze around.

But it wasn't the unfamiliar flora that was so disorienting. Sometimes when the children looked behind them, what they looked back on did not seem like where they had just been. Like a shift of kaleidoscope glass, the scene was a few degrees different, as if each passing moment brought a slightly new jungle into focus.

They saw creatures, usually dimly in the distance: the flutter of a bird or bat, or a rodent running low to the ground into the shadows. They found clear, narrow paths, which confused them until they realized that they were hunting trails trampled by small animals. It was a relief to have decoded something in a strange new place, and their discovery cheered them. The paths allowed them to move more quickly. They kept their eyes peeled for signs of the mandrill—a footprint, droppings, shrubs stripped of the sweet lantanno leaves they had heard he loved to eat, a tuft of his yellow mane caught on a thorn. Even, they feared, his colorful face itself peering through the foliage.

"It's not as bad in here as I thought it would be," said Tabba.

"We've just got here," said Jebby. "Let's wait and see."

"You'd think there'd be whorls all over the place," said Penny. "But we haven't seen a single one."

"How are we going to find the place with the shells?" asked Tabba.

"We keep walking and hope we find some sign of them somewhere," said Jebby.

"What do we do if we see the mandrill?" Tabba asked in a low voice.

"What we talked about," said Jebby. "We get the natal plums and the net and we build a trap."

No one said anything. The plan was shaky at best, and they knew it.

The path they were on became overgrown, and the children fell quiet and concentrated on ducking beneath mossy branches and swiping away small feathered vines that tickled their necks. Their feet crushed silent dents into the rubbery mats of mushrooms that hugged the ground.

The laws of nature seemed disrupted and jumbled in the Gorgonne. Leaves drifted down that didn't match the trees they came from. Odd pebbles pinged down on the path in front of the children, and sometimes they would stumble upon shafts of light that appeared mysteriously, not from the top of the canopy but in midair below it. From time to time, out of sight in the distance, they heard what sounded like the wet thud of fruit falling. It was as if the jungle were a drawer for random castoffs with no home, thrown in there and left to rattle around.

Tabba and Jebby had been Penny's guides; she had re-lied on them for knowledge about Kana. Now they were as lost as she was. Jebby squinted at the map, trying to keep track of where they were, though there were no landmarks, either on the map or in the dense jungle itself. Simon's compass was no help either; its needle drifted aimlessly inside its case.

Penny lifted her backpack a few inches off her back to let the air reach her skin as she walked. After just a few days of sweat and humidity, already its fabric was starting to rot. She took out her canteen and took a few unsatisfying sips of warm water.

"There's been no sign of the Dorado brothers or Kal yet," she said. It was obvious, of course, but it felt reassuring to say *something*, to voice some concrete fact about the strange place they were in.

"The Gorgonne is big," said Jebby. "They could be in a totally different part."

"I don't know why you keep looking at it," said Tabba, glancing over his shoulder at the map. "It's no good in here. You may as well put it away."

Jebby ignored her.

Annoyed that his stubborn insistence on walking with his nose in the map was slowing them down, Tabba took the lead, but she hadn't gone far along the narrow, leafy trail when abruptly she stopped.

"You guys, come here," she called excitedly. "Stand exactly where I'm standing. Do you feel that? This spot is definitely colder than anywhere around it."

Penny stopped next to Tabba. A moment ago she had

been sweltering, but now the sweat was drying on her brow and a chill crept over her shoulders.

"We passed through something like this earlier, too," she said to Tabba. "I noticed it, but I thought it was just me."

Jebby put out his hand, testing the air. "It's weird," he admitted. "It's definitely colder."

"But it's only right here," said Tabba, stepping in and out of the spot. "Like a draft is coming in through a window."

A normal breeze would have stirred everything over a wide area; what the children felt was confined to just a small area, as if a steady stream of cold air was sneaking in through a window or under a door. One step backward or forward and they could no longer feel it. Penny remembered the sensation of coolness that had spread through Elder's yard on her first day here, and of Grasshopper Boy describing the heat when he had put his hand through a whorl.

She scanned the foliage slowly until she found it.

"Look," she said. "It's coming from there."

She pointed up at a whorl, not much bigger than the children, that hung like a small rogue cloud in the verdant gloom between two low branches of a nearby tree. It glimmered with a low, whispery light. The foliage around it eddied gently.

The others gazed up at it.

"What *are* whorls, really?" Penny asked, more intrigued than afraid. "Why do you think they look like that, all blurred?"

"Heat, light, shadows, who knows?" asked Jebby, never eager to dwell on things he didn't understand.

"Kal makes them," said Penny. "I came through one. Even Grasshopper Boy put his hand through one." She took a step closer. "Maybe we should try to look into it."

"That would be stupid," said Jebby. "We don't know what would happen."

"We would find out," said Penny. "Where do you think it goes?" She took another step. Close up, the whorl was frustratingly opaque, like a light burning from deep inside fog.

"Stop," said Tabba. "Come on, Penny. It's not a good idea."

"What if we're *supposed* to go through one?" asked Penny.

"Just because the mandrill can go through them doesn't mean we can," said Jebby. "Or should. What if it *does* take us somewhere—somewhere without the shells—and we never make it to Palmos or the Bloom? What if we get lost? Or can't get back?"

"Remember the dust storm yesterday?" said Tabba. "Maybe there are only bad things on the other side."

Penny hesitated.

There was a small popping sound and the whorl vanished. The children waited, but nothing else happened. The place where the whorl had nestled was now just an ordinary patch of leaves.

"See?" said Jebby. "What if you had been in there when

that happened? Maybe you wouldn't have been able to get out."

"Or would have been squashed," said Tabba.

Penny had to admit the way the whorl had shut without warning was alarming enough that it had dampened her desire to investigate further.

"Let's stick to our plan," said Jebby. "It's only a matter of time before we find the shells. The mandrill will have left some sign—fur, a footprint, something that will lead us to them."

"He left that whorl," muttered Penny, but after a final glance at where the whorl had been she followed after Tabba and Jebby.

～⌇～

A little while later, there had still been no sign of the lake with the shells, and Penny was beginning to wonder if they were in the right part of the jungle at all. The path they were on unspooled without purpose through a tangle of leaves and vines and trunks that repeated endlessly in all directions.

She was at the rear of the group when she began to have the sensation they were being watched. The feeling amplified with each step she took. Her heart quickened. She caught up to the others.

"Something's out there," she whispered. "We're being followed."

"Is it him?" asked Tabba.

"I don't know," said Penny.

The children stopped and stood completely still. Penny's whole body was tensed. Without a word, Jebby took out the net and held it at the ready—as if, should they see the mandrill, he could simply cast it over him.

From the corner of her eye, Penny noticed a small pale whorl open; a tiny furry hand emerged and dived into Tabba's backpack. It seized a natal plum, then both plum and fist disappeared. From other whorls, more of the tiny sharp-clawed hands appeared, delving deftly into the children's backpacks. Penny saw a face fleetingly in the trees, then another and another. A tribe of small gray monkeys, emboldened by their success, settled above the children in the canopy to enjoy their plunder out of reach. Their eyes were like pats of melting butter, their faces fringed with ruffs of knotted fur. Their long silky tails curled under them, keeping their balance on the narrow branches.

"It's just monkeys," said Jebby in disgust. "Thieves."

The monkeys' chortles reverberated through the swimmy green depths of the jungle.

"They're laughing at us," said Tabba.

"Just ignore them," said Jebby. "They won't hurt us. There's nothing left for them to take, anyway." He lifted the net out of his backpack. "They tore it," he said angrily.

Tabba examined the tear. "I think I can mend it," she said. "It will take a little while, though."

Penny's heart was slowly returning to a normal rate. The monkeys had given them a fright, but she was relieved they had been only some pesky bandits, not the mandrill. She stood and turned in a slow circle, studying the choked, chaotic vegetation all around them. She could see small, almost imperceptible whorls hiding everywhere—hanging out like a shirttail from behind leaves, peeking out from beneath the curve of a vine, tucked in the crook of a branch. These were where the monkeys had hidden.

"They can make whorls, too," she murmured. "The mandrill, Kal, now the monkeys . . ."

"Look," said Tabba. "There are whorls all over the place up ahead." Her eyes were big and fearful as she gazed at the hazy spheres encroaching on the path.

Jebby observed the whorls grimly. He took a thin rope out of his pack. "Let's tie this around our waists," he said. "Just to be safe—so we don't get separated."

"What I don't understand," said Tabba in a wobbly voice as she took the end of the rope from her brother, "is that except for the Dorado brothers and Kal, who we don't know about, all the other teams came in here and the mandrill immediately chased them and kicked them out. So why not us? Why hasn't he gotten to us yet?"

Penny gazed all around into the dim reaches of the jungle that flickered patchily wherever there was a whorl. She tied the rope around herself, but, unlike the others, she was beginning to have that feeling of being keenly alive, as she did in the tank at the aquarium at home. She felt close to understanding something, as though some new, exhilarating knowledge was coming within reach.

"Maybe he doesn't see us as a threat," she said. "Or . . . maybe it's the opposite—animals will only attack other animals if they think they're stronger. Maybe he doesn't think he can get rid of us so easily."

"But we aren't stronger than him," argued Tabba.

"Unless we are and we don't know it," said Penny.

"Well, that doesn't help us, does it?" said Tabba in frustration. "I don't want to be here anymore," she said quietly. "I want to see Ma and Da and be back in Tontap."

Muted beams of gray light slanted through the trees. The monkeys jibbered in the branches, cackling and taunting. Suddenly a warning cry went up between the creatures, and the next instant they disappeared, whorls popping shut behind them.

"Something's scared them off," whispered Jebby.

The whole jungle fell silent. Leaves were frozen in the breezeless air. No paw stirred or tail flickered or wing opened. The children reached out and grasped one another's hands.

The excitement Penny had felt moments before evaporated. She had the same feeling she'd had the first day at Elder's, and again in the alley in Santori: that they were not alone, that some malevolent presence had infringed. The ancient, creeping awareness came over her that another animal had her in his sights, that she had become part of the age-old struggle between hunter and prey. She knew it was already too late to escape.

She heard a dull, punching thump. From the corner of

her eye, she saw a whorl appear next to them, larger than the ones the monkeys had come from, a few feet off the ground, shining brightly.

Without a sound, Jebby's hand was wrenched from her own, and Penny was jerked violently forward by the rope around her waist. She lost her balance and fell. She, Tabba, and Jebby were being dragged at speed toward the whorl, as if someone on the other side were reeling in a line. Penny saw Tabba disappear into it. Immediately the rope went slack around Penny's waist.

She and Jebby scrambled to their feet.

"Tabba!" he shouted frantically. *"TABBA!"*

There was no answer. The frayed end of the rope that had been tied to Tabba lay on the ground outside the whorl, which was glowing more intensely now, a blurred, quavering lens suspended just off the jungle floor.

Penny's heart was beating so fast it felt like it was going to burst. Her legs felt like rubber. She tried to speak but no sound came out.

Jebby was still shouting for his sister when Penny felt herself yanked for the second time. This time she fought, clawing the earth, grasping at roots and stones too slippery to keep hold of. Whatever was pulling her was immensely powerful. She was no match.

Abruptly the rope snapped, releasing her.

Instantly everything went quiet.

Jebby had disappeared into the whorl after his sister.

Penny was alone.

Shakily, she stood up. The whorl glittered furiously. A single insect whirred near her ear. A bird shrilled a piercing alarm from high in the canopy, but otherwise the silence was oppressive. She felt a terrible squeezing in her chest, as if the atmosphere were so heavy that its weight was compressing her lungs. She expected to be seized at any moment, but her legs no longer felt like part of her body and she couldn't make herself move. The rope slid down around her waist. She forced herself to step outside it, kick it off her ankles. She backed up a few steps. The whorl was almost too bright to look at. Panic surged, turning her body into a prison. She had to escape. She had to get out of the jungle. She needed air.

Penny turned and ran, crashing heedlessly through foliage. She lost one shoe. She lost the other. She tripped over rocks, stubbing her toes. Thorns slashed her arms. She didn't know where she was going, but she didn't stop. She had to be anywhere other than where she was.

She saw the whorl lodged between two trees for only a second, not long enough to stop herself before she ran straight into it.

❧ Chapter Seventeen ❧

Penny had the brief sensation of being underwater. Then it passed and she felt only air on her skin.

She was in absolute darkness.

She stopped and stood completely still.

The world she had just come from, the dense, dim, humid jungle where she had been walking and talking with her friends, was gone—gone so completely that Penny wondered if it had ceased to exist altogether. She desperately wanted to be with Tabba and Jebby again, but she didn't dare call out to them in case the mandrill heard her.

Giving in to fear would have made her situation unbearable, so through sheer will she forced herself to stay calm. She had stopped running as soon as she had realized she was going through the whorl. That meant it was still very near. It should be right behind her. All she had to do was back out of it. She reversed a few tentative steps, but nothing happened. She turned around, hands outstretched, and searched for it. She cringed at the thought that the mandrill could be right there with her and she wouldn't know it. At any second her fingertips might touch fur. Her hands groped empty air. The whorl wasn't there. There was nothing with which to orient herself. She was in empty space.

A terrible, paralyzing thought struck her: Maybe she wasn't anywhere. Maybe that's what the whorls were—nothing and nowhere. She had stepped away from everyone and everything she knew into a void. She couldn't see herself in the dark, and for a brief moment she wondered if she herself was even real anymore. It felt as if her whole body were changing states, turning to liquid, about to drain away or to evaporate as steam.

She didn't know what gave her the strength to reach out again, but she did, stretching her arms as far as she could in front of her as she took a small step forward.

Then another.

And another.

She could have been floating free in space, attached to nothing.

She reached out farther.

She whimpered.

Her fingers had touched something.

A tree.

A real thing.

She stepped closer to it and pressed her palms against its reassuring solidity, felt the papery fibers of its bark, the soft dampness of mushrooms breaking off under her fingers.

She took a deep breath and fought off the nervous urge

to laugh even as tears spilled down her face. She laid her cheek against the trunk. She was real. She wasn't nowhere; she was in a real place. And maybe Tabba and Jebby were there, too.

Slowly her senses revived. She smelled a damp nighttime smell. She circled the tree cautiously, feeling its knots and hollows. She jumped when something brushed her cheek. She reached up. Just a leaf. All the nerves in her body felt sharply alive. The trunk was thick. She kept walking. As she rounded it, she saw tiny pinpricks of lights bobbing and twinkling in the distance.

To reach them, she would have to leave the safety of the tree. It was the only thing she knew for certain was there with her. She hesitated—then she let go. She walked toward the little lights. They guttered and died, leaving her in pure darkness, before flaring to life again. She might have been deep underwater, seeing the cold flares of bioluminescent creatures drifting through some remote sunless zone. A light appeared suddenly beside her, revealing itself to be an insect, its body an incandescent bulb.

As she got closer to the swarm, the creatures emitted enough light for her to see that she was in a forest of giant widely spaced trees. The canopy was so high and thick that it formed a vault of permanent night beneath it. She trod carefully, her feet silent in deep moss. Here and there the insects illuminated pale clusters of buds gathered on vines, like the sea foam of breakers catching the moonlight. The air smelled of rain and mud, of mushrooms and sodden bark and freshly snapped ginger, of rotting cane stalks and decay, a rich, overpowering, organic smell.

She did not hear her friends, or hear anyone. Nor did she sense that another being was near. She was alone.

Then, up ahead, in the light cast by the insects, she saw something that made her stop in her tracks.

A yellow flag was staked in the ground, its folds and falls illuminated by the bright insects. It waved in a languid draft.

Heart racing, Penny walked deliberately toward it.

She reached out and lifted a corner of the fabric. It was wrinkled and dirty, but in the middle was the frayed green stitching of the parrot, wings outstretched in flight. She recognized a small tear in the lower right corner. It was the first flag, the one she had left in Tontap.

She didn't know how or why, but Helix had been here.

Carefully she unhooked the flag from the stick it was tied to. She squeezed it and held it to her chest. In the middle distance she saw the next one, rippling in a breeze as the insects passed. She glided, feet bare, through the darkness toward it. It was the one from Jaipa. She took it down. She waited and watched the insects. The swarm zigged and zagged in a slow, halting passage through the trees up ahead. After a few minutes they illuminated another yellow oblong, the third one, which she'd raised on the message pole in Santori just the night before.

As she added the final flag to the others, she saw a light in the distance that was too bright to be from the insects.

She approached it. As she got closer, she saw that it was coming from a round and very bright whorl. It looked like a sun radiating light into the dark emptiness of space.

This time Penny didn't run.

She steadily approached it.

Its light was not the false warmth of bioluminescence or the cold brilliance of moonlight. It was sunlight that streamed in, making her blink, bathing her in afternoon heat as she came right up to the edge of the whorl.

She leaned in. When her eyes adjusted, she found herself gazing out across a long, sunny valley, at the foot of which nestled a seaside town. It was as if she were looking through a window. She instantly recognized the horseshoe amphitheater Tabba and Jebby had described to her, and at its base she could just make out what must be the great stone dial that measured the time until the Bloom. Tremendous heaps of shells, like the ones the children had seen being hauled by the elephantine creatures, glistened in middens along the shoreline, ready to absorb the brunt of the Wave. An intricate maze of trenches had been dug to divert the surge around the town, which was small, just a neat huddle of stone homes climbing up one side of the valley. Penny was looking down at Palmos.

The sea was still calm. It twinkled enticingly. A brisk breeze unfurled off it, briny and fresh. A procession of people was making its way into the town along a sun-baked white road, polished smooth by shoes and hooves and wheels whose scuffle and rumble Penny could hear, mingling with the strains of music that drifted up through the valley. She smelled the pulp of mangoes and the charred scent of meat roasting over campfires, and her mouth watered. Her feet were still in the damp muck of the jungle, but her face was in the warm, bright sunlight on the other side. Here was a way out of the gloom and fear and terrible isolation of the Gorgonne. She could step through the whorl and be among people again. She could run down to the sea and rinse off the mud of the jungle, scrub away the scent of dampness and rot, fill her lungs with the clean sea air. She could see Helix. How he had been in the Gorgonne, she didn't know, but he had staked Granny Pearl's flags in the darkness, like channel markers guiding her safely to shore, and he was down there now, in the town, waiting for her.

Safety, light, life, the comfort of other humans—all she had to do was step through.

But behind her, still in the darkness of the Gorgonne, were her friends, and the shell to capture the Bloom that both Kana and Granny Pearl so desperately needed.

Penny stepped back from the whorl.

It shivered and closed. Palmos was gone. The glowing insects that had lit her way had left. Again she was in pure darkness. She stood very still, waiting for her eyes to adjust. The panic she had felt earlier was gone and instead she felt a deep, electric calm.

Again there was nothing, only silence, then she heard a faint trill.

At first she didn't know what it was, but after a moment

she recognized the sound: It was the bell—the one from Bellamy's bicycle—that Jebby had rescued from the tree, which they had kept to return to him after the trials were over. Hope spread like warmth through her.

She followed the sound blindly through the darkness. Unseen leaves brushed her shoulders; her feet made no sound in the soft earth.

She ended up at a small whorl, glimmering softly in the loop of a low-slung vine. The sound of the bell was louder on the breeze that blew through it. Tentatively Penny reached out to touch it. She drew her hand back quickly, fingers tingling.

The mandrill would be with Tabba and Jebby. He mustn't know that she was coming. Penny looked down. She had lost her shoes during her frantic flight, and the mud of the Gorgonne squished up between her bare toes. She remembered what Helix had taught her long ago, during the boredom of a drowsy afternoon in the garden at home, and she knelt and painted her arms, legs, and clothes with mud to mask her scent. The mud was cool and dank, and smelled like old leaves and earthworms. She wiped streaks of it across her face until slowly she blended in with the jungle.

When she had finished, she wiped her hands off on her tunic.

Her goggles hung around her neck. She reached up and briefly held them. They were her grandmother's, the ones she had worn every day for years on her morning swim through the cove out to the anvil rock. After Granny Pearl had stopped swimming, Penny had taken them as her own. Neither her grandmother nor her parents had seemed to notice.

Penny lifted them up and put them over her eyes.

Taking a deep breath, she stepped into the whorl.

With a sensation that felt like passing from air to water, Penny was expunged from the night world and into the low light of the jungle, the spot where she had been when the mandrill had taken Tabba and Jebby. Everything was still the same, except that the whorl into which her friends had disappeared was gone. Penny saw the tattered net and the shuffle of footprints in the dirt from where the children had struggled. There was no sign of the mandrill's footprints. He had never left the whorl—he had simply reached out and pulled the children in. Lying tattered and trampled on the ground nearby was the spiderpod silk net. They had thought they could catch him with a simple net—how childish an idea it had been!

Penny felt a moment of panic when she realized she could no longer hear the bell.

She closed her eyes and listened.

There it was, very faintly, coming from deeper in the jungle.

She followed the sound. There were no trails and she had to fight her way through the crunching undergrowth, pausing every now and then to listen. She traced the ringing to another whorl, this one cradled in the crook of a low branch.

She went through it and, to her surprise, found herself in broad daylight on a hard mountain ledge. She caught her breath as she looked down over a sheer drop. She knew the rocks below must be boulders, but they were so far away they looked like pebbles. The atmosphere was thin, and a chill breeze buffeted the sheer stone cliffs. She was quickly cold. Goose bumps rippled over her bare arms and legs. Far below bloomed the verdant jade roof of the canopy, but all that grew where she stood was a dry frost of pewter lichen, eating acidly into the rock. Higher up the mountain it was snowing; cold flakes drifted down and melted in her hair. Fearful that a gust would blow her off the ledge, she inched along with her back against the cliff until she saw the next whorl, mercifully near, nestled beneath a blunt, stony over-hang. The wind carried the broken notes of the bell from it and whisked them out over the valley.

Penny reached the whorl and ducked quickly through. She felt a slight tingle over her skin, and then she was in another place once again. Warm golden light dappled her limbs. A robin's-egg-blue sky stretched as far as she could see. Marmalade-orange plains undulated to the horizon. Slow herds of animals grazed on it. Here and there, shad-ows were anchored to the earth beneath umbrella-shaped trees. She noticed that a tree in the distance was on fire, slow flames flapping like silk cloths in a steady breeze, but to her amazement its leaves were not burning up; the bark on its slender limbs was not charred. The animals appeared unbothered by it.

Keeping an eye on the strange fire, Penny followed the sound of the bell out across the open field. A horse cocked its ears and lifted its head to watch her, still chewing the tough russety grass. The sun was so bright that she didn't see the whorl until she was right in front of it. It was sitting on the ground, where it seemed to rock back and forth slightly, like a glassy tumbleweed that had yet to build the momentum to roll.

The horse watched her as she stepped through it and disappeared.

After that whorl, there was another and another. The newest, the ones the mandrill had opened most recently, pulsed gently, emitting a warped and dreamy glow brighter than older whorls, which lingered like ghostly morning moons. Penny didn't know whether Tabba, Jebby, and the mandrill were moving just ahead of her, or whether the sound of the bell was just echoing through the whorls, but she kept going, her exhilaration greater than her fear. She had never known such freedom. World spilled limitlessly on to world, but she always ended up back in different parts of the original jungle the children had first arrived in. This was the place the mandrill kept returning to—the real world—and then there were little side worlds off it. Geography was not a cumbersome thing in the Gorgonne. The whorls were like shortcuts: You could be in one place and then, in a split second, in another, miles away—it was like moving through memory. The Gorgonne was as rich and complicated as a mind, and Penny began to feel, in fact, that she was *in* the mandrill's mind. She began to *want* to see this creature, this spinner of worlds.

Once she saw the tribe of yellow-eyed monkeys that had tormented them before. This time they leaped out of her way to observe her from a safe distance. Another time she thought she glimpsed the lumphur, riderless, its golden flanks disappearing into the jade gloom. Right after that she lost the sound of the bell. She traipsed in circles, searching for small, accidental signposts the mandrill had left—lichen scraped off a branch, a mushroom shattered underfoot—and followed them to a whorl at the foot of a tree with pale marbled bark. But this time, instead of stepping neatly across a threshold, she found herself falling.

Penny landed with a thump on a dark, swampy patch of earth. She was in a jungle, but it was darker and muckier than anywhere she had been before. Gloomy curtains of epiphytes hung down from branches, obscuring the view. Mushrooms as large as dinner plates squatted here and there. Pale ground mist cleared to reveal a smooth boulder, swirled with patterns of jade and gypsum, as cold and clammy as something unearthed from a cave. Penny started to walk and tripped over a knotty root hidden in the mist.

Suddenly she heard leaves swishing a short distance away. Something was approaching. She stopped and stood very still and watched the figure. He was going in circles, looking like someone searching for something he had lost.

Kal had not seen her yet. He was picking his way through rotting branches, unhooking thorns from his clothes. His legs were caked in mud, and blood was dried on his arms where branches had scratched him. Penny felt a brief flash of camaraderie with him—he might be the only other soul in the Gorgonne with her, and he was there by himself, too. She shifted and a twig snapped. He froze. She was surprised by how terrified he looked. Then he saw her.

They stared at each other.

"Oh," he said in surprise. "It's you."

"Hi," Penny said awkwardly.

Kal stepped over a fallen tree trunk and made his way toward her.

"Where are Tabba and Jebby?" he asked.

"The mandrill took them," said Penny. "A whorl opened suddenly and he grabbed them."

Kal stiffened when he heard the news.

"But they're still in here somewhere," Penny said. "I've been tracking them through whorls. Jebby's been ringing the bell, the one from Bellamy's bike. . . ." She trailed off, remembering that Kal's treachery was the reason they had the bicycle bell with them in the first place. She thought of the parts of the bicycle, swinging in the breeze back in the jungle near Hopper. Had that really just been yesterday? It felt like so long ago.

"If they're ringing the bell, they're okay," said Kal. "Don't you think?"

Penny was surprised that he was trying to be reassuring. "They're okay," she said. "They have to be." She paused. "Have you seen any of the other teams?"

"Lamlo," said Kal. He climbed over a rotting log and stopped in front of her. "We had just run into each other in here when the same thing happened—a whorl opened and the mandrill reached out and grabbed him and dragged him in. I saw it happen. I hid, but later I peeked through the whorl—it went to somewhere outside the Gorgonne. What about you? Have you seen anyone else?"

"No, but before we even reached the Gorgonne we heard that Grasshopper Boy and the Dorado brothers had been kicked out," said Penny. "They gave up and headed to Palmos." She took a deep breath. "Where's Seagrape?" she asked.

"I don't know," said Kal after a moment. "I really don't. I'm sorry. I opened that whorl so quickly I don't know where it went. But there are whorls all over the place. She can go through them. . . . She can find her way back. If I could bring her back myself, I would—really."

Penny studied his face. She exhaled. She believed he was telling her the truth. Now she had to stop thinking about Seagrape before she got too upset. Kal was right; the parrot was probably making her way back at this very moment. Relieved to have the company of another person—even if it was Kal—she was eager to talk. He seemed to feel the same.

"I've been following the bell through the whorls, into all these strange places," she said. "Have you been in them, too—these other places? What are they?"

"The mandrill made them," said Kal. "Whatever he imagines, he can make real. I think that outside the Gorgonne he can only open whorls before the Bloom. But in here he's free to open them whenever he wants."

"But how does he do it?" asked Penny, taking a tentative step closer to Kal. "Are they real places?"

"You've been in them—they seem real, don't they?" said Kal. "But I think they're the way he pictures things, or remembers them, or wants them to be; that's why they're so strange. I don't know how he does it. I just know that if he imagines somewhere—if it's in his thoughts—and he wants it to be there, it's there."

"And the whorls are like doorways between them," said Penny.

"Yeah," said Kal. "Sometimes between places he's imagined or remembered, and sometimes he opens whorls to actual places—like when he shows up around Kana."

"Is that how you found the Molmer egg and the Zamzee beetle and got back to the next towns so fast?" asked Penny. "You were going through whorls?"

"I opened one straight to a Blue Pit to get the Molmer," said Kal proudly. "And the Zamzee—I just imagined a place where they were coming out of the ground. That's the only time I've been able to do that—to imagine a whole new place. They were all alive, flying all over the place, and it was hard to catch one—that's how I got stung. But I caught it and got back to Santori quickly. No one would have believed anyone could have found a beetle that fast, so I had to hide outside the town for a while."

Penny was quiet, absorbing what he had told her. Insects ticked over dead leaves. The gray light faded in the distance and the jungle pressed around them.

"Why hasn't he kicked us out?" she asked at last. "He's got all the others, so why are we still here?"

"Don't you know why?"

Penny shook her head.

"Because we can make whorls," said Kal. "We're the only ones who can."

"Not me," said Penny quickly, in surprise. "*I* can't."

"I didn't open that whorl at the line," Kal told her.

Penny stared at him, confused.

"I figured it out," he said. "We can do it because we don't belong. The mandrill doesn't. I don't. And neither do you. That's why we're the only ones who can."

For a moment Kal looked as though he was going to say something else, then his face hardened and he seemed to remember that they were competitors.

"I can't help you," he said. "I have to find the shell."

"Wait!" Penny cried.

But Kal opened a whorl and disappeared into it. It closed behind him. He was gone.

Penny was still standing there, her thoughts reeling, when she heard another whorl pop open in the trees nearby. A stick cracked and leaves rustled. Something was there. Something large.

She looked anxiously around and noticed a whorl next to her, hidden beneath a plant with broad spatulalike leaves. The whorl wasn't quite like any she'd seen before. It emitted a sickly, jaundiced light. The hairs on the back of her neck rose. But whatever was in the jungle was getting closer, so she ducked through into it to hide. She found herself alone in a small sandy burrow. Instantly and unmistakably, she sensed Kal and knew that she was in a whorl that he had made. He must have been in this same spot sometime earlier. Perhaps he had hidden from the same thing that was out there now. The ceiling was so low she had to crouch. The sand was softly, continuously collapsing around the edges. The only light came through from the jungle outside. The dank, fetid stench of decay hung in the air. It was a place made by a fearful mind, and Penny wanted to get out, but through the whorl she could hear the thing in the undergrowth coming closer. Whether it was human or animal, she wasn't sure.

Suddenly the inside of the burrow began to dim. Penny could no longer see or hear anything on the other side of the whorl. In alarm she realized that it was weak and fading; it was going to close. If she didn't get out now, she'd be trapped. The sand at the edges began falling faster. Penny tried to leave the way she had come in, but it was as if some invisible, impermeable shield were sealing the way. In desperation she hurled herself at it and tumbled out. She was back in the murky, humid jungle again. She looked around, but she was alone. She smelled ginger leaves, heard the tick of insects. A spider observed her from its thick yellow web.

She turned back to the whorl, which faded before her eyes.

The mandrill's worlds were vibrant, alive, strong, and healthy. Kal's was a stunted, lifeless hollow. Not a fully realized world, but a place made in haste by a frightened, hunted mind. It had reeked of fear and desperation. What had he been so afraid of?

Then Penny looked down and saw a footprint.

A long heel, five toes, just as Tabba had described from that day the mandrill had appeared in Tontap. He had been here. Penny's heart began to pound.

She crouched and touched it, then drew her hand back sharply. The footprint was warm.

The mud cooled beneath her hand.

And then, horribly, she knew.

She turned around very slowly.

She looked at the same patch of foliage twice before she saw him, sitting there on his haunches, watching her.

She knew that, by the time you saw a predator, the predator had seen you long before.

He observed her, but nothing in his posture suggested he was preparing to attack. He was alert but relaxed. Tabba and Jebby were not with him.

Penny remained very still.

Like every creature in Tamarind, he was a few degrees off from the animals she knew on the Outside, from a divergent branch of the same tree. He was the size of a small human man, and his head, larger than any human head, rested on a thick block of shoulders. His fur was dark, twilit blue, frosted here and there with white. He was so deft and agile as he moved through the whorls that she was surprised to find that he wasn't a young animal. But it was his face that captivated her. Its hairless skin was brightly pigmented. Oblongs and streaks of color—bright yellow, royal blue, deep green, vivid red—like a gaudy oil-paint mask. Deep blue grooves and ridges carved his cheeks. His long, pendulous nose was bright red. Blond plumes of thick, long hair—like a lion's mane—flowed on either side of his face.

As she watched him, she felt a curious kinship with the beast, solitary and misunderstood. No one in Kana knew all the rich and wonderful things in his mind, how he created these places, and how alone he was in them. And he was magnificent, with his showy colors and his deep velvety fur, his body built for speed and stealth. She respected him, admired him, even. A crazy thought went through her mind—she could just walk out in front of him, talk to him, explain her case, befriend him. But, just as she was thinking this, the mandrill grimaced and his face transformed: His lips drew back and his thick yellowed fangs lengthened. His broad oval nostrils quivered. His fearsome mask darkened. He walked forward a few paces on his knuckles. His burly warrior back was broad; his curt, devilish beard as orange as a flame; and his steely hands could surely snap her neck as if it were a matchstick. She began to sweat. The mud she had painted on her skin ran down in rivulets, but it didn't matter. The mud, like the net and the natal plums, had been futile.

She expected him to attack her but, inexplicably, he turned and walked off on all fours into the foliage.

Penny stood there trembling, unsure if he was leading her into a trap or taking her to the others—or if that was one and the same. Feeling she had no choice but to follow him, she slowly picked her way through the foliage. She maintained a respectful distance but kept sight of his silvery-blue back through the leaves. He didn't seem to object to her presence. She half wondered if he was happy for some company.

He walked into a deep fern bed. Penny pushed soft, wet ferns out of her way and followed him. The damp fronds soaked her clothes, and her feet sank into the mulchy ground. Dewy spiderwebs broke against her shoulders and the rich, rooty smell of mud rose through the low light.

Suddenly she could no longer see or hear him ahead of her.

She hurried to catch up and find the whorl she was sure he had gone through.

Mud sucked at her feet as she tramped around, peering between the thick green arches. If a whorl was there, it was hidden.

Just as she was starting to feel desperate, Penny stumbled upon it, concealed beneath the feathery bridge of a tall, stooped frond.

She stepped lightly through.

～～～

She looked down to see that her feet were no longer in mud but on sunny, stony ground, scattered with what looked like shattered glass.

Lizards basked on rocks, their puffy orange throats catching like flames. The dim, suffocating canopy was gone, and above her was a hot blue sky studded with clouds. In the jungle the foliage had been so dense that it had been impossible to see any great distance, but now her view was broken only by low scrub and, in the middle distance, a tall range of jet-black rocks. Whorls hung in the leaden sky above it. Only a lone, discordant frond, the one she had ducked beneath, stood behind her, leaning in the scrap of shade afforded by a stray boulder. She stepped out of the path of a snapping terrapin, and her feet left damp tracks on the dry ground.

She noticed that the clouds in the sky were all coming from the same place, rising from behind the range of black rocks, as if a steam engine were chugging along behind them, pumping puffy white clouds in its wake. She winced as she took a step closer and her bare foot crunched on glassy shards. She heard a low growl, and the hairs on the back of her neck stood on end. She looked up and saw the mandrill sitting on his haunches near the opening to the break in the rocks.

Quickly Penny crouched in the shadow of the boulder and peered around it.

The mandrill was eating something. She squinted and saw that it was some kind of shellfish, its shell a clear, swirled flute. Her pulse quickened. She looked down. The fragments she had stepped on weren't glass; they were broken shells. A breeze picked up, parting the steam clouds, and in a chasm between the rocks Penny glimpsed light reflecting off water. The lake—it was right here!

The breeze blew toward her, and an acrid whiff of sulfur stung her nostrils. Penny thought the lake must be some type of hot springs. Then she heard the bell trilling, clearer and closer than ever before. It sounded as though it was coming from somewhere out on the water. Tabba and Jebby were here. Penny glimpsed a small stone island in the middle of the water. Her friends were there. She had found them.

But there was no way past the mandrill. She noticed that his tracks went back and forth in front of the chasm. He was patrolling the area, guarding it. Why was he keeping them prisoner instead of expelling them as he had the other teams? Was he laying a trap for Penny? Why? She could hear him slurp as he sucked out the meat and cast the empty shell to land with a tinkle among others strewn around him. She glanced behind her, to see if she could retreat then approach from another angle, outside his range of vision, but beyond the protection of the boulder it was all open ground. The whorl she had come through weakened and sputtered out.

There was no way back and no way forward.

Penny was trapped.

Steam hissed softly from the lake.

She needed a way to get to the lake. What she needed was a whorl. She thought about what Kal had said and wondered if he could possibly be right. She remembered back to the foggy morning she had woken in the rowboat, how she had been thinking so strongly of Tamarind right before the whorl had opened.

She closed her eyes and imagined being on the other side of the black rocks.

Nothing happened.

She tried again, but when she opened her eyes she was still there, on the hot earth beside the boulder. She frowned. Kal had seemed so sure.

The idea came to her, suddenly and easily, as though she had reflexively reached out and caught a ball someone had thrown to her. Penny needed to be in another place, and she needed a way to get there. A whorl was like a door or a window between places—a sort of portal.

Penny would imagine the only portal between places she could—a real one.

She closed her eyes and imagined a place she knew inside and out, a place she knew every detail of by heart.

When she opened them, there in front of her, in the side of the boulder, was a whorl. It glowed gently and promisingly in the bright day, inviting her closer. She leaned in and saw one of the *Pamela Jane*'s portholes, fogged with steam. Penny smiled. She pushed it open and wriggled inside.

Inside the cabin of the *Pamela Jane*, it was dark: the dark of a deeply overcast day. The portholes were thick with steam, but Penny could see that she was on the other side of the black rocks, out in the middle of the lake. Through her bare feet, she could feel heat emanating through the hull. She opened the hatch and climbed onto the deck. A blast of heat almost overwhelmed her. The air smelled powerfully of sulfur.

The boat was not the real *Pamela Jane*, but a version from Penny's own mind, amplified and altered by memory. The portholes were larger than they really were; their brass sparkled as they had not in years. The mast was taller in her imagination than it was in real life, the deck broader, its warp gone. The pure white mainsail was raised, set at a broad reach.

The lake was so hot that it bubbled softly. Steam clouds lingered over its surface, reducing the world to tones of gray. Around the shore was a seamless, glittering band—a multitude of shellfish clinging to the rocks, thriving just out of reach of the simmering water. The mandrill had been prying them free, feasting on the creatures that lived inside, and discarding the empty shells, which now sparkled in heaps on narrow strands of black sand beaches. One of these shells would capture the Bloom. Penny might even have a chance to get one before she reached her friends.

On the shores and in the sky all around the lake were dozens of whorls the mandrill had made each time he had come there. They were densely clustered, some nearly transparent, others strong and bright. They looked like a cosmic sweep of galaxies, fixed in the firmament. Breezes emanated from them, and it was on these that the *Pamela Jane* was sailing.

Through the steam she heard the bicycle bell trilling invisibly. Not wanting to shout and attract the mandrill's attention, Penny stood at the wheel and turned the *Pamela Jane* to sail toward it. She tacked out of one breeze and glided blindly along until the next one caught her. The winds through the whorls were scattered and unpredictable, coming from every which way. It was tricky to make progress and almost impossible to keep on course. All she could do was turn her face to feel where the next breeze was coming from. The steam obscured her view, and she expected to crash at any moment. She abandoned the idea of getting a shell before rescuing Tabba and Jebby.

A gust cleared the air long enough for her to glimpse a bare stone island, bleached white by heat, in the center of the lake. She spotted Tabba and Jebby on its barren shore. They were not tied up; they were free and unharmed, but stranded with no way to cross the boiling water. Seeing her, Jebby stopped ringing the bell for a second before quickly resuming. They waved silently and urgently to her. Penny turned the boat toward them.

Perhaps the mandrill was alerted by the pause in the ringing, perhaps he had just returned to dine on more shells, but he appeared on the far shore, his face a colorful blot against the gray.

He saw the boat.

He stood up to his full height.

He roared.

He paced back and forth a few times, then leaped into the air.

An instant later a tremendous clanging broke out in the skies, as if all the doors in a great, sprawling house were slamming shut one after the other. In a rage, the mandrill swung from arm to arm between whorls, closing them behind him. The crashing echoed deafeningly around the lake, rattling Penny's teeth.

As the whorls shut, the winds died. Penny reached the island on a fading puff of breeze. She tucked deftly into shore, and Tabba and Jebby had just enough time to leap on board as the boat passed. The *Pamela Jane* glided a little farther and came to a stop, becalmed, in the middle of the lake.

All the whorls were closed. The sails fell slack. The air was still and silent, the surface of the lake flat. There wasn't a lick of breeze to sail on. With nothing to hurry it along, a layer of steam amassed and lay stationary. Penny felt as though the air had been sucked out of her lungs. She looked around fearfully, not knowing where the mandrill would appear from next.

A shadow passed over the deck. A moment later the boat rocked dangerously. The children seized the railings to keep their balance. Penny looked up and saw that the mandrill had jumped through a whorl and landed on the top of the mast, his burly silver shoulders lustrous, his garish mask bright against the low gray screen of sky.

"Get into the cabin!" she shouted to Tabba and Jebby.

The mandrill sprang into the air and vanished into a whorl. He reappeared in a crouch on the bow just as the children dived through the hatch and scrambled down the companionway. Penny was the last one in. As she reached up, she saw him leap across the deck, saw his blue-furred toes land inches away. She slammed the hatch shut as hard as she could.

"He'll be in here in a second," she cried breathlessly.

She ran to open a porthole. It was stiff, but she forced it open with her shoulder. Steam poured in. She slung a leg through and waved to Tabba and Jebby to follow her.

"Trust me!" she shouted. "JUMP!"

⊰ Chapter Eighteen ⊱

The Shell • Field of Snares • Palmos • Like St. Elmo's Fire

P enny hit the ground.

For a moment she was afraid that the others weren't going to follow her through the porthole, but then there was a thud followed by a second thud as first Tabba and then Jebby appeared out of thin air and rolled onto the dirt on the hillside. The children had dropped not into the bubbling boil of the hot springs but onto a patch of dry land just off a darkening road. Instantly the steam dissipated. The whorl was gone, sealed shut behind them. The mandrill had not come with them.

"Are you okay?" Penny asked.

"We're okay," said Tabba. "Are you?"

"Yes," said Penny, taking a deep breath. "I'm okay."

"What was that boat?" asked Jebby. "Where did it come from?"

"And how did we get *here*?" asked Tabba.

"It was my family's boat, from home," said Penny.

As briefly as she could, she explained how she had met Kal in the Gorgonne, and her discovery that she, too, could open whorls. Tabba and Jebby listened in amazement.

Slowly the children became aware of their new surroundings. A frog disturbed by their arrival hopped deeper into the foliage. Voices came from the nearby road. People passed, heading down the hill, not noticing the children in the trees. The evening breeze was briny—they were near the sea. It cooled the children's skin, still flushed and sweaty from the hot springs. With a sinking feeling, Penny realized that they had left the Gorgonne without getting a shell. In the panic to escape from the mandrill, she had forgotten all about it.

But Tabba was taking something out of her bag. She peeled back cushioning layers of cloth and carefully handed an object to Penny.

Relief and elation flooded Penny as she saw what it was.

"You got one," she said softly. She took a shaky breath.

The shell from the shores of the boiling lake was a hollow spiral flute. Its glossy swirls lapped one another, tapering to a fine point. It was smooth and cool, clear as crystal. Little clouds of condensation were still caught in it from the steam of the springs.

"Thank you," she said.

"It isn't the only one," said Jebby, getting to his feet. "There were thousands there. Kal could already be in Palmos with one of them. It could all be over already."

Tabba stood up and peered through the trees.

"We're on top of a hill," she said. "I think I can see the amphitheater. Palmos is right down there in the valley."

The three of them hurried to the road, but as soon as they reached it they stopped dead in their tracks. The trees had broken and exposed the sky over a broad valley. Not even the whorl that had unleashed the dust storm over Santori could have prepared the children for the sight before them now.

Like a weather front that had moved in and stalled were dozens, maybe hundreds, of dark whorls in the pale violet sky over the valley. Some were small, some huge—bigger even than the dust-storm whorl in Santori. Some were static, others trembled. A few swirled restlessly. Most of the whorls the children had seen before were blurred patches, smudges that blended in with the background and were often almost impossible to detect. But there was no missing these. They were dense and opaque. The sky looked like a field set with dark snares.

Penny knew that the mandrill had opened each one of them and could be looking down from anywhere. His oppressive presence weighed heavily on the valley.

It wasn't until the children started down the hill that they noticed that it was full of people. Families huddled together, looking up at the whorls, arms around one another's shoulders. Subdued children burrowed in their parents' laps. Never had such a large festival crowd been so quiet. There was no strumming or drumming, no voices lifted in song, no celebration at all. Cooking fires dotted the valley here and there, and the air was hazy with smoke. There was a feeling of temporary stillness, of suspense, as though the whorls were storm clouds about to burst.

People were so focused on the whorls, eyes turned up to the sky, that the children passed undetected through the gathering darkness. The limestone crescent of the amphitheater held the last of the light. The navy-blue sea reposed at the foot of the valley. Tremendous middens were heaped along the shoreline, burnished orange in the last of the sunset, like the studded backs of monstrous crocodiles rising for a breath. Torches were being lit in the town, and the wagging flames seemed to suck up the last of the daylight, concentrating it, while the rest of the air grew darker.

Finally someone saw the children and pointed. The crowd melted away to let them through, opening a path to the Council of Elders.

The Council was assembled on a large, flat tablet of stone at the base of the amphitheater. Beside them was the stone dial. Its single chiseled hand, the length of a man, was pointed almost directly north, like an arrow tensed to leave the bow. Blooms past had described a deepening circle into the rocky tablet with each slow, grinding revolution of its hand. In mere hours from now, its latest turn would be complete.

Penny raised the shell over her head as she approached.

In the crowd, faces waxy from the day's sweat glowed in the torchlight. Mouths were open in small dark Os.

It's the child from the Outside!

She has a shell!

Is that really it? Does she really have it?

Penny handed the shell to Elder. The other councilmen gathered closer to examine it.

Elder looked up at the children. "You've done it," he said simply.

The children were too overwhelmed to speak. The whorls temporarily forgotten, the crowd near the platform shuffled and murmured restlessly, pressing close to try to see what was happening. Everything felt surreal to Penny, as if she were in a dream and things were happening outside her control. She tried to pay attention to what Elder was saying. Though he was just feet away, his voice sounded as if it were coming from a great distance.

"Tomorrow morning you'll walk—alone—to the Great Wave and gather the Bloom," he said. "The Wave will hold firm while one person enters and then leaves it. After that you'll have just enough time to return safely to shore with the Bloom before it breaks. You'll immediately pour the Bloom into the Coral Basin. Do you understand?"

"Yes," said Penny breathlessly. "Except I don't know where the Coral Basin is—"

"The Coral Basin will only be revealed tomorrow, after the Wave," said Elder. "You'll spend the night in contemplation, as the Bloom Catcher always has. The Council will come to collect you in the morning."

The static roar of the crowd was growing louder. Elder

nodded to two men in red silk robes, who approached the children. Then he turned to the crowd and proclaimed: "The child from the Outside is the Bloom Catcher!"

For a split second, silence fell over the valley. After all the preparations and festivities, the tracking of favorites since the first feats were done, the thrilling tales of the grueling trials, after all the miles crossed by players and ordinary people alike, it was done: A winner had been declared. And the unlikeliest of winners, at that—a young girl, an Outsider. People could not hide their disbelief. But quickly all distinguishing facts about Penny melted away, and she became a pure thing: the Bloom Catcher, the one who tomorrow would gather the Bloom and banish the mandrill back to the Gorgonne, who would close the whorls and restore Kana to safety and prosperity. A single shout went up and soon the whole valley erupted in celebration that echoed up to the whorls above, making them tremble like spiders in a giant web.

Penny felt the men in red robes lift her onto their shoulders. She reached desperately for Tabba and Jebby but was swept up and carried, feeling suddenly seasick, over the heads of the jubilant crowd and along the main street onto an empty road along the coast.

Penny was taken to a tiny palm hut on the shore of a lagoon. The people who had taken her returned to the town. The hut was a single, spare room, with a porch that faced the lagoon and a few stray palms, and, beyond them, the open sea. A meal had been left under a basket on the porch for her: a yellow bed of cassava with translucent onions, leafy vegetables, and the tiny bright bubbles of sea eggs. She had eaten ravenously, wiping the plate clean.

After she had eaten and explored around the hut, she had nothing to do, so she wandered to the end of the porch and sat down. It was fully dark now, the sky littered with stars. The whorls were concentrated far away, in the distance over the valley, and away from them the air felt fresher. Penny could see back to the road that ran through thick cane fields. Here and there were the flickering torchlights of guards posted along the route. She wished Tabba and Jebby were there, and she wondered where Seagrape was and if she was safe. A thought occurred to her and made her heart quicken: Maybe Seagrape had found Helix. It was possible. The three flags were still in Penny's backpack. She knew he was out there somewhere.

The sea purring softly against the smooth stones of the lagoon slowly lulled her, soothing her racing, disjointed thoughts. She closed her eyes. She was the Bloom Catcher. It still didn't seem real.

But it was. Her grandmother's health would be restored. Everything at home would go back to the way it had been. Penny sent a silent message out across the dark sea: *I'm coming home soon and I'm bringing the Bloom for you.*

But first there was the Wave.

It seemed impossible to believe that tomorrow the sea,

so deceptively peaceful, would rise up into a monstrous wall of water. She wondered nervously what it would be like to dive into it. And what would the Bloom look like? She remembered what the others had said that first day they had picked her up in the boat: pollen, blue-green fires, glowing sand. What if it wasn't like any of those things?

The moon came out and lit the cane like a silver sea. An insect ticked in the palm fronds, and the sea swished gently on the rocks. The cane grass stirred.

"Penny!"

Penny saw Jebby's face poking through the grass. He hissed her name again. She looked both ways. "No one's here," she said, beaming. "Come on!"

Tabba and Jebby slipped out of the cane grass and dashed across the clearing to the porch.

"There are guards posted all along the road!" said Jebby. "We had to sneak all the way here through the cane."

"I'm so happy to see you!" cried Penny.

"They took you away so fast," said Jebby. "We had to wish you luck before tomorrow."

"And we brought this for you, from Ma," said Tabba. "She and Da are here, with all the little ones."

She handed Penny a few slices of sweet bread wrapped in a banana leaf, the same kind Ma Silverling had given them the morning they had left for the first trial. Penny felt a pang—she was glad her friends had reunited with their family, but she couldn't let herself think of her own, not yet, not until she was actually on her way home. She shared the bread with Tabba and Jebby, then tore off a piece for herself.

The children had not had time to really see one another since their escape from the Gorgonne, and now they shared in more detail everything that had happened after the mandrill had seized Tabba and Jebby. Tabba and Jebby described to Penny their dizzying flight through the whorls, each of them tucked beneath one of the mandrill's arms, until finally he deposited them on the tiny stone island in the middle of the boiling lake. And Penny told them about finding the flags from Helix, and about meeting Kal, and the strange whorls she had passed through.

"So Helix really is here!" said Tabba, looking suddenly starstruck.

"I'm impressed you went through all those whorls in the Gorgonne by yourself," said Jebby. "You're brave, Penny."

A large wave lapped the shore, its foam white in the moonlight.

"Can you believe that in the morning you're going to walk out to the Wave?" said Tabba. "Are you scared?"

"No," said Penny. "Well, a bit. I wish we were all going together. It doesn't seem fair—we did the trials together."

"It's fair," said Jebby. "You were the one who did the feat. We would never have been able to do anything if you hadn't crossed the Blue Line."

"To tell you the truth, I'm glad we just get to watch from shore," said Tabba. "I can't imagine going out to meet the Wave. The three trials were enough for me."

"We've been invited to sit with the Council of Elders," added Jebby proudly.

Penny was relieved to see that her friends harbored no secret wish to be the ones walking out to the Wave. They'd come as far as they needed to. She was the one who had really wanted the Bloom all along.

"What about Kal?" she asked. "Have you seen him?"

"We heard he got here a little while after we did, but when he found out that we were already here, he ran off," said Jebby. "No one's seen him since then, but I'm sure he's skulking around somewhere nearby. There's no way he won't want to see the Wave, even if he isn't the Bloom Catcher."

"I almost feel sorry for him," said Tabba. "Almost. Then I think about everything he did—or tried to do—to us."

"Try to forget about him tonight," said Jebby. "Tonight we should just be happy."

"One thing," said Penny. "I still don't know what or where the Coral Basin is."

"No one does," said Jebby cheerfully. "It's hidden until after the Wave. We found that out for you, at least."

At a sound from the road, Tabba and Jebby hopped lightly to their feet.

"We'd better go," said Jebby. "That may be a guard coming. We aren't supposed to be here! Good luck tomorrow, Penny."

"Yes, good luck," said Tabba. "It's going to be amazing. Tomorrow morning you'll have the Bloom!" She hugged Penny, and then she and Jebby disappeared into the cane.

Penny held her breath, but no one else approached.

She felt lonely after Tabba and Jebby had left. She looked up at the hills where the whorls were clustered ominously. She thought about Kal, out there somewhere, licking his wounds. The lagoon shone, still as black glass. The tide was seeping out slowly. The sound of the people in the valley was a distant buzz only when the wind carried it, and the campfires on the black silhouettes of the hills seemed as far away as the stars.

She looked back at the road. She had thought that maybe . . . but, no, there was no one there. She didn't know if he would show up. He had disappeared once before without saying good-bye. He could do it again. She took out the three flags and hung them from the railing of the porch— a welcome—and sat down to wait.

Before long, she heard the sound of wings. In the moonlight she saw the parrot zigzagging like St. Elmo's fire over the cane, keeping pace with the person walking hidden through the tall grass below.

The parrot left the cane and landed lightly on the porch beside Penny, then flew to her shoulder and nuzzled her cheek. Relief and joy washed powerfully over Penny, and she thought she might weep.

"You're all right," she whispered.

She pressed her face against Seagrape's soft feathers and listened to the beloved rumbling sound the parrot made when she was happy.

The cane at the edge of the clearing stirred, almost

imperceptibly. It didn't rustle madly like when Tabba and Jebby had come through. The person moving through it now was as silent as a cat. Penny felt her heart thud in her chest.

She got to her feet, Seagrape still on her shoulder, and watched as he stepped out into the moonlight.

"Hello," she said.

⤜ Chapter Nineteen ⤛
Strangers • A Deep, Old Familiarity • World in Transition

Helix had been a teenager the last time Penny had seen him. Now he was a grown man. He was clean-shaven, but his cheeks were paler than the rest of his face, so she knew he'd had a beard he'd shaved only recently, perhaps that same day. His clothes were shabby but clean. His fingernails had been freshly scrubbed. Still, there was some suggestion of transience about him, of someone not wholly settled in the world.

Penny studied him, reconciling the omissions and exaggerations of memory with the real person in front of her, at once utterly different and exactly the same. She remembered how he used to hoist her onto his shoulders to lift her into the branches of the orange tree, and part of her wanted to run and jump into his arms like she used to. But it was painfully obvious to both of them: They were strangers to each other now. She saw him look behind her, saw him quickly hide his disappointment when he saw she was there on her own.

Neither of them spoke, and Penny began to be afraid that after thinking about him and missing him for so long they would have nothing to say to each other. Maybe the person so vivid in her mind all these years was only a figment, about to be dispelled. After this they would go their separate ways without even the daydream of something still to come.

"You found them," he said at last, nodding to the flags.

"In the Gorgonne," said Penny quickly, grateful he had spoken. "Where you left them for me."

"After Seagrape found me outside Santori, she flew through a whorl and I followed her, and it took me there," he said.

"Did you see the mandrill?" Penny asked.

"I did. Did you?"

"Yes."

They stared at each other, awkward and halting, but allowing the shared experience of the dark, strange place and its solitary creator to connect them for a moment.

Suddenly in the distance rain bucketed down from a whorl over the valley. Lightning lit the silvery tips of the cane and illuminated the veil of rain, and thunder reverberated off the hills. It broke their awkwardness.

"They're still mostly quiet now," said Helix. "But every now and then one of them opens up and startles everyone. Snow was coming through another of them earlier today—actual snow. And this evening there was a deluge high in the hills that caused a landslide down the coast."

"After tomorrow they'll be gone," said Penny. "At least . . . I hope so."

"They will," said Helix. He smiled at her. "Because you're the Bloom Catcher."

His smile encouraged Penny. "When I was in the Gorgonne, I remembered everything you taught me about tracking," she said. "About finding marks in the moss and looking for just part of an animal in the trees, like a puzzle piece."

"You remember that?" asked Helix. "You were so little!"

He came closer to the porch. After a moment they both sat down on the stairs. They faced the lagoon, but Penny sneaked glances at him. If, before she had seen him, Helix had existed in a fond blur in her memory, being reunited with him brought everything about him back to the surface of her mind, and almost instantly she remembered a thousand tiny things about him.

"Everyone still talks about you," she said.

Helix smiled at that. "I still think about all of you, too," he said. "At first I thought that maybe Maya and Simon might have come back with you."

"No," said Penny. "Just me. But they're coming home for a visit next week."

"For a visit?" asked Helix. "That means they don't live there anymore," he murmured to himself. "I figured Maya wouldn't, but I never knew where to picture her," he said to Penny. "How is everyone? Simon? Your parents? Granny Pearl?"

Penny told him about everyone. When she got to Granny Pearl, she began to explain that was why she had come, to get the Bloom for her, but she felt a lump in her throat and stopped.

"So that's why you're here," said Helix. "Don't worry," he said kindly. "You'll be taking some of it home for her very soon."

A breeze whispered through the cane and stirred the surface of the lagoon, and moonlight wrinkled its shallow floor. Slowly they were falling into an easy rapport—a deep, old familiarity still existed and was coming back to life.

"My old shark's tooth necklace," said Helix, noticing it around Penny's neck. "How did you get it? I left it for Maya."

"I, um, borrowed it," said Penny.

"Borrowed?"

"Well, when she moved out she left it," said Penny. "In a drawer."

"Oh," Helix said, frowning. "Well, it's not something that she'd wear anymore. She probably only wears beautiful things." He paused. "It's not something I would give to her *now*."

"She wore it for ages," said Penny quickly. "Even in the shower. And she *did* keep it."

"Or she just forgot it was there," muttered Helix.

"She used to write letters to you, in her diary," Penny said suddenly.

"And how do you know *that*?" Helix asked.

"I guess that means you don't want to know what she wrote," said Penny.

Helix laughed. "All right, you've got me," he said. "I'm curious. What *did* Maya have to say?"

Suddenly Penny felt a glimmer of betrayal—late, she knew—but powerful nonetheless. She had veered into grounds of sisterly disloyalty with no safe retreat. She hadn't seen Helix in so long—why was she telling him all this?

"She missed you," she said. "That's about it. We all missed you."

"For someone who goes snooping around reading someone else's diary, you're being very secretive all of a sudden," said Helix.

"She missed you *a lot*," said Penny. "That's what she wrote about."

"And when was the last time she wrote that?" Helix demanded.

"I don't know," said Penny. "Three or four years ago. Before she left home."

"A lot changes in three or four years," said Helix.

They fell quiet. A breeze rustled the palms. The sound of surf breaking over rocks, invisible in the darkness, carried across the water every few moments.

"Well," said Penny. "After tomorrow it won't matter."

"What do you mean?"

"You can see her yourself," said Penny. "After I get the Bloom, when we go home."

Helix just looked at her.

"You're coming with me, aren't you?" she asked.

He didn't speak for a minute, keeping his gaze out over the dark water.

"For a little while, after I saw the second flag, I thought so," he said at last. "But no . . . I can't go back with you."

Penny felt confused. Somehow she would have understood if Helix had never even shown up at the hut. But now that he had, now that they had been talking as though no time had passed, now that it was obvious to her how much he still thought about Maya, she had believed, suddenly and surely, that the whole purpose of their finding each other again was so that he could come home with her, as if everything had been leading up to this all along.

"I thought—" she began.

"Going back would be . . ." Helix paused and shook his head. "It's a crazy idea."

"What's so crazy about it?" asked Penny.

"This is my home," said Helix. "I belong here. What would I even do on the Outside?"

"See Maya," said Penny.

"And then what?" asked Helix.

"I don't know," said Penny. "You'd figure something out."

Helix laughed. "It's that easy, is it?"

"Maybe," said Penny.

Suddenly Helix was angry. "And what makes you think Maya wants to see me?" he asked.

Penny thought about how he hadn't found her after he had seen the first flag. Or the second. He had waited. Not because he hadn't wanted to see her. He was scared. He could come back to the Outside with her, but what if Maya no longer cared? Penny felt the grip of a new type of fear, one she'd never felt before, that didn't have to do with beasts or darkness or physical peril, or even the fear of losing her grandmother.

Helix's flash of anger had passed quickly.

"The whole time I watched you all sail away, I was afraid I'd made a terrible mistake," he said. "I believed that for a long time after. There hasn't been a single day that I haven't thought about all of you."

He paused.

"Your sister was my first real friend," he said quietly. "I've never had a friend like her. But we were kids when we knew each other. Things move forward, not backward. I can't go back. Too much has changed."

The tide had begun to recede and the sound of the surf was farther away.

"That's why you could," said Penny at last. "Because enough has changed."

They sat in silence, then Helix got to his feet.

"Now's not the time to talk about this," he said. "I'm happy I saw you tonight, Penny." He hugged her. "Now you need to get some rest before tomorrow. You don't have the Bloom yet, you know. I'll stay nearby tonight. Just in case. Seagrape will be with you. I'll see you after the Bloom, to say good-bye. I promise I won't run off this time. Get some sleep."

Seagrape murmured from her perch on the steps beside them. Helix stroked her silky head before he disappeared back into the cane.

Penny stayed sitting on the step for a while longer. It had been so good to see Helix, but now she felt crushed— more disappointed than she would have been if she had never seen him again at all.

"This can't be all there is," she whispered to Seagrape. "It just feels wrong."

Finally she went into the hut and lay down on the grass mat. Seagrape followed, warbling softly, begrudging but submissive. She let Penny pull her close and tuck her under one arm as she had when Penny was a small girl. When Penny finally slept and her arm fell slack, Seagrape wriggled free and hopped out to sit on the porch railing in the fresh air. As the tide ebbed, the shore shifted invisibly outward in the dark. The world was in transition, unfinished. Over the valley the whorls gathered thickly in the sky, more with each passing hour, and people slept fitfully beneath them.

PART THREE

❧ Chapter Twenty ❧

The Great Wave

Penny woke soon after dawn. The smell of the moss exposed by the receding tide had grown stronger in the night, and the air was pungent and briny. She heard the clatter of hundreds of beaks against the middens. She hurried onto the porch and drew in her breath. It had begun! In the gray light she saw that the tide had crept out in the night and the lagoon was drained, the damp shock of its soft fans and mosses and coral exposed to the air for the first time. Though she had expected it, it still felt unreal. Beyond the lagoon the milky-blue sea was receding slowly, like a storm in reverse.

In the distance she saw that the whorls had proliferated overnight and were now packed together in the sky over the town. They seemed to suck the air out of the day, and it felt hard to take in a full breath. It was morning, but the light seemed already to be fading. The cane grass looked wan. Not a blade turned or tassle shook. There was a feeling of airlessness, like before a storm.

Penny saw a woman approaching on the road through the eerie light, hurrying, carrying a bundle tucked under her arm.

"Good morning, Bloom Catcher," she said as she reached the hut. She bowed her head respectfully, a little in awe of Penny. "It's time to get ready—the elders are on their way to escort you!" She put a basket of bread down by the door, then carried a jug of water into the hut and poured it into a basin for Penny to wash.

Penny splashed her face with water and did her best to unsnarl her hair with her fingers. She put on her bathing suit and pushed her goggles up over her forehead. She ate quickly, too nervous to really taste anything. One of the councilmen was blowing the triton. The faint sound drifted through the window, growing louder as it got closer. Penny returned to the porch, where the woman was waiting with a bright bolt of cloth.

"This was made for you," said the woman, shaking out the fabric. "The Bloom Catcher always wears a cape out to the Wave. Before you dive in, let it drop from your shoulders."

The ceremonial cape was made of heavy plum-colored silk that glistened in the light. Lustrous tellin shells were stitched into a swirling pattern on its back, and the hem was weighted with heavier, iridescent oyster shells. The woman lifted it over Penny's back and tied it under her chin. Penny felt a strange, deep calm as the weight of it settled on her shoulders. She could see the Council of Elders approaching the hut on the dirt road. They were dressed in their festival finery, robes bejeweled with shells and fringed with colored palm fibers. The bald dome of Elder's head had been polished with oil and it shone in the dull light. He carried a crooked, knotty staff, which he banged on the ground when he stopped in front of the hut.

"Good morning, Bloom Catcher," he said briskly. "Are you ready?"

"I'm ready," said Penny, though her heart was already pounding.

She went down the steps and walked with the Council toward the town.

Along the edge of the coast, people had strung nets between the trees to catch fish that would be tossed up when the Great Wave broke. The shells of the midden breaks were pale and luminous. The maze of deep channels dug to absorb the Wave and deflect it back to sea lay shadowed and empty, waiting for the rush of foaming surf to fill them. At the base of the valley she could see the great hand of the stone dial. It had shifted in the night and was now just a hair's breadth from finishing its long sweep.

At first Penny thought that a flock of thousands of birds had gathered on the steep hillsides above the town, but as she drew nearer she realized that the figures were people crammed together on the long, mossy stone benches of the amphitheater. The theater twinkled with the constant glint and flash of bits of magnifying shells raised to see the Wave. Penny searched in the crowd for Tabba and Jebby but couldn't see them, or Kal, either. Her chest felt tight.

The light was not like morning at all but like the weird light of an eclipse. Whorls jammed the sky. There was a disturbance—a sudden gust of wind from one of them brought icy bullets of hail that scattered the jittery people below. As quickly as it started, the hail ceased, but the people were slow to return, leaving a gap in the crowd.

During the walk into the town, Penny had been purposely kept from facing the sea, but when they turned the final bend that brought them to the foot of Palmos she caught her first glimpse of it.

The tide had receded dramatically and the bay was empty. Where water usually was there was only rocks and sand, still wet and shiny, its nakedness new and shocking. When Penny looked out to see where the water had gone, her legs began to tremble.

A few hundred yards from shore, a towering pewter wall stood straight up from the sand. The Great Wave. It was still building. With each second that Penny watched, it loomed taller and farther from the town. It was spectacular, perhaps one hundred feet long and already fifty high, a vast bolt of gray silk flung improbably skyward. She had never seen anything so tremendous, so intimidating, could not have imagined that something so powerful and seemingly impossible could be real.

Elder handed her a spear, its tip a chunk of polished black stone chiseled to a fierce point, and a single kelp pod.

"The spear is to protect yourself in the water," he said. "And the kelp pod—when the air in it is used up, you'll know you have only moments to leave the Wave before it comes tumbling down."

Then he unwrapped the mandrill's shell from a cloth. It was crystal clear; not a single fingerprint smudged it. An orange sea sponge corked it. A gold string had been tied to an aperture near its top. Penny bowed as Elder put it over her head.

"You'll catch the Bloom in this," he told her. "On the way out, stay calm. Don't go too fast or too slow. You need to reach the Wave at the right moment. Once you're there, don't delay—dive in at once."

"All right," whispered Penny, her gaze fixed on the receding water. She felt sick and nervous. What if she didn't reach the Wave exactly when she was supposed to? Or if she ran out of air before she had gathered the Bloom? And would she even know what the Bloom was when she saw it? But Elder had no more advice for her.

He put his hand on her shoulder and squeezed it. "Good luck."

Drums rolled on the shore behind her as Penny walked out to the Wave. She used them to keep her footsteps measured. *Step, step, step.* Steady beats in the glossy sand. The rest of the world faded away.

The pace of the receding tide quickened and Penny walked more determinedly to keep up with it. The wet sand was hard under her bare feet. She walked past the middens, out past reefs lustrous and dripping in the weak light, plastered with limp sea fans and capped with mustard-yellow brain coral. A few fish left behind struggled on the sand, flapping and flailing. From the corner of her eye, Penny saw them get snatched up by diving seabirds. The Wave itself was like a celestial gray screen, empty before the action started. The air pressure changed as the water was drawn up and Penny felt her ears popping. Then the Wave stopped building and—improbably and magnificently—stood where it was.

Penny had almost reached it. She looked up at the sheer wall, dizzied by its height.

The sun came out suddenly, dazzlingly, through a crack in the clouds, injecting potent, dangerous color into the world. The Wave looked like the glassy face of a great aquamarine jewel.

Don't be afraid, she told herself. *Dive through.*

She pulled her goggles down over her eyes. She shrugged her shoulders and the cape slid off and fell at her feet. Without breaking her stride, she took a last long breath, raised her arms over her head, pressed her hands together, and pointed her fingers. She didn't hesitate.

She dived.

The first thing she felt was the cool water all over her body, a pleasant shock after the heat in the air outside. She opened her eyes.

The outside day was gone, the crowd on the hillside, the sounds of the drums. Penny saw a few fish in spinning schools, illuminated in the murky distance. A lone turtle swam past.

The first eruption of Bloom happened near her—a brief, mesmerizing blaze that hovered for a second before a school of silver fish bulleted through, devouring it before it could dissipate.

The next patch of Bloom burst open, and then everything began to happen quickly. The creatures waiting in the wings exploded forth into a feeding frenzy. An eel rippled past. A nervous school of squid veered here and there, changing colors each instant. Turtles appeared, gobbling the sudden profusion of jellyfish. A shark sliced through a huge shoal of yellow fish, and the fish spun away like fallen leaves swirling up from the pavement in the wind. Penny gripped the spear. Above her, distorted by the lens of water, she could see seabirds circling and diving, wings folded into their bodies at the moment of impact, silver bubbles clinging to their feathers as they torpedoed underwater. Creatures zipped and zoomed through the clouds of blue-green phosphorescence. It was a wild, unstoppable torrent of life.

Bursts of Bloom were happening all around, but Penny wasn't quick enough for the first few—fish and animals got

341

them first, bumping into her in their haste. A sailfish shot past and nearly knocked the shell from her neck. A razor-beaked bird almost dived right onto her.

The breath she had come into the Wave with had run out, so she took another from the kelp pod. When the next turquoise cloud burst open right beside her, she was ready. Swiftly she uncorked the shell, keeping it tilted upside down so the air stayed in it. Then she turned it upright inside the patch of Bloom. With a *glug-glug* the air was released— silvery bubbles juddering up toward the surface—and the Bloom filled the shell.

Penny replaced the sea-sponge cork and swam away. The water behind her cleared, but the mixture inside the shell glowed with rich green light. That was it. She had it. She kicked toward the face of the Wave. Elder had said she would have just enough time to return to shore before the Wave came tumbling down. But she was eager to get out.

She neared the glassy wall. She saw the flat sand on the other side of it that ran all the way to the shore and the distant blur of the steep green hills. In just a moment she would be in the open air again.

As she watched, a whorl opened on the sand and a figure appeared out of it, stumbled, and began running, barefoot and bare-chested, toward the wall.

He wasn't the Bloom Catcher, but he was coming to get the Bloom anyway.

Kal never stopped running. He dived cleanly through the prism of blue.

Penny watched as he opened his eyes and gazed around him in wonder. He hovered there, stunned and awed as flares of emerald Bloom continued to erupt everywhere. For several seconds nothing happened, and Penny thought that perhaps nothing would, perhaps any number of people could have come through the wall with no consequence.

But then a deep rumbling tremor traveled through the water. The wall was no longer stable. Fish quivered, looking around with alarmed eyes before shooting off in schools and disappearing into the blue. Turtles fled. An octopus beside Penny turned midnight blue, transformed its body into a long jet, and zoomed away. All the creatures were escaping. Penny felt herself being tugged up through the water. She looked down to see a giant shadow spreading from the base of the Wave out across the sand. She realized the shadow was from the Wave itself—the wall of water had begun to curl. In moments it would collapse and tons of water would crash down and charge toward the shore. She took the last breath from the kelp pod and let it go.

The birds had ceased diving and returned to the sky. The last of the fish had left for deeper water. It was just Penny and Kal suspended there. With no creatures to eat them, the bursts of Bloom multiplied like stars exploding in an empty solar system. Penny dropped her spear and motioned frantically to Kal to swim deeper, where they would be safer until after the Wave broke, but he was fumbling with a small vial in which he was trying to capture a cloud of Bloom. But it was already too late to try to escape.

The water was too powerful. Penny and Kal were being swiftly drawn up toward the gathering crest. Far below, the dark shadow of the Wave spread on the sand, creeping toward Palmos.

Seconds before it crashed, Penny opened a whorl.

It shone, a trembling mercurial hoop, like a bubble ring rising up from the deep.

As the Wave lost its balance and began toppling, she seized Kal's hand and kicked through.

She and Kal were suspended in some sort of empty, colorless cloud—not a fully realized world, just some interim, emergency space. They looked at each other, but before they could speak, they were shunted out of wherever they were and back into the Wave, which had just crashed. The whorl had spared them the brunt of it, but the water was charging up the shore. Instantly they were separated in the violent tumble. There was no use trying to swim. Penny opened her eyes in her goggles once, but there was so much sand clouding the water that she couldn't see anything. The lights of the Bloom had gone out. She felt air on her face for a split second and was able to gasp before she was pulled back down into the dark chaos.

Helix

From the amphitheater he saw the wall of water with a single figure in it, legs kicking froglike. He saw birds wheeling above the water and the shadowed huddles of creatures waiting in the depths. He had come to see the Great Wave, and now, of all impossible things, he was watching Penny in it. Pride and fear mixed in him, rising in his throat. When the first burst of blue-green phosphorescence erupted near her, he fought to see over the sea of bobbing heads to keep her in sight. She couldn't hear the noise of the crowd, he knew.

Everyone was so absorbed by the spectacle of the Wave and the silent pandemonium happening within it that only a few noticed the whorl appear suddenly on the sand. Helix's heart lurched when he saw the boy charge out of it.

By the time Kal punched through the wall of water seconds later, everyone in the amphitheater and surrounding hills had seen him. The wall lost its gravity-defying solidity and became an elastic blue curve stretching higher before beginning to curl over onto itself.

Helix stood on his feet as the crowd did and was part of their collective gasp of horror as they watched the two figures being dragged like rag dolls toward the crest. He began to push through people, leaping over the mossy slabs of the amphitheater, fighting to keep her in sight.

Swim, he willed her.

The water came down.

He began to run toward the sea.

⁂ Chapter Twenty-One ⁂

"Wake up," said the voice.

Penny opened her eyes and felt a breeze on her face. Her nose and throat stung from the salt. The world was sideways, which after a moment she realized was because she was lying on the ground. There was a deep, ceaseless growling overhead, as if the sky were full of planes. She felt waterlogged and light-headed. Sand was in her mouth, her scalp, her ears. She blinked it off her lashes and tried to lift her head, but it felt as heavy as a stone. Why was the day so dark? She sank back groggily onto the sand and closed her eyes. Everything felt confusing.

She heard the voice again, though she no longer knew if it was really a voice outside her body, or only her own weary mind.

"Wake up," it repeated urgently.

"Open your eyes," said the voice.

With effort, for her body was stiff and sore, Penny propped herself up on one elbow. The world righted itself. The Wave had deposited her onto a broad sandbar. Water shivered in the hollows of the ripples in the sand. Kal was nowhere to be seen. Her eyelids felt heavy and she began nodding off again. What was that sound and why wouldn't it stop? Penny felt like a very tiny creature, an ant, inside a conch, the roar of a false sea in her ears. She felt a sharp nip on her ankle, felt feathers brush her skin.

Penny opened her eyes. Seagrape perched on a weathered piece of driftwood, fanning Penny with her wings.

"Is that you talking?" Penny asked lazily. "I always thought you could but just wouldn't."

"You're running out of time," the parrot said urgently. "Look where you are."

She nipped Penny's ankle again, then flew up into the sky.

Penny watched her go. At once fear penetrated her fog. She scrambled upright and looked all around. She was at the bottom of some kind of vortex, a tunnel whose sides were made of whorls, spinning madly, crowding one another.

Now she was terribly awake. She spat out a mouthful of grit and struggled to sit up all the way. She grasped for the string around her neck. The shell was there. The Bloom was safe. It glowed softly, a lone, tiny beacon in the dim day. She clasped it to her chest.

Her grandmother's goggles were gone.

At the same instant that she realized this, a tremendous boom came from the sky, as if there had been a great collision. Penny looked up. A larger whorl had swallowed a smaller one, and as she watched, another collapsed into it, unable to resist its gravity. Seagrape circled, a green scrap aloft on the cacophony of winds.

"This way," she called.

She tilted her wings and dived toward a small tower of stone a short distance away. Penny got weakly to her feet and stood swaying. She still had the sensation that she was being tumbled in the Wave. She staggered crookedly after Seagrape. The whorls were growing denser and darker. The light dimmed with each step and the wind rose. Penny leaned into it. As she drew closer she realized what the rocky outcrop was.

The Coral Basin.

It hadn't been on the map because it had been buried for so long, its precise location forgotten until the force of the Wave had dislodged sand and sediment to reveal it: a tiny castle of old coral, with ivory crags and turrets as high as Penny's shoulders. Nestled between its towers was a deep, porous bowl, carved out of the stone by other hands long before even Elder had been born.

The wind through the whorls was growing louder and stronger, pushing Penny back. She had to grab onto the edge of the stone.

Seagrape flew in sharp, agitated jags back and forth, pecking at the wind with her beak.

"The Bloom!" she cried. "The Bloom!"

Penny uncorked the shell, grasping the sea sponge tightly so the wind wouldn't pluck it out of her hands. She cupped the shell, as though she were sheltering a small flame. She tipped it, pouring all but a few drops of the Bloom into the basin. It soaked into the porous rock almost at once, leaving a fine crystal precipitate that began to multiply in long daggers that crackled like a fire coming to life. Penny felt a tremor under her feet. The day grew so dark she could barely make out the silhouette of the coral outcrop beside her.

There was a thundering metallic racket in the sky, explosion upon explosion, as if a battle was going on overhead. A blinding blaze of light gripped the air. Penny smelled sulfur and burning, felt a confusing welter of sensations wash over her. She crouched and closed her eyes and shielded her face with her arm, still clutching the shell. The violence in the sky crescendoed, then—suddenly and completely—it ceased. There was silence.

When Penny could open her eyes again, at first all she could see was a misty-blue afterglow from the flash of light. Slowly the world became clear again.

She stood beneath a dazzling sky, empty except for a few woolly ivory clouds scudding along. A shaggy dark fringe of jungle stood in the distance, waving in the breeze, and in front of it ran the shiny seam of a lazy, narrow river. The Bloom had sunk deep into the ancient coral, and evaporated and expanded in the air, diffusing over Kana, dissolving the whorls. Penny caught sight of the last of them, like a faint husk of the moon left in a morning sky, before it, too, faded away. All that was left were fragile oblongs of blue-green crystals that studded the Coral Basin. A bee zigzagged out from the jungle and landed on the basin's edge for a moment before flying off.

It was done. The whorls were gone. The mandrill was banished back to the Gorgonne. Kana was safe. The breeze stirring the trees in the distance was just that—an ordinary breeze, not a draft from some near-invisible doorway. Everything was where it should be. Penny looked down at the shell around her neck and saw that several precious drops of Bloom still glowed in it. She looked up at Seagrape, gently aloft on the light breeze. She no longer spoke, if she ever really had.

Things still seemed strangely muffled, and in the hazy, ponderous new way Penny's brain seemed to be working, she realized it was because she had water in her ears. She tilted her head to the side and shook it, but the water was stuck. She didn't know where she was; somewhere down the coast from Palmos, she guessed. The Wave couldn't have taken her too far. Seagrape squawked and took flight across the sandbar toward the beckoning sparkle of the river.

Penny thumped the side of her head gently to try to get the water out, then followed Seagrape in the direction of the river, which flowed indolently, the breeze tripping over its surface, making it shimmer.

As she neared the rippling water, she realized it wasn't a real river after all, or at least not one that was usually there. The Wave had surged inland along a channel, and now it had reversed and was flowing back to the sea in the same deep gully. It would take her to Palmos. She waded in and grabbed hold of a large broken branch, its leaves still bright green, flapping like dozens of tiny wings. She held on, her legs trailing in the cool water, floating debris bumping gently into her. Soon enough she saw the town at the crest of the hill on her left, its limestone glaringly bright in the sun. The Wave must have carried her into the neighboring valley. When she was as close as the false river could take her, she hopped off and waded to shore. The branch continued on without her, its flock of leaves fluttering silver in the breeze.

The noon light was gleaming on crystals of salt spray still hanging in the air, and the shadows were shrinking under the palms as Penny climbed the hill to Palmos. At the top, she paused to catch her breath and look out. The great and magnificent Wave that came only once a generation was gone and the sea was mellow and blue. Thanks to the deep trenches and high middens, even the parts of the town closest to the shore had been spared. The worst that had happened was that the Wave had gobbled the sand from the bay. The middens that hadn't been washed away shimmered in the sun, crabs tapping and clattering as they strutted over them. The air smelled of rich earth and briny sea and the newly exposed rocks of the shoreline. The world felt broken open, transformed.

Penny walked down into the town to find it unnaturally still and quiet. A lonely festival streamer flapped in the wind. Her footsteps rang hollowly against the walls.

The streets were rinsed clean, but here and there a stranded fish lay dead on the cobblestones. She caught sight of the cloak that she had worn out to the Wave, washed up in a heap in a gutter, like a drowned animal, but it was sodden and, in her weak and weary state, it was too heavy to carry.

Kana was safe, but something wasn't right. Penny turned a corner and saw part of the amphitheater at the end of a street. It was deserted, its white limestone glaring in the sun. Where was everyone? In the distance, between buildings, she saw that the single hand of the stone dial had finally concluded its generational revolution and lay fixed in stony slumber at the base of the valley. The breeze changed direction and she heard a low, rhythmic chant coming from farther inside the town.

Seagrape's shadow fluttered silently on the street in front of her as Penny followed the sound to a hut with a broad thatched porch where the Council of Elders was gathered, faces grave. She didn't see Elder. Women sat outside on the hot earth around the hut or crouched beneath wrinkled shadows of palms. Someone caught sight of Penny and alerted others. The chanting ceased and people scrambled to their feet. A councilman crossed the dirt yard to meet Penny.

"You're safe!" he cried in relief. "Sound the triton to bring everyone back," he told one of the women, who immediately ran off down the street. "Everyone's searching the coast for you," he said to Penny. "Come this way." He took Penny's arm and led her urgently to the hut.

"What's in there?" she asked, but he didn't answer.

Feeling as if she were floating in a dream, Penny walked up the steps, passed through the doorway, to enter the dim hush of the hut. The burlap curtains were drawn and it took several moments for her eyes to adjust. When they did, she was transfixed by the sight of the boy lying on a mat in the middle of the floor.

Kal's skin was pale. A woman knelt beside him, pressing his hands between her own to warm them. Other women took turns waving a big palm leaf nearby to keep fresh air flowing over him. His body was wrapped in a rough blanket. One of his arms was splinted. His lips had a blue tinge that made the hairs on Penny's neck rise, and for a moment she felt like once again the Great Wave was bowling her over and there was nothing beneath her feet: Kal was dead. But as she held her own breath, she saw his chest rise and fall.

"He was found caught at the bottom of one of the trenches," said Elder, whom Penny saw standing nearby. "He hasn't woken up."

Penny had buried beloved pets in the yard at Granny Pearl's house, cradled baby birds fallen to their doom from their nests. She had watched Simon and her father neatly club struggling fish that the family would later eat for dinner. But she had never seen a person—let alone such a young person—so close to death.

In revolt against this affront to the natural order of things, it was as if the hour had stopped around them, the day come to a standstill. Through a crack in the curtains, the sun hung stationary in the sky. Not a breeze stirred the palm fronds. Pinpricks of light filtered through the mesh roof. Seagrape perched motionless on a stool near the foot of Kal's mat. The only motion was the trickle of sweat down the faces of the people keeping vigil. The heat was oppressive, but cold emanated from Kal. He breathed shallowly, and there were long pauses between each breath. He was between worlds.

Penny had to look away. Her gaze fell on Elder's hands clasping the top of his cane. They were as wrinkled and spotted with age as Granny Pearl's were. Suddenly, powerfully, with every fiber of her being, Penny wished she were with her grandmother. She wanted to hide in the safety of her arms, feel the hand that had smoothed her hair back from her face and checked her forehead for fevers since before she could remember. Somewhere in the distance she heard the triton sounding.

Kal murmured in his sleep and Penny turned back to him.

She took a small step closer.

He was just a kid, like her. But, before he had even finished growing, he was disappearing. He looked so fragile and small, a ghost of the boy she had met days ago. The bruise on his forehead had faded to a shadow—how ridiculous that it had healed while he would not. Seeing him like this, the memory of his treachery seemed hard to recall. She remembered their conversation in the Gorgonne, how secretly happy he had seemed to talk to her. It felt, for a surreal moment, that they had been fighting for the same thing, on the same side, all along.

They had *not* been on the same side, though: He had destroyed their bike, sabotaged them, broken the rules, and he'd run out to the Wave after her and caused it to topple and almost killed her—he was her enemy. But somehow what had happened no longer mattered; it was as though the Wave had swept it away.

She felt numb, as if she were outside her own body, but she knew what she had to do.

Feeling her hands shaking, she reached up until she felt the shell around her neck. Carefully she pulled its string over her head. She knelt down and took out the sea-sponge cork and looked at the last of the Bloom. There were only a few drops left. Before she could change her mind, she tilted the shell until it touched Kal's lips. The coldness of his skin startled her and she almost dropped the shell, but she recovered and held it firmly and poured. Kal swallowed, murmuring through his sleep. She tipped the shell until the last of the Bloom drained out.

There. There was none left.

None left for Granny Pearl.

It was all over.

The full weight of what she had done settled on her.

Penny dropped her head. She felt dizzy.

She had made it so far—all the way back to Tamarind, to Kana. She had faced the terrifying octopus in the depths of the Blue Pit and secured a deadly Zamzee beetle. She had navigated the whorls through the strange and twisting depths of the Gorgonne, saved her friends, and returned with a shell from the boiling lake. She had been hailed as the winner of the competition—the Bloom Catcher—and had dived fearlessly through the great wall of water to gather the precious Bloom, and she had filled the shell with it. She had been brave, always. But after all that, she had nothing to show for it but the empty shell, almost weightless in her hands. The Bloom was gone, used up on a person who until moments ago had been her enemy.

Penny turned so she didn't have to see Kal anymore.

"There's nothing I can do to help Granny Pearl," she said. The room was still and silent. Dust motes rolled softly. "Things can't go back to the way they were, can they?" she whispered.

"No," said Elder. "They can't. I'm sorry."

Penny reached up for the goggles around her neck before she remembered they were gone. She began to cry.

She inhabited a pure feeling: sorrow. She lost all sense of time. The women who had been there had left. The hut was quiet.

Gradually her tears subsided. She became dimly aware that life outside had begun to buzz along again. Someone had opened the curtain, and through it she could see that the water moved, the sun shone, the breeze caught the leaves, the birds flew, the palms brushed the sky. The unnatural hush had been replaced with sounds of life resuming: cart wheels rattling over cobblestones, stray crabs being gathered into buckets for dinners later that night, the clank and clatter of the middens being dismantled, the whistle of nets being cast out to catch the fish that had returned after the Wave. People were breaking camp and preparing to return home to ordinary life. Seagrape was no longer on the stool and must have flown out of the hut. The last of the water from the Wave drained out of Penny's ears. She could hear sounds again, sharp and distinct. She wiped her eyes on her shirt.

With or without the Bloom, it was time to go home.

Then she remembered Kal lying cold behind her. If he had woken she would have heard, but there had been no sound. Maybe she had been too late, or maybe the Bloom didn't work. She dreaded the inevitable grim news.

She heard Elder saying her name. She had forgotten he was there.

"Look," he said. He nodded to Kal.

Steeling herself, Penny turned around.

The change was evident. The color had returned to Kal's face. His breathing was slow and even, the breathing of someone sleeping deeply.

"He's resting," said Elder. "But he'll wake. When he does, he'll have to face the consequences of what he did. But . . . because of you . . . he'll live."

The relief that flooded Penny was bittersweet. The Bloom *did* work.

Elder rose. His flowing silk robe was bright. His polished head shone. He held his jeweled cane firmly.

"I have to go and call the Bloom Festival to a close," he said. "You'll be able to open a final whorl to go home, but you don't have long." He paused and looked at Penny kindly. "You aren't returning home with what you came for," he said. "But you've swum in the Bloom. You're different now."

Elder left, and Penny looked back at Kal. She hesitated, then reached out and squeezed his hand. His skin was no longer cold but warm, flush with life. His eyes opened. He looked around the room and down at his own body lying there. With difficulty, he swallowed. He tried to lift his head, but he was still too weak. When he spoke, his voice was raspy.

"We were in the Wave," he said. He was quiet for a moment, gathering his thoughts with effort. "You opened a whorl for us to get out before it crashed."

"Not for very long, though," said Penny. "The water still caught us."

Kal's thoughts became clearer as he woke. He managed to sit up a little way.

"You could have made a better one, if you hadn't tried to take me with you," he said.

"Maybe," said Penny.

"Where's the Bloom?" he asked, looking for the shell around Penny's neck.

"Most of it went to the Coral Basin," replied Penny. "The whorls have closed. The mandrill's gone."

"And the rest of it?"

Penny was silent.

Kal looked at her.

"Oh," he said quietly. "I see." He looked wonderingly at her, then, exhausted, lay back and closed his eyes. "You probably won't believe me," he said at last. "But I'm sorry. I really am. I meant to open a whorl inside the Wave, but I misjudged. I was just going to get a little of the Bloom for myself and leave right away. No one was even supposed to know."

"Why did you want it so much, anyway?" Penny asked finally.

When Kal opened his eyes, he wasn't looking at Penny but out the window at the bright square of the sky.

"It's hard to explain," he said. He was quiet. "When I was younger, I was sent to live with my aunt in Tontap," he said at last. "My mother couldn't take care of me anymore. There were too many kids and my father was never there." He paused to clear his throat. "I hated Tontap. I don't know when it started, but I got the idea that if I became the Bloom Catcher, my parents would hear about me and one of them at least would want to come and bring me home. Everyone in Tontap would know that I was important. After you won, I was so mad. I felt like it should have been me—I was the one who deserved it. I'd wanted it for so long.

"Then I thought that even if I couldn't be the Bloom Catcher, I could still have some of the Bloom, that maybe it would give me some kind of power. It felt like my last chance. I know now that I won't go back home; it's too late. I think I already knew it. But I thought I could still have *something*, something for myself." He looked at Penny.

359

"So that's why I did it. Not to mess things up for you. I'm sorry."

They were quiet as Penny absorbed what Kal had told her. It was easy to see how when he was a homesick young kid he had thought that being the Bloom Catcher would change everything—would make him powerful and accepted, could even be the thing that helped him go back home. As time went on, he couldn't give up the plan—the idea itself still made him powerful. Probably he had even wanted to prove that he was better than the people he was so unhappy among. Penny could identify with feeling on the outside of things, with not belonging. But, even when she was lonely and unhappy at school, she had always had her family. So, when she looked at him here now, she felt not anger but overwhelming sadness for him, for how lonely he must have been for so long.

"You must hate me," he said.

She looked at him, small and alone on the mat. He was the only one who had wanted the Bloom as much as she had, who needed it as badly, who had pursued so single-mindedly the idea of what the Bloom could do and believed so wholly in its power to change things. He had believed in its magic, too.

"No," said Penny. She shook her head. "I thought I did before. But I don't. I'm glad you're okay. And glad the mandrill has gone back to the Gorgonne and Kana is safe."

It was over, for both of them. They were released. Penny felt a strange, heady freedom, the newness of life without an all-consuming purpose. She had the sense, kneeling there, that in another life she and Kal might have been friends. But in this life there was the bicycle, and the Bloom that was gone, and the fact that she couldn't stay in Kana any longer, anyway.

"I have to go now," she said. "But I hope, I don't know— I hope things work out for you."

"I'm going to be in trouble," said Kal. "Huge trouble."

Penny nodded. "Yeah . . ." she said. "But maybe just for a little while. I think that in the end, everyone will just be happy that you're all right."

Kal looked skeptical.

"I know that Tabba and Jebby will be," said Penny. "You should be friends with them, I mean really friends. They're great."

For a moment Kal's sadness parted and he looked hopeful. With effort, he sat up and reached out his hand. Penny took it in hers, and not knowing what else to do, they shook hands. It was a strangely formal, adult gesture that made them both feel self-conscious, but they could not think of anything better.

"Good-bye," she said.

"Good-bye," he said solemnly. Before he let her go, he squeezed her hand tightly. "Thank you," he said.

Penny left the hut. Everyone else was gone, but two women had stayed behind to tend to Kal, and they slipped quietly

inside as Penny went out. Down the hill, between the buildings, Penny could see the limestone crescent of the amphitheater, which began at the edge of the town and curved
around the valley. Below it lay the blue sweep of the sea. As
Penny walked down the steps from the porch, she saw Tabba
and Jebby running up the street toward her, out of breath.
When they saw her, they sprinted the last of the way and
almost barreled into her.

"Penny!" Jebby cried. "We're so happy to see you!"

"You looked so small in the Wave!" said Tabba, embracing her. "We were so scared when it crashed!"

"When the whorls closed, we knew you were all right
and must have gotten to the Coral Basin," said Jebby. "We
were looking for you up and down the coast, but we ran all
the way back here when we heard the triton. . . ."

"We just passed Elder," said Tabba. "He said you gave
the last of the Bloom to Kal and he's going to be all right
now. Is that true?"

"It's true," said Penny.

Tabba and Jebby just looked at her.

"Oh, Penny," said Tabba, her eyes filling with tears.
"There's none left for . . ."

Seeing Tabba's tears made Penny feel sad again.

"It's all right," she said hoarsely. "My grandmother
would have wanted him to have it. I have a feeling it only
works in Tamarind, anyway. And I'm glad that Kal's okay."

There was nothing else that could be said about it.
Penny cleared her throat.

"Tell Bellamy I'm sorry about his bike," she said.

"We already have," said Jebby. "We saw him last night, and Rai."

"They're down there now—look," said Tabba. "On the top step of the amphitheater. See—they're waving."

Penny looked where Tabba was pointing and could just make them out, Bellamy sitting, Rai standing on the bench beside him, looking up the hill. When she saw that the children had seen her, she swung her arms wildly back and forth over her head. Even from a distance Penny could see that she was smiling. And Bellamy was waving, too—he must not be that angry about the bicycle. Penny waved back at them.

The Council of Elders had assembled for the last time on the platform at the bottom of the valley, and the amphitheater was filling with people again. Penny searched for Helix. He had promised he would say good-bye this time. And where was Seagrape? Penny heard Elder's voice, echoing off the hills.

"People of Kana," he boomed.

His voice was as strong and clear as a bell. The crowd stopped shifting and rustling and murmuring, and fell so quiet that Penny could hear the flapping of a bird's wings. She held her breath. Seconds later, Seagrape appeared and landed on Penny's shoulder. Penny sighed in relief. She waited until she saw Helix, running up the hill toward them. He embraced Penny wordlessly, lifting her feet off the ground, and she hugged him back, resting her head on his shoulder. When her feet touched the ground again, Elder was speaking.

"The end of the competition did not unfold as it could have," he shouted, his voice resounding up through the valley. "But what matters is that the Bloom is complete. The whorls are closed; the mandrill has gone back to the Gorgonne. The last few drops of the Bloom were given away in a moment of great need to the person who required it most. The danger has passed. Kana is safe and will prosper for another generation. When the triton sounds for the last time, the festivities will be over."

It was time to open the final whorl. Penny did not know how she did it—somehow she just imagined it, clearly, strongly, and there it was, shimmering in the middle of the yard. Mist slowly swirled and eddied inside it and, as she watched, it began to glimmer more brightly. She turned to Tabba and Jebby. They didn't have long.

"Would you do something for me?" she asked. "Would you be nice to Kal? He needs some friends."

"We will," promised Tabba.

Jebby raised the bicycle bell and rang it.

Penny hugged each of them fiercely. They hugged her back.

Seagrape nuzzled Penny's cheek and wove back and forth. Penny stroked the parrot's smooth feathers, felt the hard, smooth mineral crescent of her beak as Seagrape gnawed her knuckle gently. Penny's heart felt heavy. Then the bird lifted her wings, and Penny felt a rush of air as Seagrape's talons left her shoulder for the last time. She flew away, leaving a painful absence in the place where she had been. Penny watched her glide out over the valley, wings opened on the wind, her shadow rippling over the earth below.

Cool white mist rolled out of the whorl and touched Penny's skin. In the distance the triton sounded. Its low, sonorous note rang out across the blue slopes of the swells, over all the people gathered in the amphitheater, up the shining green hills and into the bright sky.

Penny stepped into the whorl. The sound of the triton faded and Kana fell away. Behind her for a moment she heard the bicycle bell trilling a furious farewell.

It would not be a passage through a rough storm, or a dark night lost and alone. This would be simple. The ground had already been covered, the journey already made. This was just the last step, a light hop across.

At the last second, Penny looked behind her. She reached out her hand.

When the mist cleared, Penny became aware that she was in the cabin of the *Pamela Jane*—the real *Pamela Jane*, in the tiny cove at home, its water lapping blue-black against the pale sand of the beach. Helix stood next to her in the cabin. Through one of the boat's portholes, the lights of Granny Pearl's house twinkled on the hill.

"Come on," said Penny, barely able to contain her excitement. "We're here!"

She hurried up the companionway and opened the hatch, then climbed onto the deck. The night air was soft on her face. She paused and breathed in the scent of home— salt, vegetables in the garden, oranges in the grove. A warm breeze blew the boat gently on its mooring. A new rowboat was tied to the stern. She and Helix climbed in and, with four strong strokes, Penny had rowed them to the small crescent beach.

"Go ahead," he said. "I'll be there in a minute."

"Should I tell them you're here?" she asked.

"No, not yet—wait," he said.

Penny left him there and ran lightly up the hill. The grass was damp under her bare feet. She didn't call out, suddenly terrified that she was too late. She bounded up the porch steps and was about to dash through the screen door when she saw Granny Pearl sitting in her rocking chair, a blanket in her lap, a soft fur of insects flickering around the tiny light burning at her feet. Penny threw her arms gently around her. For a long time now she'd been too big to sit in Granny Pearl's lap, but she snuggled into the chair beside her. The two of them were small enough to sit side by side.

"I'm so happy to see you," murmured Penny, burying her face in her grandmother's arm.

"I've been waiting up for you," said Granny Pearl. "I had a feeling you'd be back tonight." She hugged Penny close and kissed the top of her head.

"I was in Tamarind," said Penny. "A different part than

we had ever been in before. A place called Kana. And Granny Pearl . . ." Penny dropped her voice and sat up to face her grandmother. "Helix is here," she whispered excitedly. "He came back with me. He's down by the cove. He didn't want me to tell anyone he was here yet."

Granny Pearl smiled and closed her eyes.

"Good," she said. "I knew when I saw all the signs—I knew it was time for him to be here again. That it was the right time. No, don't call him—wait until he's ready. We'll see him soon enough."

"I tried to get the Bloom for you," said Penny. She was so tired but had so much to say. "I was close—but then . . . I gave it to this boy who really needed it."

"The Bloom?" asked Granny Pearl.

"The stuff that would make you better," said Penny. "What you sent me to get for you."

The chair creaked softly as Granny Pearl rocked.

"I didn't send you there to get anything like that for me, Penny," she said. "I don't even know what the Bloom is. I knew you had to go back to Tamarind—that there was something you needed to do there, something for yourself. And I hoped that you'd find Helix, too, and that maybe he'd come back with you."

Penny felt confused. "But . . ." she said.

Granny Pearl pushed Penny's hair behind her ear.

"I'm an old lady, Penny," she said. "I won't be around forever. All I want is to know that you'll be all right when I'm not here one day. And for you to know that, too."

Penny pressed her cheek against her grandmother's arm, felt her soft, papery skin, the warmth from her body. In the garden, crickets chirped, and in the distance, the sea broke over the far reefs, sounds Penny had known since she was a tiny girl. They were part of her, embedded, like Granny Pearl herself, in her deepest, oldest memories.

"You'll have to tell me everything tomorrow; it's too late tonight," said her grandmother. "And I hear your parents coming out now. You can imagine how worried they've been. They've searched up and down the coast in the boat, even though they knew you weren't there. If Maya and Simon hadn't come home yesterday, I don't know what they would have done."

Voices came from the house, and Penny's parents appeared in the doorway. They looked worried and exhausted, but when they saw Penny, her father heaved a sigh of relief and her mother cried, "Penny!" and rushed out to greet her.

In the next moment they were all embracing her—her mother wiping away tears, her father gathering her up in a hug that lifted her feet off the ground. Maybe tomorrow she'd be in trouble; right now they were too glad to see her.

Simon and Maya had heard the commotion and hurried outside, and then they were hugging her, too. Penny hadn't seen them in months and she squeezed them back, hard.

"You went without us!" said Simon.

Penny saw Maya looking at her with a sort of proud wonder—Penny had been in Tamarind so recently that its magic still hung around her. She had been there now, too, not as just an infant or a little kid, but in her own right.

"What was it like?" Maya asked. "Was it like it was before?"

"Did you see anywhere you remembered?" Simon asked.

It was so good to have her family all together that it was all Penny could think about. It had not been like that for a long time. Her heart felt as if it would burst.

Her mother was still fussing over her, running her hands through Penny's hair. She tilted Penny's face to look at her. "You really are in one piece, you're sure?" she asked.

"Did you—" asked Maya, but everyone was speaking at once. Penny glanced past them, down toward the cove, but didn't see Helix. He had said not to tell them yet. She would let him come up in his own time. She began to tell them about Tamarind—about Kana and Tabba and Jebby and the mandrill and the whorls—but then she yawned, suddenly overwhelmed with tiredness. She could hardly keep her eyes open.

"It's time for bed," said her mother, steering her toward the door. "We'll all be able to talk in the morning."

Simon helped Granny Pearl to her feet and everyone went inside.

Penny brushed her teeth and changed into her pajamas. In her room she paused when she saw the empty perch in the corner, feeling an ache. She climbed into bed and pulled the sheet up to her chin. Lying there, she felt different from how she used to. The room was the same as it had always been, but it seemed smaller, somehow, or perhaps it was that she seemed bigger, and the room too small to contain all the new things she had felt and seen and done. Maybe Elder was right: Swimming in the Bloom had changed things.

Outside, in the lane near the house, the seedpods had finished shedding. Most had blown away; only a few stray bits could be seen here and there in the grass. The leaves on the orange tree were dark green beneath the moon. The sky was clear and peaceful. The *Pamela Jane* lay calm on her mooring, and out beyond the cove, the darkly milling sea broke softly over the far reefs.

As Penny drifted to sleep, she heard Granny Pearl shuffling softly down the hallway, heard the familiar tap of her knuckle on the door frame.

"Good night, my darling," her grandmother whispered.

Penny was already asleep.

Granny Pearl tucked the sheet gently around Penny's shoulders, kissed her forehead, then quietly left the room.

Helix

After Penny had run up the hill, Helix had stopped and stood amid the dark mangroves at the edge of the cove. He looked up at the house, the windows lit and welcoming, as he remembered them. He had not seen this place in seven years.

He hadn't known until the last minute what he would do.

"It's in the past," he had told Penny the night before the Bloom.

But the past was always a part of the present, real and vital, and when the moment came and the chance appeared—the wavering lens of the porthole burning bright in the daylight in Palmos—he had known exactly what to do. Something that Penny had said had stuck in his mind, that things had changed enough that now he *could* go back.

He stood on the shore of the cove and watched them all on the porch—hugging Penny, talking. They were too far away for him to see how their faces had changed, but he knew their shapes, the drift and timbre of their voices. They went indoors. Lights went out inside, but the porch light was left burning.

He was still standing there, breathing in the damp night air, when he saw Maya step back outside by herself. She stood on the porch, hair tucked behind her ears, feet bare, tugging her sweater around her waist in the cool spring night, looking over the garden, where in a few weeks the cocoons would rattle softly in the breeze through the milkweed patch, and out beyond the garden to the darkly turning sea. She was right there, in front of him. Real and present. Not a memory, not a feeling in his heart. The real person. A shiver went through him.

He stepped out of the shadows onto the open beach.

She saw him. Her hands dropped to her sides and she stood very still. Then, as if a wind had picked her up and set her in flight, she began to race silently down the hill toward him.

Behind Helix, the whorl he had come through glowed dully then dissolved. The dark portholes on the *Pamela Jane* sank away, too, until they were invisible across the cove. The school of snappers had retired under the hull. The sea beyond the cove was dark beneath the clear night sky. Helix felt the earth solid beneath his feet, felt himself anchored firmly in the world. He began to walk up the hill toward Maya.

Acknowledgments

I am forever grateful to Jean Feiwel for helping to bring the world of Tamarind into being by opening the door to these three books and the adventures of Maya, Simon, and Penny. And to Amanda Punter, Carmen McCullough, Emma Jones, and Wendy Shakespeare, whose guidance and insight strengthened these characters and their stories immeasurably. And to Lexy Bloom and Julia Holmes for their astute counsel and essential support during the earliest, foggiest days of Penny's story taking shape. Sarah Burnes and Caspian Dennis remained fiercely unwavering in their commitment to this book, and Emily Settle steered it deftly through the publishing process. Finally, I'd like to thank my dad, whose steadfast encouragement has always been a gift.